Michael Hartmann, married with two children, is a lawyer. He lives in Hong Kong, where for a number of years he has specialised in international criminal law. He has had seven previous novels published.

Some reviews for previous novels:

A WEB OF DRAGONS
'A powerful story of drugs, gold and treachery' – *Edinburgh Evening News*
'Action aplenty in a fast moving adventure' – *Yorkshire Evening Post*
'A multi-level story bulging with sub-plots and side tracks' – *Guernsey Evening Press*

THE PHOENIX PACT
'An intricate adventure thriller of arms dealing, financial intrigue and duplicity' – *Bookseller*
'A breath-taking thriller, tough and uncompromising, told at a frantic pace. Great stuff' – *Liverpool Daily Post*

TIGERS OF DECEIT
'A chilling and powerful study of the Far East heroin empire' – *Bolton Evening News*
'All the essential ingredients for a thriller – suspense, suspicion, savagery, deceit, romance' – *Dumfries & Galloway Standard*
'Intriguing . . . excellent . . . It has that hallmark of all the best thrillers – you can't put it down' – *South China Morning Post*

Also by Michael Hartmann

**Tigers of Deceit
The Phoenix Pact
A Web of Dragons**

Horses of Vengeance

Michael Hartmann

Copyright © 1992 Michael Hartmann

The right of Michael Hartmann to be identified as the Author of
the Work has been asserted by him in accordance with the
Copyright, Designs and Patents Act 1988.

First published in 1992
by HEADLINE BOOK PUBLISHING PLC

First published in paperback in 1993
by HEADLINE BOOK PUBLISHING PLC

A HEADLINE FEATURE paperback

10 9 8 7 6 5 4 3 2

All rights reserved. No part of this publication may be
reproduced, stored in a retrieval system, or transmitted,
in any form or by any means without the prior written
permission of the publisher, nor be otherwise circulated
in any form of binding or cover other than that in which
it is published and without a similar condition being
imposed on the subsequent purchaser.

All characters in this publication are fictitious
and any resemblance to real persons, living or dead,
is purely coincidental.

ISBN 0 7472 4011 6

Printed and bound in Great Britain by
HarperCollins Manufacturing, Glasgow

HEADLINE BOOK PUBLISHING PLC
Headline House
79 Great Titchfield Street
London W1P 7FN

MELANIE
for her criticism, her encouragement
and her eternal patience

AUTHOR'S NOTE

Corruption by government officials is a regrettable fact of life in many countries. Fraudulent immigration practices are a scourge and history shows that attempts have been made to secure diplomatic immunity both to aid criminal purposes and avoid the retribution of the law. It must be stressed, however, that this is purely a work of fiction. The countries mentioned have been chosen because they advance the plot and for no other reason. For example, at the time of writing, Peru had only an honorary consul in Hong Kong. The characters in this book are entirely imaginary and bear no relation to any person or actual happening.

Chapter One

The bomb was not large. It fitted snugly into the shell of the video cassette recorder, the kind of item ten thousand tourists purchased in Hong Kong every month. The cassette recorder itself fitted snugly into a suitcase, packed securely with shirts and trousers, all the clothing new, all purchased for cash off market stalls in Causeway Bay. The timing device could be reached easily: one turn of a switch, that was all. Every wire, every connection had been checked.

It was five-fifty in the evening. The pick-up time was on the hour. A metallic-gold Mercedes 500SE sedan, unusual elsewhere but nothing special in Hong Kong, would collect him from the hotel for the drive to the airport. The driver, he had been told, was a business associate, a man called Tselentis, half-Cantonese, half-Greek. They had never met before and would never meet again.

A black leather travel wallet lay on the bed next to the suitcase. It contained an Australian passport and a return air ticket to Manila in the Philippines. He would plant the bomb and walk straight through immigration into the departure lounge, mingling with the hundreds of passengers waiting to depart to their various destinations. Everything was set.

But Bruce Rexford was troubled, more troubled than he had ever been. One man, one target, that he could deal with. That's the way it had been for twenty years. But a bomb like this was indiscriminate. God knows who would be killed. If he had any choice, he would walk away from this assignment, drop the device in the harbour, let it sink into the silt. But walking away was impossible. This was an inner sanctum assignment, a Red Scroll directive. There was no such thing as refusal.

Nerves chewed into his gut like viral cramps. He was nauseated by what he was going to do, terrified . . . yet deep down, in the most savage part of him, he was excited too. He went one last time to the bathroom, running water into the basin and splashing his face. He stared at himself in the bathroom mirror. What had happened to all the years? He was forty-seven and looked every day of it, a thick-set, ageing salesman who liked the booze too much: thinning rust-red hair, a filigree of purplish veins in his cheeks, milky green eyes the quality of cheap jade.

He felt suddenly very tired, exhausted beyond belief. 'Please God,' he said out loud to a God he knew didn't exist, 'let this be the last time.' Then, with the resolve of one of Dostoevsky's damned, eternally haunted by demons, Bruce Rexford turned back into the room where the suitcase lay waiting.

As the taxi slowed to a crawl, joining the snarled-up lava-flow of traffic heading towards the Cross Harbour Tunnel, Dave Whitman could feel the tension oozing out of him. An involuntary smile – pure relief, pure anticipation – came to his face. Bloody great, he thought, ten days of sun and sand on the Thai island of Phuket; no more eighteen-hour shifts at Police Headquarters, no pagers beeping on his belt, no more interminable conferences, no more surly accused, just the three of them lazing away the days together: snorkelling along the coral reefs, windsurfing, drinking wine at night.

Danny, his son – nine years old last month – sat next to him in the back seat of the taxi, engrossed in a pocket-sized electronic game that had been bought for him to take on holiday. The two of them would be flying to Phuket that evening. Hannah unfortunately had work to finish. But she would be joining them in two days time. It was the first time the three of them had been on holiday together in more than two years.

Hong Kong was a great city but it was like New York, a constant cauldron. The pressure got to you after a time.

Hannah had been struggling with her fashion design business, spending half the year travelling the world, the other half fretting about finance, while he had been snowed under with police work. And the strain of it had begun to tell; little time for each other, barely enough for Danny. So a couple of weeks back the decision had been made. To hell with it, they would take some time off.

Time . . . in Dave Whitman's dog-eared book of values, it was the ultimate commodity. And they had been squandering it. But not any more, he thought. From now on they were going to get their priorities right. Phuket was just the beginning.

With the taxi crawling along one of the elevated flyovers that fed into the harbour tunnel, he had a panoramic view out over the water. Fragrant Harbour, that was the meaning of Hong Kong. Over the years, however, the translation had taken on a certain irony. You could smell the pollution from a hundred yards. Even so, polluted or not, it made a magnificent sight.

To Dave Whitman it had always been the crowded, rumbustious essence of this Cantonese souk in the underbelly of China. Across the water in Kowloon the lights were coming on. It would be dark soon. But everybody was still buying and selling, making, delivering. Ferries and lighters, tugs and sampans, a vast raggedy pageant of vessels, were still criss-crossing the luminous pewter water.

Time . . . in a few short years this overcrowded, hardselling, exquisite bloody city would be reverting to Mother China. Then what? Where did it leave a man like him?

Dave Whitman had spent fourteen years in Hong Kong. He spoke the Cantonese dialect fluently, knew every street and alley; loved and hated the place with equal passion. At present he held the rank of Superintendent in the Organised Crime and Triad Group. He was one of the supposed highfliers in the territory's police force. And sure there was a future for good men, that was the official line – a limited one.

But he was thirty-six now. In just four more years he would reach that mythical hump between employable experience and geriatric redundancy. Hannah had been at him for years to go into business. One thing was for sure, he would have to start making some decisions about his life.

But not this evening, not over the next ten days. The purpose of Phuket was to get away from problems like that. Who knows, he thought wistfully, maybe Hannah will make the breakthrough she's been slaving to achieve. Then I won't need to be a menopausal expat cop any more worrying about my future. Then it will all be taken care of: jogging every morning, a token seat on the board, raising our son while she's in Paris or Milan playing hardball with hemlines. Not a bad job, not bad at all . . .

Laughing softly, he threw an affectionate arm around his son's shoulder. But Danny, engrossed in the buttons and beeps of his game, wriggled away. 'C'm'on, dad, I've nearly got to a thousand points. It's almost a record.'

Dave Whitman smiled down at him. 'Tomorrow morning we'll be on the beach at Phuket. Aren't you just a bit excited?'

Concentrating fiercely on his game, punching the buttons, Danny replied with a big smile. 'Sure. I just wish mum was travelling with us, that's all. I thought running your own business meant you could do what you liked.'

Dave Whitman gave a rueful grin. 'Most of the time it means just the opposite. Your mum has clothes to design for some people in Canada—'

'I know, the spring collection. She told me.'

'Well, those people want samples of the designs before she flies off on holiday. They're not prepared to sit around losing money while she gets a suntan. That's business.'

'But why can't Scott do the samples? Mum says Scott is her right hand, her muse – whatever a muse is.'

'Scott is important, sure. Scott is mum's design assistant. But it is your mum's business. She designed those clothes and she's the one who has to make sure they turn out exactly the way she thought of them in her mind. No passing the buck – that's business too.'

'Sounds worse than school,' said Danny, very matter of fact. 'I thought it got better as you got older.'

4

Dave laughed.

Playing the buttons with the skill of a pianist, Danny asked him. 'Do you make much money having your own business?'

'If you work hard, sure. And you're lucky.'

'Mum can't be too lucky then.'

'Why do you say that?'

'She works all the time and still doesn't have any money – that's what she says.'

Unable to contain his smile, Dave Whitman tousled his son's hair. 'One of these days her luck will change, you'll see. Perseverance, Danny.'

'Perseverance? Is that another lesson in business?'

'That's it.'

Danny looked up at him with a freckle-faced grin. 'I hope her luck does change. Then maybe we can go on holiday together every year.'

'Yes, that would be nice, wouldn't it?' Very nice indeed, thought Dave.

Four years ago, brimming with confidence, Hannah had started China Girl Fashions, determined to break into the export fashion market for herself. She had had everything going for her too – talent, ambition, a top-rate name in the trade – everything pretty well except, as Danny had said, her share of luck.

Four years now . . . and all of it a grinding struggle, first to clear the overdraft that crippled her company, then to earn enough to meet the overheads, the preposterous rents they charged in Hong Kong, the salaries of Scott Defoe, a pattern maker, a cutter, two pressers and four sewing girls. It often surprised him that Hannah kept at it with such dogged determination. But it was wearing her down. She was the one, he knew, who really needed this break.

Every day of the year the road outside the departure terminal at Kai Tak Airport was a chaos of double-parked vehicles, hooting horns and people stumbling over their luggage.

As his chauffeur jostled for position, Geraldo Gomez, the

Consul General of the Government of Peru, physically had to restrain his irritation. Good or bad, he was pleased to be getting out of Hong Kong. Four years was enough for any man. 'Hurry, hurry,' he muttered to the chauffeur. 'There's a spot there. Can't you see it? Mother of God, this damn place!'

The black BMW with its consular corps sticker pulled in to the pavement and Gomez stepped out. He was in his late fifties, swarthy and olive-skinned. In his youth he had been a striking man. But he was balding now and running to fat with one drooping eyelid, the result of a minor stroke. 'Take the luggage to the Cathay Pacific counter,' he instructed the Chinese chauffeur. 'First class – the London flight.' Then he helped his wife from the car.

It was the month of May, building into a fierce, hot monsoonal summer. Gomez had to mop the perspiration from his face with a handkerchief. He looked red-eyed and harassed. Through the glass doors he saw a number of press photographers. 'They're not here for me are they?' he muttered to his wife. 'I don't think I can face them.'

But his wife Eva, a woman of Latin looks and Wagnerian proportions, was made of sterner stuff. 'The press knows nothing,' she said. 'Ignore them. You're making too much of this, Geraldo. A couple of ridiculous complaints, pah!'

Gomez, however, was not reassured. His wife didn't know the half of it, not even half. He hesitated, dreading the prospect of a confrontation. But what choice did he have? If he wanted to fly out of this awful town, he had to go through those doors. The Peruvian Consul General to Hong Kong wiped his brow again. He was a very troubled man.

'Come,' said his wife. 'We can't wait out here all day. The exhaust fumes and the heat are unbearable.'

'Yes, Eva, of course.'

As he stepped nervously towards the sliding glass doors, Gomez glimpsed a small dapper man, Chinese, climbing from a Mercedes a little further up the pavement. The Chinese man, also in his middle to late fifties, nodded politely. Gomez replied with a bilious smile.

'Who was that?' asked his wife as they entered the con-

·course. She had seen the man before but couldn't place him.

At that moment, however, Geraldo Gomez was thinking only of the press. He walked in a straight line, eyes focused on a distant point, not looking left or right. *Madre de dios*, he was praying. None of the journalists even looked at him. He got past them and stopped, sweat dribbling down his temples, knees weak with relief.

'Who was that man?' his wife asked a second time.

'His name is Gao Xin,' Gomez replied. 'New China News Agency. You've met him before. Effectively, he's the number two Beijing diplomat in Hong Kong.' Then a thought came to him. 'Oh heavens, no,' he groaned. 'He can't be on the same flight as us. He's such a calculating little man. I'm sure he knows why I'm being recalled to Lima. The Chinese know everything that goes on in Hong Kong, I tell you, Eva, just everything.'

'I don't know why you're worrying about this whole affair,' snorted his wife, who had not been told the truth. 'You should give it the contempt it deserves. Anyway, Geraldo, what harm can a little man like that do to you?'

Twenty yards down from the Cathay Pacific first-class counter Dave Whitman waited in an economy-class queue for the flight to Phuket. Danny, trying to break his record again, sat on their battered suitcase playing his electronic game.

At six foot, dressed in jeans, a faded blue shirt and joggers, Dave Whitman stood a head taller than most of the others in the queue. He needed glasses for reading these days, which he hated and invariably forgot to carry. But that apart, he had aged pretty well.

There was a loose-limbed look about him, the look of a runner, a man who ran every day. His face was angular, a little raw. He could look forbidding on occasions. But the gauntness was saved by a mop of dark brown hair that fell over his forehead and an easy, boyish smile. Hannah, biased of course, had summed it up long ago – all sinew, bones and sex appeal.

Danny possessed the same long-legged build. But in every other respect he was Hannah's son: much finer boned

7

with corn-coloured hair, a host of honeyed freckles across· his cheeks and big, round, Delft-blue eyes. Like Hannah too, he was constantly on the go, fiercely competitive, sharp as a whip. But he was a nice kid, not a bully, not too precocious. He got on well with people, kids and adults alike.

Glancing up from his game and seeing the huddle of pressmen near the doors, Danny asked. 'Dad, what are those reporters waiting for?'

Dave Whitman gave a casual shrug. 'Who knows, some celebrity arriving for a flight probably. A movie star, a football player.'

'Do you reckon whoever it is could be on the same flight as us?'

Dave smiled down at him. 'Not in tourist I expect. But yeah, why not? Everything is possible.'

'Oh no,' mumbled Geraldo Gomez to his wife. 'I was right. Look who is with us on the flight, it's going to be purgatory.'

Gao Xin smiled politely as he took up his position in the first-class queue behind them. 'So you are travelling to London too?'

Gomez grimaced in reply. 'Just in transit. We are returning to Lima. And you?'

'My daughter is studying for a doctorate at Cambridge University: physics at Pembroke.'

'Very nice.'

'I shall be spending a few days with her.'

'So it is purely private business?'

'Yes, purely private. And yourself?'

'Just a holiday,' said Gomez a little too quickly.

'That will be nice.'

'Yes, we hope so.'

As their conversation dried up, both men noticed the crowd of pressmen suddenly elbowing their way towards a small party that was entering the concourse. The party was headed by a tall hulk of a man, well-tanned and muscular, his silk shirt open to his abdomen, a gold medallion of St

Christopher around his neck. He stopped, grinned for the cameras and began answering questions.

'Who is he?' asked Gao Xin.

'I have no idea,' Gomez replied with distaste.

But young Danny Whitman knew exactly who it was. 'Dad, it's Gideon Hildebrand,' he said, awe-struck, his electronic game forgotten. 'Is he going to be on the same flight as us?'

'I doubt it,' said Dave. 'He's probably flying to Europe.' He recognised him too. Hildebrand, a one-time Dutch Mr Universe, was now a Hollywood action star. There had been something in the papers about him completing a martial arts movie in Hong Kong. He had been on the television a couple of times.

'Do you think he'd mind if I asked for his autograph?' asked Danny. 'Gee, Gideon Hildebrand!'

Dave Whitman grinned. 'Go and ask him,' he said. 'Just don't make a nuisance of yourself, that's all.'

As Hildebrand reached the small group at the first-class counter, he smiled engagingly at Gomez and his wife. 'Sorry about all this,' he said in a thick Dutch accent. 'I am afraid it is part of the job.' Then he turned again to pose for the paparazzi.

As the flashlights burst around Hildebrand's head, Bruce Rexford, dressed unassumingly in brown slacks and an open-neck shirt, entered the terminal. He was carrying a suitcase. He came so close to the first-class counter that he was physically jostled by the anxious pressmen. He stopped, face empty of emotion, and put down the case. He waited patiently until the melee began to clear, then he walked silently on. The suitcase, however, remained.

Dave Whitman saw the man walk past – almost as tall as himself, sturdily built, heavy wedged face with thinning red hair – but the image barely registered. His attention instead was proudly focused on his son. Danny, shy but determined, was edging closer to the film star.

As the photographers dissipated, Hildebrand saw him and smiled affably. 'Hi there. Gideon Hildebrand is my name. A bit of a mouthful, hey kid. But once you know it, you don't forget it. Would you like an autograph?'

'Yes, please.'

'Have you seen any of my movies?'

'All of them – on video mainly.'

Hildebrand laughed. One of his aides, a pretty young woman, took out a large black-and-white publicity photograph. 'So, what's your name?' asked Hildebrand.

'Daniel Whitman,' said Danny with the grave seriousness of a nine-year-old.

'Okay, so I'll just say here: To Danny, my good friend, with best wishes—'

And at that moment the suitcase exploded.

Dave Whitman was aware only of a vast flash of light that seemed to sear his eyes. He was thrown back, engulfed in a thunderous concussion and, for a moment, lost in a tangle of arms and legs, must have lost consciousness. He tried to struggle up, but it was so hard. What had happened? He found himself on his knees, his vision blurred by blood. Around him people were screaming, clutching at their wounds, running in wild panic. Then he began to realise . . .

Oh God, no, Danny! All he could think of was his son. He looked towards the source of the explosion, to where he had seen Danny standing moments before. The roof above had been shattered, bursting the sprinkler system. Water showered down on the carnage in an eerie silver spray. But he saw no movement.

He staggered to his feet, blood and water streaming down his face. He began to run, shouting: 'Danny! Danny!' Then he saw the small figure sprawled on the floor, lying next to the bomb-blasted body of Hildebrand. Oh God no, this couldn't be happening. It was impossible. He knelt beside his son and lifted the small body into his arms. His voice was barely a whisper, his soul was being torn apart. He murmured to his son. 'Please, Danny, just open your eyes, please, please my darling.' But there was no response, there never would be. His son was dead.

Chapter Two

For six hours Kai Tak Airport had been sealed off. Even at that early stage everybody in the departure lounge knew the carnage had been horrendous. The wail of ambulance sirens filled the night. The terrible keening of shell-shocked survivors hugging their dead was a sound nobody would forget. Squads of blue beret police, Hong Kong's quasi-military, had interrogated everyone, checking their travel documents, searching their hand luggage. A number of passengers had been taken away, others told they could not leave.

Bruce Rexford, numb, elated and yet destroyed inside, a churning mass of contradictions, had been asked the standard questions: where had he come from, why had he been in Hong Kong? It was superficial stuff, but the police were not so interested in the content of his answers as the reactions when he gave them. Maintaining a cool totally relaxed composure had been the key; a bland exterior to hide the rot inside.

Just before midnight, his flight had been granted clearance and he had flown back to Manila, back to the Ermita District, back to Del Pilar Street, where the whores stood shoulder to shoulder under the neon signs and the pavements throbbed to the sound of Tagalog and rock . . . back to the Red Lips Bar which he owned: his sanctuary, his *mea culpa* retreat.

Now, seven days later, he lay on his bed in his room above the bar, naked, his scarred body glistening with sweat, trying to ride out the fever. There was always a reaction after a hit but never before had it been as bad as this. This time he was on the verge of disintegrating totally.

13

A book lay next to him, a yellowed copy of Graham Greene's *The Power and the Glory*, another story of a tortured individual seeking salvation. Another man lost in his private hell of inadequacy.

Scattered across the floor in a sodden pile lay copies of newspapers. The headlines, days old now, screamed up at him –

JAPANESE RED ARMY OUTRAGE

In a statement to the press, the Japanese Red Army, a tiny cell of fanatics, dormant for a decade, had claimed total responsibility for the Kai Tak bombing. It was, proclaimed the announcement, a blow against Japanese and US imperialism in Hong Kong, itself a cancerous symbol of British imperialism. Long live the people's revolution! The running dogs of capitalism were doomed! Christ, even he couldn't believe it – propaganda from the sixties, madmen lost in a time warp.

Six people killed, twenty-two wounded, some maimed for life. It was, howled the world's press of every political persuasion, a deed of unimaginable savagery: blind, butchering terrorism. And they were right, dear God how right.

Rexford knew the names of the six dead now, each face seared into the bruised sinew of his conscience. A slaughterhouse of celebrities; Geraldo Gomez, the Peruvian Consul General, and his wife of thirty years, Eva Maria; Gao Xin, a senior Beijing diplomat stationed in Hong Kong; Gideon Hildebrand, the martial arts movie star; Mary O'Connell, his publicity secretary, and finally, one nine-year-old boy with blond hair and freckles, everybody's image of a perfect kid, a boy named Daniel Whitman.

With the media attention on the diplomats and the Hollywood movie star, the boy's death had received the least publicity, a little maudlin sympathy for the parents, some sentimental nonsense in the Sunday tabloids. But of the six it was the boy who haunted him most.

And suddenly he was back all those years, back in that malarial, bamboo gulag north of the DMZ, standing there shivering with terror, while Conrad Fung smiled, as cold as a cobra, and offered him cigarettes . . .

'You have made a wise decision, Bruce. You are a young man with many talents. Why die so needlessly and in such pain? You have seen how that one man died. Three days it took. Three whole days. Imagine that divided into seconds. You have heard his cries of agony during the night. I am sure you thought it would never end. From this day on, you and I are entering into a special relationship, you understand that, one that can never be broken. Your past no longer exists. That is one of the prices you must pay. Your family in Australia, your parents, your brothers and sister – forget them. But I regret it does not end there. You see, you must mark the passage from one life to another, mark it in a way that never allows you to go back, never lets you even think of trying to reclaim it. Do you understand, Bruce? You must do something so much against your instincts that it will scour your soul. Only then can you be the sort of man we can trust. There are two persons waiting outside in the sun. One is your SAS friend captured with you. He is wounded and very sick. The other is just a boy. His father works for Saigon. The boy himself is incorrigible. How old is he, you ask? What does that matter? He is maybe nine, maybe ten. Just an urchin. To earn your right of passage Bruce, you must kill them both. And we shall film it so that you will always know – until the day you die – that there is a record, a record which can be shown to the world. Two deaths, Bruce, that is all we ask. Is that too high a price? Two deaths and your salvation is assured.'

Killing his mate, Johnny Dean, in front of the whirring cameras had been bad enough. But Johnny God bless him, had made it easy. There had been no begging, no heart-rending pleas, just a spit in the face and a stream of delirious obscenities. *Fucking arsehole, fucking motherfuckin' traitor, go on then, do it, you bastard!* There had been the knowledge too that, even if Johnny didn't know it, he was giving him the easy way out: one bullet between the eyes, no pain, just oblivion, no more torture, no torment.

But with the child it had been different. A single tear ran

down the boy's face. The liquid doe-like eyes begged him. And, with the cameras whirring just inches away, catching every twitch of every nerve, Fung made him put the pistol into the child's mouth . . . the final cruelty. The child was a stranger. Just one quick shot and it was done. But it was never done, never over, it would always be with him. Bruce Rexford reached out for his scotch. Why in God's name did that kid at the airport have to be so close? Why did fate, the malicious whore, have to conspire that way?

The telephone next to his bed began to ring, but he ignored it as he had every other call. The extension, however, was picked up downstairs in the bar and a minute later there was a cautious knock on his door.

Isabellita, one of his bar girls and his mistress of the moment, came into the cluttered room. 'There is a man on the line. He has phoned several times. He says he must speak to you.'

Rexford knew who it would be, Conrad Fung circling like a vulture. Fuck him, he thought. But he knew that if he didn't answer him now, Fung would just keep phoning and phoning, wearing him down. Rexford picked up the phone, indicating to Isabellita that she should leave the room.

'I have been asked to pass on congratulations,' said Fung, his voice, as always, as quietly menacing as the sound of acid eating into metal. 'The Red Scroll people are delighted. For an operation planned at such short notice, it was perfectly executed. You have proved yourself again, my friend.'

'I didn't want to do it, you know that. The fucking thing was a disaster.'

'Ah, of course, the killing of the innocents, the slaughter of the lambs . . . that disturbs you. When innocent people die it is never good. It disturbs us all. But please believe me, there were compelling reasons. Do you think we would have ordered it that way otherwise? We are not monsters, Bruce.'

'But the boy, a poor goddamn kid . . .'

'The boy was an accident of fate. Nobody can be blamed. He could just as easily have been run down by a car.'

'But he wasn't. I killed him. He hadn't even started his life and I killed him.'

16

. Fung sighed. 'Why do you eat yourself up this way? Why not admit it to yourself – just once – that deep down you relish these operations. After so many years, your self-flagellation rings a little false, my friend.'

'Fuck you, Fung.'

'Ah yes, fuck you – the good old Aussie response.'

'Say what you've got to say and get off the line.'

'It's been said already. Our faith in you, Bruce, is constantly renewed.'

Rexford slammed the phone down. His head flopped back on the sweat-drenched pillow. Fuck you, Fung . . . hollow threats, always the same, a pygmy spitting at the knees of a giant.

A cold, humid wind wafted in through the open window and he began to shiver. With the call finished, Isabellita came back into the room. She knelt next to him, her brown face full of puzzlement. 'Why are you lying here naked? Why is the window open? If you are sick, why can't I call a doctor?'

'Why?' he gave a long sigh. 'Because the sickness is here in my head, that's why.'

She smiled, raising a scarlet-painted fingernail to her full, dark lips. 'Then let me soothe you. I know how.' And she began to caress him, her tongue tracing patterns down his chest.

For a moment Rexford was angry, ready to push her away. Did she really believe that every ill could be cured by concentrating on the crutch? But how could he blame her? That was the sort of woman she was, the kind of woman to whom he had committed his life.

The Philippines had been well chosen all those years ago when Fung had settled him . . . a country where all power was corrupt, where the warlord and the assassin were revered, where there was no extradition, a palm-fringed Third World cock-up of a country where the women were lovely and the beer was cheap and the children on the streets broke your heart. That was all he deserved of life now.

There was ice in an ice bucket on the side table and Isabellita took a cube into her mouth. 'Ice cold,' she murmured, 'That's how you need it tonight.' She took his erection in her hand and brought her mouth down on to it. Rexford gasped with the sharp, brilliant pleasure of it. But it was only momentary, relegated quickly, a subsidiary emotion. For, even as he was brought to orgasm, that face of the young boy from the newspapers haunted him . . . another child's face in the ghost-driven gallery of his mind.

Chapter Three

Eight days had passed since the death of his son. But Dave Whitman remained in a disbelieving daze, still unable to comprehend the reality of what had happened. It couldn't be true, not a fibre of his body would accept the fact; it was some cosmic practical joke, that was all. The universe had gone into aberration. But the balance would be reset and Danny would be back with them again . . . Danny laughing as if nothing had happened, the puppy-like energy of him, the joy of hearing his voice again in the cold vacuum of the apartment. God could not take him, no God could be that cruel. Dave Whitman had seen the small coffin lowered into the ground but he still could not accept the reality of it.

For Hannah, mercifully, it had been different. For the first few days, after the initial wild hysteria, she had been in a state of collapse, doped on tranquillisers, unable to get out of bed, barely aware whether it was night or day. For those few days she had been possessed by a kind of madness. It had been impossible for her to attend the funeral. But the catharsis of that madness had had a healing side too, easing her slowly back to reality, to an acceptance of Danny's passing.

That morning, when Dave Whitman had struggled out of a drugged sleep, he had found Hannah sitting on the balcony, a mug of coffee in her hand. There had been a calmness about her, a new kind of strength, no more trembling of the fingers, no more tears brimming in the eyes. She said she had been awake all night, most of it spent there on the balcony of their Pokfulam apartment staring out over the waters of the Lamma Channel. And she said that for her the

19

time of mourning was over. That didn't mean that Danny would be forgotten. That could never happen: Danny would always be part of her, forever in her heart. But life had to continue. The most important thing now – the only thing – was to cherish his memory and to prove that no life is ever wasted . . . that nobody, not even a nine-year-old child, ever dies in vain.

'What do you intend to do?' he had asked her. And she had replied that she intended to commemorate his name in the only way she knew how.

'How is that?' he had asked, too thick-headed, too numb still to comprehend. And she had said that she intended to start that day on a line in children's fashionwear – bright pert outfits, full of fun and sunshine, zest and cheekiness. She was abandoning women's fashion. From now on she would concentrate on children's wear. And she was going to sell them all over the world, she said, this time nothing would stop her. That was how she was going to commemorate Danny's memory, by using the skills God had bestowed upon her.

She had showered and dressed then, carefully choosing her clothes and matching jewellery, slowly applying her make-up as if this day was unlike any other: a renaissance, a rebirth of courage. When the time came to leave the apartment, however, to meet the world again, she hesitated at the door, suddenly afraid. Dave went towards her but she held up her hand, smiling, and said. 'No, I'll be fine.' Then she had driven to her tiny factory premises across the harbour in Tsim Sha Tsui and Dave was left in the apartment just as dazed, just as lost.

Delia, their Filipino amah who had been with them since Danny's birth, who cherished Danny like her own son, had brought breakfast which he ate in morose silence. Then, for some reason which he couldn't divine, Dave Whitman walked through to Danny's room.

Not once since Danny's death had he been in that room. Delia had lovingly cleaned it every day, Hannah had treated it as a shrine, but he hadn't been able to bring himself to go in. This time, however, he lingered at the door summoning his courage. Then he entered. There was a silence about the room, an unnatural stillness. The soft toys on his bed, the old tiger that he had had since he was five, the giraffe, the koala from friends in Australia, were all too neatly arranged. A Snoopy poster hung on the wall above the bed: 'Just when I knew all of life's answers they went and changed the questions.' Danny's drawings were on the wall, photographs of him in his mini-league baseball team. On his desk was a hand-drawn anniversary card; two stick people wearing huge smiles sitting on a bench holding hands and inside the words: 'For the best mum and dad in the world, love you lots – Danny.'

Dave Whitman picked up the card. But, as he did so, his hand began to tremble. He was a strong man, he had seen more than his fair share of life's tragedies. He had always believed he could cope. But not now, dear God, this was impossible to bear. The tears welled up in his brown eyes, hot and stinging. His chest felt as if it was going to burst. He turned towards Danny's bed but suddenly his legs were weak. He fell to his knees, clutching the card, and now the tears streamed down his face. He couldn't hold it any longer. And he said out loud, 'Oh God, why couldn't it have been me?' And, for the first time, he began to sob, great racking sobs that shook his whole body. 'Oh Danny, my son, my son,' he prayed, 'please forgive me.'

It was ten that morning when he went to the phone. He had climbed up from his knees, he had dried his tears. Hannah had shown the way. Now was the time for him to follow.

Since the day they had returned from honeymoon ten years ago, Hannah had tried to convince him to leave the police, to find a job in the private sector, in finance or real estate; something button-down and prosperous. So many times she had said it to him: *you can't stay in the police forever; you can do it Dave, any job you wish*. But he had resisted the move. He didn't know why, lethargy maybe, the fact that when he was old he wanted to look back on his life and have something more than just cash in the bank . . . the hard, inescapable fact that he liked being a cop.

Being a cop was no big deal, he knew that. He wasn't a big deal person. He wanted his life to be full and he wanted happiness, not too much more. But being a cop had taught him one thing – to track down criminals. And, if Hannah had her way of commemorating Danny, so did he, the oldest way known to man – to seek justice, to exact revenge.

Hannah might seek to ensure that Danny hadn't died in vain by distilling his laughter and his boundless young boy's charm into the colour and cut of cloth. But for him it was more simple, primeval. As the Old Testament decreed, an eye for an eye, a tooth for a tooth . . . the ancient song of vengeance. There would, he swore silently to Danny that morning, be an accounting. If it took him the rest of his life, there would be retribution.

With slow deliberation he dialled the number of the Organised Crime and Triad Group, the office where he worked. He got through to reception and asked for Superintendent Lampton, Christopher George Kerwell Lampton – Kit, his best friend in the force and Danny's godfather.

Kit and he had come to Hong Kong in the same intake to join the Royal Hong Kong Police, two footloose characters fed up with England and fascinated by the Far East, bugger all use to anybody then, amazed even to be offered the job. They were both superintendents now, both in the OCTG. He and Kit had done their fourteen years together, totally different characters and close as brothers.

When Kit came on the line, there was a tone of sympathetic caution in his voice. 'Hi, how are you feeling?' he asked. 'Are you bearing up?'

'I'm okay,' said Dave. 'I'm coming back to work.'

He never wore suits if he could help it, that was one of the perks of being a cop. Hannah dressed him in casual gear she purchased at factory prices from other fashion houses. He looked a little bit too upbeat for his own comfort sometimes but Hannah liked it and he could live with it happily enough. His transport was a motorbike, a black Suzuki 750GSXR. Hannah hated motorbikes and drove a venerable BMW. But in the interminable spaghetti of Hong Kong's

·traffic the bike got him around quicker and cheaper than any car.

At eleven-thirty that morning he drove into Central, to the offices of OCTG at Police Headquarters on Arsenal Street. He had worked there for the past two years but that morning he saw it with fresh eyes. Now it had become a means to an end.

The operational wing of the Organised Crime and Triad Group, the Bureau, as it was called, was under the command of a senior superintendent. His name was Tom Mackay. Tom had four divisions under him. Dave led C Division, Kit led B. On arrival, Dave went straight to Tom's office.

Tom Mackay was a Scot, ruddy faced with sandy hair, a big man, well over six foot. He had been a good sportsman in his day, strictly mud, blood and rugby, and had the broken nose to show for it. He was aged somewhere in his mid-forties, a Hong Kong veteran. He was married to a wee woman, a Chinese, who ruled his life. Tom liked his beer, he spoke his mind. He got angry when the need arose but he had compassion. All in all, he was a good boss to have.

Dave came straight to the point with him. 'I want to be on the Kai Tak investigation,' he said. 'I know that Kit is heading it up, that he is working with Special Branch on the Japanese Red Army claim. But I also know that it's not as simple as that. There are other angles that need investigation, a hundred and one tangents. You can't accept anything at face value, not in a case this big. Put me on anything, Tom, I don't care. Let me just feel I'm part of the team.'

'I wish it was that easy,' said Tom Mackay. 'But you know the situation when there's a personal involvement, Dave.'

'There are no written rules.'

'I accept that. But—'

'Tom, please, that was my son who was killed. Can you imagine how I feel? I'll be no good for anything else, you know it. Let me at least be part of the team. You've got kids of your own. Don't shunt me off into a siding like somebody

23

recuperating from an illness. I have to know what's happen-. ing, I have to play a part. I'll go mad otherwise. Harry, my deputy, can take over the day-to-day stuff in my division. I'll help him out whenever necessary. I'm prepared to put in eighteen hours a day, I don't care.'

Tom Mackay was uncertain. As Dave had said, there were no written rules for situations like this. Instinctively, though, he knew it was courting trouble. On the other hand, as Dave said, he had kids of his own. God forbid he was ever in Dave's situation: he knew how he would feel. 'Okay, give me time to think about it,' he said. 'I'll come back to you.'

Dave and Kit Lampton went out for lunch to a local Wan-chai restaurant, nothing expensive, some sizzling beef, white rice and beer. It was the first full meal Dave had eaten since Danny's death.

'You're looking shit,' Kit told him. 'Are you still running?'

'Not since Danny's death. Just can't get myself into the mood for it.'

'Then start running again. And eat. You look like a Belsen case. I'm over two hundred pounds. I feel guilty just looking at you.'

Kit Lampton was a big man too, big and beefy and affable, a man who was full of jokes and hoary tales and a considerable amount of bullshit. He loved sport, loved organising things. You wanted a police golf tour, you spoke to Kit. You wanted fancy gifts for the New Year ball, you spoke to Kit. He had no respect for rank. You can't breathe when you're brown-nosing, was his credo. He had never therefore been the favourite son of the hierarchy. But he was a top-rate operator, that's what redeemed him. He got the job done.

Kit's marriage had broken up less than a year ago and he had taken it hard. But he was over it now, on the surface at least, always happy to joke about her. 'She's emigrated to New Zealand,' he said, trying to get Dave's mind off the one subject that possessed him. 'South Island, down next to the Antarctic. Suits her personality admirably. She's even got married again. Some monosyllabic chicken-sexer from Invercargill. God honest truth, that's what she tells me. Their idea of an exciting life must be to take a six-pack of Steinlager and go watch a glacier melt. She wanted the settled life, well, she's got it. A picket fence, a pick-up truck, two canaries and a mortgage. What's the world coming to, Dave? I've been replaced by a bloody chicken-sexer!'

For the first time since Danny's death, Dave found himself laughing. In its own small way it was a revelation. Slowly, like a man crippled, he was rediscovering the world.

After lunch they returned to the offices of OCTG. Kit had meetings to attend with Special Branch on the Japanese Red Army issue. Dave had nothing to do but sit in his office, flip through files, do a little of his division's admin work and wait. It wasn't until late afternoon, close to five, that Tom Mackay came to his office.

'I can't promise mainline action,' he said.

'I don't need it. Anything, Tom, anything at all.'

'So long as you appreciate that.'

'Of course.'

'Good. Then you're on the team.'

That evening, as the neon lights of Tsim Sha Tsui came on and their electronic glow flooded through the window of her small office, Hannah Whitman was still bent over her design board. All day she had worked like a woman possessed, the door locked, taking no calls, allowing no interruptions. Drawing after drawing had been rushed off, thrown on to her desk or falling to the office floor. She had never been in such pain, never experienced such love. Never in her life before had she felt such soaring inspiration.

Around eight, exhaustion finally set in. She unlocked her office door and collapsed into her chair, leaving her drawings where they had fallen. Not a sound came from the office area or the small factory next to it. It seemed as if everybody had left, everybody with the exception, of course, of Scott Defoe.

Scott came in with a cup of coffee, put it on the desk in front of her and, without saying a word, began to collect her drawings, studying each one in turn.

Scott was a New Yorker like Hannah, Brooklyn born, a young designer who had been her right hand in the business since its inception. He was small for a man, almost diminutive, serious looking with grey eyes and black hair. He always spoke softly. He was gay, he made no pretence about it. He worked hard, he was loyal beyond sensibility and, as a sounding board for her creations, he was perfect.

'So, what do you think?' asked Hannah in a tired monotone. 'Is there anything there even halfway worthwhile?'

Scott finished with the last drawing, reverently placed it on the desk, then he looked up and there were tears sparkling in those grey eyes of his. 'Oh heavens,' he whispered. 'Danny is alive here. They're beautiful, Hannah, more beautiful than anything you have ever done.'

At seven that night there was a meeting in Tom Mackay's office. Dave and Kit Lampton were there. The others were Henry Tang who was from Special Branch, the political wing of the police, and Stan Tarbuck, the Legal Liaison Officer at the US Consulate, their FBI contact. For Dave's benefit, progress to date was summarised.

At Kai Tak itself, a team of officers had sorted meticulously through the scene of the blast, collecting and plotting every fragment and shard of the suitcase bomb, three thousand five hundred pieces in all. The pieces were still being analysed, but one item, the brand logo from the suitcase, spoke for itself.

'The suitcase was made in the Philippines,' said Henry Tang, their Special Branch man, who fancied himself as an intellectual and always wore a bow tie. 'The logo bears the words FLY HI. The factory that manufactures the suitcases is in Pagadian, a town on the island of Mindanao. That's an area where the New People's Army, the Filipino communist insurgents, have operated for a long time.'

'How does that tie in with the Japanese Red Army?' asked Dave. 'I always assumed they operated out of Japan or, at a push, the Middle East.'

26

'Not always,' said Henry Tang. 'For several years now the JRA has had a base of operations in the Philippines. If it suits them, they team up with other armed groups. We know, for example, that several recent kidnappings of Japanese businessmen in the Philippines were a joint venture between the JRA and the New People's Army. They shared the proceeds.'

'So the origin of the suitcase would support the JRA claim that they planted the bomb?'

Henry Tang shrugged. 'I don't want to go that far. It fits, let's put it that way. It adds a little corroboration.'

'Do you have anything to suggest that the bombing was not the work of the JRA?'

Stan Tarbuck, the FBI man, replied, 'No, nothing. We know the JRA is operational, we know they have the manpower, we know they have the ability to get into Hong Kong. Let's face it, economically, what they say about Hong Kong is right. The Japanese and the Americans do have huge investments here. Hong Kong is a capitalist dream working. You can smell it, you can feel it. It's exactly the kind of target they would choose.'

'But why plant the bomb right next to that particular small group of people,' asked Dave, 'one a consulate officer from Peru, one a diplomat from Communist China?'

'They were standing at the first-class counter, maybe that accounts for it,' said Tarbuck. 'Making sure the fat cats were taken out.' But it was said without conviction.

'It still seems strange to me. Why wouldn't they go for an American-owned building here or a Japanese aircraft, something more obviously identifiable? It's almost as if they were specifically targeting those particular individuals, not just slamming the system.'

'It's a valid observation,' said Tom Mackay, 'one which has been worrying me too – which brings us on to the individuals themselves. Gao Xin first. I received some information this evening which might interest you all. Gao Xin has a daughter studying physics at Cambridge University. Gao Xue is her name. Xue in Mandarin means snow. It seems that Gao Xue went to her tutor a day or so back and confided in him, just about gave the poor old bugger a stroke . . . said that her father had been intending to defect, to seek political asylum either in Britain or the USA, and that she was positive he had been murdered, killed for political motives.'

The news stunned everybody. A new dimension had been added to the investigation, a potentially mind-blowing one too, considering Hong Kong's special relationship to China.

But Henry Tang, the SB man, was dubious. 'Gao Xin was essentially an admin person, a backroom bureaucrat. Even if he was defecting, what kind of information could he take with him? I'm sorry, it makes no sense. Why would the Chinese wish to kill one of their own in such a catastrophic fashion? Nobody operates that way, not any more. If you ask me, the daughter, this girl Gao Xue, is fantasising, post trauma hysteria. It's not unusual.'

'Maybe,' said Tom Mackay. 'But we still need to look into it.' He turned to Kit. 'I want you on a plane to the UK tomorrow night. It's been cleared through Interpol. Special Branch are in agreement. Go up to Cambridge, spend a bit of time with her, speak to her, sound her out. Speak to those people who know her well. Maybe it is just hysteria, as Henry says. But maybe there's more.'

Kit couldn't help a smile. Cops didn't get to travel too much, not with expenses paid. It had been a couple of years since he had been back in England.

Tom Mackay turned his attention to Stan Tarbuck. 'What have the FBI been able to dig up on our movie man, Hildebrand? Anything yet that would smack of motive?'

Stan Tarbuck shook his head. 'Zero. He was strictly a muscle man, body and brain. No known political connections. Did what his agent told him. Outside of the movies, the most controversial thing he ever did was promote high-fibre food. No suggestion he was in debt, no gangland connections. Squeaky bright and clean.'

'What about the deranged fan angle, the John Lennon syndrome?' asked Dave.

'Yeah, we've considered that. But the experts tell us that with psycho fans it's a love-hate thing: they like to get in close, use a small-calibre gun, a knife maybe, make the death dance something intimate. Apart from that, the bomb was too sophisticated. No Dave, everything points to a professional hit.'

'Back to the JRA again?'

'Afraid so.'

'What about the publicity secretary?' asked Tom Mackay.

'Mary O'Connell? From what we know, nice girl, mid-twenties, totally harmless,' Stan Tarbuck answered. 'Our people back in the States are still investigating but I think we can discount her.'

'So, out of the people killed, if we're looking for a personal motive, that just leaves Gomez and his wife,' said Dave. 'Is there anything there?'

'Yes, maybe there is,' said Tom Mackay. 'It's a long shot, I admit. But there might just be something. And that's where you are going to be involved, Dave. From what we've learnt over the past couple of days, our Mr Gomez wasn't exactly in the running for the most honest diplomat of the year. He and his wife weren't returning to Peru for a holiday. He had been recalled.'

'Why's that?' asked Dave.

'We've learnt that there had been complaints,' said Tom Mackay. 'Complaints that he was involved in the corrupt sale of residence visas.'

Dave blinked. Peruvian residence visas? He almost wanted to laugh. To blow up an airport over some Peruvian residence visas? A long shot, Tom had said. Hell, it had to be twenty thousand to one! Okay, United States visas maybe – way out at the far edge of what was possible. But Peru? Half of Hong Kong didn't know where it was!

Tom Mackay read his thoughts and smiled at him across the desk. 'Don't knock it, Dave, you might just be surprised. The Peruvian Government has taken it seriously enough to send out a team of investigators. They arrived this morning, closeted themselves in the Consulate and will be working all weekend. Kit was going to liaise with them but now that he is heading for England, that's your job. They expect you at the Peruvian Consulate first thing Monday morning.'

'Okay,' said Dave.

'Like I said, it's a long shot, don't expect anything,' said Tom Mackay. 'We're covering the bases, that's all. But once in a blue moon . . . well, who knows?'

It was gone ten that night before Dave and Hannah eventually returned to their apartment. Hannah had telephoned ahead asking Delia to prepare a dinner for them as she had always done in the old days, the days before Danny's death. The table was laid, the best cutlery set, a French Chablis was on the ice.

As they sat at the table, they were both emotionally exhausted. But they were filled too with a new resolve. And there was a special new closeness between them, a closeness they hadn't felt for many months.

Over the past couple of years their marriage had been under strain. It had been subtle, unspoken, but there all the same, especially since Hannah's business had bogged down in the financial mire. She had pressed Dave too often to get out of the police and his reluctance had been the source of some bitter arguments. For months, if they were truthful with each other, the only real focus of their marriage had been Danny. And now Danny was gone.

But sitting at the table that night, sharing the wine and their sorrow, they began, gently, uncertainly, to reach out to each other again. Who else did they have now if not each other?

After dinner, Hannah showed him the sketches she had rushed off, thirty or more, all in the space of one day and even to Dave's untutored eye they were good, bright with colours and innovations, friendly and eminently wearable. Hannah knew they were some of the best she had ever done, and she was bubbling with excitement. 'I've decided on a name,' she said, 'a name for the whole range – Danny's Rags. What do you think?'

Dave liked it – yes, the name was irreverent, cheeky, hinting at the sophisticated, great for a city kid.

Hannah looked at him and her blue eyes were dazzling. 'They're going to sell, Dave,' she said. 'I know it. And the smile of every child who wears one of the outfits – whether

30

he's American, Chinese, French, it doesn't matter – will be a memory of Danny's smile. That's my final gift to him.'

Dave watched the first tear spill down his wife's cheek. She was a beautiful woman, petite, flaxen-haired, slim as a reed, as ethereal as a ballet dancer; yet combative too, fiercely and physically so.

'Come,' she said to him. 'Come through with me.' She reached out to take his hand and together they went through to their bedroom.

The clothes slipped from her body and she stood naked before him. Although she was petite, her breasts were high and full and her waist, flowing into her hips, traced a line no artist could match. She looked vulnerable yet proud, enticing and brave. Her skin was as pale as autumn sunlight.

'Oh God, I need you so much,' she said.

'I love you,' he whispered. 'I always have. I always will.'

She came to him, her breasts bobbing, her nipples the colour of champagne. Slowly, she undid his shirt, button by button. The shirt slipped from his shoulders to the carpet. He was so thin, she thought, so physically ravaged by Danny's death. Yet the strength showed so clearly too, the muscles in the abdomen and in the broad sweep of his chest.

They kissed then, standing there, their bodies locked, before Dave led her to the bed. Both of them were crying now. And like two lost souls, clinging together in a great void of space, filled with fear and buoyed with hope, they made love together.

Chapter Four

The room where the initiation ceremony was held was a mildewed basement beneath a rice shop in the old part of Western close to the waterfront, the praya as it was called. It was an area of poor folk: coolies and hawkers and opium smokers. But it was an area too where the old Chinese values were held dear. And that was what brought Chan Sau-fuk to this place.

Chan – Hector Chan as he liked to be called in the European circles of his business – was sixty years old, a lawyer. He had founded his own firm, a firm of twenty lawyers now. He was a man to be reckoned with in Hong Kong. As a young man, he had taken his degree in law at Oxford University and to outsiders, to those who did not really know, he seemed greatly impressed by all things English. He dressed like an English gentleman, belonged to the best clubs, kept an apartment in London's Mayfair. But, despite his British affectations, Hector Chan was deeply, mystically Chinese, pure Han from generations back.

Many years ago, as a young lawyer with few contacts and fewer friends, when the big expatriate firms, the British with their 'old boy' network, ruled the roost, Hector Chan had fallen upon hard times. That is when he had been approached and asked if he would represent certain persons in their business affairs. He had agreed and he had prospered and naturally he had fallen in league with those who had made him successful.

That was why now, today, he was the *Heung Chu*, the Grand Incense Master of an outlawed Triad society, the society known as the Wo Shing Wo.

The Triad, the secret brotherhood of heaven and earth, had been the foundation of Chan's reputation and riches. Triad influence turned the testimony of witnesses in both civil and criminal cases. Triad interests gave him opportunity for investment. Triad cash paid his fees.

Very few knew it of course, very few indeed. To belong to a Tong, a Triad society, was a criminal offence. To most people Hector Chan was an articulate product of Hong Kong's special place in Asia, a product of its internationalism, more Western than Oriental, a man who appreciated the bouquet of a good Bordeaux, every inch an assimilated gentleman. And that suited him perfectly.

The climax of the ceremony was approaching. In the small basement the joss smoke hung in pale layers like mist. Hector Chan took the gold chalice – the chalice filled with wine, sugar, cinnabar and the ashes of the yellow parchment listing the thirty-six sacred oaths – and set it close to the chopping block.

The cockerel was brought forward. Its legs were tied with four red tapes and each recruit held one of the tapes as the shivering bird was laid upon the block. Hector Chan recited the ancient incantation and the recruits repeated his words in an awe-struck monotone –

'The cockerel's head sheds fresh blood,
Here among us is loyalty and righteousness.'

Then, with one blow, the Vanguard severed the cockerel's head and, their cheeks spattered with its blood, the recruits let go of the red tapes. Hector Chan dipped the severed head, still oozing blood, into the chalice while the Vanguard wrapped the carcass in joss paper and recited –

'Ah Kat, the cockerel, you have done evil.
Our new members punish you tonight.
Now they know how traitors are treated,
Their coffins will be joss paper . . .'

Hector Chan went to the altar, taking a silver needle

threaded with red cotton. Then, standing in front of each recruit, he repeated to each of them –

> 'The silver needle brings blood from your finger.
> Do not reveal our secrets to others.
> For, if any secrets are disclosed,
> Blood will be shed from the five holes of your body.'

Each finger was pricked and blood squeezed into the chalice, mingling with that of the cockerel. Then each recruit knelt around Hector Chan and, to each in turn, he handed the chalice so they might drink from it, chanting all the time –

> 'After drinking the red flower wine,
> You will live for ninety-nine years.'

Then each was allocated a protector and to each protector a *laisee* packet containing money was given, a sign of due homage. And with that, the ceremony was done, the new recruits inducted.

Hector Chan was pleased. He always ensured that the ancient rituals were followed to the letter. There was no better way of ensuring loyalty. Make a man, especially a simple man, feel that he had entered some mythical brotherhood, that the whole was greater than any individual, and he never betrayed you.

Hector Chan went to a small side room in order to take off his robes, the white robe resembling the dress of a Buddhist monk, the prayer beads, the red headband and the single grass slipper that all officials wore in memory of the magic sandals salvaged from Siu Lam Monastery by the First Five Ancestors of the brotherhood. He was folding them into a briefcase when Wong Kam-kiu, a lower official in the Triad, entered.

'May I have a word?' asked Wong, who was a timid, mousy individual, a small-time accountant and emigration consultant. 'I have been trying to reach the Foreign Boy for

35

days. It is most worrying. I have no idea where he is but I must speak to him.'

'He travels a great deal,' said Hector Chan. 'He must be out of Hong Kong. What do you wish to speak to him about?'

'It's about the scheme we had together,' said Wong, 'the Foreign Boy and I. Remember, it was you who brought us together, the scheme with Gomez.'

Hector Chan remembered only too well – and regretted it immensely. Thank God he had only been a broker. Things had turned bad with Gomez, very bad indeed. 'What about it?' he asked, stiffening. 'Perhaps I can help.'

'I'm just so worried,' said Wong. 'I mean with Gomez being recalled and then dying that way. What happens if the police question me, what do I say, what do I do? I'm at a loss.'

'Have you destroyed your records?'

'Yes, yes, of course, every last one!'

'Then I don't see the problem. Gomez will never have kept records himself,' said Hector Chan. 'If you are questioned, you conducted your business with Gomez in a perfectly legitimate manner. Say that and no more. They can prove nothing.'

'But I worry so much,' said Wong, wringing his hands. 'What happens if they *do* find out? What happens if I am put in jail? You know my wife, you know how sickly she is. Her heart condition gets worse every month. The child is sickly too and my business just doesn't earn enough. You know all that.'

Hector Chan gave a bland smile of sympathy. It was important to show concern even if all you felt was irritation. 'If any ill luck should befall you, your family will be looked after. You know that. The brotherhood will stand by you.'

'But it's more than a question of money,' wailed Wong. 'My wife is a very fragile person. The Foreign Boy promised me protection. He said he would see to it that I came to no harm. That's the only reason I ever agreed to the scheme. He must get us out of Hong Kong. That's the only way. Please, I must have his assurances.'

'I'll see what can be done,' said Chan stiffly, searching for some way to wash his hands of the affair. 'I'll try to contact Tselentis and talk to him. But you're a *Pak Tsz Sin*, remember that, an official adviser to the brotherhood, a White Paper Fan.'

'Yes, yes, I understand,' blubbered Wong.

'Then stay firm. Remember your rank. And whatever you do, don't panic.'

As arranged, Dave met the Peruvian team at their consular offices in Central at nine on Monday morning. He wasn't expecting much.

The team consisted of just two, the country's director general of consular staff, a shrewd but disarmingly affable individual by the name of Miguel de Haan, and a woman, Maria Ramirez, thirty or so, plump and pretty, who had been hauled out of the embassy in London to take over as consul in Hong Kong.

Miguel de Haan did virtually all the talking. 'I'll be frank,' he said. 'No diplomatic hedging. This may seem like a problem of minimal importance to you – a few visas, perhaps a little bribery – but I must tell you that we have a scandal of very great proportions about to break in Peru. It won't bring the Government down but there will be many red faces, many questions to be answered. The press in Lima are already printing stories, demanding an investigation. In short, we need your help, Mr Whitman. Tell me, what do you know about the extent of the problem?'

'Very little,' said Dave. 'As you say . . . a few visas, perhaps a little cash passed under the table.'

'There is no need for me to tell you of the great movement of people from this part of the world at the present time.'

'There's a lot of people leaving, I know that,' said Dave. 'They want to be out before 1997 when China takes over the government of Hong Kong. It's becoming a stampede to some countries, Canada, Australia . . .'

'There are people leaving mainland China too,' said de Haan, 'people getting permission to join relatives, people trying to escape the difficult conditions they live under.

From Asia generally there is a great migration of people. Ninety-five percent of it is orderly, controlled, legal. But five percent – the five percent that concerns us – is not.'

'What specific problems do you have in Peru?' asked Dave, thinking that, in respect of Chinese anyway, they had to be small.

Miguel de Haan gave a wry smile. 'Three years ago we had a settled Chinese population in Peru of just twelve thousand people. Do you have any idea how many Chinese – and not just from Hong Kong, I include the mainland here – have settled in Peru since then, people we are sure have used tainted papers, visas obtained through corruption? Fourteen thousand, Mr Whitman. Yes, fourteen thousand. And the problem is not just restricted to Peru. It is the same in Venezuela, Colombia, Argentina. For a country of our size fourteen thousand is a vast number. I don't blame the immigrants themselves. They are anxious, they are poor, they want to make a new life for themselves. They will not be deported. What is done is done. But an uncontrolled flood like that, a flood of people who do not speak our language, who have no cultural ties, a flood caused by rampant corruption . . . no, no, that must not happen again.'

Dave was surprised by the figures, his attitudes beginning to change. 'But can you prove this corruption?' he asked.

'It will take time, of course. Here in the consulate we have thousands of files, one for each family, files covering mainland China, Taiwan, Hong Kong. In Lima, our capital, there are many more. Within a few weeks we hope to have more accurate figures for you, names and addresses of people who need to be questioned. Of course we have no jurisdiction to question them ourselves, not in Hong Kong. That is where we will need your help.'

'What about Gomez himself? Presumably he was up to his neck in it?'

'He had the disease, Mr Whitman, the disease called greed. Maria can tell you more about it.'

Maria Ramirez opened a buff file which she had on the table in front of her. 'The late consul,' she said, 'did not come from a wealthy family. The only income he had was

38

his salary. Yet he appears to have enjoyed a life style disproportionate to his earnings, remarkably so: two homes in Lima, a ranch near Huacho, a luxury boat, sports cars, racehorses. We know too he kept Swiss bank accounts. The late consul obviously relished the trappings of luxury. Even the watch taken off his body was a gold Rolex.'

'What about the wife?' asked Dave. 'Did she come from a wealthy family? What about relatives? Is there any money there?'

Maria Ramirez shook her head. 'The wife came from a middle-class background. Her father was a schoolteacher. There is no wealth in either family.'

'There can only be one source of the money,' said Miguel de Haan with undisguised bitterness. 'That is from the corrupt sale of residence visas, Mr Whitman, thousands upon thousands of them. As soon as we have more information, in a few days time, we will seek your aid.'

Hannah could hardly believe it. It was Friday night already, close to midnight. Scott had left a few minutes ago and now it was just her, alone in her office. What had happened to all the days? They had passed her in a blur.

She had never known it before, the frenetic energy, the constant compulsion, the determination to see in cloth and colour, in buttons and stitching, all those images spinning in the Catherine wheel of her mind. She was resolved that the samples would be ready within record time: she couldn't wait. Everything had to be done on the turn.

What in the past had taken days was now taking a matter of hours. For most of that week, she and Scott Defoe had worked until one or two in the morning, alone in the factory together long after the other workers had gone, arguing over fabrics and accessories, pushing for perfection. Scott had been working flat out on the spec sheets, as tireless as her.

In the beginning there had been sixty drawings but they had been edited down now to just twenty-five pieces; the twenty-five pieces that made up the spring collection, her *first* collection of Danny's Rags.

Not content with available prints, determined that the

look must be one hundred percent right, Hannah had painted her own patterns – bright and cheeky, full of antics – and sent them to be run off, pushing business colleagues for immediate results, even phoning them at home. Nothing would hold her back, not lack of money, lack of past performance, nothing. She was, she knew it, and relished it too, a woman possessed.

The staff worked with her all the way. Nobody complained, nobody demanded extra pay. Somehow they all knew, the pattern maker, the sewing girls, all of them, that this collection was inspired.

Wearily, Hannah got up from her chair. It was time to go home. Dave would be waiting for her. He never went to sleep until she returned. He had been so good, so patient. She went out into the factory. It was very quiet, very hushed. She looked at the sewing machines and the rolls of fabric, the racks of samples and the brown paper patterns scattered on the tables . . . they were all her altar. And suddenly she was aware of his presence, ethereal, invisible, so full of love. An exhausted, radiant smile settled on her face . . . it was the spirit of Danny skipping next to her. He had been with her all the time.

On the Monday morning – one week exactly since their first meeting – Dave received a call from Miguel de Haan. At last the waiting was over.

'Maria and I are still scratching the surface of the files,' he said, 'but there is one name which keeps coming up. It is the name of a Hong Kong travel agent who arranged charter flights for many of the immigrants. It seems he arranged flights for whole blocks of families, two or three hundred a time, and on a regular basis.'

'Can you give me his name?'

'He calls himself Eustace Yu,' said de Haan. 'The company he runs is called Double Happiness Vacations. I have the address here.'

Double Happiness Vacations was across the harbour on the Kowloon side. It was situated in an old building in the teeming back streets of Yau Ma Tei, a stone's throw from the typhoon shelter. Hawkers stood on the pavement outside peddling fried squid and bean curd, obscuring posters of the Swiss Alps in the window.

Eustace Yu was a fat, seedy individual who chain smoked behind a desk littered with papers and brochures. The visit of a senior *gweilo* cop didn't surprise him in the least. With the death of the Peruvian Consul at the airport and all the publicity he had been expecting a call.

Yes, he told Dave, he had had dealings with Mr Gomez, very many dealings. He knew him well, in business that is, not socially. He had arranged charter flights to Lima in Peru, flights for immigrants and their families, immigrants who had their visas. Most flights left from Hong Kong, a few from Taiwan, some even from Indonesia. It depended on the best rates available at the time.

Dave asked him if he took any part in helping the immigrants to obtain the necessary visas.

'I did nothing like that. You can check my files,' said Yu candidly. 'I had nothing to do with the immigration side. I am busy enough as it is. I am a simple travel agent, nothing more.'

'To do the charter bookings, you must have had an arrangement with somebody,' said Dave.

'Yes, naturally. I had an arrangement with an immigration consultant,' said Yu. 'He gave me the lists. I gave him a small commission in return.'

'What is the name of this consultant?'

A cigarette dangling from his lip, Yu searched through his files, trying to give the impression that the name had escaped him. It was all bullshit. They were probably first cousins, thought Dave.

'Ah yes,' said Yu, 'I have it here. He has an office on Hong Kong Island. It is in Western, near the Magistracy there. The man's name is Wong – Wong Kam-kiu.'

The office was just off the Pokfulam Road. It was a grubby little ground-floor place squeezed in between a repair shop and a picture framer. Above the door was a hand-painted sign in Chinese characters which read: Utmost Fidelity Consultants. The door was open.

There was just one person in the office. He was a scrawny, middle-aged man in a suit and tie. He was balding with moles on his chin. Thick bottle-bottom glasses sat on the end of his nose. When Dave entered, he was hunched over a dusty computer pecking away with two fingers. A half-finished lunchbox sat next to him. The smell of soy sauce and cabbage filled the room.

'Are you Wong Kam-kiu?' asked Dave, showing his warrant card, speaking fluent Cantonese.

Wong jerked up, his glasses almost fell off. 'Yes, that's me. Why, what do you want?' he squeaked. 'It's nothing serious, is it? I mean, I can't imagine . . .'

Dave stared at him in surprise. When a cop walked in to ask questions, there was always a reaction, even with perfectly innocent people. But nothing like this. This was a reaction of a different kind, a reaction he had seen many times before, the pop-eyed look of a startled rabbit, the response of a very frightened – and very guilty – man.

Dave pulled up a seat, his instincts racing. His face was gaunt at the best of times but there was a sudden hardness to it now, a glacial look in the eyes. 'I believe you advise people on emigration matters,' he said.

Wong remained glued to his chair. It was incredible, even a straightforward question like that appeared to floor him. 'Yes, yes,' he muttered. 'That's right.'

'What countries?'

'Canada mainly. Hong Kong people like to go to Canada. And Australia too. America, England, a few to New Zealand. Yes, South Africa now, yes a few there . . .' He was babbling, falling over his words.'

'South America?'

'South America? No, not too many.'

'Come now Mr Wong.'

'Well, yes, a few, just a few.'

'Let me ask you about one country in particular.'

'Yes?'

'Peru.'

'Peru? What about it?' Wong visibly gulped.

Dave was amazed. What in the hell was it? Was the man that frightened by a simple bribery investigation? He stared straight at him, face hard. 'Have you ever handled immigration into Peru?'

'I must check. I have a file here.' Wong half rose from his chair.

'Surely you don't need a file, Mr Wong.'

He fell back. An elbow caught his lunchbox which toppled to the floor. Wong fumbled to pick it up, cabbage all over his fingers. 'Yes,' he said in a mournful voice. 'Yes, I have advised some people.'

'How many people, Mr Wong?'

'Without checking my records—'

'I'm not after exact figures.'

Wong fell into a stupefied silence.

'The figure I've been given,' said Dave, 'is fourteen thousand or more. About ninety-nine percent of your recent business, I would imagine. Is that right?'

For a moment it looked as if Wong was going to vomit into his lunchbox. Then he protested in a weak voice, 'I don't know why you are asking me all these questions. I did nothing wrong.'

'Why are you so frightened, Mr Wong?'

'Frightened? I'm not frightened. But you come barging in here. It was all legal, everything. They were business migrants, all wealthy people.'

'Wealthy? Are you sure? If so, why Peru, Mr Wong?'

'They saw the opportunities.'

'And how much were they paying for their papers, Mr Wong, these *wealthy* people you advised?'

Wong removed his glasses, polishing them furiously. 'I'd have to check. Each country has different charges.' His mouth was opening and shutting like a fish.

Dave decided – right or wrong – to go in harder, to hit him straight in the midriff. 'You know what I mean about paying: I mean monies to the consul.'

'There were standard fees.'

'No, Mr Wong, I mean money under the table.'

43

Wong's eyes popped. 'Are you accusing me – ?'

'You were paying the consul, weren't you, paying Mr Gomez massive amounts. It was one huge scam.'

Wong's fingers started to tremble. A dribble of spit rolled down his chin. 'I want to see a lawyer,' he stuttered. 'You can't come in here and make wild accusations like that. I refuse to answer any more questions.'

'Who was with you, Mr Wong? Who was pulling the strings? The scheme was too big for you, too complex. Fourteen thousand emigrants, men, women and children . . . emigrants from here, emigrants from the mainland. You didn't originate the scheme, you didn't organise it all on your own. Who was it, Mr Wong?'

Wong shook his head like a man with a terrible nervous affliction. 'Nobody. I don't know what you mean.'

And at that moment – acting on pure, primal instinct – Dave took the quantum leap. His eyes bored into Wong. He was silent for a moment. Then he said. 'Gomez, your partner, was killed at the airport, killed in that bomb blast. Do you know why, Mr Wong?'

Wong gawked at him, his mouth fell open – and Dave knew. In that fraction of time, eye to eye, with not a word said, right then he knew that he had struck the vein of gold.

Wong pushed his chair back, away from his desk, as if Dave carried a deadly plague. 'I know nothing about that,' he stammered, his voice close to hysteria, 'nothing, nothing at all.'

And Dave's temper snapped. 'Oh yes you do! You know a great deal, Mr Wong. It's written all over your face. And you're going to tell me. I don't care how long it takes. A week, a month, it's all the same to me. I don't think you comprehend the depth of the shit you've landed in. This could well be murder. Innocent people have been butchered, one of them just a nine-year-old boy. Either you come clean and tell me everything you know – everything! – or I'm going to crucify you. Do you understand what I'm saying? Make it easy on yourself or make it hard. It's your choice. But in the end you'll talk.'

'Why are you doing this to me?' wailed Wong, his arms in

the air. 'The Japanese Red Army did the bombing. Everybody knows it. Why are you trying to involve me? I'm not going to say another word. I want a lawyer. I'm a respectable man!'

Dave climbed to his feet, his fists clenched. Respectable? Christ – Wong stank of fear, reeked of it. Whatever he knew, whatever he was hiding, may have started out as bribery but it had grown into something greater, darker, a hundred times more sinister. He could see it in Wong's eyes. The man knew his life was on the line. But why? Why? As he stood there, Dave tried desperately to control his temper but it was next to impossible. All the time he could hear the explosion of the airport bomb in his ears, he could hear himself shouting for his son, oh God, please Danny, please, don't be dead!

Wong was gawking up at him, at his face, at his clenched fists, eyes frozen like the eyes of a rabbit trapped in a cage with a python.

'You're happy to make your money out of crooked schemes aren't you?' hissed Dave. 'Yes, until they go wrong, until they get too big and dangerous for you. Then you sit here and crap yourself. What are you going to do now, run back to your protectors, back to your big brothers? Look at you, you can't even hide that. You're a Triad. That's where this thing started. I can see it in every line of your face. And now you think that your brothers will fork out the cash, pay for some fancy lawyer to protect you. You think it's going to be played by the rules: fair play, the right to silence. Well, you're wrong. Because this time the rules have changed.' Dave spun away from the desk, walking towards the door. 'And do you know why? Because you see, Mr Wong, my *respectable* little man, that young boy who was killed at Kai Tak . . . he was my son.'

For five minutes or more Wong Kam-kiu sat paralysed at his desk. He had never been more frightened in his life. How could this have happened? How could it all have gone so wrong? Oh merciful heaven, he thought, what was going to happen to him now?

He remembered that night when Gomez had phoned, he remembered what a state he had been in – drunk, belligerent – shouting at him over the phone. He remembered Gomez telling him that he had been recalled to Lima, telling him that everything was going to come out, that he was going to make a clean breast of it, arrange some sort of deal. He had no other choice, he said, it was the only way to avoid jail. The names of all the people, the money, everything, it was all going to be out on the table.

He remembered afterwards, in a lather of panic, phoning Tselentis, lucky to get him in town, telling him what Gomez had said, begging him for advice. And Tselentis, in a mad panic too, telling him to hold tight, to do nothing. 'It will be all right,' Tselentis had promised him. 'We'll deal with it, don't worry, somehow it will be handled.'

And how had it been handled? They had blown up the airport, that's how. Madness! He was in greater danger now than ever before. He needed help, he was *entitled* to help. Something had to be done. Fingers shaking, he rummaged for his telephone book to find the number of one man at least he could trust. He dialled the number and was put straight through – through to Hector Chan. 'The police have been here,' blurted Wong. 'They know all about the scheme. I told you it would happen, I told you!'

'Did you say anything?'

'Nothing, I swear!'

'I'll arrange for you to be represented by one of my associates. Wait there in your office, I'll send him now. In future you don't say a word to the police without him being present. Is that clear?'

'Yes, of course. But I must still speak to the Foreign Boy. He must help me, that was our agreement.'

'I'll give you his number,' said Chan, clearly shaken himself. 'But be careful when you phone him and from where. Don't use your own line. I'm sure Tselentis will see you are protected. Trust him. But, in return, you must involve nobody else in this thing. Is that clearly understood? Nobody at all.'

*

The Cantonese who knew him well called Dimitri Tselentis *Gwei Chai*, the Foreign Boy. Although his mother was Cantonese, his father had been Greek, a Greek merchant seaman, and in truth, Tselentis looked more Greek than anything else, every inch a foreigner.

Tselentis travelled throughout Asia most of the year attending meetings, monitoring investments. He was a difficult man to contact. It was fortuitous that he had flown into the Philippines from Japan that afternoon and had taken his normal suite at the Manila Mandarin. If that had not been the case, Wong Kam-kiu would never have contacted him.

In a supplicating whine, all pride abandoned, Wong begged him. 'You must get me out of Hong Kong. Please, Dimitri, myself, my wife, my child. How can we stay after what has happened? But we have no money. And my wife is so ill, her heart, you know how it is.'

Tselentis tried to calm him. 'Don't panic,' he said. 'All the police have against you is bribery. That's all you did. You did nothing else, you know that. How bad can it be? At worst it's a few months in jail. But they have to convict you first and how can they with Gomez dead? You'll be safe, don't worry—'

'But it's not just bribery now, don't you see? That cop – the father of the boy – he wants to drag me into the bombing, the bombing at Kai Tak!'

'That's absurd. You knew nothing about the bombing.'

'But what if I'm arrested? What about my wife, how will she cope? And what about my child? Please, Dimitri, you promised, you said I would be protected.'

'You will be.'

'But I need more than words.'

'You trust me, don't you.'

'Of course, Dimitri, of course.'

'Then leave it with me. Just give me a few days.'

'You promise?'

'Yes, I promise.'

When the phone was down, Tselentis sat for a time,

blanched with shock. Oh God, it was happening, it was all catching up with them.

But what should he do? Wong couldn't be left there, stewing in Hong Kong. He'd tear himself to pieces, self-destruct. He had to be got out, away from the cops. He wished he could do it himself, put the whole thing in hand. But it had to be discussed. There was no way he could act unilaterally, not with a crisis of this kind. He had no choice. He had to talk to Conrad Fung – he just prayed to God the man would act rationally this time.

Chapter Five

When Tselentis drew up, there were guards at the main gate of the estate. They were local Filipinos dressed in sweat-bleached fatigues, each of them festooned with bandoliers of ammunition, each conducting himself with that peculiar mix of menace and indolence that they perceived as the essence of *machismo*.

It had been a long drive from Manila. Tselentis was tired and hungry and anxious. He knew that at the main house there would be a chance to shower and change, a superb dinner, the best wines, no doubt a woman too to share his bed. But he was dreading the meeting, dreading every moment of it.

Why did Conrad Fung always have to revert to violence? The man was addicted to it like a drug. When he had spoken to him about Geraldo Gomez, he had never thought – not in a million years – that anything so drastic would be done. How could Fung even have contemplated it? Of course he had known the ramifications if Gomez talked, he had known exactly how far they would stretch. He had always appreciated the fact that drastic action was needed. If Gomez had to be killed, if there had been no other choice, no choice at all, then all right. But dear God, how could Fung think of carnage like that? All those people, just innocent people. It was insane.

Fung had deliberately pulled him into it too, making him an unwitting accessory. Such an innocent request . . . just drive a business friend to the airport. He had known it was more than that, it always was. But dear God, not a bomb! Conrad Fung was a psychopath. Tselentis had always guessed it. Now, when it was too late, he knew it for sure.

For Tselentis, what made it worse was that he had never understood the need for violence: so cruel always, so wasteful. His Greek father had been a trader who haggled deals from Sarawak to Yokohama. His mother, as a girl, had bribed her way on to a boat when southern China was falling to Mao Tse-tung's communist armies. Buying his way out of trouble was in his blood.

All violence did was bring misery on your head. Not in any way, not emotionally, not physically, was he built for it. He was as short as a jockey, as round as a watermelon: a half-Oriental, half-Hellenistic humpty-dumpty with a five o'clock shadow at one in the afternoon. He was no matinée idol. But he made up for it with his brain. Wealth, he always said, was the best aphrodisiac on the market. And wealth he understood, wealth in all its forms. He knew how to manage it and move it. A hostile takeover, that sort of violence he could understand. The rest was anathema to him.

It was half a mile to the main house along a dirt road that ran through sugar cane fields and palm plantations. Conrad Fung had bought the place eighteen months back when he had made the Philippines his main base. He enjoyed the role of a landed baron.

As Tselentis drew up outside the main house, a great rambling mansion of a place, he saw Fung waiting for him on the long, covered veranda at the front. What, he wondered, made the man so analytically brilliant one moment and such a sadistic fool the next?

Fung Chi-man, Conrad, as he preferred to be called, came down to meet the car. He was in his mid-fifties, slim and dapper, a man who ate sparingly and drank little. He had a dark, sallow complexion. He wore glasses and his black hair, always oiled and brushed back, was thinning badly. It was a hot evening but he wore a tie, a maroon one with conservative stripes. He liked formal wear. He was rarely without a jacket, never seen in anything other than a lounge shirt.

At first glance, he seemed to be cut from the standard

50

mould: very much the discreet Oriental businessman, dry as dust. But Tselentis knew him better, he knew of the hot blood running, he understood Fung's soaring ambitions, not just to be rich, oh no, much grander than that. At one time too he had been seduced by those ambitions . . . but that was before he really understood, before he became locked in.

As he came across to the car, Fung had an air of irritation about him. 'What are these problems with Wong?' he said. 'Why must we bother with him? If the Hong Kong police press him too hard, he pleads guilty to bribery, serves a few months and it's done.'

'It's not just bribery any longer,' said Tselentis with as much pluck as he could muster. He was always the yes man, the adjutant, the financial technocrat, but not this time. 'Wong says the cop who saw him knew all about Gomez. He wasn't buying the airport story about the Japanese Red Army. He knew that somehow Gomez had been a target.'

'This policeman,' said Conrad Fung, 'you said something about him on the phone. The father of the boy . . .'

'Whitman – he's the father of the boy who was killed in the bombing. And according to Wong, he was spitting fire. Wong says he came at him like a tank. We have to do something, Conrad, do it fast. If Wong gets arrested and starts pointing the finger, he's going to point it straight at me. I'm the one who convinced him to act as front man. He's never heard of you. I'm the one in the firing line.'

There were drinks on the veranda. Tselentis poured himself a strong brandy, topping it with soda. He was in a state of nerves and Fung could see it.

'Calm yourself,' he said. 'Nobody thinks rationally when they are so highly strung. Sit down, enjoy your drink and then tell me what you suggest.'

Tselentis was surprised at Fung's composure. He took a long gulp of his brandy. 'I don't think we have any choice in the matter,' he said. 'We have to get Wong and his family out of Hong Kong. I know he has a sick wife and child. I know it's going to cost us. But it's a damage-control exercise.'

'Will he be able to work?'

'At some menial job.'

'So we must support him?'

'Partially.'

'For how long?'

'Until this thing has blown over.'

'It could run on for years.'

'Then we'll just have to support him for years,' said Tselentis, pushing as hard as he could. 'Please, Conrad, trust me on this one. What's Wong made out of the scheme? Peanuts. How's it going to hurt us?'

'But the police are already on to him, Dimitri: you seem to ignore that fact. Possibly they have enough already to arrest him on bribery charges. Even if he gets away, builds a domestic nest for himself in Singapore at our expense, they can still haul him back.'

'Then put him somewhere Hong Kong can't reach him – Taiwan.'

'Taiwan deports people all the time. Extradition under another name, you know that.'

'One bridge at a time. If that happens, we deal with it.'

'How?' Fung seemed almost amused.

'Wrap him in cotton wool. Wall-to-wall lawyers. Keep his family supplied with cash. Just show the poor bastard we care.'

'And if we do that?'

'Then he'll hang in there, I know it. He'll keep his mouth shut.'

'Aah, Dimitri, the incurable optimist. The believer in the innate goodness of man. The man has one interview with a police officer and seems to have fallen apart at the seams.'

But Tselentis wouldn't back down, not this time. 'Please, Conrad, listen to me. Let's not do anything rash. If we keep Wong sweet, he'll ride out the storm. Trust me. Let's play this one low key. It will cost us a little but it will be cheap in the end. I'm not even asking you to pay. Just give me the go-ahead, that's all.'

Fung smiled. 'Very well,' he said.

'You agree?' Tselentis was amazed.

Fung nodded. 'Yes, I agree.'

'Okay, so I'll get on to it,' said Tselentis, relieved.

Fung's smile broadened. 'Don't worry, Dimitri. Leave it to me, I'll see that our little friend is given all the help he needs.'

That night at dinner they were joined by Conrad Fung's protector in the Philippines. His name was Eduardo Paredes, the senator from Mindoro. Paredes was very influential, a one-time ambassador to the UN. He was the man who ensured that Fung's residence in the country remained free of bureaucratic interference. Fung paid for that protection, of course, paid in all sorts of ways.

As Tselentis had anticipated, there were women available, three high society whores brought down from Manila – one American, one Korean, one Filipino. Paredes, a big blustery Latin full of charm and empty talk, liked women very much. That, Tselentis knew, was the foremost reason for their presence.

Relieved that the Wong matter had been so amicably resolved, riding on one of those artificial highs that follow prolonged periods of tension, Tselentis was looking forward to a night in bed himself.

As for Conrad Fung . . . well, he could live with women or without them. But when the fancy did take him, they were always women who could be hired and dismissed. Always the flesh, Fung said, never the soul. For Fung, women were a commodity.

Dinner was served in the main dining room, laid as if for a state banquet. The cutlery was sterling silver, each glass handcut crystal. Although Fung rarely drunk it, the wine was the best vintage. An aquarium of tropical fish lined one wall of the room, ensuring good *fung shui*. Luck, like everything, Fung believed, could be controlled.

There was no business discussed at dinner, no dry finance, not with women present. That was one of Fung's quirky little rules. Paredes monopolised most of the conversation, rambling on about his prowess at deep-sea fishing or something equally inane. Tselentis had little time for the man.

Towards the end of the meal, Fung was called to the

telephone. It was New York on the line. Five minutes later he returned, a thin smile on his face. He poured himself a little cognac, sure sign that he was pleased and leant across to Tselentis. 'That was Edgar Aurelius on the line,' he said. 'We may just have a buyer for Marada Cove.'

Tselentis was stunned. If it was true, it was the best business news he had received in months.

Even Fung, normally so poker-faced, was visibly relieved. 'Edgar described it as a very positive enquiry,' he said. 'It's a Texas conglomerate, leisure people. They want to have some preliminary talks. Protecting our financial position is going to be critical. I want you to go over. I want you to join Edgar.'

'Yes, of course. When do you want me to go?'

'In a couple of days. You'll be away a week or so.'

'No problem at all.' Unable to keep the grin off his face, Tselentis knocked back his cognac and poured another. Well, well, he thought, so the age of miracles is still with us. Marada Cove. The stone in their financial kidney might just be passed . . .

Marada had been one of Fung's Napoleonic follies. It was a massive hotel and condominium complex on Isla Marada, one of the more northerly islands that made up the Florida keys. Fung had initiated the multi-million dollar scheme five years back. Tselentis had argued against it all the way. 'You want the bottom line? It's crazy,' he had said. And from day one it had been a disaster . . . arguments with the architects over the design, zoning hassles, soil problems, strikes -- everything that fate could invent to doom a project. Initially the Hilton group had shown an interest in managing the hotel. Then it had pulled out. To date they had sold less than ten percent of the condo units and there was still no deal on the hotel. There was no other way of expressing it – Marada Cove was crippling them.

Later that night, Paredes, unable to contain his lust, retired to his room with one of the women, the Korean, the one Tselentis had fancied. The passion of his lovemaking drifted out across the night air. Even Conrad Fung, who was walking with Tselentis in the gardens, looked abashed.

'I've been thinking about that policeman, the one who threatened Wong,' said Fung, 'the one whose son was killed in the bombing.'

'What about him?' asked Tselentis, glass of cognac in hand, pretty drunk by that stage of the night.

'He must have pushed hard to be on the case. It can't be normal procedure, not to investigate a case in which your own son has been killed.'

Tselentis shrugged. He had no idea.

'And the way he went at Wong in that way, not caring about the rules, like a wounded bull.'

'Can hardly blame him,' said Tselentis. 'I mean, hell, having your only son blown away like that. Such a terrible bloody waste.' The Kai Tak bombing still appalled him, terrified him and, half-drunk, Tselentis let the words slip out. 'Why did it have to be done that way, Conrad? What possessed you? Tell me, I just don't understand—'

Fung came at him with the mesmerising speed of a black mamba striking. 'Understand what? What is there for you to understand? That was my business, my affair! You don't know half of it, not half. All you have is a bundle of assumptions. There were good reasons, compelling reasons. Don't you ever question me again on something like that – something you know nothing about – not ever! Do you understand?'

Tselentis reeled back, astounded by the ferocity of Fung's words. 'I'm sorry,' he muttered, the yes man again.

They walked on through the gardens in silence. A peacock called from the far side of the lawn, a mournful, shrill call that cut through the distant grunts of Paredes in his room with the Korean whore.

Tselentis, churning inside, wanted to walk away, to go back into the house and find his own woman. But he dared not leave. So he walked on, staring morosely at the ground.

Fung's tempers, however, could rise one moment and die the next. With him there never seemed to be an aftershock. His thoughts had returned to Whitman, the father of the murdered boy.

55

'He worries me, Dimitri,' he said, 'this man, Whitman. He is so obviously on a crusade, pursuing his own private vendetta. A man driven is a dangerous man. He cuts corners, he exceeds limits. But most of all, unlike sensible men, he doesn't know when enough is enough. He does not know when to close the file and move on to something else. I think we must keep an eye on him, a very close eye indeed.'

Tselentis washed back the last of the cognac from his glass. 'That's all very well,' he said, 'but how do you get close to a *gweilo* cop of his rank?'

Fung gave a slow, condescending smile. 'Dimitri, I'm surprised at you. Does your brain cease to function when you are sulking? There is always a way, you should know that. Our profession is money, our business is influence, our trade is information. What better combination could there be?'

Dave had a breakfast meeting with Miguel de Haan and Maria Ramirez. They met in the Marriott Hotel across from Police Headquarters.

'The man who organised the paperwork for the immigrants was Wong Kam-kiu,' Dave told them. 'Wong was the one paying the sweeteners to Gomez. At least, the payments were made *through* him. He didn't initiate them. Wong is a small-time Triad. He has a couple of convictions, petty fraud and the like. He wouldn't have had the vision to originate a scheme this big. He was in it up to his neck but strictly as a worker not a boss.'

'Who could the bosses be? Do you have any idea?' asked de Haan.

'It's early days yet,' said Dave. 'There could be a higher echelon Triad influence, I just don't know. But I tell you one thing, Wong is a very frightened man. And he knows a great deal.'

'He could face criminal charges for bribery,' said Maria Ramirez. 'Maybe his fear is natural in the circumstances.'

'No, it goes deeper than that. The minute I walked into that office he fell apart. It was written all over his face.'

'But what else could there be other then bribery?' asked de Haan. 'It couldn't have anything to do with Gomez's death. That was a random terrorist attack.'

'Was it?'

De Haan blinked, taken aback. 'What do you mean?'

'If it was the Japanese Red Army – and nobody has proof of that yet – why must the attack have been *random*? Why couldn't it have been targeted at specific individuals?'

'At Gomez?'

'Possibly.'

De Haan was dismayed. 'But the terrorist announcement said it was a general attack against US and Japanese imperialism. Those words were quite clearly stated.'

'A smokescreen perhaps.'

'But why target Gomez? What possible reason?'

'I don't know,' said Dave. 'At the moment I'm just following my nose. I'm not saying I'm right. I could be going in circles.'

'I hope to God you are,' said de Haan, shocked by the implications of it.

'All I'm saying is that we have to dig deeper. You said that Gomez had a ranch, two houses, cars, boats. How big was the ranch, for example?'

'Very big,' said Maria Ramirez. 'Many cattle, many buildings, a stable of thoroughbred race horses.'

'That would have cost a great deal of money. Am I right?'

'But there were a great many emigrants he let in,' she answered. 'Fourteen thousand or more.'

'Sure, I accept that. But reduce those fourteen thousand down to families. Divide by four. What do you get? About three and a half thousand families. Many of them too are from mainland China, remember that, people with special permission from Beijing to join families already in Peru . . . farmers, artisans, people who would find it difficult to scrub up five hundred dollars, let alone five thousand.'

'What are you saying?' asked de Haan.

'If Gomez had the sort of assets you describe, then he was being paid to do something more than rubber-stamp hopeless immigration applications. And the money wasn't coming from the immigrants either, it was coming from another source.'

'But why? What earthly reason could there be?' De Haan

was struggling to overcome his incredulity. 'Some scheme perhaps to make the emigrants carry drugs? That's ludicrous. Columbia, Peru – that's where drugs are grown! What else could there be?'

'The answer has to be in those files you possess,' said Dave, 'the application forms for immigration.'

'But those forms deal with so many things,' said Maria Ramirez. 'Family links in Peru, education, health, financial status. It could take us years to check everything.'

'Stay with the important stuff,' said Dave. 'Financial status – start there.'

There was silence. Both de Haan and Maria Ramirez saw the force of his argument. But the logistics involved were frightening. They would have to double-check every stated figure with banks and savings institutions. They would need more people. Lima would scream. What was the purpose of it all? Was it worth it? The bribery could be proved. What more did they need? Whitman himself admitted he could be going in circles.

'Do you have any comprehension of the size of the task?' asked de Haan.

'Take a number of sample files,' said Dave. 'A cross section. That will cut down the workload.'

'Even so . . .'

'If you need extra manpower, I can provide it. I have officers available. They can do most of the leg-work for you. They're highly competent people at this sort of thing.'

'No doubt but for that they will require access to our consular files,' said de Haan, a little stiffly. 'And those, as you know, are protected by the Vienna Convention. I do not know how my superiors in Lima will react. I wish it was as easy as you suggest.'

'I'm not suggesting it's easy,' said Dave, his voice flat and businesslike. 'I'm suggesting a way to take this thing further, that's all. I appreciate it has political ramifications. Maybe your superiors in Lima feel they have enough already. But Gomez is dead, that fact can't be ignored . . . and somewhere along the line your government has been the subject of a massive fraud. The ball is in your court now. It's a matter for you.'

Miguel de Haan nodded. 'I will have to consider the matter,' he said. 'It may take a few days.'

'Okay,' said Dave. 'I will wait for you to come back to me.' He smiled politely as he got up from the table but inside he was boiling with frustration. He wanted to get moving now, get things done. But the politicians had to have their say. And until they had, what more could he do?

Chapter Six

The morning after Kit Lampton returned from England, there was a task force meeting in Tom Mackay's office. Kit, looking badly jet-lagged, was there together with Henry Tang from Special Branch and Stan Tarbuck from the US Consulate.

'Gao Xin's daughter was a nice kid,' Kit reported. 'A near genius according to her tutors at Cambridge. But nervy, highly strung. Put bluntly – neurotic as hell. The death of her father clearly knocked the stuffing out of her. She had nothing in black and white to prove that her father was flying to England to defect. She said they spoke on the phone a few times but it was all pretty veiled. It was more a kind of *feeling* she had.'

'What about her father's murder?' asked Tom Mackay.

'It gets worse, I'm afraid. The murder, she said, had to be a natural consequence of his intention to defect. Cause and effect, a rule of physics I suppose. She says he would have been carrying information in his head, information damaging to Beijing. Papers as well, secret documents and the like. That's why they would have killed him.'

'Is that it?' asked Henry Tang.

'Yeah, I'm afraid it is.'

'Just a young girl's feelings, nothing more than that?'

Kit gave a stoic shrug. 'That's about the sum of it, yeah. But we had to check it out: close the door at least.'

'It looks like it's closed as far as Beijing is concerned too,' said Tom Mackay. He handed each of them a phototstat copy of a diplomatic note –

Comrade Gao Xin was at all times a loyal member of

the Party and a distinguished representative of the People's Republic of China. We can find no evidence of internal or external enmity against him sufficient to motivate an attempt on his life. It is our conclusion that he died an innocent victim of the bombing outrage. We have accordingly closed our file.

'We received it yesterday through the Political Adviser's Office,' said Tom. 'So the options get smaller.' Tom turned to Stan Tarbuck. 'What about Hildebrand, any fresh developments?'

'Nothing. Loved his folks, loved his gym, always finished his movies on schedule and stayed clear of fatty foods. The man was a walking lesson in moral behaviour.'

'The girl, his publicity secretary?'

'Just a sweet kid.'

'What about the twenty or so persons wounded?'

'We've checked each one,' said Henry Tang. 'Ordinary citizens . . . businessmen, holiday-makers. Nothing to raise a moment's concern.'

'So what's left?'

'We're back where we began,' said Henry Tang. 'The Japanese Red Army. I don't think we can argue about it any longer. We have to accept they were responsible. A case of blind, senseless terrorism.'

For the first time Dave spoke. 'Maybe not so blind,' he said. 'Maybe not so senseless either.'

Henry Tang looked at him. 'Do you mean the Gomez affair, the stuff you've written in your report?'

'Yes,' said Dave bluntly. 'I mean exactly that.'

A supercilious smile settled on Tang's face. 'I know how anxious you are to involve yourself in this investigation, Dave. Believe me, we all feel terrible about your son. But rubber-stamping a few visas the cause of the Kai Tak bombing . . . surely you're not serious?'

Wong Kam-kiu was working late that evening. His wife had phoned down from their apartment on the tenth floor to say that his dinner was waiting but he still had a few papers to finish. It was seven o'clock, he was just about to lock up, when the telephone rang. He didn't recognise the voice. But the man knew him, using the Cantonese familiarity of his name, Ah Kiu.

'I have a message from *Gwei Chai*,' he said. 'He wishes to see you, Ah Kiu, he wishes to talk to you. He can make things right.'

'Did he say that? That's wonderful!' Wong was flooded with relief. 'Where is he, when can I see him?'

'He is only in town for one night. He is at a meeting now, a business meeting in a building near you. He would like you to go across, Ah Kiu. That's what he said.'

'Of course. Right away. Did he say anything about all of us leaving? Did he say anything about my family?'

'There is no need to worry, that's what he said.'

'Oh good, thank you, thank you.'

Wong was given the address of a business called Sinotech Trading. Excitedly, he telephoned his wife to say that he was going out to meet Tselentis, that arrangements had been made and everything was going to be fine. He asked that his dinner be kept warm and hurriedly closed the office.

He had always known that Tselentis would come through for him. He was sure that some arrangement had been made for them all to be settled elsewhere, Taiwan maybe or Malaysia, out of harm's way. Tselentis had a decent heart. Although he wasn't full-blooded Chinese, he was a Wo Shing Wo. They were both members of the secret brotherhood of heaven and earth; they had drunk from the chalice together, the chalice containing the wine and ashes and cockerel's blood. In such circumstances trust was implicit.

It was dark outside, warm and humid. A damp May mist was drifting in from the sea. The neon lights were on and the tea houses were full. Wong bustled along the crowded pavements until he reached the building just east of the market. It was a ramshackle place, ten or so storeys high. All the windows were barred, each one blotted with a rusting air conditioner.

He searched for the main entrance and discovered that it was at the side of the building down a narrow alley. It was locked, but there was an intercom system which allowed him to speak to the offices inside the building. He searched the board for the name of Sinotech Trading. His glasses were misted from the warm damp air and he had to rub them with a handkerchief. He looked closer, squinting. But the name wasn't there. Strange, he thought. He checked again. But there was no mistake.

He stood for a moment, face to the board, puzzled and worried. Something was wrong, very wrong. His pulse began to race. Oh no, he thought, suddenly terrified, no, Tselentis wouldn't do it, he wouldn't betray him. They were brothers, both Wo Shing Wo. No, it was impossible. There had to be some mistake. He must have the wrong address. He spun around – and found himself facing three men.

For a moment, in the wet, grey-black gloom, they were little more than shadows, kitchen workers perhaps out in the alley for a smoke break and a talk. Wong Kam-kiu stood rooted, watching them. Then, head down, he tried to scurry away. Instantly the three men moved to cut him off.

'Who are you?' stuttered Wong. But they did not respond. Wong glimpsed the squat, square-shaped meat cleavers in their hands and his belly turned to water.

On a silent signal the three men began to close in on him. One of them smiled, a smile of terrifying, exquisite menace. Wong shrank back against the wall. He was going to die, he knew it, be slaughtered here like an animal. He let out a small moan. It wasn't fair. What had he done? He was paralysed with terror. But in that terror came a sudden, frenzied urge for life. He stared at the three men, his eyes darting from face to face. He focused on the one who was smiling and some deep instinct told him – yes, he was the one.

He hung back a moment, cringing. Then, using the wall as a springboard, he hurled himself outwards, straight into those curled-back lips and smiling teeth. His elbow caught the man in the throat and they both went down on to the wet concrete, slipping and punching and flailing with their arms. Wong shrieked as a blade sliced open his shoulder.

But the pain of it only spurred him on and, scrambling up, he burst away, running, stumbling, screaming for help. He heard them pursuing him, heard their grunts of surprise. They were so close they could almost touch him. He knew he could never outrun them, he was too old, too weak, not three men.

Directly ahead the alley was blocked with dustbins. But there was an open door too. He could see steam billowing out, smell the duck and the soy sauce, hear the chefs bellowing at the waiters. Despairingly, slithering in a mulch of rotting vegetables, he flung himself into the kitchen. 'Help me!' he shouted in Cantonese. 'Help me!'

A dozen faces turned, staring at him in horror. But nobody moved. Wong barged his way through, still pursued by the three. In his terrorised flight, his elbow hit a wok standing on a stove and a shower of shrimps and boiling fat hit his legs. He half spun, screaming with pain. He saw a blade slash down, ripping open his jacket, and in desperation he clawed for the swing doors that led from the kitchen into the restaurant.

He saw more faces, customers at their tables turning in amazement, waiters gawking. And that's where the three caught him, set upon him like baying hounds on a cornered fox. In among the crowded tables, with customers fleeing in panic, they rained in blows, cleaving open great wounds.

Wong raised his arm to ward off a blow that would have split open his skull and felt the blade hack clean through the bone and sinew of his wrist. In a daze of petrified disbelief he saw his severed hand fall to the floor. Blood was everywhere, blinding him.

He fell to his knees, sobbing, 'Help me please!' he clutched at a tablecloth, trying to pull it around him as if it could offer protection. A blow cracked into his ribcage with such force that he retched blood. He tried to crawl under a table, tried to curl up. He was slipping, slithering in his own blood. He was dying. Then dimly, far off in a distant universe, he heard the shout – police!

Wong did not see the two men at the corner table, did not see the two off-duty detectives with revolvers in their hands.

65

But he heard the shout and for the first time in his life he blessed the police. A shot rang out. He heard a grunt, a shout of pain, and one of his pursuers dropped to the carpet next to him. They were so close they were almost embracing. The man was making peculiar sucking noises from a bullet wound to his chest. He was dying too, thought Wong, strangely satisfied.

The surgeon at Queen Mary was very matter-of-fact. He saw chop wounds similar to Wong's every day of the week. 'He has lost a great deal of blood,' he told Dave. 'Two arteries were severed. We sewed his right hand back on. Whether that will be successful we don't know. We also sutured one incision to the neck. He had four deep wounds to the upper back, three to the arms and one to the left thigh. One of the chop wounds glanced the lung. But otherwise no vital organs were affected. If he can deal with the shock, he may pull through.'

'Any chance of speaking to him?'

'Not at the moment.'

'When?'

'It will be a few days. He is heavily drugged.'

'What about the assailant, the one who was shot?'

'He died early this morning, shortly after midnight.'

'Could I see the body?'

'If you wish.'

'If I may.'

Dave hated mortuaries, hated the clinical smell, the stainless steel and the stillness and the knowledge that one day a place like this would be his temporary repository too.

The man was older than he had expected, well into his forties. As a street goon he should have retired years back. Like many low-life Triads, he sported a number of tattoos on his chest and upper arms. But there was one that stood out for its clarity. On his right forearm was the image of an ink-green dragon, scaled and ferocious, obviously in full flight but surrounded by a halo of fire. It was a symbol he had never seen before.

It took twenty-four hours to obtain full details on the dead assailant. His name was Szeto Chi-chui, born in mainland China, a resident of Hong Kong since the mid-Seventies. He had a string of convictions to his name: blackmail, wounding, criminal intimidation, all the classic indicators of a Red Pole, a Triad grunt, one of the foot soldiers.

Special Branch had nothing on him. They were given a photograph of the tattoo but it meant nothing to them. There was no suggestion that it was related in any way to the Japanese Red Army. The JRA, after all, were intellectual radicals, anarchists, Trotskyists, they didn't have much use for gangland tattoos.

Later that day, Dave telephoned Miguel de Haan at the Peruvian Consulate to give him the news. He wanted him to know what had happened to Wong Kam-kiu and he didn't want to spare the details.

'It is a terrible thing,' said de Haan.

'Yes it is.'

'Will he live?'

'We hope so. Do you have any news yet from Lima? Are you going to take this thing further or not?'

There was a silence. 'I have not heard from Lima yet,' said de Haan. There was a further, deeper silence. Then he said: 'But on my own authority, yes – we are taking it further.'

For three days Wong Ling-mui sat by her husband's bed in the Queen Mary Hospital. She had left her son with an aged aunt, the only relative she had in Hong Kong. For three days she waited, expecting her husband to die. How any man could survive such an attack she did not know. But Wong Kam-kiu clung to life. He would not give up. On the third day he came out of his coma. His eyes opened, he recognised her and he whispered. 'You must find out who did this to me. Why was I attacked? Ask everybody. Why me?'

In her heart Wong Ling-mui knew already who had done this to her husband. It was Tselentis, the one they called the Foreign Boy. Her husband had spoken to Tselentis begging to be taken out of Hong Kong, he had gone to meet

67

Tselentis the night he was attacked. Tselentis *had* to be the one. But, because she was a dutiful wife, she would ask. If nothing else, she would confirm what she already knew.

For five days she tried. But she had no success. She disliked the men her husband associated with; they were Triads, she knew it. But she expected at least some loyalty, some help to pin the blame. She found none. Her husband's colleagues shunned her as if she was a leper. None would tell her who, none would tell her why.

There was only one who gave her aid. In desperation she telephoned the lawyer, Hector Chan. Her husband had told her that Chan was a close colleague. Secretly she believed he was a high official in the same Triad. But he had earned a reputation as a man of integrity.

'I have heard some rumours on the street that your husband's business associate, Mr Tselentis, may know something,' he said, 'but I cannot believe it. I will try to contact him, to speak to him. I have done some business with him in the past. But what is more important is that your husband gets well and that you stay strong too.'

That same night five thousand Hong Kong dollars in an envelope had been delivered to the apartment. As her husband had said, Hector Chan was a man of honour. But, as for all the others, as for Tselentis and his kind, they had shown their true colours.

Wong Ling-mui had a bad heart, the doctor had told her she could not expect to live many more years. Her child, Chi Chi, was sickly too. They had next to no money. They had a few savings for their old age from the business with Peru but nowhere near enough. They would have emigrated to another country, Canada or Australia, if only they could. But they were too old, they did not have the qualifications. They had to remain here in Hong Kong. But without friends, without help, surrounded by enemies, how would they ever survive?

When she knew they had been abandoned, that they had all sided with Tselentis against her husband, Wong Ling-mui knelt in front of the three-tiered altar that she kept in the tiny tenth-floor apartment above her husband's office. The highest tier was dedicated to the god of heaven, the middle tier, where joss sticks smouldered, to her ancestors and the lowest tier to the god of earth who protected the household. Only in these spirits, only in the supernatural, was there any assurance. She had always known it and now it was affirmed. Men were no better than rats . . . vermin who devoured their own.

Wong Kam-kiu had a police guard twenty-four hours a day. But it was just short of a week before the doctors considered him well enough to be interviewed. Dave went alone to see him.

Wong, shrivelled and pallid, still on a drip, would not look him in the eye. 'I don't want to talk to you,' he said in a feeble voice. 'You shouldn't be here.'

'I'm about the only friend you have right now,' said Dave. 'What do you think will happen when you limp out of here? Do you think it's over, that it was just a friendly warning? You know better than that. They'll come at you again. They'll keep coming at you until they finish it. Work with me, cooperate and I'll be able to protect you.'

A pathetic half-moan, half-sob came from between Wong's chapped lips. But he didn't speak.

'You're a small fish,' said Dave. 'I know that. I'm not after you. Why be sacrificed by the bastards who did this to you? I can recommend a full immunity. Consider your wife, consider your baby child. You've only got one life. Don't be stupid, don't throw it away.'

Wong shook his head. He was almost demented with fear. 'You don't know what you're asking me to do,' he muttered. 'It's impossible, impossible.'

'Why?' asked Dave.

'I can't tell you.'

'Why?' Dave asked again.

'No, please . . .'

'Gomez was murdered at the airport, wasn't he? He was murdered because of this Peruvian thing. There was a plot to kill him. That's why you're so frightened.'

Wong screwed his eyes shut, trying to block out the words.

'Help me,' said Dave. 'Help yourself, help me.'

69

But Wong wouldn't answer. He wouldn't say a thing.

Three days later, on the afternoon of his eighth day in hospital, Wong Ling-mui came to her husband. She told him that there was a conspiracy of silence, that none of his old colleagues would help in any way, that they had all shunned her and allied themselves with Tselentis. She asked if even one of them had been to the hospital to see him, to ask after his health and comfort him. None, he said, not one.

The only man with any honour, she told him, was the lawyer, Hector Chan. He had sent her cash, enough to keep her going. But all the others had abandoned them to their misery, just because they were poor, because they had nothing in life.

Wong lay in bed, struggling to hold back the tears. It was true. Tselentis, whom he trusted, had tried to murder him. Not one friend had come to their aid. Apart from Hector Chan, a man of dignity, a man to trust, they were snakes in the grass. 'What do I do?' he begged his wife. 'Tell me, what must I do?'

She took his hand. She looked at him, her eyes very dreamy, and said that she had found a way. 'We must return home,' she said. 'We must all be together, the two of us and our son . . .'

Dave received the news at his office in Police Headquarters. 'What are the doctors doing?' he demanded. 'Are they nuts? Wong can hardly walk. He's got more stitches in him than the Bayeux Tapestry. How can they let him go?'

The sergeant phoning from the hospital did his best to explain: 'The doctors say they tried to reason with him. But he demanded his discharge. His life is in no danger, his wounds are beginning to heal. They have no choice, that's what they say. The ambulance is leaving now. If you wish, I've still got time. I can stop him.'

'No,' said Dave, 'leave it. What for? We don't have enough to arrest him, not yet. You'll have to let him go. We're in the same fix as the doctors. But follow him home. Keep the apartment under surveillance. Is that clear? I want

. it watched around the clock. Twenty-four hours a day.'

Dave put down the phone. What was the stupid bastard playing at? It made no sense at all.

Last night Wong Kam-kiu had slept in his own bed again. He had kissed his son goodnight. He had seen his wife undress, seen her poor, faded body, the tiny breasts not strong enough to succour a bird. He had held her hand in the darkness. He had listened to the whirr of the ceiling fan above their head.

Now, in the harsh brightness of the morning, he gazed out of his tenth-floor window at the rooftops all around. He could see so much, there were so many memories there . . . plywood huts and wire cages in the corners of the rooftops where beggars slept at night, baskets of cuttlefish drying in the sun, potted plants, television aerials, grey concrete walls and white shirts hanging out to dry.

For the first time in months he was suddenly aware too of the smells he had known since childhood, the rich fetid algae of the harbour, the pungency of soy sauce and egg noodles from a tea house on the second floor. His ears detected sounds, the constant hum of traffic, a couple of old mothers haggling over the price of *choi sum*. And, closer still, the tremulous call of a songbird in its cage. This was all he had known all his life, this square mile of the island called Western: his Hong Kong, his China. And it had betrayed him.

Wong Kam-kiu looked at his wife, who lay on the bed. The last few days had taken so much out of her. She was so pale and thin, her skin as translucent as molten wax. 'Are you sure there is no other way?' he asked.

'None,' she replied.

Wong nodded. He knew she would not change her mind. But the commitment, once irrevocably made, was terrible in its consequences. Painfully, swathed in bandages, he limped across to the cot where his son, Chi Chi, lay sleeping. They had wished for a son for so many years.

'We must not lose courage,' said his wife. 'We must not hesitate.'

He looked at her, his eyes pleading. But she was resolved, he could see it. She would not waver.

'How can these people who have caused us such grief go unpunished?' she said. She smiled at him as a mother would smile at a child. Then she said in a voice tinged with sadness. 'We owe it to our ancestors, we owe it to ourselves. The god in heaven has given us no other choice.'

Chapter Seven

It was done at last. The blitzkrieg was over: finished, completed. Hannah could hardly believe it. It was nine o'clock at night and everybody was gathered around – more a family now than just workers in a factory – while Scott lifted the last sample. 'There,' he said with a poetic flourish, 'the final thread.'

There was much laughter and chattering. The sewing machines had fallen silent. The work was done. Hannah thanked everybody for their efforts then walked through to her office and flopped down in the big leather chair in the corner – her curl-up chair, she called it.

The collection was ready. How they had done it in such a short time she could only wonder at. But that was half the work, maybe the easiest half too. Because now – somewhere out there – she had to find a market. And that scared her to death.

Scott came through to her office. He poured himself a coffee from the percolator on the side table and eased himself down on to the carpet, legs out, back against Hannah's desk. He looked as tired as she did. 'Well, how do you feel?' he asked. 'Elated?'

She smiled, shaking her head. Elated? No. There was never any exhilaration or lightness of heart when a job was finished, only a sense of relief, a slow dissipation of tension . . . a desire to sit down and not think or do a single thing. But this time, yes, if she was honest with herself, there was another feeling too, a feeling of deep, abiding satisfaction.

The collection was good. It was original and it was wearable. It had a voice. For the first time ever she knew that all her talents had gelled. Twenty-five pieces, that's all, the twenty-five that made up the spring collection of Danny's Rags, but beyond all doubt it was the best work she had ever done.

'So now New York,' said Scott.

'Into the tiger's mouth.'

'Rubbish.'

'It's a hard world out there, Scott. They stone you to death with indifference. I've got no illusions.'

'I'll tell you what, my sweet lady, the world out there will be a sad excuse of a place if it doesn't take Danny's Rags to its heart. You'll do just fine.' He winked at her. 'Always remember though, put your shoulder to the wheel—'

'Keep your nose to the grindstone?'

'And never lose your head while all about you are losing theirs!'

Hannah giggled. 'Sage advice, Scott, I'll remember it.'

She got back home at eleven-thirty that night. Dave was watching a video on television. He always waited up for her.

'There's some cold chicken in the fridge,' he said. 'Some salad niçoise and white wine. Have you eaten yet?'

'No. Have you?'

He grinned at her. 'I thought I'd wait for you. Let me get the wine.' He went through to the kitchen, calling back to her, 'How are things going at the factory?'

'We've finished.'

'Tremendous! The whole collection?'

'The whole thing.' The way she said it sounded so flat, like such an anti-climax, not the way she wanted it to come out at all.

But when Dave returned with the two glasses of wine, he was beaming. 'That's fantastic,' he said. 'God, I don't know how you did it so quick. So, what now?'

'Now comes the hard part, trying to find a decent market.'

'What will you do,' he asked, 'send the samples across to Sonny Weiss?'

She shook her head. 'Scott and I have been talking. Sonny is not the right man. He's just too settled. He makes a living and that seems to be enough for him these days. All the spark has gone out of him. Look at the last couple of years, Dave: what has he really done for me? Anyway, I don't know that children's wear is his thing. Scott says I have to go over to New York myself, get in and see a top-flight sales organisation, convince them to take on the collection.'

Dave smiled at her. 'I agree,' he said. 'You've put so much into the collection already. Sonny Weiss will market it in a mediocre sort of way. But that's the worst death of all. Scott is right. This time you have to go for broke.' He raised his glass in a toast to her success. 'So when are you leaving?'

'Tomorrow afternoon. Scott got me a seat.'

'Wow, no hanging around.'

She gave a guilty smile.

'Any idea how long you'll be away?'

'A couple of weeks maybe. As long as it takes.'

Dave came across to her. He refilled her wine glass. There was a slow, smouldering smile on his face. 'But we've still got tonight,' he said. 'All the time in the world.'

They showered together first, soaping each other, kissing under the soft waterfall. It was languid and lovely, their bodies slipping against each other, oiled with the perfumed suds. He soaped her back and her breasts. His hands went down over her stomach, down to the wet centre of her and she wanted him so badly, more than anything in the world. Dave dried her in a huge, warm, peach-coloured towel and then she dried him. And they laughed and kissed.

He carried her to the bed. The curtains hadn't been drawn. They looked out over the waters of the Lamma Channel and the sea under the moon was liquid gold. He possessed her slowly, with great tenderness, kissing her all the time, her neck and throat, her lips and breasts. It was lovemaking in its purest, most sublime sense. And, when it was finished, for the very first time since Danny's death, Hannah slept without an ache in her heart.

★

Dave woke early, before the dawn. He slipped out of the bed and quietly, so as not to disturb Hannah, put on his running vest, his shorts and shoes. Not since Danny's death had he run, but there was a time to begin everything again, a time for this too. He took the elevator the twenty floors down to the ground and, running slowly at first, began the climb up into the green-clad central hills of Hong Kong.

He followed the paths that circled the reservoirs above Aberdeen, gently increasing his pace, enchanted by the silence, by the silver-soft mist in the trees. A couple of kites, great, wing-spread brown birds of carrion, circled above him. Occasionally he would catch a glimpse of the factory buildings down in Aberdeen, dull grey-black slabs jammed tight together. But they could have been a million miles away.

He ran ten miles, his mind filled with Hannah, filled with the glorious sensuality of their lovemaking and the fact that everything seemed so right with them now. Despite the great aching void of Danny's death, a void which would take years to fill, so long as she loved him, there was some meaning to his life.

When he got back to the apartment, Hannah was still asleep. Hannah could work late, all through the night if necessary, but she could never get up early. She was not, as she put it, a morning animal.

Dave showered and dressed and had some toast and coffee that Delia, their amah, had made for him. Before leaving for work, he scribbled a short note which he stuck on the mirror of Hannah's dressing table. 'I'll be back for lunch,' it said. 'We'll go to the airport together.'

There was a meeting that morning with the forensic people who had analysed the remains of the Kai Tak bomb. The device, they said, had not been complex. It had consisted of a simple timing device connected to a battery and a primer and then to the explosive substance itself, a plastic composition containing cyclonite, usually known as RDX. The bomb had been packed into the body of an Akai video cassette recorder and that unit placed into a suitcase. It was a device that could have been made by just about anybody with the basic skill and access to the materials.

The painstaking recovery of all the pieces of the bomb had, however, resulted in two physical exhibits of particular importance. The first was the small metal logo – FLY HI – which proved the suitcase to be of Filipino origin. The second was potentially of much greater significance.

Despite the shattering force of the bomb blast, part of a thumbprint had been discovered on one of the shards of the suitcase. The print was blurred. But the fingerprint experts were confident they could make a match, not enough for evidential purposes in a court of law, but enough at least to help confirm they had the right man – if and when they ever found him.

Dave got back to the apartment just after noon. Hannah had two suitcases to take with her on the flight. One contained the samples which Scott had packed at the factory, the other her personal belongings. They drove out to the airport together in Hannah's old, ink-blue BMW . . . to the exact same building where their son had died.

Hannah had been dreading it. That was why Dave had driven there with her. For them both it was unnerving. Yet it was strangely moving too, like coming, penitent, before a shrine. The area of the bomb blast was still blocked off with hoarding. There were no wreaths, no plaques, just builder's paraphernalia. But somehow, as they passed the place, amid all the noise and bustle, for a few moments, it was as if the world was shrouded in silence. They sensed the spirit of their son, sensed his love, his laughter, every precious essence of that perfect young soul. They stood, hands held, both striving to hold back the tears. 'Oh God, I loved him so much,' whispered Hannah. Dave wished he could answer but his heart was bursting.

They walked to the check-in counter. They were still holding hands. As they waited in the queue, Hannah looked up at him, her blue eyes glistening. 'Sometimes I feel so frightened,' she said.

'Frightened of what?' he asked.

'Of everything . . . frightened of life. Frightened of failing in New York when this time – for Danny – I want to succeed so badly. Frightened of coming back empty-handed. Frightened of losing you.'

Dave squeezed her hand, amazed that she should think such a thing. 'It's nerves, that's all,' he said. 'First, you're never going to lose me – no chance. And as for New York, you're going to be a smash hit, I know it.'

'And if I'm not, if it's a disaster?'

He looked into her eyes, a smile on his lips. 'So we're a little poorer. So what? Your collection is important, I know that. My investigation is important too. It's everything to me at the moment. But we mustn't blind ourselves. Danny is in our hearts, that's where he really is. And that's where he'll always belong.'

At three that afternoon Dave got back from Kai Tak. He walked into his office at Police Headquarters to find Kit Lampton waiting for him.

Kit had a grin of expectation all over his face. 'You're wanted at the Peruvian Consulate – now, now, now! Get on your motorbike, my lad. Your lady friend, Maria Ramirez, needs to speak to you. She sounded pretty excited.'

'What's it all about?'

'I haven't a clue. Something about the immigration papers, about it being under their noses and, oh yes – you were right all the time.'

Maria Ramirez sat behind a mound of consular files, her plump face shining with triumph. 'I know the reason for it,' she said: 'I'm sure I do – the reason why Gomez was paid such huge amounts, the reason for the whole immigration fraud.'

'Okay,' said Dave, his own excitement mounting. 'Best begin at the beginning.'

'As you suggested, when I began to check the immigration files, the first thing I looked at was the financial status of each immigrant. I went through a dozen, maybe two dozen files, and I began to notice something strange

78

Mr Whitman . . . a surprisingly high number of wealthy business immigrants, millionaires in fact – multi-millionaires.'

That jolted Dave's memory. Yes, Wong had told him that his clients were business migrants, wealthy people. It had struck him as strange at the time too.

Maria Ramirez continued. 'Now I love my country, Mr Whitman, but I am not naive about it. Millionaires go to Los Angeles and London. They buy villas in the south of France, in Cannes, not Lima or Trujillo. Why would so many wealthy people wish to settle in my country? Why would they wish to start businesses there and buy homes? It made no sense.'

'So?'

'So I took a sample of these wealthy ones – just five – and looked into their backgrounds.'

'And the results?' asked Dave.

'Startling, Mr Whitman, truly startling. Let me take the first applicant. His name is Heung Wah-bor. In his papers he described himself as the owner of a manufacturing company here in Hong Kong – watches and clocks and the like. He wished to start a similar factory in Peru, he said. That was the basis of his application. And on the surface it did look good, very good for us indeed. Do you know how much money he transferred to Lima? Five million United States dollars. That money went, it was physically received in Peru, and Mr Heung followed it. But when I checked into his company here, I discovered that it had no premises, nothing. It was a bundle of papers in a company registry. Do you know how Mr Heung really made his living in Hong Kong? He was a taxi driver. Do you know how he is living now in Peru? In a one-bedroom apartment with his wife and three children. Do you know how much money he has left in his account? Five hundred pesos.'

'And the others you checked?'

'The same story, exactly the same. There was another applicant called Poon. He owned a chain of supermarkets, so he said.'

'Do the supermarkets exist?'

'Yes they do – but Mr Poon never owned them. He was a fish hawker, he had a stall in Wanchai market. He sold squid and prawns. He never owned a property, he never owned a car.'

'How much did he transfer?'

'Two and half million.'

'Any trace of it now?'

'None.'

'Did all five applicants transfer similar sums?'

'Similar, yes.'

'And now those funds have disappeared?'

'All they have in their accounts is enough to pay the rent and buy bread. They are all poor people. It was never their money. They carried it, that's all. They were pack mules – donkeys.'

Dave nodded. Suddenly it was all so obvious, staring them in the face. 'Money laundering?'

'Yes, Mr Whitman,' she said. 'Money laundering. What else can it be?'

'What sort of amounts are we talking about?'

'There were seventy or more applicants sprinkled among the others who classified themselves as business migrants. Even at four million each, that's close to three hundred million.'

'Bloody hell!' Dave was staggered by the figure.

'And Hong Kong makes such fertile ground,' said Maria Ramirez. 'Think about it from the viewpoint of the money-launderers. What do you have here in Hong Kong? First, a thriving commercial city. Second, an easy banking system which does not check large amounts of cash flowing in. Third, a stream of people desperate to find another country before the Chinese take over in 1997. But people whose options are limited. Easy prey . . .'

'Bear with me a second,' said Dave, interrupting her. 'Run this past me slowly. I understand the basics, that the grubby twenty-buck bill collected on the street for a shot of crack has to be turned into legitimate mainstream money. I understand there's literally billions being moved every year – a bigger business than Bank of America and Lloyds of

80

London combined. But in this instance, with these immigrants, how did the cash get physically out of the United States and into their accounts?'

'There could have been fifty ways or more. It might have been physically smuggled out, put into the false bottoms of suitcases, inside tennis balls or cans of deodorant, even screwed up in candy wrappings. Bank drafts might have been sent by fictitious relatives, small enough not to be recorded by the US authorities but many of them, dozens in a matter of weeks. There might have been disguised wire transfers. But let me give you a practical example – Mr Heung Wah-bor, the owner of the non-existent factory. He was interviewed yesterday by our people in Lima. A copy of the interview has been faxed through to us. I have an English and a Spanish copy. Here, take the English one. Look to the top of page three. You may find it illuminating.'

Dave took the document from her, turned to the page she had indicated and began to read . . .

Mr Wong came to me on many occasions with boxes full of cheap watches. He laughed. He said I was now a watch manufacturer, a maker of gold watches. He gave me shipping documents to sign, banking documents too. I signed everything without asking. The watches, I know, were sent to America. Payment was received for those watches in the form of letters of credit. The letters of credit were given to my bank in Hong Kong and the monies went into my account. Within six months I had over five million dollars. But the watches that were sent to America were just rubbish, worth nothing. I knew the money had to be illegal. I became very frightened. I told Wong I did not want to be part of the scheme. But he said it was too late. He came one night with some men to my house, Triads – Wo Shing Wo – and said that if I refused to go ahead, my family and I would come to harm. So what could I do? I came here to Lima. I was given a small commission to help me settle here, five thousand dollars. But the other money, the big money, I never saw. All I wanted was to get a foreign passport for my wife and family, a passport to protect us for the future. That is all. I wanted no trouble.

Dave handed back the fax. He could see now how it had worked. 'But didn't anybody question anything in Lima?' he asked. 'Didn't they think it strange that suddenly they were getting an armada of millionaires?'

Maria Ramirez gave a resigned smile. 'A little money under the table, Mr Whitman, and people look the other way. That is the way of things. How many hundreds of millions go into Colombia every year that cannot legitimately be accounted for, how many millions into Venezuela?'

'So the huge amounts paid to Gomez make sense. He wasn't just turning his eye to some bogus applications, he was oiling the wheels of a money-laundering scheme.'

'When he was recalled,' said Maria Ramirez, 'it must have disturbed many people, no doubt many powerful people too, especially if they believed he might talk.'

Dave looked at her. 'So he was murdered, is that what you're saying?'

'No, I cannot say that,' she answered. 'But you know, Mr Whitman, in Colombia, in the city of Medellin, the capital of the cocaine trade, a bomb was used to assassinate a judge. It made a crater a metre deep in the road and killed twenty-two innocent people – for just one judge.'

Filled with certainty now, positive in his mind that the Japanese Red Army claims had been nothing more than a smokescreen to disguise the murder of Gomez, Dave telephoned Kit Lampton from the consulate offices. 'It's all falling into place,' he said. 'The Peruvian thing wasn't just bribery, Kit, it was a massive money-laundering machine. And Wong Kam-kiu is the lynchpin. I underestimated the little bastard. He wasn't just filling in forms, he was helping to manage the whole thing. No wonder he was crapping himself. If he goes down, he's looking at ten years or more. Where is he now?'

'Still holed up in his apartment,' said Kit. 'It's been over a week since he discharged himself from hospital. The place is locked and barred. Nobody has come out, not even the wife. The air-conditioners are running. That's the only sign anybody is there.'

'Then let's go pick him up,' said Dave. 'If we can get him to talk, the whole house of cards is going to come tumbling down, I know it.'

Wong Kam-kiu's apartment was in an old, ramshackle building typical of Western: a slum tenement with unpainted walls, a coffin of a elevator and bare wires dangling everywhere.

It was standard in Hong Kong for apartments to have two entrance doors, an outer iron grill and an inner wooden door. In case they had to force an entry, Kit had brought two constables with metal cutting equipment.

Kit rang the doorbell. They waited. There was no answer. They rang again. Still no answer. They rang a third time. They listened for a noise, footsteps behind the doors or a voice calling, but there was nothing, only the persistent drone of the air-conditioners.

'Okay,' said Kit cheerily. 'Let's indulge in a little arc welding, shall we?'

Dave stood back watching the two constables cut their way through the lock of the outer iron grill. There was still no sound from inside the apartment. In a couple of minutes it was done. The iron grill was thrown open and the constables began to prise open the lock of the inner wooden door.

Dave stepped a little closer. He was becoming aware of a strange, distasteful smell. Kit smelt it too. 'What in the hell is that?' he said. Initially Dave shrugged it off as a blocked drain or some rotting vegetables out on the fire escape. But the smell was too distinctive for that.

The smell grew stronger. It was fetid, gaseous, thick, the all-pervasive odour of burnt animal horn and rancid milk. He glanced at Kit who had smelt it too and could see from the apprehension on his face that he was thinking the same thing. Both had been on the force too long not to recognise it. When at last the inner door was thrown open, the stench rolled over them like an invisible cloud of poisonous gas. 'Oh Christ,' muttered Kit, shoving a handkerchief over his nose and mouth. 'I hate this side of it, I just hate it.'

Inside the small apartment the stench was so thick that Dave felt he could physically scrape it off the walls. He saw that cloth had been jammed into the space beneath the front door, sealing in the stench. He made his way down the narrow, cluttered passage. He stepped past the toilet. It was empty. Then he came to the first bedroom. Its door was ajar. He held back a moment, dreading what he would find, then pushed it open with his foot.

On the nearest bed lay the body of a woman, her face gazing up at the ceiling. Decomposition made her almost unrecognisable. At the time of her death she had been wearing a yellow silk nightgown which, with the swelling of the body, had slipped open showing the decaying blackness of her flesh. Body fluids had seeped out. They stained the bed all around her and stained the wooden floor.

On the second bed, in the far corner under the window, lay the body of a child also bloated with gases. It too lay on its back staring up at the ceiling with glazed jelly eyes. A single pink rose, wilted now, dry as straw, lay on its chest.

Dave was standing in the doorway, trying to stop himself from gagging on the stench, when he felt one of the constables touch his arm.

'Excuse me, sir,' said the constable.

'Yes, what is it?' said Dave.

'You'd better come through to the kitchen, sir. There's something you have to see.'

By the time the mortuary van arrived, the police had been forced to cordon off the area around the building. Reporters and photographers crammed the street. The pavements were filled with curious onlookers. They saw three shining aluminium body boxes – ominous in their functionalism – carried out of the building and loaded into the mortuary van.

Now that the terrible stench had been released from the

sealed apartment, neighbours on the same floor, on the floor above and below, had been forced to evacuate their dwellings. They sat out on the street complaining about their ill fortune. How could they ever sell their homes now? They were ruined. Nobody would buy homes with such terrible *fung shui*.

Standing in the crowd was a man, a labourer by the looks of him, dressed in dusty jeans and a sweatshirt. He had been watching events from a roasted meat shop on the corner of the street. Now he walked forward, speaking to a police officer on crowd control. 'What happened?' he asked.

'Some man went crazy,' said the officer. 'Murdered his wife and kid, then killed himself. The bodies have been up there over a week. The man must have sealed up the apartment and put on the air-conditioners before he killed himself.'

'Any idea of his name?'

'All I know is that he ran that office there, the one on the ground floor.'

The man in dusty jeans knew exactly who ran the office on the ground floor. And within an hour the news of Wong Kam-kiu's death had reached the Philippines.

Hannah had been gone three days now and it seemed like a month. That morning, early, Dave ran up into the central hills of the island. Mist shrouded the high ground. As he ran, he relished the sensation of being wrapped in silence, lost in pearl-grey cloud, alone with just the steady pulse of his breathing. He was running longer and faster every day.

He got back to the apartment at seven, brown hair slick-wet around his face, and took the lift up to the twentieth floor. When he entered, the telephone was ringing. It was Hannah on the line.

New York was thirteen hours behind Hong Kong. It was six in the evening there, still yesterday. 'Hi, how are you?' said Dave. 'How was your trip across?'

'Still a little jet-lagged,' she said. 'Otherwise I'm okay.' But she sounded more than tired, she sounded badly down, depressed and discouraged.

'Have you been able to see any sales organisations yet?'

'A few,' she answered in a disheartened voice.

'And?'

'Always the same – thanks but no thanks, we have all the merchandise we can handle right now. I go to places on 7th Avenue and they tell me to look downmarket. I go to places on Broadway and they tell me the collection is too chic, strictly 7th Avenue. I'm being pushed from pillar to post. I just don't know what to do for the best. This afternoon, in desperation, I even gave Sonny Weiss a visit.'

'What did he think?' asked Dave, fearing the answer.

'Sonny?' Hannah gave a despondent laugh. 'You know Sonny. He looked, he clucked. It's very good, he said. I've seen him more excited over a glass of warm beer. But he'll take it on, that's something, I suppose.'

'You haven't given it to him, have you?'

'No, not yet.'

'Don't,' said Dave. 'Sonny has to be the option of last resort. I know you must be feeling pretty dejected right now. It's a hard town, everybody is hustling. But you've got to give it time. It's only been a couple of days.'

'Long enough to know which way the wind is blowing.'

'There's got to be hundreds of agencies out there, good ones too,' said Dave angrily. 'Don't give up on yourself. It's not like you. You're jet-lagged and you're feeling down. I know what it's like. The greater the hopes, the greater the disappointment. But come on, New York is your town. You were born and bred there. Don't take no for an answer. Get out and do some hustling of your own.'

She laughed. It was a tired laugh and depressed, but it was a laugh all the same. 'You're right,' she said.

'Bet your life I am.' Dave knew she would be okay. Hannah never stayed down for long. She was far too gusty a lady.

Dimitri Tselentis learnt of the death of Wong Kam-kiu when he dined with Conrad Fung at a small, exclusive restaurant in Manila's Makati District.

He had just got back from Florida. He and Aurelius, Fung's Wall Street attorney, had been negotiating the sale of Marada Cove. The uncompleted complex was costing them half a million a month. Either they dumped it or they sank. It had been two weeks, two crucial weeks, of hard, no quarter bargaining and they were almost there. Tselentis had flown back to the Philippines a happy man – only to be hit with the news.

'What do you mean, he killed himself, his wife and his kid too? Oh shit, no! How could that have happened?' He was dismayed, horrified. 'I thought we agreed to help him,' he said.

'I did intend to help him,' Fung answered in a reed-thin voice of icy control. 'Unfortunately Dimitri, events pre-empted me.'

'Events? What kind of events?' Tselentis was still shaking in disbelief. For Wong to kill himself was one thing, but his wife and child too. What kind of pressures could have driven him to an insane act like that?

Fung nibbled at his starter of terrine d'anguilles. 'It seemed that Wong got himself into a private street grudge, I don't know what about. He was attacked in an alley near his office. It was a miracle he lived.'

'But he killed himself, you say?'

'I presume the pressures must have got too much for him. He was a weak, jellyfish of a man at the best of times. It seems he discharged himself from hospital, went home, killed his wife and child, put on the air conditioners to keep down the smell, sealed the apartment and then killed himself too.' Fung sipped his soda water. 'Such things happen, Dimitri. Under pressure some men crack. They lose their minds.'

Tselentis gulped at his claret, unable to rid himself of the terrible images swimming in his mind. There was more to the story than Fung was telling him, he knew it. Fung was behind it, he had to be. He had given an undertaking and gone back on it. He had betrayed his word. 'You don't seem too upset,' he muttered, staring down at his plate.

There was a vague look of contempt on Fung's thin, sallow features. 'I'm not,' he said. 'Wong was a danger to us all – especially you, Dimitri.'

'But I don't want to see him dead.'

Fung smiled, humourless and cold. 'Look at it this way, the ledger is clear: no debits, no credits. Doesn't that satisfy your accountant's mind? There is nobody left who can implicate us in the Peruvian operation. There is nobody who can point to the fact that we are ready to do the same in Chile and Brazil. Now you can return to Hong Kong without worrying. Our clients are happy. We are happy. Nobody wants to see people die. But if the tide of events carries us to a safer shore, must we complain? I am sorry for that woman, I am sorry for that child. But all in all, it has worked out well. Who can threaten us now? So drink your wine and enjoy it, Dimitri. It's business as normal again.'

They came down a long passage harshly illuminated with neon light. It was eight in the morning but it could have been midnight. At the end of the passage, in front of a locked door, stood a police constable on guard.

'Is he awake yet?' asked Dave.

'He awoke about an hour ago,' replied the guard.

'Okay, let us in,' said Kit Lampton.

The door was unlocked. Dave and Kit Lampton entered the darkened room. It was sparsely furnished with just a single, iron-frame bed and side table. Two wooden chairs stood in a corner. A ceiling fan softly whirred. Curtains covered the windows and the walls were bare.

The figure in the bed, head propped up with pillows, looked across at them. All Dave could see in the gloom was the outline of a skeletal face. But the eyes he could see, the eyes were everything and they were huge, like the eyes of an Auschwitz survivor, blank and yet accusing, full of terrible memories; eyes that said: you have never known, you will never be able to comprehend what I have seen. They were the eyes of Wong Kam-kiu.

Chapter Eight

On the advice of the doctors, they returned later that day when Wong Kam-kiu was a little stronger, when he could sit up in bed and speak his piece.

Dave talked to him in a very quiet voice as if he did not want to disturb the monastic hush of the hospital room. 'That evening when we found you in the kitchen, that first evening when we spoke, you told us that you wished to cooperate, to be a witness. That is why, as you know, we had you smuggled out, that is why we called for three coffins, to make it seem that all three of you were dead. You are safe now. You are free to talk. But I must ask you first, do you still wish to cooperate? Do you still wish to be a witness?'

Wong Kam-kiu murmured to him in Cantonese, 'That is my only reason for being alive.'

'You know that I cannot give you any guarantees of full immunity? You know that what you say may be used against you if there is a prosecution? You do appreciate that?'

'That doesn't matter. My life is irrelevant. I don't care about jail.'

'I have a tape recorder,' said Dave. 'Take your time, don't worry about us, say whatever you wish.'

Wong Kam-kiu looked at the far wall, focusing on nothing, for a long time. Then, after several minutes, with a small cough, he began. He spoke haltingly as if remembering events that had happened decades earlier. Occasionally, he would fall into deep, melancholy silences, staring fixedly into space. But, like the drip of sap from a broken leaf, drop by oozing drop, the facts slowly fell to earth . . .

'It began when I was introduced to *Gwei Chai*, the Foreign Boy. There was a scheme, you see, a scheme in which I could make much money . . . or so I believed. I will not tell you who introduced us. He is one of the few good men I know, a man of trust. In any event, he had nothing to do with the scheme. It was just the Foreign Boy and I.'

'What kind of scheme was it?'

'It was a scheme to launder money, to get money to South America, white powder money. We had immigrants moving it for us. The Foreign Boy knew Geraldo Gomez, the Consul of Peru. Gomez, he said, must be paid and in return he would issue visas, not ask questions. I paid Gomez a great deal, I paid him every month. I found the people who were willing to go and I did the paperwork. Gomez never questioned the documents. So long as he had his money he was happy.'

'How did you find the people?'

'It was not difficult. I found poor people. Peru offered them a passport, that is all they wanted. With that passport they could return to Hong Kong as a foreign citizen. They could go to Brazil or Argentina, to Europe maybe. The passport . . . that is what I sold them.'

'What went wrong with the scheme?'

'Wrong? Gomez was recalled, that's what went wrong. Too many people in his country were asking questions. Why so many Chinese? Why all these poor people from Asia? We should have kept the numbers smaller. But it grew and grew. Gomez did not come from a powerful family, he had few friends. He was certain he would go to jail for corruption. So he drank too much. He was very frightened. One night, he telephoned me, he said he was going to make a deal with the security police in Peru. No jail provided he told them everything . . . all the details, all the names.'

'What did you do?'

'I was very frightened too. So I telephoned the Foreign Boy. I told him, I told him everything Gomez had said.'

'What did he say?'

90

'He said I must not worry. He said I must just sit tight, he said it would be dealt with.'

'What happened then?'

'Then there was the bombing, the bomb at Kai Tak.'

'What did you think?'

'It was murder, the bomb had been used to kill Gomez, murder of so many people . . . your son, just so many. I went mad, mad in my head. I was the first the police would question. I could go to jail for murder. I had to get out of Hong Kong.'

'Why didn't you go? Didn't you have money?'

'No, never. The money, the big money, was always promised but it never came. Wait, I was told, always wait. I had just a few savings, not enough to live in a new country. So I telephoned the Foreign Boy. I asked for help.'

'What help did he give you?'

'Help? He cut off my hand, he chopped my body – that's the help he gave me. He betrayed me. They all betrayed me, all those ones I had called my brothers. Who could I go to? Where could I hide? They had all turned their backs on me.'

'So what did you do?'

'My wife knew there was no way out. As a family in this life we were doomed. If I was attacked again, if I was killed, how would she survive without me? She could not work. Her heart was bad. How would our son, Chi Chi, survive? They were both so sick. We had such little money. So we spoke. She told me she had prayed and knew what must be done. First, she said, she and Chi Chi must be placed beyond harm's reach, sent to a place where they could never be threatened again.'

'She asked you to kill both herself and your son?'

'At first I said no, I could not do it. How could I kill the ones I loved so much? But she said we had no alternative. The god of heaven had decreed it.'

'Did you kill your son?'

'I played with Chi Chi for some time, we played with his toys. Then I suffocated him with a pillow. He struggled a little but not for long. Afterwards, I placed a rose upon his chest. Then I sat for a long time with my wife and we cried together. I said I did not have the strength to kill her too. I said it would be best if she went away, back to China. But she said she had to join Chi Chi to care for him in the other world. She said I should not lose courage. So I tied her arms with string. We said goodbye. Then I suffocated her too. It was very easy. She hardly struggled. She wanted so much to go.'

'Why did you stay alive?'

'So that I could testify, you see, testify against those who had betrayed us without any fear for my wife and child. Now, whatever I do, whatever I say, they cannot be harmed.'

'But why stay with the bodies so long?'

'My wife and I agreed, a solemn agreement . . . she must not be touched, she must be left for a full week there in the apartment.'

'But why?'

'Why? So that she could decompose. That was her wish, to turn black and awful to look upon. The reason, you see, is that she wished to become a ghost, a fierce and gruesome ghost.'

'A ghost? Why?'

'Because we agreed that my testimony was not to be our only justice. From the other side of the grave, in the spirit world, my wife would haunt the ones who had betrayed us. That way none of them would escape, not in this life or the next. She would haunt them as an apparition for their nightmares. She said the words to me . . . they will learn, she said, that even the meek, even the humble can exact an awesome revenge.'

After that, with the talk of the death of his wife and child, Wong Kam-kiu could say no more. He fell into a long silence, lost in another world. He was gently crying.

It had been enough, though. Dave was chilled to the marrow, more than enough for one day . . .

The following day they returned to continue the questioning. They sat by the bed in the darkened room and Dave asked him. 'Who is *Gwei Chai*, the Foreign Boy, the one who betrayed your trust?'

Wong Kam-kiu answered in a dry voice. 'His name is Tselentis. His father was Greek, his mother Cantonese. His mother is still alive, she has a shop in Hong Kong. Tselentis is a financier, a trader. He deals in black money. They say he moves many millions.'

'Where can we find him?'

'He travels a great deal. Most of the year he lives in hotels. He travels all around Asia. But he has an apartment in Hong Kong. He has a business here too, a trading company.'

'Do you know, did Tselentis originate the money-laundering scheme or, like you, did he also take instructions?'

'There was somebody, yes . . . a more powerful man.'

'Who was this man he answered to?'

'I do not know.'

'Did he not say anything about him?'

'No.'

'Did you not ask?'

'There are some things,' said Wong, 'that you never ask.'

The records showed that Dimitri Tselentis was forty years of age, born in Hong Kong, a Greek national. He was divorced with no children. The only immediate family he had was his mother, a Cantonese woman who ran a general store in Aberdeen on the south side of Hong Kong Island, and an uncle, a deep sea fisherman.

In all the records, Tselentis listed his occupation as a director of companies. His business address was in Admiralty, Tower One. A check of the premises revealed that it was the registered office of a company named Hellenic-Oriental Trading. Hellenic-Oriental had a number of agencies to distribute goods in Asia. A glossy brochure was obtained from reception listing the goods. Dave read through the brochure and on page six found what he was looking for – a range of Filipino-manufactured suitcases called FLY HI.

A comparison was conducted between the fingerprints of

Tselentis registered with the ID Bureau and the single print found on the fragment of suitcases at the bomb site. Twelve points of exact comparison were needed for legal certainty in most jurisdictions. The print found on the shard of suitcase was blurred and smeared at the edge. Seven points, therefore, was the best that could be done. But there was little doubt about it – they had the man who had carried the bomb.

Immediate steps were taken to locate Tselentis. It was discovered that he was out of Hong Kong. The manager at his office in Admiralty could not assist. 'Mr Tselentis will be back in a while,' was all the man could say. There was no point in approaching the mother, she would only alert her son, and, at this early stage an Interpol Red Notice was too public.

The decision was made by Tom Mackay that the mother should be kept under discreet observation. Tselentis himself would be placed on the Watch List so that when he returned they would immediately be informed. But he was not to be stopped at immigration control. When they picked him up, they wanted it to be in circumstances of their choosing.

There was a party that night on Park Avenue held in some baronial coop apartment owned by the heiress to a bra and knickers empire. Sonny Weiss had telephoned her hotel in the morning. 'Why don't you come with me?' he had said. 'It's a bash for some new hotshot frog designer. The rag trade will be there in force. You want to meet some fancy people with connections? Okay, this is your chance.'

Hannah accepted without hesitation. Any opportunity – no matter how slim – to meet somebody who might help her with her collection was an opportunity she couldn't miss. So far, she had struck out badly. She was getting more desperate by the day. So she had put on a black cocktail dress, a creation designed by herself, and Sonny Weiss, short and fat and happy, with a Pancho Villa moustache, had escorted her there.

Hannah was a New York girl herself. Her parents, both

now deceased, had been Czech immigrants, Ashkenazi Jews who had somehow over the years abandoned their Jewishness as an unwanted old-world tag in the new. Her father had been a bookseller, her mother a violin teacher, both intellectually rich and financially poor. Hannah had been raised in Queens in an old brownstone with a deli downstairs, a world away from the WASP grandeur of the Park Avenue apartment where the party was held. It was, however, everything she had ever dreamed of, a vast shimmering fantasy that went on from room to room – Chinese red silk wall coverings, regency chairs, exquisite oil paintings in rich gold frames, wood that shone, amber lighting, Mozart music at the perfect pitch – a glittering showpiece of wealth.

'Some place, huh, babe,' said Sonny with open-mouthed avarice. Then, seeing a small male huddle of acquaintances, he pulled her over. 'I'd like you to meet Hannah Whitman. She's from Hong Kong. Has a great new line in kids' clothing. Knockout stuff. You should examine it some time.'

The male chorus chirped dutifully back but, from the way they ogled at her, it was obvious that kids' clothing was the last thing they wanted to examine. It irritated her. Put a group of chauvinists together with a whisky in each hand and you were back in the stone age. The talk in the group centred either on how the city was going to shit or the fact that half their colleagues were booked for triple by-passes in the fall. Not one of them spoke to her about her new line and when she tried to raise the subject, all she received in reply was a vacant, lecherous grin.

When the buffet was served, she managed to break away. At least she would have the comfort of eating with the company of her own frustration. She took a petite serving of salmon and red caviar, had her champagne glass refilled and found a safe corner to sit.

'Do you mind if I join you? There appears to be a chair free next to you and I hate eating standing up.' The voice was mellow, cultured, distinctly European. Hannah looked up. 'My name is Sam Ephram,' said the man. 'A glass in one hand, a plate in the other, it is always so impossible.'

He looked down at her with a brown, courteous gaze, the

95

barest shadow of a smile on his lips. He was not tall, about five foot eight inches. He had a square-cut face with a strong jaw line. He looked to be in his late thirties and clearly came from Mediterranean stock. His black hair was cut short and frosted at the tips. She saw that it came down to a devil's peak at the centre of his forehead. His eyes were very dark, very expressive, and he had olive skin. Hannah was impressed, almost flustered.

He paused a moment, politely seeking her permission to sit, and only when she nodded did he do so. 'You must be in the fashion business,' he said, speaking slowly with a fine, strong timbre to his voice. 'Everybody here seems to be.'

She nodded, for some strange reason flushing a little.

'What do you do?'

'I'm a designer.'

'I very much envy people who are creative. Whatever work we do, we all have our share of pain and aggravation. But for you at least, well, it has a clear value. At the end of the day there's a new creation, something unique, something more than just money moved.' That barest shadow of a smile remained on his face. 'What kind of clothing do you design? Women's fashions?'

'I used to, yes, but I've recently moved into children's fashions. What line of business are you in? Not the creative side, I take it?'

He smiled, showing fine white teeth. 'Sadly no, much more prosaic. I'm in finance.'

'Do you work here in New York?'

He shrugged. 'Yes, much of the time. But I also travel a great deal. And yourself?'

'Hong Kong.'

'Ah, Hong Kong, a fascinating place. I like it very much. Except in the summer of course. Then it is hell on earth. Do you have your design studio there?'

'I design and produce there, yes, and sell here in the States.' She gave an uncertain smile. 'At least that's the theory. Times are a little tough at the moment. And you, what sort of finance are you in, bonds, equities?'

'Trade finance . . . wherever an opportunity presents

itself. I have my own small business.' He smiled again as if embarrassed to go into too much detail, a sure sign that whatever it was, it was big.

'You're not American,' said Hannah.

'No, although America is my home.' He smiled again. 'I have my green card now. By origin, though, I am Israeli. And you?'

'Born in New York – and Jewish too. Went to design school here. So I'm as American as apple pie.'

'Or gefilte fish . . .'

She laughed. She didn't know why but she felt almost nervous in his company. There was something very provocative about him. At one time he accidently touched her arm and she felt it tingle. But at the same time he was approachable too. Her heart beat a little faster. Perhaps, she thought, just perhaps. And stuttering a little, she said. 'I'm over here trying to market a new line in children's clothing. A tough market . . .'

He looked directly at her, his cheeks deeply tanned, a small cleft in his chin. 'You are having problems?'

She gave a small, slightly embarrassed smile. 'Let's just say I'm not getting anywhere too fast at the moment.'

'Even in hard times,' he said, 'quality will sell.'

'Yes, that's what I was banking on.' She tried to make a joke of it. 'The fairy-tale solution . . . the triumph of talent over the system. It makes a good movie theme. I don't know about anything else.'

'Does your new line have a name?' he asked.

'I call it Danny's Rags.'

He grinned, disarmingly boyish. 'I am surprised. I would have expected something more . . .'

'Predictable? Kiddy-like?'

'Yes, maybe. Why such a name?'

She paused for a moment, holding back the small surge of emotion. Then she said very softly, with such clear, ringing sadness. 'Danny was the name of my son.'

He said nothing for a time, just sipped his drink. Then, in a soft voice, he asked her. 'How old was your son when he died?'

Tears sparkled in her eyes.

'I'm sorry,' he said. 'I should not have asked. It was very wrong of me.'

'No, no, it's good to talk about it. I'm the one who should be sorry. He was nine years old, nine years and one month.'

'So young, I'm sorry.'

She didn't know why but, once it was out, she felt compelled to tell him everything then, every last detail of Danny's death and her determination, using the only skills she had, to commemorate him. As she spoke, her voice faltered with emotion and she expected to catch a look of embarrassment on his face, a kind of withdrawal that had been the inevitable reaction so far. But there was nothing of the kind. He listened attentively and sympathetically until she had finished. Then, calling a waiter across, he had her champagne glass refilled.

There was a short silence before he spoke. 'I am not in the fashion business, not directly,' he said. 'But I am here tonight, which means of course that I have certain contacts . . . a few friends, a few old acquaintances. I cannot promise anything. But I would very much like to see your new range. Would you mind?'

'No, of course not, I'd be delighted.'

'How about tomorrow?'

'Yes,' she answered, flustered, 'yes, tomorrow would be fine.'

'Say around noon? Then we could have lunch together – if you're not busy, of course.'

'Lunch? No, I would enjoy that. Thank you.'

'Where are you staying?'

'At a hotel on East 42nd.'

'Good,' he said. 'Then I can come to the hotel, we can look at the samples and afterwards have lunch.'

She gave him the name of the hotel and, very formally, he handed her his business card:

Trade Negotiations International Inc.
President
Samuel Ephram

He rose from his chair. 'Until tomorrow then,' he said with that solemn heart-stopping smile.

Hannah watched him walk away through the crowd. She took a deep breath, trying to control her excitement. At last, she thought, at long last, somebody who at least is interested.

By the time they met the following day, Hannah was in a state of high anxiety. When Sam Ephram entered her hotel room, that soft smile set against the lean cheeks and that mesmerising gaze in his eyes, she was so nervous she was shivering. He sensed it too. But nothing was said. She had the twenty-five samples laid out on the bed. 'Pick them up, look at them. Tell me what you think,' she said.

He examined each item carefully, the material, quality of workmanship, the overall effect of each design. He had an eye for an article, that was obvious. When he had finished, he pondered for a moment and all the time Hannah's heart was beating against her ribcage like the wings of a trapped bird.

Then suddenly his face was lit by a broad, generous smile. 'I think they are wonderful,' he said. 'If I had children, this is exactly what I would want them to wear. They are bright, they are chic. They are clever. I'm amazed you have not been able to interest anybody in representing you yet.'

Her relief was so palpable that she had to find a seat. She was grinning foolishly, she knew it, but she could do nothing to stop herself.

They went to an elegant midtown restaurant for lunch. Sam Ephram excused himself to make a telephone call but was back within a couple of minutes. They both ordered a salad of salty preserved duck and sweet lobster which they washed down with California Chablis.

'Earlier this morning I spoke to a friend,' said Ephram. 'He is a very nice man, very approachable. You would like him, I think. He runs a small sales organisation from offices at 1407 Broadway.'

Hannah felt her heart leap. If you stood outside 1407 long enough you met everybody in the fashion business. It was where 7th and Broadway merged, the best of the best addresses.

'I hope you don't mind, but I told him your story . . . about the death of your son and your determination to remember him. He was of the same opinion as me. It is very touching, a story of courage too. If courage is matched to talent, he said, then it deserves to be rewarded. He asked me to look at your samples and give him my opinion. That was why I had to go to the telephone a few minutes ago.'

'What did you tell him?' she asked.

'Exactly what I told you.'

'And what was his answer?'

He gave a quick, bright smile. 'We have an appointment with him at four this afternoon.'

The friend's name was Joel Grossman. He was the president of Pan-Perfect Sales, one of the fastest growing, most respected sales corporations in New York. Hannah had been trying to get in to see Pan-Perfect for days. Joel Grossman surprised her. She didn't know why but she had expected a dynamically dressed, hard-punching sales tycoon, the soap opera image. Instead, at four that afternoon, she found herself in the chaotic, cluttered office of a round-faced, totally unpretentious individual who had a photograph of his son's barmitzvah on his desk, laughed all the time and had a wonderful knack of putting everybody instantly at ease. Joel Grossman ordered coffee and brownies – brownies were his addiction, he said – studied her samples and then went off to discuss them in private with his staff. Within twenty minutes he was back. 'We're unanimous,' he said. 'We would be delighted to represent you.'

Sam Ephram took her for dinner that night to a small Italian restaurant. The decor was wonderful, Hannah ate a steamed bass with zucchini that melted in her mouth. But she was too giddy, riding far too high, for mundane senses to prevail. At last everything she had worked for, everything she had dreamed of, was happening to her.

'Joel Grossman was very impressed with your work,' Sam Ephram told her. 'Joel relies very much on his instincts, he has a *feel* for fashion and he has done brilliantly well so far – as brilliantly as you can do, he says.'

She laughed. 'I could never hope—'

'No, no, he thinks you have great talent, Hannah.'

'I'm sure they were just compliments.'

'Don't let the laughter and the brownies fool you. When he has to, Joel can cut a person off at the knees without blinking. He's a businessman, a very successful one. They were not just compliments. When he says you have a great future, I trust his judgement.'

Hannah raised her wine glass, tipsy with the excitement. 'Well, here's to his judgement.'

Sam Ephram smiled. 'But, as you said the other night when we first met, talent alone does not always triumph over the system. You will need financial backing, you will need professional advice on how best to promote the Hannah Whitman image.'

She laughed again, dizzy with the flattery of it all, the wine going to her head. 'Isn't it a bit too early to think of promoting my image?'

'It is never too early,' he said. 'The world of fashion moves fast, Hannah. Names explode on the scene. In one season the design label of a new star can be selling all over the world.' He smiled at her, exuding quiet, well-judged confidence. 'And that's what Joel and I think you are capable of being – a new star in the fashion world.'

Hannah could hardly believe all this was being said to her. Just yesterday she was nobody, going nowhere, ready to pack up her bags and fly home. Now suddenly words like 'star' were being tossed around her head like confetti.

Sam Ephram filled her wine glass. 'You can be a rich woman, Hannah.' He saw the look in her eyes and laughed. 'You think this is all a dream but I can assure you it is not. This is the real world, the world of sudden opportunity – it is your world, Hannah, the fashion world.'

Hannah was laughing but at the same time her mouth was

bone dry. It was all happening so fast. 'Are you saying that you would like to back me financially?'

His dark eyes gazed into her face. 'Only, of course, if it is your wish too.'

'Oh God yes,' she exclaimed. 'I could think of nothing better, Sam! That would be fantastic.'

'I don't want to push you in any way. I know that it must be like a crowded dance floor in your head at the moment. But over the next few days, when you have had a chance to settle a little, a chance to think . . .'

She was laughing like a girl on her first date who had drunk too much wine. 'It's crazy, isn't it?' she said. 'Here we are talking about all these things – corporate images, fashion labels – and we haven't sold a single garment yet!'

'But we will,' he said, 'wait and see – hundreds of thousands of them.'

It was impossible to sleep that night. At three in the morning her head was still spinning. Hannah lay on her bed in her hotel room and all she could think of were the incredible events of the past thirty-six hours. How in the world had it happened to her? An empty chair near a buffet table – my God, in years to come she would be telling that story! She went through every event again in her mind – the hotel room with the samples on the bed, the lunch, the drive together to Joel Grossman's office. She pictured Joel Grossman, the coffee and brownies, his lovely teddy bear laughter . . .

But all the time her thoughts kept spinning back to Sam Ephram. And it wasn't just the good fortune he had brought her, it was more than that. Hannah had never met a man who combined such solemn, beguiling reserve with such overpowering sexuality. It sounded so stupid but in his presence she felt like a teenage girl. Was he married? Did he have a lover? What secrets were hidden in his past? Listen to me, she thought, I'm romanticising like a teenager too! Not once in ten years of marriage, despite all the travelling, despite all the propositions, had she been unfaithful to Dave. Not once had she even been tempted – until now,

102

that is. And with the realisation came a sharp stab of guilt.

On an impulse, she booked a call to Hong Kong. She had to tell Dave what had happened. He had to be the first person. It was late afternoon there already, thirteen hours ahead. With luck she would get him at the office.

At first, when he heard her voice, Dave was worried, expecting the worst. 'What time is it over there? It must be about three in the morning. Are you okay?'

'No, I'm fine, I'm just fine. I've done it, Dave, I've broken in! I've got a financier who wants to back me and this afternoon Pan-Perfect, the best, the most dynamic sales force in the whole of New York, agreed to take on my collection. I just can't tell you how I feel darling, I'm floating on air.'

'That's great. And financial backing too. My God, how did it happen so fast?'

'I met this man at a cocktail party. Sam Ephram is his name. I got to telling him about the collection and how I came to design it. He said he wanted to see the samples.'

'And?'

'And that was it! He liked what he saw, he lifted his rod and the waters of the Red Sea parted. It was incredible.'

'But how did you get to this company, what did you say its name was?'

'Pan-Perfect. Sam Ephram knew the president of the corporation. They're personal friends. All it took was twenty minutes. Dave, darling, the whole thing is like a dream.'

'I think it's great,' said Dave, 'absolutely great. What did I tell you? Just keep hustling. I knew you would do it. What's this guy, Ephram like? Is he old, young?'

For a second – she didn't know why – Hannah hesitated. 'Sam? Oh, you'd like him, Dave. He's charming. A nice man.' She was straining to find the right words: innocuous, bland descriptions. 'He's your age, late thirties, a few inches shorter, dresses well . . .'

Dave laughed, teasing her. 'Good-looking?'

'He's dark, going a little grey. Yes, he's good-looking, I suppose.'

'Rich, good-looking, charming. Sounds like a real hotshot. I hope I'm not in trouble.'

Hannah gave an awkward laugh. 'Come on darling, don't tell me you're jealous?'

When the phone went down, Dave sat for a while. The news was fantastic and Hannah deserved her success, every moment of it. He was delighted for her. But, as pleased as he was, something worried him because, beneath all the excitement and enthusiasm, there had been a kind of reticence as if Hannah was holding something back, something to do with this guy Ephram who had suddenly come into her life.

No, that's crazy, he thought, trying to shake himself out of it. She only met him a day or so ago. How can you sense something like that on a call made from halfway around the world? It was the middle of the night in New York, she couldn't sleep, she was in a spin. You're imagining things.

But despite the rationalisation, the small nagging doubt wouldn't leave him. Hannah had joked with him, saying he was jealous. Well yes, he thought, perhaps he was . . .

Chapter Nine

Madam Ma Mei-ling was a small woman, a little brown Cantonese sparrow, proud and industrious. She had fled to Hong Kong as a young woman to escape the communists and for forty years had run her shop in Aberdeen on the south side of the island. The Good Well Provision Company, she had called it and that was still its name. It overlooked the harbour where the junks crammed in their hundreds and most of her customers were the junk people. She sold rice and soy sauce, sugar and oil, all the provisions poor folk required.

She had married in Hong Kong and seen her husband die. She had raised a child on her own. She was now sixty-five years old, her hair pure white, tied back in a bun, her face a handsome mask of weathered wrinkles. Her back was bent, she suffered badly from arthritis. Yet she kept her shop open twelve hours a day, seven days a week with just one assistant, a woman nearly as old as herself. She still used an abacus. She made a fair profit, saved her money, kept plenty of gold and planned to keep working another ten years. On the waterfront of Aberdeen she was an institution.

That evening, however, Madam Ma felt poorly. She didn't know why. She felt dizzy, a little disorientated. There were pains in her chest. Her elder brother, Ma Chi-wan, seventy years of age, a deep sea fisherman with his own junk, had returned to harbour that day. They had planned to have supper together. Madam Ma still had work to do before she closed the shop. But for some reason she was unable to concentrate. Her fingers trembled on the beads of

105

the abacus. A glass of water would help, she thought. But when she tried to rise from her chair, the pains in her chest intensified. Oh dear, she thought, oh dear.

She saw her brother enter the shop and called to him in Cantonese. She saw the look of concern on his face. But then she remembered no more . . . only the strange sensation of falling in slow motion to the wooden boards of the floor.

Ma Chi-wan – Uncle Ma, as everybody knew him – was the one who got the news to his nephew. 'Your mother has had a heart attack,' he said. 'It happened just a couple of hours ago. She was in the shop and she collapsed.'

Dimitri Tselentis felt himself go cold. 'How bad is it? Is she all right?'

'The doctors have got her in intensive care. They are doing tests and things. I have to be honest with you, they tell me it's bad, Dimitri, that it's touch and go. But you know your mother, she has a will of iron.'

'Where have they got her?'

'In the intensive care unit at the Adventist. I'm phoning from the hospital now. I saw her a couple of minutes ago. She had wires all over her and still she was trying to give me instructions about the shop. See what I mean about a will of iron.'

'Tell her I'll get on to the first flight I can,' said Tselentis. 'I'm dropping everything. I'll be there tomorrow. What about the doctors, Uncle, are you certain we've got the best?'

'Don't worry about the doctors, they are doing everything they can. But you must come, Dimitri, you're the only son. With you by her bed I'm sure she'll pull through.'

The following day, on the first available flight, worried sick about his mother, Tselentis returned to Hong Kong. He touched down at four in the afternoon and, in trepidation, entered the building where, just a few weeks earlier, the bomb had exploded.

With Wong Kam-kiu dead, there was no way the cops

106

could know anything about his involvement in the bombing. But even so, just being there, appreciating his potential vulnerability, was a nerve-racking experience. When he presented his Greek passport at immigration and the officer seemed to take an inordinate time pondering over it, he felt the hairs on the back of his neck begin to rise. But then, just when he was beginning to panic, the man stamped the passport without a word, and Tselentis was through. It was just as Fung had said – business as normal again.

A taxi took him direct to the Adventist Hospital on the island on Stubbs Road above the Happy Valley racecourse. On arrival, he went straight up to Intensive Care where he found his uncle waiting. He and his uncle hugged and Tselentis asked him. 'How is she doing?'

'The doctor is in with her now. She's holding her own,' his uncle said. He gave a smile of encouragement. He looked worn out, as if he hadn't slept all night.

When the specialist came out, Tselentis introduced himself. 'How is she?' he asked anxiously. 'Is she any better?'

'Yes, much better. Your mother is a lucky woman. We managed to catch her in time. We've put her on an anti-clotting drug, TPA, which seems to be working well. We'll have to keep her in the Intensive Care Unit, monitoring her condition, for a couple more days. But then, if all goes well, we'll be able to move her to a general ward.'

'And after that?'

'A slow, steady recuperation, Mr Tselentis. The first six weeks is always crucial but if your mother takes it easy, avoids unnecessary stress, I see no reason why she can't make a full recovery.'

'So she's going to make it? I mean, she's not in any danger?'

'Her condition is being permanently monitored on an ECG machine. She's responding to the drugs. She's not overweight, her blood pressure is good. She should do just fine.'

'Oh thank God. Can I see her?'

'Yes, of course, go through. But not too long. She's been through quite an ordeal. She's very tired.'

His mother lay in bed, wires running from her body. Against the stark white of the pillows, she looked so brown and wrinkled, so small and frail. He called to her in Cantonese, the language they always spoke together. She opened her eyes and a smile lit up her face. He sat by the bed, taking her tiny brown-blotched hand in his. 'I've just spoken to the doctor. He says you're going to be fine. But you have to take it easy, no stress, that's what he said. So I don't want you worrying about anything. I want you to relax and I want you to get well.'

'I won't worry,' she answered, 'and I promise to relax. But in return you must promise to keep an eye on the shop for me.'

He laughed softly, shaking his head. She was incorrigible. 'Why do you bother with that shop? You should sell it. You don't need to work. I can keep you, you know that.'

'What would I do with myself if I didn't work?'

'Enjoy life.'

'I enjoy life in the shop.'

'Will you at least come and stay with me in the apartment?'

'Your place is so big, Dimitri, so grand.'

'What's wrong with that?'

'I like being where I am, close to the water, close to my friends. Your apartment is not a place to live, it's a place to visit.'

'Then come and stay for a little while at least, just until you're stronger. I've got a room for you there, a maid, everything.'

'I'll think about it.'

He squeezed her hand. 'You're so stubborn, you know that.'

'Of course I am,' she said, a mischievous twinkle in her eyes. 'That's why I'm still alive.'

Tselentis remained in the room with his mother for another hour until it was time for her medication. Then he sat outside in the open air talking to his uncle while the old man smoked cigarettes and talked about the good old days when Tselentis's mother had been just a girl – and beautiful too – and they had both come to Hong Kong with no money, no family, nobody but each other to rely on.

Tselentis stayed at the hospital until eight that night when he was finally satisfied that his mother was settled and would sleep peacefully through the night. He checked that the massive arrangement of flowers he had ordered by telephone arrived, he assured himself that his uncle would get home safely and only then did he catch a cab to his Mid Levels apartment set high on the slopes of the Peak.

He owned the penthouse on the thirtieth floor of the block. Although he rarely spent more than a couple of months a year in it, he had spent a fortune furnishing the place and kept an amah employed full time. Inside the apartment, he poured himself a stiff cognac, put on some classical music – he loved Bach – and flopped down in one of the big easy chairs. He was beginning slowly to unwind.

His mother's heart attack had scared the life out of him, he made no bones about it. But she was going to pull through. With a little rest, she was going to be as good as new. And suddenly everything looked so much rosier. No doubt about it, after a bad scare life was that much sweeter. A small celebration was in order, he decided, a few drinks with a good-looking woman to talk to and help him unwind. He knew just the place too, one of his regular haunts.

By nine-thirty he had bathed and changed. He went down to the parking basement where he kept his metallic-gold Mercedes 500SE and his red Porsche. He chose the Porsche – he felt in a sporty mood, the Mercedes was too sedate – and headed out of the building. As he turned out of the entrance and drove away down Po Shan Road under the spreading banyan trees he glimpsed two men sitting in a small Japanese car opposite the block. They were obviously waiting for somebody and he took no further notice.

It took him half an hour to get to the club in Tsim Sha Tsui East on the far side of the harbour. It was called the Jade Palace and was a hostess club, extravagantly glitzy, outrageously expensive, packed every night with Japanese and Korean businessmen, each with a hostess sitting next to him who charged a small fortune per hour for the pleasure of her company. Tselentis often brought business associates here to celebrate a deal but tonight the pleasure was just for himself.

One of the hostesses came to his table. She was Chinese. Her name was Charity, she said, Charity Choi, and she would very much like to sit with him. She was dressed in a *cheong sam* of peacock blue. Her hair fell to her shoulders in a shimmering black waterfall. She was petite and curvaceous and possessed a smile so provocative that Tselentis could almost see the sheets being turned back. 'Sure,' he said, 'come and sit with pleasure.' He ordered a bottle of champagne. The band was playing, there was laughter all around him and Charity, he was sure, was going to be the best lay of the decade. No doubt about it, Hong Kong was a good place to be.

At one in the morning, with Charity Choi on his arm, he decided it was time to go home. He had drunk enough to fire his sexual drive, not too much, he hoped, to impair the performance. He was feeling very amorous. A contented smile sat on the dimpled swarthiness of his face. As he stood on the pavement outside the club waiting for the valet to bring the Porsche, he swayed a little, laughing, while Charity pressed herself against him. He kissed her neck and she giggled. Her skin was milky soft, as smooth as the satin of her dress. Earlier, at their table, drinking champagne and eating oysters, they had agreed three thousand Hong Kong dollars for her services. Charity could drive a hard bargain. But just the smoothness of her skin, thought Tselentis, made it worth every cent.

When the Porsche arrived, Tselentis opened the passenger door so that she could climb in. When she sat, her *cheong sam* rode up high showing the full stretch of her legs; beautifully shaped, sheer and enticing. Tselentis had eyes for nothing else. He did not see the man in the doorway of the club speaking into a mobile telephone. But even if he had, he would have thought nothing of it. After all, mobile telephones in Hong Kong were as common as swimming pools in Bel Air.

★

In the past hour a brisk wind had risen, bringing drizzle and mist in off the sea. Dave could hear the wind moaning around the tall obelisk of the apartment block. Through the rain-speckled windshield he had a clear view of the entrance lobby, all glass and marble and potted palms. The message had been radioed through: Tselentis was due any minute now. Good, he thought with grim determination, he had waited long enough. It was time for the arrest.

Officers of his rank didn't normally make arrests. But this arrest was different, unique. This arrest was his obligation, his privilege. Nobody could usurp this one from him.

He saw the red Porsche come up the driveway and pull into one of the visitors' parking bays in front of the lobby. A man climbed out. He was short and round, black hair, swarthy complexion – Tselentis. Dave's pulse began to race. All right, you bastard, he thought. Now this is where you begin to pay.

It began to rain harder. Tselentis and his woman were laughing as they ran from the car into the lobby. But Dave was oblivious of the rain. He entered the brightly lit lobby with a sergeant at his side, one of his most trusted men.

Tselentis was across the far side waiting at the elevator doors, his arm around the woman, whispering to her and giggling. They were so wrapped up in each other that they had no idea Dave and his sergeant were standing just five paces behind. The elevator doors opened. The two of them entered – and Dave stepped in right behind them.

Tselentis gawked at him. It was close to one-thirty in the morning and he was a stranger. But he said nothing and Dave maintained the silence too. The sergeant stepped into the elevator, the doors hissed shut and it began the ascent to the penthouse on the thirtieth floor.

Slowly, very deliberately, Dave removed the police warrant card from his wallet. He turned to face Tselentis who was backed into a corner. 'Are you Dimitri Tselentis?' he asked.

Tselentis's eyes popped. 'Who are you?'

'My name is Whitman, I am a superintendent in the Royal Hong Kong Police.'

Like a vole plucked up in the talons of an owl, Tselentis gave a sudden squeak of doomed surprise. For a moment he looked as if he was going to faint.

'You are under arrest,' said Dave. 'The charges are murder. They relate to the bombing at Kai Tak Airport, the killing of six people and the wounding of twenty-two others.'

'Oh Jesus no, you can't think – ' Tselentis gagged, throwing a hand over his mouth to stop from vomiting.

In a monotone, Dave recited the standard caution. 'You have the right to remain silent but anything you say will be taken down and may be used in evidence.'

And all the time Tselentis protested, 'I knew nothing about it, I swear to God.'

The doors of the elevator opened at the thirtieth floor. Dave gestured at Tselentis to step out. 'I suggest you unlock the door to your apartment and let us in,' he said.

Tselentis fumbled with his keys. He was pleading with Dave in a shell-shocked, shivering moan. 'I promise to God, I had nothing to do with that Kai Tak thing. Your evidence is wrong. You have to believe me. I could never have done anything like that, never.'

Dave took the keys from his hand, opening the door himself. As he had expected, the penthouse was extravagantly furnished, a rich man's den. He spoke to his sergeant in rapid Cantonese, instructing him to take the woman to one of the other rooms and hold her there. Charity Choi, ashen with shock, was led away without protest.

Tselentis had retreated to the far side of the lounge. 'You're the father of that boy, aren't you?' he said.

Dave answered in an unforgiving voice. 'Yes, I am. The boy you killed.'

Tselentis was on the verge of tears. 'Oh God, how do I convince you I had nothing to do with it?'

'Tell me the truth, that's how.' Dave walked to the doors that led out on to the balcony and opened them. Warm, wet air gusted into the air-conditioned stillness of the room. The harbour spread below him, an infinity of murky black water and diamond lights. The wind was blowing in hard from the

112

northwest, pushing clouds of mist before it. Dave felt the wind on his cheeks but it did nothing to quell the rage building inexorably inside him. He turned back to Tselentis. 'Tell me what part you played in the bombing. Tell me the truth and maybe then I'll be convinced.'

For a moment it looked as if Tselentis was going to answer. But then, with a small moan of despair, he turned his head away. He knew that one word said wrong – one word out of place – would condemn him forever. So he said the first thing, the most obvious thing, to keep Whitman at bay. 'I want to see a lawyer. I won't say anything until then.'

Dave's face became instantly a raw, forbidding mask. He stepped closer to Tselentis, grabbing his arm and pulling him towards the open doors on to the balcony. 'I'll ask you once again. What part did you play?'

'I want to see a lawyer. I'm entitled to make a call.'

'You're entitled to nothing.'

They were out on the balcony now, out in the swirling sea mist and the wind. Tselentis tried to resist but the grip on his arm was too strong. All he could do was protest feebly, 'You can't do this to me. I have rights too!'

'Rights?' Dave glared at him. 'My son was nine years old. He hadn't even begun his life, he was just a kid – and you talk of rights!' He grabbed the lapels of Tselentis's jacket, almost lifting him off his feet, and the blind, boiling rage that had been building inside finally burst out. He hauled Tselentis over to the balcony wall, slamming him against it. Tselentis cried out in pain. He tried to resist. But he was a head shorter than Dave, half-drunk, unfit and flaccid, while Dave was fired with a murderous fury that cared nothing for the consequences.

Dave heaved him upwards with such force that Tselentis was half over the balcony, arms flailing. 'Help me!' he called. 'Somebody for God's sake help me!' But his cries were rushed away on the wind.

'Now I'll tell you something,' said Dave, his voice low and lethal. 'We know the brand of the suitcase that carried the bomb, a brand you sell.'

Tselentis was squirming in his grip, struggling hopelessly to get free. 'But there are thousands of those suitcases. They're everywhere, in every shop!'

'Not with your fingerprint on.'

'My fingerprint?' Tselentis's eyes bulged in horror. 'No, that's wrong, that can't be!'

Dave heaved him further up, further outwards.

'All right, all right!' shrieked Tselentis. 'I must have touched it. But I didn't know what was in the case, I swear to God!'

'You wanted Gomez dead.'

'No, no!'

'Don't lie to me, you bastard. You knew he was going to talk when he got back to Peru. That's why you had him killed. That's why the suitcase was taken to the airport. You knew all along.'

'You've got no proof of that!'

'I've got all the proof I need. Enough proof to hang you – I've got Wong Kam-kiu.'

Tselentis was stupefied. 'Wong? No, no, that can't be right. Wong is dead.'

Charity Choi had been taken to the study. But the room looked out over the harbour and, at an angle, it had a view of the balcony too. Smoking furiously to try and calm herself, she stepped over to the window – and that's when she saw what was happening. 'They're fighting out there,' she said to the sergeant. 'One of them is going to be killed. Look, look!'

The sergeant pulled her back from the window. But he had seen the two figures too. 'Wait here,' he commanded her. 'Don't leave the room.' Then he ran out towards the balcony.

Dave spat out the words, forced to shout above the swirl of the wind. 'Three body boxes went down to the street. But one was empty. Wong was still alive. You had tried to butcher him like you butchered my son and Wong is going to see you in hell.' All the time as he spoke, he was forcing

Tselentis higher and further out over the balcony. His head was close to bursting. Somebody had to pay, somebody had to pay for the death of his son.

Behind him he heard a call in Cantonese. 'No sir, don't do it, please.'

'Get back, Sergeant,' he shouted. 'This is my business. One step nearer and I promise to God he goes over.'

Tselentis cried out in terror. 'No, no, please don't! Oh God, don't tip me over!' Dave's face was only inches from his. Tselentis had never seen a look of such remorseless intent. He clawed hysterically at the smooth marble of the balcony wall trying to find a grip. But there was none. His body was being lifted relentlessly higher. He twisted his head, staring down through the mist to the black well of the ground thirty storeys below. 'Please, no!' he shouted. Oh God, he was going to die. This madman wasn't going to stop. And his spirit broke. 'All right, I'll tell you everything!' he shrieked.

But the grip on him remained just as tight. There was no pulling back. He was still hanging there, out over the black void. He looked into Dave's eyes, as remorseless as ever, and his soul shrivelled. 'Please!' he begged. 'Oh God, please!'

'Then tell me – and no lies, not one.'

'No lies, I promise. Oh God, where do I begin? I had to supply a suitcase and video cassette recorder to a man. That's how my fingerprint must have got on the case. I took it to his hotel. But I promise to God I didn't know why. I thought it was for smuggling. I didn't think he was going to kill anybody. I drove him to the airport and dropped him there. But there was nothing else – nothing, I swear!'

'Who told you to supply the suitcase and the video cassette recorder? Who was it? I want his name.'

'No, no, please.'

'Everything, I want everything.'

'If he ever finds out – oh God – he'll kill me.'

'He'll kill you or I'll kill you. It's your choice.'

'All right, all right!'

'Then tell me.'

'His name is Fung – Conrad Fung.'

'Did he order the bombing?'

'Yes, yes, it was Fung, he was the one who ordered it!'

'No lies.'

'No, God help me, I promise, it was Conrad Fung!'

Only then did the iron-hard clamp on him relax, only then was he allowed to slip back. His feet touched the balcony floor but he was so weak at the knees that for a moment Dave had to hold him up. Tselentis wiped the spittle from his lips. 'Please,' he murmured, 'let me go inside, let me sit. I don't think I can stand . . .'

In silence, Dave led him back inside, closing the balcony doors, shutting out the wind and the clouds of mist. Tselentis collapsed into a chair. He tried to smooth down the windswept tails of his balding hair. His short, podgy fingers were trembling.

'Who is that woman, the one you brought up with you?' asked Dave.

'Just a hostess I picked up in a club. She knows nothing, I promise. She's not involved in any way.'

Dave motioned to his sergeant. 'Okay, take her downstairs. Get her a taxi. She can go.'

'Could I have a brandy?' Tselentis requested feebly.

Dave went across to the liquor cabinet. There was only the best cognac, all XO. The glasses were crystal, the beer mugs too. Only the best of everything, he saw. He poured two stiff drinks. He needed one himself to steady his nerves. He had always been an ethical cop, one who obeyed the letter of the law. He could hardly believe he had taken it so close to the point of no return out there. Had it been intentional, a game of brinkmanship aimed at grasping the truth, or had he gone mad, all the grief returning, had he lost his mind? He would never know, not for sure. And the truth was, he didn't care. Results, that's all that mattered to him now, finding his son's killers and bringing them to justice: wild justice maybe but justice all the same.

Dave handed a glass of cognac to Tselentis who cupped it in both hands, not trusting one, and took a deep gulp from it.

Dave took a deep gulp too. Tselentis's protestations of innocence had a ring of truth to them. But there was one aspect that troubled him, one that required an answer. 'If you knew nothing about the bomb, why would this man Fung have ordered you to deliver the suitcase and the VCR, why would he have told you to drive the killer to the airport?' he asked. 'Didn't you smell a rat?'

'I knew there was something happening, yes, money laundering, smuggling, but God, never anything like that . . .'

'But you drove this man to the airport.'

'Yes.'

'Why you? You're not a chauffeur.'

Tselentis shook his head in confusion. 'I wish to God I could tell you for sure. It's been crucifying me for weeks. There can only be one reason. Fung knew I wanted to cut myself loose, we had had so many arguments, and this was his way of dragging me back in. That's all it could be, making sure – unwitting or not – I was involved in a massacre, that I got blood on my hands. Then there'd be no way I could break free. You've got to know Fung, you've got to understand him. That's the way his brain works. He must have a hold over everybody. Fung doesn't have friends, Mr Whitman, he has captives.'

'The killer,' said Dave. 'I want to know about him. This man you delivered the goods to, the one you drove to the airport, had you met him before?'

Tselentis shook his head. 'No, never.'

'What do you remember of him?'

'He was European. He sounded Australian to me, a thick, flat accent. I'm not sure of his age, forty-something.'

'His name?'

'He was booked into the hotel under the name of Noonan, Paul Noonan. But whether that was his real name or not, I don't know.'

'Can you describe him?'

Tselentis searched for the words. 'Yes, he was thickset, not fat but heavy. He had a face like a retired boxer, I remember that, very puffy and beaten about with veins in

117

his cheeks. And yes, I remember that too – he had red hair.'

Red hair? And suddenly it all came back to him . . . that was the man who had walked past him at the airport just seconds before the bomb exploded. They had been so close he could have reached out and touched him. The realisation of it hit Dave so hard that for a couple of seconds he was lost for words. He had seen his son's executioner.

Tselentis was gulping at his cognac like a man sucking for oxygen. He turned his face up to Dave and there was a look about him of a small frightened boy. 'What do you think will happen to me?' he asked.

Dave answered flatly. 'You'll go to trial.'

Tselentis's mouth fell slack. 'I'm not a killer, Mr Whitman. All right, I've been money laundering for years, I'll admit that. But I wouldn't intentionally harm anybody. You believe me, don't you?'

Yes, Dave did believe him. There was no pretence left in Tselentis, all the lies had been stripped away. Tselentis was telling the truth. But Dave wasn't going to admit that to him, not yet. 'It doesn't matter whether I believe you or not,' he said. 'It's a matter for the jury.'

'The jury?' Tselentis was trying to bring it all into focus, the whole horrifying, slow-grinding process of the criminal law. 'But surely they'll believe me. I promise to God, Mr Whitman, I had nothing to do with it.'

Dave shrugged. His jaw was clenched tight, there was a purposeful look of cynicism on his raw-boned features. 'It goes according to the evidence,' he said in a hard, flat monotone. 'You've been Fung's partner for years. You were behind the Peruvian scheme. You knew Gomez was going to betray you. You supplied the video cassette recorder that contained the bomb, you supplied the suitcase. You even drove the assassin to the airport. Wong Kam-kiu – who can link you to Gomez and supply a motive for the bombing – will swear you ordered his murder to keep him quiet. Weigh all that up yourself. What do *you* think your chances are?'

Tselentis had shrivelled into his chair, totally crushed. 'If I'm found guilty, what will happen to me?'

'The death sentence.'

'Oh God . . .'

'It won't be carried out, it never is,' said Dave, 'not in Hong Kong. But after the Chinese take over in 1997, well, they put a bullet into the back of people's heads for small-time theft. How a mass murderer will fare then . . .'

Tselentis couldn't bear to hear any more. His face was bloodless. 'What must I do?' he mumbled. 'Please help me.'

'As I see it, you only have one choice,' said Dave. 'Make a full statement, agree to testify against Fung and his accomplices and hope for an immunity.'

'Against Fung?' There was a fresh look of terror on Tselentis' face. 'Do you have any conception of what you're asking me to do? If I testify against Fung, I'm a dead man.'

'With your testimony, he'll be behind bars – out of the way and harmless.'

'Behind bars or not it'll make no difference. The man has power, influence. He buys people. You don't know him. You don't have the first idea.'

'It's your choice,' said Dave. 'Do you want to go down as a murderer or as a man who tried at least to do what was right?'

Tselentis stared into his brandy for a long time, trying to control his trembling. 'Will you protect me?'

'Yes,' said Dave, 'we'll protect you.'

Tselentis looked up at him. Then he said in a very low, timid voice. 'All right, God help me . . . I'll cooperate.'

For Hannah, from the moment it began, it was a glorious evening, one of the most memorable of her life. Sam Ephram collected her at nine. He took her to Delmonico's for dinner, he ordered one of the great red wines of Bordeaux, a Chateau Margaux, and in the warm, rich wine-light, their glasses touching, he told her of their first sales. Saks Fifth Avenue had ordered the entire range – not just a selection, he said, but every last item! Bloomingdales had followed suit. For a new designer it was almost unheard of, stunning news, a total vindication of Joel Grossman's faith in her. And more sales were following, the best stores and boutiques, everybody was clamouring for a look at the

119

samples. The word was out, Danny's Rags were the hottest new items on the market. They were going to need more duplicates, they couldn't cover the ground unless they had them. Joel was being swamped with enquiries.

As the second bottle of Chateau Margaux was opened, in a giddy night of triumph, there was still more news. Sam told her that *Women's Wear Daily*, published internationally, the trade magazine that everybody in the business bought, had telephoned Joel wanting to do an article, a full-page spread on Danny's Rags. 'You are on your way,' Sam said to her. 'Nothing can hold you back now.'

They seemed to have a million things to talk about. They didn't finish the meal until close to midnight. They were one of the last couples to leave, lingering over liqueurs. As they rose from the table, both of them light-headed with the wine, Sam slipped his arm around her waist, reaching down to gently kiss her on the neck.

The presence of him was overpowering, a heady essence of charm and sensuality blended to perfection. It took resolve of will to rebuff him, no matter how gently Hannah did it. 'Let's not spoil it,' she said. 'You're an attractive man Sam. But I'm married. I love my husband very much. It would be wrong.'

'You're right,' he said. 'I'm sorry. I didn't mean to upset you.' And, as if it was the most natural thing in the world, he took her hand, friend to friend, smiling down at her.

The valet brought his car, an English Jaguar xjs, and they drove back through Manhattan together. 'I know it's late,' he said, 'but there's a couple of matters I would like to discuss with you. How about a nightcap in my apartment? I have champagne on the ice.'

She hesitated a moment. He smiled at her, that deep brown gaze that made her mouth go dry, and she answered. 'Yes, that would be nice.'

Immediately she had said it, in that small oasis of silence that followed, Hannah felt a dart of guilt. She had never done anything to betray Dave's trust in her before, she had never been to another man's apartment alone. But tonight was different, she told herself. There were so many plans to

120

be made, so much to celebrate. And, apart from that one moment when they left the restaurant, more a compliment than an intrusion, Sam had been a perfectly understanding friend.

The apartment was not large. But, as she had expected, it was exquisitely elegant. The colours of it reflected Sam Ephram's heritage, all beiges and whites and desert ochres. It was lit in amber gold, highlighted in simple pools of perfection by the green-black onyx of a sculpture or the scarlet richness of a Bokhara carpet. There was no clutter, no fuss, even the oil paintings on the walls were austerely abstract. Sam Ephram put on soft music. She recognised the haunting evocation of the Spanish spirit in Rodrigo's *Concierto de Aranjuez*. The effect of it all, the music and the sumptuous simplicity, the stunning views of Manhattan, took her breath away.

'I hope you like it,' he said. 'For six months of the year this is my home – when I am not on a plane to London or Tel Aviv or living out of a suitcase somewhere. I like uncluttered surroundings. It is perhaps a little of the Bedouin in my soul.' He smiled at her, his eyes liquid black, enticing and unfathomable. Then he laughed. 'Now that champagne I promised you.'

While he went to the kitchen to collect the bottle, Hannah walked to the window for a better view out over the glittering spires of Manhattan. There was a photograph on a sideboard. It was of two young men in olive green uniforms, both festooned with bandoliers of ammunition, both arm in arm, grinning at the camera under a harsh Middle Eastern sky. 'I didn't know you were in the army,' she said.

He called to her from the kitchen. 'That was a lifetime ago. That's my brother, Muli. We were both in the paratroopers.'

'Where is Muli now?'

'Still in Israel. Very settled, very married, very happy.' He came through, poured champagne into two tall, fine-stemmed glasses and handed her one. 'To life,' he said. They drank from the glasses and she felt wondrously light-headed. They sat next to each other on a soft leather sofa listening to the music. Their thighs touched, she could sense his warmth. In every way she was achingly aware of him.

'In a night full of news, there is one other piece I have for you,' he said. 'Joel had a meeting with Maceys Northeast this morning. They are showing considerable interest in ordering. Joel says he should have something definite within the next forty-eight hours. But, because of the large quantities involved – it's for the whole northeast chain – Maceys say they will require certain guarantees.'

'What kind of guarantees?' she asked.

'They relate to financial viability, that's all, the ability to supply the necessary quantity and quality on due date. You're a new designer. It's understandable.' He fell silent, sipping his champagne. Then he said. 'I hope I can give those guarantees on your behalf . . . provided of course you have no reservations about our proposed partnership.'

'No, of course not. Why should I?' she said. 'I thought all that was agreed.'

'Good, good. Then the problem is solved.' He turned to her, that solemn brown gaze seeming to look right through her. He sipped his champagne, never once taking his eyes from her. 'You are a very beautiful woman, Hannah.'

'Please, Sam,' she said, shaking her head, 'you know I'm married.'

But it was as if he had not heard her. 'I must tell you that from the moment I first saw you, I was captivated by you. Can you blame me, though? All men must feel the same when they look at you.'

Her smile was pure nervous reaction. Her heart was pounding, part desire, part fear.

He took the champagne glass from her hand and, leaning towards her, let his lips brush hers. It was like ice consuming fire and she shuddered through her whole body. 'No,' she murmured, 'please don't.' But she hardly heard the words herself. Sam Ephram kissed her cheek then gently touched her throat, and she could do nothing, neither push him away nor move into his arms. She had never been with a more desirable man in her life, the nearness of him, every

122

touch, was irresistible. But she had never betrayed Dave before and he was such a good man, a man she loved so much.

Sam Ephram kissed her on the lips with more force this time, pulling her close so that her breasts were hard against his chest. And still she could do nothing. He looked at her, smiling softly. But she could see the puzzlement in those penetrating black eyes, perhaps the faintest spark of anger too. And at that moment she knew that everything hung in the balance. He was the bedrock of her success, her guardian, her genie. Without him she would be lost. She felt his hand on her knee, felt it caress the inside of her leg. Her whole body was electric, she had never felt this way before, never, never . . .

'I'm sorry,' whispered Sam. 'I must have you. I'll go mad if I don't.'

'No,' she answered, 'this is so wrong, we mustn't.' But his hand was climbing higher and there was just no way she could resist him. She let out a sigh, hesitating . . . then, half defeated, half triumphant, she opened her legs to him.

There was a hastily called meeting at two that afternoon in Tom Mackay's office. Dave had not slept, he had not eaten, he had been on the go since Tselentis's arrest twelve hours earlier. Critical decisions had to be made, decisions that would irrevocably alter the course of the investigation. He could sleep later.

The first priority had been to obtain as much information as possible on Conrad Fung. He was the chief target now, the fountainhead of the crime. But CIB, the Criminal Intelligence Bureau, had next to nothing on him.

Conrad Fung . . . Fung Chi-man, born in China's Guangdong Province during the Second World War, exact date unknown, the son of peasant farmers. Came to Hong Kong in 1968 during the bloody unpheavals of the Cultural Revolution. No marriage recorded, no children. Profession: import and export merchant. Arrested twice in connection with drug trafficking, discharged before trial on both occasions for lack of evidence. Believed to have Triad connections, the Wo Shing Wo. No criminal record, no other known facts.

The Americans, however, had more. Stan Tarbuck, the Legal Liaison Officer at the US Consulate, brought with him an intelligence report just faxed from the FBI archives in Langley, Virginia.

Stan, a big blond bear of a man, a former gridiron player, six foot four, two hundred and thirty pounds, was by common agreement a star. Although he had no jurisdiction in Hong Kong and was there strictly in an advisory role, from the very beginning he had been an integral member of the investigation team. Without his enthusiasm and skill they would still be way behind.

'Fung first came to our notice six years back,' he said. 'At that time he was laundering money for various Middle Eastern syndicates, Turks and Lebanese. But he was ambitious and hustled a share of the Colombian market too. From the beginning he was big, very big.'

'Tselentis talks of a company called SCI,' said Dave. 'Any record of that?'

'Yeah, Sino Commercial Investments. That's when our records first show Tselentis getting involved. He and a guy called Aurelius, Fung's attorney, were on the board. In the first couple of years we reckon SCI moved close to half a billion. Everything Tselentis says ties in.'

'What happened to the SCI operation?' asked Tom Mackay. 'Did you manage to break it?'

'We tried, yeah. But without much success. According to the report, we turned one of the SCI accountants, a young Chinese guy. He started working on the inside for us. It was looking good too.'

'And then?'

'Then the poor guy was wasted. He was found in his kitchen one morning shot through the head. It had been made to look like a break-in, an everyday crime, but we're certain it was a professional hit.'

'Any way of linking Fung or the others to it?'

'None. They had been down in Florida at the time drinking daiquiris in Palm Beach. Shortly after that, Fung

124

packed up house and moved off-shore.'

'Any evidence that he's still laundering?' asked Dave.

'Is the Pope Catholic? Sure he's still laundering. Our intelligence suggests he's still in big with the Colombians. But he's a smart bastard. He has lots of friends. He stays well back, protected by a phalanx of little men, the fall guys. We've culled a few of them, confiscated a few million. But it's peanuts.'

'Where's Fung living now?' asked Tom Mackay.

'The Philippines. Has a ranch down there. He's a real philanthropist too if you believe the bullshit his friends put out – has a wing named after him in the local hospital, pays for the running of a local school. That's how you buy protection these days, that's how you keep your little coterie of senators and generals sweet.'

'What does your profile on Fung tell you?' asked Tom Mackay. 'Could Tselentis be telling the truth? The use of a hired killer, for example, this red-haired Aussie?'

'Sure, fits the profile.'

'In your opinion, could Fung be behind the bombing?'

Stan Tarbuck did not hesitate. 'Absolutely,' he said. 'No doubt about it.'

'And the Japanese Red Army claims?'

'As Dave says, a smokescreen.'

Tom Mackay turned to Dave. 'You made the arrest, what do you think? Assuming we ever get Fung and his accomplices into court, what kind of witness will Tselentis make?'

'Terrified but convincing.'

'Convincing enough to send them down?'

'Yes,' Dave answered. 'All the way.'

Tom Mackay looked around the room, at Kit Lampton, at Henry Tang from Special Branch. 'Okay then,' he said, 'are we agreed that we go to the Attorney General's people and recommend an immunity?'

There was no dissent, not one voice.

Dave got up from his chair. He felt gritty-eyed – a headache was coming. But he was satisfied. All the evidence pointed one way now. Fung had been the driving force

125

behind the Peruvian money-laundering scheme. Fung had ordered the Kai Tak bombing, he had been the one who hired the assassin. Fung more than anyone bore responsibility for the death of his son.

Hannah lay beneath Sam Ephram on the silk Bokhara carpet, dress cast aside, her breasts bare, thinking to herself: this is crazy but I feel like a virgin with him. She was totally under his control. His mouth came down on to her nipples, warm and liquid, and she gasped out loud. He was marvellous. With her head thrown back, she ran her fingers over his sun-kissed back. He was softer than Dave, not as exercised or sculptured; there was not the same feeling of sinew and muscle. Yet there was no fat, just a perfect, silky smoothness. In the warm lamplight his olive-brown body seemed to glow.

Sam Ephram lifted her legs, stroking them as he took off her panties, and at his first touch she was a wet, unfolding secret aching for him. Then she fumbled to strip him naked too, kissing his neck and chest, tasting the warm muskiness of his skin. He knelt next to her and Hannah saw the bursting velvet of his manhood. She heard him whisper. 'You're more beautiful than I ever imagined. The most beautiful woman I have even seen.'

Then, almost fiercely, he pushed her back, her shoulders on the carpet, and he was into her, strong and tight, as hard as burnished steel. At first he barely moved, no more than the soft lapping of his thighs like water against a boat. But then, when every nerve in Hannah's body was crying out, he began to move faster, his mouth covering hers, his tongue probing with the same rhythm as his loins, faster and harder until she was gasping with every thrust and suddenly, amazed at the quickness of it, she was in a spasm of complete fulfilment.

As she lay limp, trying to catch her breath, Sam Ephram looked down at her, smiling, a sheen of perspiration on his forehead. She could still sense the pulsing strength of him inside her. 'That was just the beginning,' he whispered as he began to move again, slowly, with an oil-smooth rhythm.

'Just the beginning of many good things to come.'

At five-thirty that evening Dave entered the small cell where Dimitri Tselentis was being held. Tselentis sat on the edge of the concrete bunk, the prison blanket over his knees. He was puffy-eyed and unshaven. His cashmere suit was crumpled. He smelt of stale brandy and sweat and fear. He said nothing but there was a look in his eyes of terrified expectation, the look of a condemned man waiting to know if he has been reprieved.

Dave released him from his agony. 'It's been officially sanctioned,' he said. 'We have a deal.'

Tselentis nodded, his shoulders slumping, a look of exhausted relief on his face. He was too tired for words.

Dave spelt it out for him. 'You must tell us everything you know about the Kai Tak bombing and what led up to it. You must testify at the trials of all those responsible.'

'What about the earlier money laundering, the stuff that goes back years, the unconnected stuff? Surely not all that too?'

'Don't worry, we don't want you in court for the next twenty years. The Kai Tak bombing, that's the deal. Honour your side of the bargain, see it through to the end, and we'll honour ours. A new identity, a new place to live – proof that life after death isn't just a myth.'

When Dave got back to his apartment that evening, he was emotionally and physically exhausted. But he was elevated too. The breakthrough had been made. The investigation was fully focused now. At last the enemy had a face.

He estimated it would be around six-thirty in the morning in New York, thirteen hours behind Hong Kong. It was far too early, he knew that. Hannah would never be awake. For Hannah eight in the morning was the crack of dawn. But she wouldn't mind being awakened, not this time, not with news like this.

Dave dialled the number of Hannah's Manhattan hotel and, when he got through, gave the room number. Almost a minute passed. He was beginning to think he had been cut off when the hotel telephonist came back to him. 'I'm sorry,' said the telephonist, 'but there's no reply from Mrs Whitman's room. She doesn't appear to be in.'

Chapter Ten

Mike Le Fleur was a Canadian, the extradition expert in the Attorney General's Chambers – the man who would help them bring back Conrad Fung. Dave had an appointment with him at two that afternoon.

The AG's Chambers in Hong Kong employed over a hundred expatriate lawyers drawn from a dozen Common Law jurisdictions. Most Hong Kong Chinese preferred the more lucrative pastures of private practice so it was left to the expatriates – English, Irish, New Zealanders – to fill the void. Legal mercenaries perhaps but no more mercenary than lawyers anywhere else in the world.

Mike Le Fleur had begun his career in the arctic regions of the Yukon, prosecuting Eskimoes for rape, or lumberjacks for criminal damage whooping it up in Whitehorse. It was a long way from extraditing Triad heroin traffickers to New York. And extradition, they said, could be a minefield. But if so, Mike had found the map because so far he hadn't blown his foot off.

Mike read the first rough, hand-written statements by Tselentis and Wong Kam-kiu. 'I don't see a problem,' he said. 'On what they say, there's a clear *prima facie* case against Fung. More than enough here to drag him back for trial – provided we can find him, of course. Where is he, do you know?'

'We believe he's in the Philippines,' said Dave.

Mike pulled a face. 'That's a problem. We have no extradition treaty with the Philippines.'

'Don't we have any *ad hoc* arrangements?'

'Disguised deportations, you mean, passports suddenly

129

not in order? Sure, once in a blue moon, if we can get the Filipinos motivated. But that's a big if. How well connected is Fung?'

'Too damn well – senators, generals.'

'Forget it then. We'll never dig him out that way.'

'So, provided he remains in the Philippines, he's safe, is that it? The fact that he's a mass murderer doesn't matter a damn.'

Mike shrugged. 'The Israelis had to abduct Adolf Eichmann from Argentina and he was a mass murderer in the major leagues. How far do you think they would have got following the kosher line?'

Dave grinned. 'Are you suggesting abduction?'

Mike laughed. 'No, I'm afraid I'm not.'

'Okay, so we have to find some way of getting Fung out of the Philippines – a kosher way. Assuming we can get him into a country with whom we have extradition arrangements, even if he's only there for a couple of days, just a visitor, what then?'

'Get him in transit in Anchorage, Alaska, on his way to the North Pole,' said Mike. 'It doesn't matter. All he has to do is be there. If all he wants to do is buy a bottle of scotch in duty free and take a pee, that's good enough.'

'But what if we have to entice him there in some way? Can he claim entrapment, abuse of process, anything like that?'

Mike smiled from behind his gold-rimmed glasses. 'You can trick him, cheat him, stuff him into a box and mail him, it doesn't matter. If you can get him to a country with whom we have a treaty – the USA, Canada, Australia, most of Europe and the Commonwealth – then Dave, the murdering little bastard is ours.'

Dimitri Tselentis, who was in a small holding cell in the offices of OCTG, had to be dragged out of a dense, exhausted sleep. Dave gave him a mug of hot coffee laced – totally against the rules – with cognac.

'I need your help,' he said. 'We have to find a way of getting Conrad Fung out of the Philippines. But time is critical. We can only keep you under wraps for so long. Once Fung discovers you've been arrested, he'll dig a hole so deep we'll never get him.'

Tselentis slurped at his coffee. He looked terrible, his eyes and face swollen, black stubble on his cheeks. 'Thanks for the cognac,' he said. 'I needed it.'

'Fung can't spend his whole life in the Philippines,' said Dave, unable to suppress his anxiety. 'He has to come up some time for air.'

'Just give me a second,' said Tselentis, 'let me try and clear my head. What date is it?'

'The twenty-nineth of May.'

'Wednesday?'

'Yes, Wednesday.'

Tselentis gave a small grin. 'In which case you won't need to get him out of the Philippines – he's out already.'

A smile settled on Dave's face. 'Where is he?'

'Right now?' Tselentis checked his watch. 'If the plane left on schedule, he's a couple of hours out over the Pacific heading east.'

'The United States?'

'Yeah, Miami.'

'How long is he going to be there?'

'Fung is going to keep his time short. He gets nervous in the US these days. He's flying there to sign the sale agreement of a leisure complex he has down in the Florida Keys. There's a couple of minor points still to be ironed out but nothing he won't agree on.'

'So how long would you estimate?'

'Twenty-four hours maximum – maybe less.'

Immediately Mike Le Fleur was informed, he gave Dave instructions over the phone. 'Okay,' he said, 'we can do it. The extradition treaty with the US allows for an emergency arrest procedure before the full bundle arrives – provisional arrest, it's called. But we still have to request it through diplomatic channels, that means the British Embassy in Washington, and we still have to supply certain papers.'

'What kind of papers?' asked Dave.

131

'First, a certified copy of the arrest warrant.'

'No problem. That'll take an hour.'

'Second, an outline of the case.'

'How detailed?'

'A page, that's all.'

'We've already got it.'

'Last, as much personal detail on Fung as you've got, his photograph, if possible, and his flight number into Miami.'

'Okay, once I've got the stuff to you, what then?'

'Then I fax it to the British Embassy in Washington and put through a phone call too, ring some alarm bells.'

'And then?'

'Then,' said Mike, 'all we can do is sit back and pray that between them the British Embassy, the US Justice Department and the Florida Marshalls get their act in order.'

As Conrad Fung stepped off the United Airlines flight at Miami International, he heard his name being paged at the airline desk. He went across, instinctively worried. 'Yes,' he said, 'my name is Fung. What is it?'

The UA woman behind the desk, blonde and chubby, smiled at him. 'A telex message for you sir.'

Fung opened the buff envelope. The message, just two sentences, read –

> TSELENTIS ARRESTED HONG KONG.
> SUGGEST YOU TAKE APPROPRIATE ACTION.
> HECTOR CHAN.

'Is everything all right sir?' The woman had seen the way Fung had blanched.

'No,' he replied, 'I'm afraid it's not. There's been a sickness in the family.'

'Oh, I am sorry. Not serious I hope.'

'I'm going to have to fly back to Manila immediately. When does the flight take off?'

'Not until late this afternoon sir. But it's fully booked, I'm afraid, even first class.'

'Don't you have any other flights?'

132

'Not direct to Manila, no sir. If you fly to San Francisco, there's a flight tomorrow morning though.'

'No, that's too late. What about flights to elsewhere in Asia, Korea, Japan?'

'There is a flight for Tokyo via Chicago. But it's leaving in thirty-five minutes. The booking is already closed.'

'Surely you can get me on,' he said. 'You must have provision for family emergencies like this. Please.'

The woman gave him a sympathetic smile. 'I'll see what I can do. Let me check, sir. You wish to fly first class?'

'Any class, it doesn't matter. I can pay cash, credit card, whatever you please.'

The woman typed in the code and checked her monitor. 'Yes,' she said, delighted to be of assistance, 'there's one seat available in first class. What about your luggage?'

'No luggage, just what I'm carrying.'

'It's gate 18, sir. Straight down the hallway. They'll deal with the ticket formalities and boarding pass there. You'd better hurry, though.'

'Thank you.'

Fung turned away from the desk – and almost collided with the two men who had been standing behind him. He tried to go past them but they blocked his way. Both had looks of stony seriousness. Both wore navy-blue blazers and grey slacks and both were built like Spanish fighting bulls.

'Mr Fung Chi-man – Mr Conrad Fung?'

Fung stared at them in horror.

'I am United States Deputy Marshall McNair,' said the taller of the two. 'My colleague is Deputy Marshall Alvares. We have a warrant for your arrest. It is for the purpose of your extradition to the British Crown Colony of Hong Kong.'

Sitting in the US Marshall's office two hours later, hands manacled, fingerprinted and processed, Conrad Fung was ranting like a man in the demented stages of paranoia. Edgar Aurelius had never seen him like this before, no matter how bad the crisis. He was sitting opposite a stranger.

Fung's hands were clenched tight into white-knuckled

fists. 'It was Tselentis, the filthy half-caste bastard! He must have pointed the finger at me. But why, Edgar? That's what I don't understand. I told him they had no evidence, none! The spineless, traitorous – how could he have done this to me? They must have squeezed him somehow, blackmailed him. It's that crazy cop in Hong Kong, the one whose son was killed in the airport bombing, he's got to be behind this. I tell you, Edgar, the man has lost his mind. He's waging a one-man war, some kind of insane jihad! He's got to be stopped. What about bail? I don't have to spend a night in this pigsty, do I?'

'You can't underestimate the seriousness of the charges, Conrad – six murders, twenty-two attempted murders. I think in the circumstances, for you to realistically hope for bail—'

'I'm entitled to bail, I demand bail! They've got no evidence, Edgar, how many times must I tell you that? They've squeezed Tselentis and the fat half-caste bastard has lied through his teeth for them. I'm only visiting this country. I'm a Filipino resident. What right have they got to pick me up? They've got none, none!'

'I regret Conrad, they have every right. You're not immune from arrest, not unless you're a diplomat.'

'So that's it, is it? They have every right, you're not immune from arrest unless you're a diplomat. What does that mean? That you're going to give up on me, leave me here to rot? You do, Edgar, and I promise, you'll go down with me – you and all the others.'

Aurelius tried to keep his temper. 'Nobody is leaving you to rot, Conrad. And there's no need for threats. We'll get you out of this mess. But I'm a corporate lawyer. We need a criminal man for this.'

'Then get one,' spat Fung. 'Get the best.'

Edgar Aurelius had been Conrad Fung's personal attorney for ten years. In many ways they were alike, both as brilliant, both as embittered, both men living on the fringe of society, manipulating it but never part of it.

Aurelius had been born humpbacked. He was small in stature, mousy-haired and pale, not a wholesome man to look upon. Since childhood he had needed special bifocal glasses and since childhood he had been at odds with the world.

He had flown down from New York to meet Fung, to tie up the loose ends of the Marada Cove sale and perfect the written contract. He had been waiting at the airport when Fung was arrested. He was stunned by events too, desperately so. In many ways, his future was equally at risk. He had known nothing of the Hong Kong airport bombing – there was no way he could be connected to that – but if Tselentis was cooperating with the Hong Kong police, there were other matters, money-laundering matters, that could send him to jail for years. He was frightened, sick to the stomach with it. The temptation was there – a compelling one too – to board an aircraft and fly south that minute, to find some bolthole, Chile or Bolivia, until the troubles were over.

But strangely, despite the fear and although he knew Fung was a despot, a psychopath, the fact remained that a decade back he had sworn allegiance to him . . . not in words, nothing that simple, but in his actions, yes, by climbing to wealth with him, by being his confessor and adviser, by riding out the crises of the past with him. Edgar Aurelius was no sentimentalist. He was too good a lawyer, too acerbic, too objective. But he believed that there was, in its truest sense, a kind of brotherhood between them now.

Fung had taken him, humpback and all. Fung had given him riches, Fung had given him power. For that some loyalty was owed. And nowhere did it say that loyalty was the prerogative of those without physical blemish.

In Hong Kong, when the news of Fung's arrest was received, the Commissioner of Police consulted with the Governor and it was resolved to break the news to the public that the Japanese Red Army claim had been a hoax. The Kai Tak tragedy had not been the work of terrorists, it had been the design of common criminals – murderers – and the mastermind behind it was now in a Florida jail awaiting extradition.

At Police Headquarters there was an air of jubilation. It

was good o'l blood-and-glory stuff, an example to the public that the police were capable of delivering the goods and a morale booster for the force itself, one of those occasions when it felt damn good to be a cop. Tom Mackay wanted Dave sitting next to him at the news conference. He deserved it, he said. This had been his case, his hard-earned success. Dave, however, declined. He had his own reasons, he told Tom, purely private ones.

For Dave the investigation had always been an intensely personal, inward experience and the last thing he needed – no matter how well-meaning – was the maudlin, re-dredged sympathy of the Press. At two-thirty that afternoon, while reporters and camera crews packed the conference room at Police Headquarters, he sat in his office, alone with his thoughts, gazing out over the green-grey waters of the harbour . . .

When the news of the arrest had come through, he had expected to be as jubilant as the others. But there had been no elation, no triumph, only a strange sense of anti-climax, and later, for reasons he did not at first understand, a deep, aching sadness for the loss of his son, a sadness more acute than anything he had felt since the funeral.

So Conrad Fung was now in lawful custody, so the wheels of justice were beginning to turn. When eventually Fung was surrendered to Hong Kong, he would be tried by a jury of his peers. Society, with due process, would exact its toll. But what good was any of it? Would it bring Danny back to life? Would it remove that sense of inestimable loss that remained with him every minute of every day? Justice was what he had sworn to achieve, justice was all he had. But at moments like this it was at best a bleak and forbidding comfort.

There was a Kipling poem, something about keeping your head while all about you are losing theirs. It served to describe the situation well, thought Aurelius. And keeping his head meant, first, ensuring that the sale of Marada Cove was agreed and signed before it fell apart and plunged them into financial chaos.

That was why, still stinging from the shock of Fung's arrest, within an hour of leaving him, he had set up an urgent meeting with the purchasers, the Texas Sun team.

Aurelius had booked into Miami's Inter-Continental on Chopin Plaza. The meeting took place in one of its conference rooms at nine the following morning.

Aurelius opened the proceedings, hoping to finish it right there. 'For the sake of the sale, and as a gesture of good faith, I'm pleased to tell you that my client has agreed all your remaining proposals,' he said. 'Unless there are other matters you wish to raise, that, I think, leaves only the signatures.'

Helen Power, the leader of the Texas Sun team, a Dallas attorney, tall, slim and tough, regarded him across the table, her face as expressive as a sheet of aluminium. 'Why this sudden haste, Edgar?'

'No haste, Helen, I assure you, a natural desire to conclude an important business deal to our mutual benefit, that is all.'

'Could one of the reasons be the fact that your client's principal stockholder is in jail facing extradition?'

Inwardly Aurelius reeled. Christ, the cow – how had she found out so soon? There had been nothing in the Miami papers that morning, nothing yet on television or radio. He smiled stiffly. 'You appreciate, Helen, that the seller is a corporation. One of the stockholders is presently under arrest, yes, that's true. But surely you don't intend to visit the alleged sins of one individual on the corporation as a whole.'

'Please, Edgar, no first-year corporate law. Don't bullshit me. Marada Cove is built on laundered cash – there are still soap suds coming out of the foundations. I'm surprised your client didn't call it Little Colombia.'

Aurelius held his temper. 'You have no grounds for making allegations of that nature, Helen, no grounds at all. This deal is a good one for us both. If we can just try and take the emotive language out of this—'

'I am sorry, Edgar. In the light of what we've learnt overnight, Texas Sun needs Marada Cove like it needs a

137

crock of nuclear waste.' Helen Power rose from her chair, her two colleagues rising with her. 'There will be no signatures, there will be no sale. It's just such a damn pity that you have wasted our time.'

Aurelius barely heard them leaving the room. He sat hunched over the table staring down at the uncompleted contract documents, a glazed look in his eyes like a boxer struggling to recover from a knock-out blow.

Marada Cove was a disaster of the first degree. But he had no illusions, he knew there was worse still to come. With Fung in jail, it was obvious what must follow. Once the Colombians received the news, they would cut them off. No discussions, no excuses, the cash would cease to flow. Within the week, their money-laundering empire – the source of ninety percent of their income – would have shrivelled to nothing.

Without a continued cash flow, without steady profits, the Marada Cove project could not be financed. It would collapse into bankruptcy, the banks would call in their loans, guarantees would be activated, assets seized. The entire corporate network that had taken a decade to build would fall around them like a house of cards. They would never be able to recover, never, not even if Fung was set free. They were staring into the face of ruin.

Fung had to be told, of course, and told immediately. In times of crisis – like a financial Houdini – he invariably found a way out. Aurelius just hoped to God he had recovered some of his wits since his arrest yesterday.

It took an hour to discover that Fung had been moved to the Metropolitan Correctional Centre in South Dade County, the federal holding centre where he would be kept until extradition proceedings had been completed. Aurelius hired a limousine service and drove out there, arriving just before noon.

Edgar Aurelius was not a criminal attorney. Jails were alien places to him. He had expected the pre-trial detention facility to be housed behind towering walls of faded limewash and huge wooden gates bolted with iron, every layman's vision of penitential hell. To his amazement, from the outside at least, it resembled a sprawling leisure complex; rolling lawns, tennis courts, even a small lake with rowing boats on it. Typical Florida, he thought, even the prisons looked like retirement condos.

Inside, however, the depressing air of incarceration was more evident. Aurelius was booked in, searched, then led through to the interview room, a small box of a room painted cream, just big enough for a desk and two wooden chairs.

When Conrad Fung was led in, he looked tired and haggard. There were bruised bags of fatigue under his eyes. The anger was there still, patently visible, the red-eyed look of an incensed caged animal. But Aurelius could also see that Fung had had a night to contemplate, a night to let the raging paranoia subside. He was thinking again, calculating his options, planning how to fight back.

Fung waited until the guard had gone and the door was closed. Then he asked in his reed-thin voice, 'What about the criminal attorney, have you got one?'

'It's being arranged, Conrad. It takes time, though. I want the best, somebody with the right reputation, an expert in extradition. I'm speaking to people. I'll have somebody by tomorrow.'

'Then why are you here?'

Aurelius took a breath, steeling himself. 'I have to tell you, I had a meeting with the Texas Sun people this morning. They know about your arrest. Somebody – God knows who, the FBI, the Hong Kong police – has fed them a story about Marada Cove being built with criminal profits. They've dumped the deal, Conrad. There's no sale. We're back at square one.'

'Then sue them.'

'It was subject to a written contract. We have no grounds. Even if we could, it would just tie us up in court for the next three years.'

'What about the Colombians? Have you heard from them?'

'Nothing yet. But it's going to come.'

139

Fung nodded. He knew well enough.

'Without a cash flow, without money coming in . . . well, I don't have to spell it out. We need eight to ten million over the next six months, Conrad. We're already up to our eyeballs with the banks. This damn Marada project has got us mortgaged to the hilt. Everything is encumbered. I don't think I can squeeze any more out of them, not once the word gets out.'

Fung listened, a look of malevolent stoicism on his pinched features. 'Then we must look elsewhere,' he said.

'But where?'

'Khalil – speak to him.'

Aurelius blinked. 'How can Khalil help us?'

'He'll know,' said Fung. 'Don't worry about that. The nature of the business is our affair, Khalil's and mine. Contact him, remind him again of the many favours I have done him in the past. Tell him that I need his help in this one extra thing, we'll share the profits fifty-fifty. As capital he can use the money in our shared account, the Cayman one, Fate. Tell him also that if he does this thing for me, I will be forever in his debt.'

When Dave awoke it was still dark. Kit and Tom Mackay had taken him out drinking last night, a long hard session ending some time around one in the morning at a club in Wanchai crowded with US sailors and Cantonese bar girls. It was the first time in years Dave had been so truly, blindly drunk.

He climbed groggily from bed, walking to the window and looking out across the waters of the Channel. The dawn was the faintest aurora of rose pink behind the distant black colossus of Lamma Island. He looked at his watch. It was ten minutes to six. Hung-over or not, his body clock always worked. He fumbled for his running vest and shorts, finding it difficult to keep his eyes open.

The telephone rang and he knew it was Hannah. He picked up the phone. It was still the evening of the previous day in New York and her voice was full of merriment as if she was somewhere – or with someone – she liked very much. 'Let me guess,' she said. 'You're putting on your running kit.' And she laughed. 'I've just heard about the arrest of that man Fung – there was a newsflash on the radio – it's wonderful, darling. You must be over the moon.'

'It's been a good couple of days,' he answered, realising how sluggish and thick-headed he sounded. 'We've got the extradition ahead of us, though, and that could take time. Like everything in the law it can get technical and drawn out. How are things with you?'

'Just brilliant,' she said. 'I can't believe it. Every day is like the Fourth of July. It's all happening so fast, darling. But I'll tell you all about it when I get back. Can you pick me up at the airport on Sunday?'

'Sunday? That's great. Yes, of course.'

'I'll fax the flight details through to Scott at the office. I'm missing you like crazy, you know that. I can't wait to get back.'

'I'm missing you too.'

'You'd better go on that run of yours.'

'There's just one thing before you go . . .'

'What is it?' she asked.

Dave paused for a moment, his mouth dry. 'Tell me,' he said, 'where were you the other morning?'

His question was followed by an abrupt silence. The breath caught in his throat as he waited for an answer. Oh God, he thought, why had he even raised it?

'When was that?' asked Hannah defensively.

'I telephoned your hotel. It must have been around six-thirty in the morning, your time. The woman on the switch-board said there was no answer from your room. She must have tried for a minute or longer.'

There was another silence before Hannah answered, a little too quickly, 'Oh then, yes. I must have been out walking.'

'Walking, you?' It was impossible for Dave to disguise his disbelief. 'At that hour, in the middle of New York?'

'I couldn't sleep, that's all. I woke up around six. There was nothing worth watching on the TV so I took a walk. I'm in midtown Manhattan, Dave, even at six-thirty I was

141

almost crushed to death by joggers!' She laughed but Dave could sense how forced it was. 'It's been a whirlwind,' she said. 'I can't explain. You have to be here to understand. But everything has been turned on its head darling – my sleep included.'

He ran hard, high up into the hills, up into the white blanketing mist that covered the Peak. He ran to the edge of his limits until his legs ached and his lungs burst, seeking out the physical pain to mask the other feelings. Was he imagining it? Was it just him? Yes, maybe it was a whirlwind for her across in New York. But, whirlwind or not, he knew Hannah and he knew she never got up at six-thirty in the morning, she never went walking. What could it be then? Could she have been with another man, with Ephram? Oh God no, just the thought of it was like a blow to the heart. What was the matter with him? He was eating himself up with jealousy and for what? One unanswered phone call. Hannah loved him, he loved her. Couldn't he leave it at that? But deep inside the first small seed had been planted, there was no way he could ignore it . . . the first seed from which such huge doubts grew.

The news conference given the previous afternoon and Fung's arrest in Miami were headline news in the Hong Kong morning papers. On his way to the office, Dave bought copies of the *South China Morning Post* and the Chinese-language *Oriental Daily*. Then he rode out along the Eastern Island Corridor to the working class area of Shau Ki Wan.

Just off the highway, on Po Man Street, close to the waterfront, he came to an apartment block. It was thirty storeys high, tapering, a brown-tiled pencil of a building with no balconies and dark, copper-tinted windows that reflected the light. Local residents referred to it in Cantonese slang as the Chocolate Cock. Its official name, however, was Benevolence Villas.

There were a number of hole-in-the-wall garages on the street where cars were repaired, there were shorter, ten-storey industrial buildings and nearby was a fish market. But the apartment block itself was isolated from all that behind a high wall that was sculptured and painted green to resemble bamboo. A short concrete driveway led from the street up to the entrance.

Dave parked his motorbike in front of the entrance and entered the building. The lobby was small, decorated in beige marble. Two attendants, both dressed in the regulation brown uniform, sat behind a desk. The older of the two was the regular concierge, the younger was a police officer. Dave gave proof of his identity and took the elevator to the twentieth floor.

This was the place that had been chosen as the safe house for both Wong Kam-kiu and Dimitri Tselentis. This is where they would be guarded until Conrad Fung was back in Hong Kong, tried, sentenced and safely de-fanged behind bars. There were two apartments per floor. Wong was in 20A and, directly across the lobby, Tselentis was housed in 20B.

Dave found Tselentis in 20B. He was looking better, more rested. But the accommodation wasn't much to his liking. 'Not exactly the Ritz, is it?' he complained. 'I've been here less than an hour and already I'm going crazy. How big is this place, fifty square feet? A self-respecting mouse would feel claustrophobic.'

Dave dropped the *South China Morning Post* on the table. The Chinese-language newspaper he was keeping for Wong. 'Conrad Fung was picked up in Miami,' he said. 'It's front-page news. Thanks for your help. It went like clockwork. The US Marshalls picked him up at the airport.'

Tselentis smiled, a secret joke. 'What did you do when you got the news? Have a few drinks, I expect.'

Dave grinned. 'Yeah, a few.'

'Hung-over?'

'A little.'

Tselentis walked across to the window, the copper-tinted glass that acted as a one-way mirror, and looked out towards the man-made finger of Kai Tak Airport where the bombing had taken place, the reason for all of this, for everything.

143

'Treat Fung with respect,' he said. 'Don't treat him as just another gangster, some Triad big brother with puffed-up ideas of his own importance. He's more than that . . . much, much more. He has connections – and not just a couple of lap-dog senators in Manila. He has a network of people here in Hong Kong, a network in the Middle East.'

'What are you trying to tell me?' asked Dave.

'I'm trying to tell you that Fung is a powerful man.'

'I know that.'

'You think you know but you don't – none of us do, not really, not even those who are close to him. It's not just a question of having a few street thugs on call or some coke barons who feed him business. It goes way beyond that. Fung has a way of mustering support when he needs it, support that seems to come out of nowhere. Take that bombing at Kai Tak. Where did that Australian come from? I had never seen him in my life, Fung had never said a word about him. But in a matter of days there he was. I mean, just conjured out of nowhere. And it can be terrifying, I have to tell you, bloody awesome on occasions.'

'I don't underestimate him,' said Dave. 'But he's behind bars now, his wings have been clipped.'

'Have they?' Tselentis gave a cynical laugh. 'Don't bet on it. You might have him behind bars but you've still got to get him out of the United States. And how long do you think a man like Fung – with his connections – can screw up the system.'

'That's a matter for the lawyers now.'

'Oh yeah? Wait and see. You have to keep Wong and myself alive long enough to testify and that's not going to be easy. Believe me, despite all the smart talk, I'm crapping in my pants here.'

Dave smiled.

'And at the end of all of that – assuming you get him back and assuming my neck is still connected to my head – you have to secure a conviction in front of a jury of everyday people, Hong Kong people, vulnerable people.'

'It's been done before,' said Dave.

'Not with Fung it hasn't.'

'So?'

'So what I'm trying to tell you,' said Tselentis, 'is that until you have done all these things, you will have a fight on your hands . . . believe me – the fight of your life.'

Chapter Eleven

The Ermita District of Manila was buzzing that night. There were plenty of tourists in town, the kind who sought out the strip joints and nightclubs, Aussies swilling beer, pink-faced Brits wanting to get laid, and in the biggest numbers, US servicemen, sailors mainly, hungry young animals denied pussy and beer during the two months at sea and determined to even the scales in the span of a few hours. The Red Lips Bar on Del Pilar was packed with them all. The band was beating out a deafening rock. The third strip show of the night had begun. Cash registers were ringing and Bruce Rexford was a contented man.

It was just after midnight when one of his bar girls tapped him on the shoulder and shouted to him above the cacophony of sound. 'That man by the entrance, the Chinese, he says he wants to talk to you.'

'What's it about?'

'Personal, he says.'

With a grunt of irritation, Bruce Rexford left the bar. The man was short, a little podgy, aged somewhere around fifty. Rexford noticed the cheap suit, the sweat stains on his shirt. 'Yeah, how can I help you?'

The man smiled politely. 'Is there somewhere perhaps a little quieter?' His English was fluent, barely accented.

'Can't this wait until some other time? You can see how snowed under we are here.'

The polite smile remained on the waxy moon face. 'I am afraid it cannot, Mr Rexford. If you have a room perhaps?'

Rexford led him through to his office behind the bar, shutting the door to block out some of the bedlam. He sat behind his desk, gesturing to the man to take a seat. Then he asked. 'So, what is your business Mr, er?'

The Chinese man lit another cigarette. 'We have a mutual acquaintance, Mr Rexford . . . a man by the name of Fung.'

Rexford stiffened. 'What about him?'

'No doubt you have heard of Mr Fung's arrest?'

'It's been in the papers.'

'So you must know the nature of the charges he faces. It is a most worrying state of affairs, Mr Rexford, regrettable in the extreme. There are two witnesses. One is named Wong, the other is named Tselentis. They are the ones who will testify against him. If they do so, if the matter comes to trial in Hong Kong, great harm could be done. I am sure I do not need to elaborate.'

Rexford could feel his heart thudding in his chest. 'What has this got to do with me?' he asked, far too belligerent.

'I am here to tell you that a decision has been made, Mr Rexford, a regrettable but necessary one. And I am here to seek your assistance in putting that decision into effect.' The Chinese man smiled, his cheeks puckering into dimples. Cigarette smoke curled around his mouth. 'I am sure you know exactly what I am talking about, Mr Rexford. I am sure you know what is required.'

'Who are you?'

'My name is irrelevant.'

'Who sent you?'

'We are colleagues, Mr Rexford, you and I . . . you see, I bring you a Red Scroll directive.'

Rexford heard the words and slumped back in his chair. He closed his eyes. *Mother of mercy, here we go again* . . .

'The two witnesses must be killed, Mr Rexford. For them to testify, for certain facts to emerge, would be intolerable. I am sure you understand that.'

Rexford did not reply. At that moment his thoughts were on his old mate, Johnny Dean, just bones now in some unmarked grave in the north of Vietnam. Who got the better deal, Johnny? he thought. Look at me now. At least you have oblivion, mate . . . peace by a more permanent name.

'You have a number,' said the Chinese man, 'a code number that identifies you.' He passed a slip of paper across the desk. 'That, I think, will prove that I have authority to speak.'

Rexford picked up the paper. The number was burnt into his brain. Yes, that was it: 8832. It could be a small town telephone number, some outback town in Australia. No fancy code name – Barbarian, Pilgrim, White Rabbit – just that number, the precise dullness of bureaucracy.

'You must remember,' said the man, 'that the witness, Tselentis, can recognise you too. He was the one – the small portly gentleman of mixed blood – who drove you to the airport. In disposing of him you will be protecting yourself too.'

Rexford got up. There was a bottle of scotch and glasses on a side-table in the corner. He went across, his heavily wedged features suddenly very drawn, very pale. He poured himself a stiff tot, offering none to the Chinese man. The old hopeless frustration was boiling up inside him, the compulsion to smash the desk top with his fist: *no, enough is enough, I won't do it any more! I've killed enough bloody people!* But what was the good of it? He was chained like Prometheus and every time they plucked his liver out, it just grew to be plucked out again. He returned to his chair, a dark shadow of anger on his face. He stared fixedly at his glass, swilling the whisky around until it formed a tiny amber whirlpool.

The Chinese man smiled, the same blank puckering of his lips. He had been advised to expect a similar reaction . . . the silent, impassioned anger that berated the cosmic unfairness of it all. But for all of that, he had been told there was an instinct in Rexford, a scent for blood and a skill in the hunt, that made him the perfect killing machine. Admittedly he was growing older now, slower, heavier. The drink – that amber liquid in his glass – was eating him up. But he would be good for this one last job.

'You have worked for the directorate for many years,' said the Chinese man. 'Your loyalty has been appreciated.'

Rexford gave a grunt of disgust, drinking back his whisky and coughing.

The Chinese man continued unperturbed: 'A time comes, Mr Rexford, when loyalty should be repaid. Kill these two witnesses and you will never be called on again. This will be our last request.'

Rexford stared at him, disbelieving. It took a moment for the import of what was being said to sink home. 'This is the last time? This is it?'

'Yes, Mr Rexford, as you say, this is it. When the assignment is completed, a quarter of a million dollars will be paid into your account. What do Westerners call it, a golden handshake? After that you can live your life in peace. You will never be called on again.'

'And the film.'

'Ah yes, the film . . . that must remain with us, Mr Rexford. That is the guarantee that you will not tell of the Red Scroll, betray us in any way. But if you honour us with your silence, we will honour you with our good faith.'

Rexford sat at the desk, stunned. For how many years had he prayed for this?

The Chinese man rose from his chair. He removed a buff envelope from his jacket pocket, placing it on the desk. 'The two witnesses are being held in Hong Kong. We do not know the location, not yet. But we have people working for us in that regard. There are instructions in the envelope, names and telephone numbers. You have worked with Fung's people in Hong Kong before, you will work with them again.' He walked to the door but turned before he opened it. 'Good luck, Mr Rexford,' he said, 'and good hunting.'

Five in the morning . . . the last drunken customers, a group of Aussies, had lurched out singing *'Waltzin' Matilda.'* No more music, no more people, just the stale smell of smoke and beer. Bruce Rexford hadn't left his desk. Slowly, as the night wore on, he had drained the scotch. It was a cliché, he knew it, he read enough books, a tormented man and his booze. But booze was good because booze deadened the soul, it kept a man's conscience in a state of torpor.

There had been a time once, twenty thousand millenia

ago, when he had been just an average kid. Bobby McLean had been his name . . . just an everyday kid with no comprehension of what lay ahead. He had come from a big family, aunts and uncles, brothers and sisters everywhere – all Adelaide folk, South Australian to the core – a proud family, proud of their country, proud of their sons. Everything had been as it should be back then – good mates at school, girlfriends, Saturday mornings working in his dad's shop, fixing irons, selling plugs. But he had never wanted that, never the humdrum things. He had always wanted to be a hero, to go out and conquer the world. What a fool. If only he had appreciated then how fate made idiots like him their playthings.

Phuoc Tuy Province, operating with Australia's Special Air Services Regiment. Long-range reconnaisance, they called it: parachute drops into Laos followed by three weeks living like rats in monsoon mud. He had loved it too. Shows what a crazy bastard he must have been. Loved it until that September in the rains, that September when they walked into the ambush.

Johnny Dean had taken a bad head wound and shrapnel in the gut. The other three had stood no chance. He had managed to drag Johnny out of the killing ground and the hunt had begun. No radio, no flares, no way of calling for help, just his wits and his will to keep them both alive. And for ten days he had stayed ahead of them, ten days with Johnny delirious and himself half cracked, ten days it took for the NVA to catch him.

Later, much later, Fung told him that he had killed six NVA in the chase. The story had drifted back through the hills how one Aussie carrying a wounded comrade had eluded them for so long. That's the story Fung heard, that's what brought him to that malarial hill camp above the DMZ.

In the camp the North Vietnamese had a prisoner, some Cambodian irregular, accused of some heinous crime he had long forgotten. An example was going to be made of the man, they said – to encourage the others. An example . . . God in heaven, three days they took to finish him, three days that stretched the outer limits of time. They boiled him in water until he shrieked like a stuck pig, they flayed skin off his back, they castrated him, they broke his bones and then, finally, they crucified him on a tree. For all that time the man's demented howls filled the camp, echoing over the empty hills. To witness death like that, so cruel, so totally beyond comprehension, changed a man forever.

And that was to be their fate too, these two round-eyed, shitface Aussie SAS men who had brought them such grief. Every night the guards goaded him in pidgin English. 'Tomorrow nail you to tree. Yeah, yeah, boil your hands until like pork meat. Tomorrow, you see!'

And he had snapped. Courage can only take a man so far. Physically exhausted, bereft of hope, emaciated, humiliated, he had finally broken. At that moment in time he would have done anything – killed his whole family – to avoid dying the way that Cambodian had died.

When Conrad Fung had arrived at the camp, he was ripe for the plucking . . . and he had wept at Fung's feet with gratitude.

Johnny Dean had never witnessed the torture of the Cambodian. He had been lying delirious on a bamboo cot burning up with gangrene. But if he had, if he had heard those howls, he would have understood . . .

'Today when you shot your friend and executed that boy in front of the cameras, Bruce, you welded a bond between us that can never be broken. You are now one of us. There is a body lying out in the hills near the ambush site. It has no head, much of it has been burnt with phosphorus. But it wears your clothes, it carries your dog tags. Soon it will be found and the remains of "Bobby McLean" will be flown back to Australia for burial. Your old life is gone, Bruce, now you begin the new. You will be given money, a place to live. And in return what do we ask? Only that once every few years you employ your specialist skills for the Red Scroll. You will learn that we are not common murderers, Bruce, we are men of honour, a very distinct and special brotherhood. But remember always that there is no going back to the old life. If you attempt it, you will be hunted down, just as you were in the hills. Remember also that we

152

have the films. If they are published, Bruce, the world will never know what really happened here, it will only know what it sees. Do you understand me? All the world will see is a man voluntarily shooting his comrade and then executing a young boy – a war criminal, that's what they will see. Imagine – at face value – the shocking brutality of it, even in twenty years time. Imagine the shame for your family. Do they deserve it? Do you really wish to be remembered that way? No my friend, what you did today took you out of the old world and into the new. You can never go back now. Don't even think of it. But there is no need to mourn. You have a new life ahead of you. The Red Scroll embraces you, embrace it too.'

In the months that followed, they indoctrinated him in the philosophy of the Red Scroll, why it stood alone, why it did what it did. They perfected his new identity, they gave him his new life in the Philippines. It seemed that he was bound to them for eternity. But now suddenly, after all the years, they were releasing him, unlocking the shackles. The impossible had happened . . . and all it would take was two more lives.

Scott Defoe glimpsed her first as she came through the doors at the top of the ramp and even at that distance he could see the change. Success like hers created its own special aura. 'There she is, Dave!' he exclaimed. 'Just look at her. All the pizzazz in creation!'

And indeed it was so. There may have been a slight look of strain in the face – the trans-Pacific flight would have tested the stamina of an astronaut – but Dave couldn't remember a time when Hannah had looked so radiantly self-assured. There was just one moment when she first saw him, when their eyes first met, that he thought he detected some hesitation, almost, crazily, a kind of nervousness in her face. But that had to be wrong. Because her smile, when it came, melted any doubts.

Abandoning her luggage trolley, Hannah came into his arms. She was delicate and lithe, as weightless as a flower. They kissed and Dave felt the wetness of tears on her cheeks. 'What's the matter?' he asked. 'Why are you crying?'

She shook her head, laughing and crying at the same time. 'It's nothing. I'm being silly, that's all. It's just so good to be back.'

Then Scott Defoe was upon her. 'You did it, my darling, you conquered the world!' And like a couple of ecstatic kids, caught up in the giddy euphoria of it all, they hugged and kissed and laughed while the airport crowds swirled around them.

When they got to the car, Hannah took a copy of *Women's Wear Daily* from her travel bag. 'Page three,' she said. 'Hot off the press.'

Scott found the page and began to read. 'Oh my word,' he said. 'It's brilliant, Dave, listen to this – ' And he began to exclaim with unabashed glee: 'Kids today want clothes that are fun, even a little zany, clothes that smile at you from the rack and say "Come on, buy me". Hannah Whitman's designs do all this and more. For originality and pure unabashed wearability, her new line, Danny's Rags, has to be next spring's hottest new range.' He kissed her, ecstatic. 'What did I tell you? I knew it all along. This confirms everything. I'm going to have it etched in bronze!'

Dave said nothing, just stood there, smiling. But at that moment, for the very first time, he understood that nothing would ever be quite the same again. Hannah was going to be a fashion star. The glittering life style, constant travel, business pressures – it was all there waiting for her, a dazzling diamond-rimmed trap. But once she was locked in, what then? He loved her too much to begrudge her success. But success, he knew – megasuccess like hers – was a potent force. It welded things together but it shattered them too. How would Hannah feel in two or three years time married to a plain Joe cop?

He didn't know why he was feeling so insecure. But so much had happened – Danny's death, Hannah's success – nothing was firm beneath his feet any more. He didn't want to lose her, it was as simple as that. Hannah was all he had left.

★   ★   ★

That night they had a light dinner, just grilled fish with a watercress salad. Then they sat listening to slow, smoky jazz and talking. Dave told her in detail about the investigations. He told her how events had suddenly gelled to enable them to arrest Fung in Miami, about the steps that lay ahead to get him extradited, and how there was still one man outstanding, the assassin with the red hair, the Australian who had carried the bomb. When Dave spoke, it was with quiet, almost solemn satisfaction. But Hannah shared in that satisfaction too. Despite everything that had happened to her – the excitement of her success and the emotional turmoil of her affair with Sam Ephram – hardly an hour went by when she didn't think of her son and feel the pain of his passing all over again.

Near midnight, they went through to the bedroom. Hannah showered first then Dave followed and she knew they were going to make love.

All the way back across the Pacific she had dreaded this moment, terrified that somehow, when they began to make love, in some indefinable way, Dave would know that she had been with another man. He was suspicious, that was so obvious, suspicious of her true relationship with Sam Ephram. Nothing had been said, not yet, but it would. Dave could never bottle worries up inside himself for long.

When he came out of the shower still drying himself, she was oddly surprised at how hard and spare he looked, so much taller than Sam, his skin so much paler, almost Nordic in comparison to Sam's dark olive tones. This is crazy, she thought, he's my husband and I'm staring at him like a stranger!

They climbed into bed together, Dave switched off the light and they lay for a time in silence. Hannah knew then that he was building his courage to ask the question, the one question that might open the floodgates and drown them both. But it had to come, it had to be asked.

When Dave did speak, there was a tremor in his voice as if each word was causing him pain. 'There's one thing,' he said. 'Don't get angry but I have to know. It's about Sam Ephram.' And he fell silent again.

'What about him?' she asked.

'Are you attracted to him?'

'What are you trying to say?'

'You know . . .'

'Have I had an affair with him?'

'Have you?'

Hannah reached under the sheets to take his hand and she could feel how rigid his whole body was, every muscle tense with expectation. 'No,' she replied in a whisper, lying with all her skill, terrified of losing him. 'No, I haven't had an affair with him. He's an attractive man, he's moved heaven and earth for me. I owe him a great deal. But you're my husband, you're the one I love.'

'It's crazy, maybe,' he said, his voice strained. 'It's just that on the telephone sometimes . . .'

She gave a gentle, teasing laugh. 'I hate long-distance calls. I'm always rotten on them, you know that.'

He laughed too, as much a sign of relief as anything, and came close to her, his lips brushing hers in the darkness.

'I love you,' she said. The words came out very simply, clothed only in sincerity. And it was the truth. She did love him. The fact that she also had feelings for Sam Ephram, that she was caught up in a compelling, fatal attraction, would never change that fact.

Dave gave a small sigh, gently kissing her neck, and she knew his doubts were dispelled. There were times, she thought, when men could be as naive as puppies and for that brief moment she was laden with guilt.

But then Dave's mouth came down on to her breasts, so warm, wet, perfectly pressured, and she shuddered, moaning out loud, all guilt forgotten. His tongue traced delicious patterns down from her erect nipples, down over the milky curve of her breasts. 'Oh yes,' she said, her voice suddenly husky. 'Oh yes, please, just like that.' His mouth did marvellous things to her, bringing every nerve alive. She thrust out her legs, opening herself and his tongue was there. She arched her back, never wanting him to stop. She had forgotten how patiently expert he was, how well he knew every yearning part of her. He was building her emotions, first a slow, solemn andante, delicious beyond description, then faster, with more force, building to a wild scherzo that had every nerve in her body burning. 'Oh yes!' she shouted. 'Oh God, yes!' And in a brilliant burst of starlight, suddenly she came.

She lay back for a moment, satiated. Then she pressed herself against him, gasping at the rock-hard surge of his erection. He came over her, heavy and yet buoyant, kissing the lobes of her ears, kissing her neck and biting into her shoulders. And briefly, in the crowning crescendo of her feelings, as he came deep inside, Sam Ephram intruded. But then the image was extinguished and everything was Dave . . . his lips, his body, the exquisite hardness of him, every touch and liquid kiss.

Normally the jet lag hit Hannah ha— she would sleep for twelve straight hours or longer. Bu— at night she awoke once, around four in the morning. —re was a full moon that night. They never closed the cu— ns, not fully. Their bedroom had an uninterrupted view —t over the Lamma Channel and a silver light, pale as gossamer, fell upon the bed. Hannah looked down at the slumbering form of her husband. The thick brown mane of Dave's hair lay tousled around that raw-boned, handsome face. He looked so strong, so quietly dependable. Maybe not a jet-setter sporting Gucci clothes and a tan from St Tropez, maybe not a man to sweep you off your feet and promise you the world. But a man to have faith in, she thought, a man to trust.

What do I do, thought Hannah, how long can I live a double life like this? She leant down, gently kissing him on the cheek and a smile came to Dave's lips. For a moment he looked almost like a schoolboy and, still asleep, gave a contented sigh. Damn you, thought Hannah. Why can't you be an unadulterated bastard? Why can't you be a drunk or a self-centred bore? Why do you have to be such a decent man?

Zachary Hedgewood was one of the brightest attorneys at the Florida bar. He had experience in extradition work and a good reputation with the courts. He was also young,

157

abrasive and arrogant. Edgar Aurelius knew that Fung would not like him. But likes were not important. What mattered was getting the job done and Hedgewood, they said, knew every device in the book.

They met on Monday morning at the Metropolitan Correctional Centre. Zachary Hedgewood arrived in a canary yellow Ferrari. He was a square-set individual, plumpish, going grey at the temples, a very smooth operator.

When Conrad Fung was brought into the interview room, Hedgewood took immediate control. 'We can talk freely in here,' he said. 'You don't have to worry about hidden cameras or bugging devices.'

Fung coldly weighed him up. 'What about my bail?' he asked.

'In the United States there is a presumption against bail in international extradition proceedings. The onus will be on us to prove special circumstances. Right at the moment, Mr Fung – unless you can pull something out of the hat – we have none. Going to court to apply for bail would be a waste of your money and my time.'

'Then how long must I remain here?'

'The extradition treaty gives the colony of Hong Kong sixty days – just over eight weeks – to submit its evidence.'

'Must I remain here all that time?'

'Yes, Mr Fung, you must.'

Fung blinked but otherwise remained inscrutable. The outraged panic shown at the time of his arrest had given way now to an icy, totally focused concentration. 'What about their so-called evidence? Will you get a chance to cross-examine the witnesses?'

'There's no oral evidence, Mr Fung, not from the Hong Kong witnesses. It's all done on the papers – affidavits and the like. An extradition hearing doesn't decide guilt. Its function is to decide whether there is enough evidence to warrant sending you back for trial.'

Fung digested the information, inscrutably passive. 'When the papers arrive in sixty days, what then?'

'Then the matter will be sent down for hearing before a federal magistrate.'

'How long must I wait for that?'

'Another month or so.'

'So I could be locked up here for three months before I get a chance to contest this travesty. Is that your system of justice in the United States, Mr Hedgewood?'

'If time is all that counts, Mr Fung, you can always waive extradition, return voluntarily to Hong Kong.'

Fung smiled but it was a lethal smile, filled with malice. 'To face trumped-up charges in a kangaroo court run by decadent English colonialists. No, Mr Hedgewood, I will not be returned like a lamb to the slaughter. This is a matter of principle for me.'

'Principle . . . aah yes, of course.' Hedgewood gave a smile of undisguised cynicism. His thoughts were obvious: for all your inscrutable ways, Mr Fung, you are a murdering son-of-a-bitch if ever I saw one.

Zachary Hedgewood departed after half an hour, driving back to his Palm Beach office. But Edgar Aurelius remained with Fung in the interview room. There were other matters to be dealt with, private matters . . .

'What about Khalil?' asked Fung. 'Has he agreed to this new business I proposed?'

'I spoke to him over the weekend,' said Aurelius. 'It took some convincing but yes, in the end he agreed. He'll move on it immediately. We've agreed amounts, we've agreed dates. If this thing you have with him – whatever it is – goes well, it'll save our bacon.'

'Have you given him full signing powers on the Fate account?'

'He has carte blanche with it.'

Fung leant back in his chair, an enigmatic smile settling on his face. 'Good. Without seeds, Edgar, there can never be a crop. We know that, don't we, you and I. For ten years now we have scattered seeds of goodwill all over the world . . .'

Aurelius said nothing. Fung had a tendency to indulge in these flights of imagery. But he would get to the point soon enough.

159

'And now, I think, it is time to start reaping a few crops. If I am to defeat this extradition, Edgar, I must have the tools to do it. I must have something solid to give that pup of a *gweilo* lawyer you have hired for me.'

'Is there no way we can get to the witnesses in Hong Kong? The case against you rests or falls on them. Hector Chan, your man in Hong Kong – I've got him working on it already.'

Fung shook his head with a mirthless smile. 'Don't concern yourself with the witnesses, Edgar. They will be dealt with, I am sure of it. Yes, get Hector Chan working. But you and I should look to other matters.'

Aurelius knew when to leave well alone. Fung had his own collateral power base somewhere out there in Asia. How the witnesses would be dealt with or by whom he didn't want to know. 'What other matters?' he asked. 'You obviously have an idea.'

'Do you recall, Edgar, when they arrested me? I said I was a Filipino resident, I said they had no right to arrest me. Do you recall what you said in reply? I recall it very well. You said to me: you are not immune from arrest, not unless you are a diplomat.'

Aurelius simply shrugged. He had no idea where this was leading.

'Those were your words Edgar – *unless you are a diplomat*. And it started me thinking . . .'

Aurelius couldn't believe it, he couldn't be talking about immunity under the Vienna Convention. That was insane. 'You can't mean it,' he said, 'not diplomatic immunity.'

'Reaping the crop, Edgar, that's all I am doing, bringing in the corn.'

'For Chrissake, Conrad, do you have any idea what this would entail? Just think about it a moment—'

'I know what the problems are, Edgar. Don't preach to me. To secure diplomatic immunity, first I must be a diplomat. But it can be done. There are ways. There are men out there, powerful men, men who are beholden to me. All it takes is some parchment and sealing wax, a little economy with the truth.'

160

Aurelius was shaking his head in disbelief. Fung came up with some unique ideas, but this one was pure madness. 'Having some government minister beholden to you is one thing Conrad. But getting him to accredit you as one of his country's ambassadors—'

'If the price is right, Edgar.'

'Not everything has a price.'

'No. But everything has a *value*.'

'What do you mean by that.'

'Political office is unstable. If a man's corruption is exposed, what choice does he have? He must resign. In third world countries, poor countries, fundamentalist countries, resignation is often not enough. In such countries the man goes before a firing squad. Political office has a value Edgar, that's what I'm saying. Life has a value.'

'No, what you're saying is that everybody is open to blackmail.'

'A small country, Edgar, an insignificant country. Surely an ambassadorship can be granted without too much concern. It has been done before.'

'Then you tell me, who do we go to? Who do we blackmail for this diplomatic appointment?'

Fung held back for a moment. Then he said in an almost offhand manner, 'What about Ibrahim al-Ghashmi?'

'Ghashmi? You can't be serious!'

'Why not? Look at the money we've moved for him, look at the schemes we know about. Ghashmi is a member of the Presidential Council of the Yemen, he's Minister of State for External Affairs. We couldn't ask for anybody better.'

'He's a hothead Conrad, you know that. Look at the trouble we've had with him in the past. He's a reforming zealot one day, a butcher the next. Ghashmi should be the last man on earth we deal with.'

'Why? Because he has a violent temper, because he is unpredictable?'

'Yes, both those things! You never know where you are with the man. He can turn on you like a rabid dog. I'll have to deal with him, remember, not you. I'll be the one who has to fly to Sana or whatever the damn capital is called, I'll

161

'be the one who has to take a step back into the Middle Ages.'

'So who must I go to, Edgar, tell me, perhaps the President of France or the Pope? We don't deal with gentlemen, it's not in the nature of our business. We take them as we find them. Yes, Ghashmi is unpredictable – so you guard against it. But he's no fool. He's a survivor. He'll go along, he has no choice.'

'He'll see it as an act of betrayal, Conrad, and that's exactly what it is. I warn you, we're making a bad enemy.'

Fung gave a snort of dismissal. 'I'm swamped with enemies, Edgar. What harm will one more do me? I have to fight this thing. I can't sit passively and wait. You're mistaken if you think I'm going to languish here for the next five years while that lawyer of yours argues legal points all the way to the Supreme Court. That's the weak man's option, not mine.'

'Even if you get this ambassadorship, it doesn't mean the State Department here will accept it. You realise that?'

'Yes but think of the pressure, Edgar, think of the political pressure.'

'The State Department is a tough nut to crack.'

'Don't worry, it will crack.' There was a look of implacable resolve on Fung's sallow features. He was a man transformed, frighteningly so. 'It can be done, Edgar. We need the will to achieve it, that's all. I *want* that diplomatic immunity.'

After Aurelius had departed, Conrad Fund returned to his cell. The other prisoners – drug traffickers mainly and fraudsters – were playing cards or watching baseball on television. But he had no desire to do either. He lay instead on his bed, hands behind his head, gazing up at the ceiling.

When he had first been arrested, he had experienced a great, blinding anger but also a great fear, a fear that he had never known before. The anger remained with him still, burning inside, but the fear had gone. He knew now that he would never be extradited, he would never stand trial. Not once in his life had he been defeated. There had been setbacks, yes, every man has those, but never a defeat. What he had been unable to achieve on his own, he had achieved with the assistance of the Red Scroll.

The Red Scroll would deal with the witnesses in Hong Kong, he knew it. No communication was required to reassure him. It followed as night followed day. Those of the brotherhood looked after their own.

That afternoon Aurelius flew back to New York. Bookings had already been made for him to fly to the Yemen via London in forty-eight hours time. In his absence, one of his associates would go down to Miami to hold Fung's hand.

Edgar Aurelius understood the checks and balances of corruption as well as any man. Since associating himself with Conrad Fung, he had been forced to make them a forensic speciality. Corruption was like sex, an intimate coupling. It bound people to each other in a special way. There was trust involved, a giving and taking. It was wrong to say there was no honour among thieves. In the business of money laundering there had to be honour and it was an honour he was going to betray.

Ibrahim al-Ghashmi was going to react, there was no doubt about it. When you blackmailed a man, diplomatic dexterity played no part. You required just one skill – the ability to convince him that you were able to follow through with your threat. That was your only protection. When he reached New York, Aurelius took a limousine straight to his Wall Street office. Two days was barely enough to fashion that protection.

The villagers who knew him called him *Sau Nga*, which meant Flat Nose. Pang Wai-ping was proud of the nickname. As a young Red Pole, a fighter, in the Sun Yee On Triad, he had been smashed across the face with a length of bamboo in a fight with some Big Circle boys from across the border. His nose ever since had been a rubbery mush, the nose of an old boxer, not attractive but distinctive, a nose that indicated a man's pedigree.

163

Pang Wai-ping was now forty years old, of Chiu Chow descent. He had a number of businesses but the small barbecued meat shop that he ran in Sha Tau Kok in the far north of Hong Kong's New Territories, right on the Chinese border, was where he could mostly be found.

That evening, as Pang Wai-ping closed up his shop, he was in a pensive mood. An hour earlier he had received a phone call. It had been from America . . . a voice from the past, from a man he knew as Khalil Khayat.

He and Khalil had not done business in over two years. But now Khalil was back and he wanted to do business again, big business, very big indeed.

Pang Wai-ping could make a great deal of money, enough to make him a rich man the rest of his days. Even so, he had been tempted to reject the offer out of hand. In the past, doing business with Khalil had always meant doing business with Fung Chi-man . . . Conrad Fung, they called him. And Pang wanted nothing to do with Fung, nothing at all. Fung was now in jail for that crazy Kai Tak bombing. Fung had always been bad luck, even more so now. Khalil, however, had sworn that this was a totally independent deal. If so, that might just be acceptable.

Pang Wai-ping walked slowly home through the village, stopping to greet his neighbours. It was the Year of the Monkey, an auspicious year, his necromancer had said, a year in which a man willing to take risks could make much money. Yes, it was tempting. But still he worried, he worried a great deal. What was the good of money without the freedom to enjoy it?

Dmitri Tselentis was not an early riser; ten in the morning for him was the crack of dawn. When Dave arrived, he had only just got out of bed, at the insistence of his permanent police minder, and was sitting in the kitchen in his dressing gown eating bacon and eggs.

Dave tossed him a copy of the morning newspaper, a regular routine now. 'How long is it going to take you to get shaved and dressed?'

'Why, what's the big rush?'

'We're starting on your extradition affidavit. The sooner all the papers are on their way, the sooner Fung is back in Hong Kong.'

Tselentis gave him a quizzical look. 'You seem cock-a-hoop this morning. You've been like this since your wife returned from New York. What happened, get your leg over again last night?'

Dave grinned. 'You can be a crude bastard, you know that.' In a strange kind of way, he was getting to like Tselentis. He was a likeable man.

Tselentis grinned back, rummaging through the paper to find the business section. 'The greenback is taking a hammering. Take my advice, stick to the yen.'

Dave laughed. 'You're talking to the wrong man. I've got to think twice before I buy new spark plugs for my bike.'

'Even with your wife about to become the world's Coco Chanel for ten-year-olds?'

'I'm afraid so, even with that.' Dave poured himself a mug of coffee. 'What do you reckon, is Conrad Fung sitting in his Miami jail doing the same as you, checking the Dow Jones?'

Tselentis gave a dismissive shrug. 'By now he's too financially stuffed to care about the Dow Jones.'

'I know that Florida Keys deal fell through, thanks to the FBI. But I thought Fung had millions.'

'Fung?' Tselentis gave a cryptic laugh. 'He should have millions. But it doesn't work that way, not with Fung. Prudence is not a word too often found in his vocabulary. If Fung had to dump all his debts right now he'd tilt the globe ten degrees. Aurelius and I tried to teach him a little financial caution. We would have done better pushing snow up Everest with our noses. If you've got a good thing, flog it to death. That's Fung's economic philosophy.'

'What about his money laundering? He must still be making big bucks with that?'

Tselentis shook his head. 'If you were a hard-assed Colombian, would you trust fifty million a month to some Chinese guy sitting in a federal lock-up facing extradition for murder? The money laundering will be dead by now.'

Dave gave a satisfied grin. 'Stuffed on all fronts – couldn't happen to a nicer guy.'

'Stuffed maybe. But don't write him off just because he's down. The man may be the world's number-one asshole but he has grit. I can't take that from him. This is when he'll come out fighting.'

'How?' asked Dave. 'What's he capable of doing?'

'You want my opinion?'

'Very much so.'

'I think he'll fight this thing on three levels. That'll be his strategy.'

'What levels are they?'

'First, the legal. Get the best lawyers money can buy and tell them to stuff up the system, argue every point no matter how crappy. Who knows, he might get lucky on a technicality and walk free. In the US weirder things happen every day.'

'That's the first level,' said Dave. 'The second?'

'Second – the extra-legal.'

'What do you mean by that?'

'By that I mean trying to plant me in the ground before I get a chance to testify – hired killers, Triads, some cop who is prepared to put strychnine in my beer. If I'm history, Fung walks away into the sunset. Nice ending for him, pretty shitty one for me.'

'And the third level?'

'Financial. Without money, levels one and two are non-starters. Fung has got to try and keep his empire together. He needs money, big money, and he needs it fast.'

'So what are his options?'

Tselentis poured himself a coffee – white with three sugars. 'He'll go back to making profits the way he did in the old days when he was muscling his way up and needed to raise capital. He still has the connections.'

'Connections for what?' asked Dave.

Tselentis gave a knowing grin. 'What's the quick road for riches for every Cantonese crook? How to get yourself the three Ms – money, mistress and a Merc – all in six weeks.'

'*Pak fan*, white powder?'

'You got it first time. Heroin. And why not? Along with cocaine it's the biggest business in the world. You think rock stars make good bread? Believe me, they don't compare – and they have to pay tax.'

'Who would he deal with? Do you have names?'

'God knows. I never got involved in that side of it, I wanted nothing to do with it. I was there for the financial deals, the laundering, that's it. Fung had a whole network of people . . . here, Thailand, the Middle East. I could give you a dozen names but I'd be guessing. Whenever times were tough he dipped into the powder. A few sales, a quick fix of cash and the merchant bankers were smiling. He's done it in the past. You asked for my opinion – I think he'll do it again.'

Chapter Twelve

The customs officer on duty at Kai Tak Airport that morning watched the man in the business suit take the green route through customs control. There were, he noted, two suitcases on his trolley. 'Are you travelling on your own?' he asked.

'Yes I am,' the passenger replied.

The customs officer checked the baggage label, seeing the name Frank Lorenzo, home address: Auckland, New Zealand. 'Two suitcases, Mr Lorenzo?'

'One contains samples.'

'Open the case please.'

The passenger opened the first of the cases revealing stainless steel tubes, bolts, hinges and springs that lay, like professional photographic equipment, in beds of foam rubber. 'I am a dealer in machine tools,' he said.

The officer removed a length of black steel tubing from its foam rubber bed. It smelt of grease. No sign of contraband, no trace of drugs. Each month thousands of businessmen came through customs with samples of goods they wanted manufactured in Hong Kong, everything from dolls that sang national anthems to electric curling tongs. If Hong Kong had a true national flag, a sample would be its central emblem. The officer replaced the black steel tubing. 'I hope you have a profitable stay,' he said.

Bruce Rexford smiled politely. 'Thank you, I hope so too,' He was back in the killing grounds – and his tools of trade were with him.

Hector Chan, the solicitor, senior partner of Chan, Wai and

Kon, gave a troubled burp, a bilious sigh caused more by tension than anything else. Since this crisis had begun he had not been a well man, not well at all.

With Conrad Fung's arrest in Miami, he had been dragged in far too deep in an attempt to assist him, forced to take far too many risks. He should not be involving himself in these matters, not so directly. It was blackmail, pure and simple. He was the Grand Incense Master, the Dragon Head, not some lowly Red Pole. But what choice did he have?

First, that caustic little hunchback from New York, Aurelius, Fung's acolyte, had been on to him demanding that his people pick around in the dirt to find something to help contest the extradition. Then there had been that disturbing visit from the man he did not know but who clearly knew him only too well.

From his accent, he had sounded Yunnanese, a podgy chain smoker in a cheap suit. The man had refused to give his name or any particulars of himself. But he had been clear enough in his demands. The two witnesses who would testify against Fung were to be located. Where the man had come from and who he was Hector Chan didn't know. But the man had known a frightening amount about him, his history, his rank in the Triad, his past dealings with Conrad Fung. And throughout their meeting, behind that irritating smile and the foul cigarette smoke, the implication had been there . . . if you fail in this and Conrad Fung falls, you fall with him.

As it turned out, obtaining the information had not been difficult. It was a notorious case; too many people involved, too many fingers in the bureaucratic pie. They had found a station sergeant in Police Headquarters, a man in debt to the loan sharks, who had located the information in a file and passed it back in payment of his debt. It had not been difficult at all but it had been risky, far too risky.

But it had not ended there because now, this evening, he had to pass the information to another stranger – and here in his own office too! Matters were becoming intolerable.

It was dark outside. His law partners and the staff had

170

gone home. Only his private secretary remained. But he still had this distasteful business to conclude. Chewing mournfully on an antacid tablet, he rang through to his secretary and said in Cantonese. 'Very well, you may send him in.'

The door to his office opened. A European man entered, a big man, heavily built, a man with purplish veins in his cheeks and rust-red hair.

Bruce Rexford smiled, holding out his hand across the desk. 'I apologise for keeping you, Mr Chan, but after hours seemed to be more convenient for us both.'

'Yes, yes, far better,' said Hector Chan. He didn't like the look of the man at all.

Bruce Rexford took a seat in a leather chair. Chan sat too, his complexion very chalky, nervously rubbing his hands. Rexford knew all about Chan from the instructions he had received in Manila. They said he was a Triad, Wo Shing Wo, a mob lawyer. That's why it amused him to look at his office, at the pretensions the man had built around himself, the airs and graces of a pukka professional.

It was very old-world, one of those offices that looked as if it had been occupied forever, every item of furniture chosen for its dark, polished antiquity. There was a faint odour, the mustiness of ancient papers: testaments and contracts, dry wax, mortgages and old ink. Even those papers that had been printed by computer possessed an air of instant age, altered by jurisprudential osmosis into a respectable Dickensian maturity. It was impressive, no doubt about it. What had Shakespeare said about making a better world? The first thing we do, let's kill all the lawyers.

'You require an address, I think,' said Hector Chan, wanting to get the meeting over in the shortest time possible. 'I have it for you. It is a residential apartment block called Benevolence Villas. Both men are being held on the twentieth floor.'

Rexford took the paper from him, placing it in his wallet. 'Knowing the location, Mr Chan, is of great value. Thank you. But that is only half of it. Knowing the movement of these two men in advance . . . when Tselentis may visit his mother, when they may go to court, to the doctor, when

171

they may be taken out for some air to fight the claustrophobia . . . that is critical.'

Hector Chan gave a dubious shrug. 'I really don't know. You are asking a great deal. That will be difficult.'

Rexford smiled disarmingly. 'I am sure you will find a way. There must be many people you can call upon, many people who owe you a kindness. I will keep in touch every day. I have your private number. You do appreciate how important this is, Mr Chan, for you, for me – for everybody involved.'

The following morning, in the exhausting humidity of the early June weather, Rexford took a taxi out to Shau Ki Wan, to the address Chan had given him in Po Man Street.

The building stood on its own close to the water. It looked out over the harbour towards Kai Tak, an ugly brown stick of an edifice thirty storeys high. But, from the outside, it clearly served its new purpose well. There were no balconies, just smooth, tiled walls, and the windows were anodised a dark copper with no way of seeing in. The only windows at the rear were for the kitchens and bathrooms, little more than arrow slits of frosted glass. There was no external fire escape.

Rexford walked through the open iron gates and up the short concrete drive to the entrance. Inside the lobby two security guards in dull brown uniforms sat behind a desk. Rexford glanced at the board on the wall above their heads listing the names of the tenants. 'I'm here to see Mrs Huang, twenty-fifth floor.'

'Is she expecting you?'

'We have business to discuss.'

The elder of the two nodded, pointing towards the elevators. It was a grubby, cheap block in an industrial neighbourhood. Rexford had calculated that there would be no telephone check with the apartment first, no need to give his name. As he waited at the elevator, he glanced back at the two guards behind the desk. The younger one, the one who hadn't spoken, was watching him all the time. He had an eager, cocksure look about him. He was a cop, sure as day.

The elevator doors opened. Rexford stepped in and pressed the button for the twentieth floor, the floor on which the two witnesses were being held. He wished to see how well it was guarded. The elevator ascended with agonising slowness, hovered at the twentieth and, with a tired hiss, the doors opened.

An iron grill barred his exit. He took in the double padlock, the sturdiness of the structure. Christ, he thought, it's a fortress.

'Can I help you?' A young Chinese man was sitting on a wooden chair in the lift lobby close to the fire escape door. Rexford glimpsed the leather cross slash of his shoulder holster. He took in the fact that the fire escape door had been padlocked.

'Is this the twenty-fifth floor?'

'No,' said the man.

'Sorry, my mistake.'

Rexford took the lift back down again. He left the building, stung by the extent of the security. He had never had to make a hit this difficult before. A bodyguard or two, that's the worst he had had to contend with in the past. He walked down the driveway on to the street and stood for a time. There was no way he could hope to get to the witnesses, each in a separate apartment, dispose of them both and then get away, not while they stayed up there on the twentieth floor. Too many obstacles, too well guarded. It would be suicide. There was only one viable option – to hit them when they came out into the open.

He walked a few paces down the street looking around. There was the smell of fish in the air from the nearby market. On the opposite side of the street, facing the apartment block, were a number of auto repair shops, tiny, grubby places, one-man businesses. One of the repair shops was empty. He went across to it, turned and looked back at Benevolence Villas.

A dry smile came to his lips. That was one small advantage at least. From where he stood, he had an uninterrupted view up the driveway and straight into the entrance lobby.

★

Later that morning he made his second contact. The man was known to him only as Fat Kwok. He was a hawker, said the instructions, who sold sugarcane and coconut juice under a flyover on the Mei Lei Road in Kowloon.

They met in a teahouse in Shau Ki Wan only a few minutes walk from Benevolence Villas. Fat Kwok was a stolid peasant, crude and slow, growing old like himself. He wore a T-shirt, shorts and plastic sandals. As his name implied – in English at least – he was heavily overweight, his belly distending the T-shirt into the shape of a barrel. There was a tattoo on Fat Kwok's forearm, the tattoo Rexford had been looking for: a dragon, its reptilian wings outstretched, soaring through a ring of fire.

It was the mark of the Flaming Dragons, Conrad Fung's personal Tong, the ageing guard he had formed back in the days when he was new to Hong Kong and hungry for power. The Flaming Dragons bore no wider allegiance, only to him. They were Conrad Fung's brownshirts, his private SS. At one time there had been thirty or more of them but now there were just a dozen still alive and out of jail. But they were still paid a monthly retainer, still kept on hold for when the need arose.

Fat Kwok knew of Fung's arrest in Miami – the whole of Hong Kong knew, it had been front-page news – and he was clearly a frightened man, frightened of losing his monthly retainer, even more frightened that he might have to do something now to earn it.

'I am going to need four of you,' said Rexford. 'There is a small auto repair shop on Po Man Street, number sixteen. I want you to lease it immediately, today. Whatever it costs I'll pay. Put in a car, some tyres, tools . . . get working.'

'Why?' asked Kwok. 'None of us are mechanics.'

'Across the street from the shop is an apartment block. The police are holding two witnesses there. Do I make myself clear?'

Fat Kwok looked suddenly very grim.

'Four men, including yourself,' said Rexford. 'I must know what is happening at the block twenty-four hours a day, I must know every movement. It could take time, weeks. So I want patient men, steady men. One word leaked out, a screw-up caused because one of you is a drunk or an addict, a *do yau*, and you will be answerable to me. Do I make myself clear in that too?'

Fat Kwok looked across the table at this *gweilo*, this ghost man with the red hair and the pale green eyes and the chest on him like a bull. There was the smell of death about him, the smell a hangman has. 'Yes,' he said with great deference, 'it is very clear.'

Dimitri Tselentis may have possessed a genius for figures but when it came to the sequence of ordinary human affairs, he managed somehow to get everything about face and upside down. It was critical, however, that he get his thoughts in order. Dave had learnt from hard experience that a confused witness, no matter how sincere, was a defence counsel's dream. That was why, no matter how many times they had to go back over events, no matter how many redrafts were necessary, he was determined that the extradition affidavit Tselentis signed before the chief magistrate would be in logical sequence, devoid of hearsay and evidentially compelling. In the final analysis, it was on this single document that success or failure against Fung depended and nothing was going to be left to chance,

Tselentis, however, boxed up in the apartment for a full week now, felt the frustrations more keenly. 'What are you trying to do, win the Pulitzer Prize?' he complained. 'How many more times do I have to go over this bloody thing?'

Dave grinned at him. 'As many times as it takes, I'm afraid. This is the basis of the extradition and the eventual trial too. We've got to get it right.'

Tselentis got up from the table. 'It's five-thirty. Enough already. We're not trying to break speed records too. What about a beer?'

'Yeah, a beer sounds good.' It had been a gruelling day but Dave was satisfied. The draft affidavit was twenty-five pages long. It needed expanding in a few places, some of the incidents required further clarification, but they were getting there.

Tselentis returned from the kitchen with two cans of beer, cracking them open and sitting back at the table. 'What about Wong across the lobby in 20B?' he asked. 'Have you started on his affidavit yet?'

'I start that after yours.'

'That should be a bundle of laughs. If you think you're having a tough time with me, wait until you try and get two coherent sentences out of that poor demented schmuck. The police boys tell me he sits in his apartment all day staring at the wall just drooling, muttering all the time about his wife and kid.'

'Clinical depression,' said Dave in quiet sympathy. 'I think that's the term.'

'What's the prognosis for him? What do the shrinks reckon? Is he going to pull through or is he headed down the long, slippery slope?'

'He's having a tough time of it,' Dave admitted, 'but he'll come through in the end. He's on medication, the psychiatrist is seeing him every day.'

'The truth is, I feel damn sorry for him,' said Tselentis. 'He and I are going to have to make our peace one of these days. I never intended him any harm. It was Fung and his goons. I need to explain that to him.'

'I already have,' said Dave.

'What was his reaction?'

'It's still a very emotional thing with him. He's all knotted up inside, not thinking too rationally.'

'So he still thinks I'm responsible, that his dead wife is across there in the other world pursuing me in my nightmares? I tell you, if anybody is pursuing me in my nightmares, it's not her.'

'Give him time,' said Dave. 'We're all on the same side now. Fung is the enemy, not you. He knows that . . . he just has to come to terms with it, that's all.'

Fat Kwok, bent over the open bonnet of a wrecked car, saw the motorcyclist drive away from Benevolence Villas at six-thirty that evening. It was near the end of his watch, his first full day in the auto repair shop. Rubbing his grease-blackened hands on a piece of rag, he retired into the shop. A mobile telephone lay on a bench. He picked it up and dialled.

One block away, in a tiny, single-room apartment bare of furnishings, Bruce Rexford answered the call.

'The *gweilo* cop, the tall one, has driven away.'

'Which direction?'

'Towards Central.'

'Anybody on the bike with him?'

'He was alone.'

'Any cars following?'

'None.'

'Any sign of other movement?'

'None.'

'When does your watch end?'

'Half an hour.'

'Who takes over?'

'Six Fingers Wu.'

'Tell him to keep in touch.'

'Okay.'

In the corner of the room stood a chair and a fan. There were no other items of furniture. At night Rexford slept on a sleeping bag. When the call was ended, he walked across to the chair and methodically logged the details in a notebook. A book lay on the floor next to the chair. It was a yellowing, dog-eared paperback of John Steinbeck's *Cannery Row*. He had started it that morning. He would finish it that night. At times like this – waiting for the kill – books were Bruce Rexford's solitary companions.

Chapter Thirteen

The Republic of Yemen – two hundred thousand square miles of mountains and desert at the foot of the Arabian Peninsula, that western wedge of land that glared across the narrow straits into the shoulder of Africa and guarded the southern entrance to the Red Sea. It was a land as old as the Old Testament, the ancient kingdom of Sheba where frankincense and myrrh had been cultivated, a desolate sprawl of ochre red desert and blistering blue skies that led inland into the Rub Al Khali, that great burning nothingness the Arabs euphemistically named the Empty Quarter.

A few years back it had been two separate states, divided into north and south. That's when Conrad Fung had first dealt with Ibrahim al-Ghashmi, moving goods through the southern port of Aden when Ghashmi had commanded the garrison there. But now the Yemen was united, its capital here in the northern mountains in the ancient walled citadel of Sana.

Ghashmi had received advance notice of the arrival but had no idea of the reason. He obviously presumed it concerned the management of his 'external investments'. Why else would Edgar Aurelius be flying in? When he learnt the true reason, God only knew what his reaction would be.

There was a government official waiting for Aurelius on the tarmac, a man sent by Ghashmi. They did not drive into the city but instead headed north, deeper into the mountains, taking stone bridges over the wadis, driving past turbaned nomads tending their flocks.

Ghashmi kept a home up here, a place on the edge of civilisation in this awesome wasteland where he could hunt

179

with his hawks in the traditional way. Ghashmi was a soldier, a stern traditionalist, a man who believed in stoning for adultery and the taking of a hand for theft. He was a devout Muslim, a man of the desert. But he was also avaricious; he craved wealth and he craved power. It was a schizophrenia that warped his personality and it was that aspect of the man Aurelius feared the most.

Aurelius had expected a home of bricks and mortar, he had expected gardens and date palms. Instead, in the early evening, they came across a bleak set of bedouin tents close to a stony well.

Ghashmi was waiting at the entrance to the central tent dressed in olive-drab military fatigues. He was not a large man. But he was cut and chiselled by the desert in a way that gave him a charisma as hard as granite. Every feature was distinct, the hooked nose, the slashes of age in his cheeks, the jut of the jaw, the black line of his moustache. There was nothing soft about him, not an ounce of fat, everything seemed to consist of muscle: flesh, mind and will.

Ghashmi came forward to meet him, shaking his hand in genuine friendship, Aurelius wondered how long that would last. 'Welcome my friend, welcome. I hope your journey was not too long. Come, you must rest. We'll eat a little and talk. Then tomorrow, if you wish, we'll hunt together. How does that sound?' His smile had the radio-active energy of a CAT scan.

The tent was woven from the hair of black goats and smelt of it too. Inside, oriental rugs and cushions covered the floor. A basin was brought and a brass pot filled with water so that Aurelius could wash his hands. Then they lounged on cushions. A bolster had been brought for Aurelius, a small concession to the physical disability of his hunched back, but still he found it incredibly uncomfortable. Ghashmi of course flourished in such spartan surroundings.

Coffee was served in tiny porcelain cups: black and sweet made in the Turkish style. While they drank, the conversation was kept to matters of no consequence, the world, the

weather, hunting. It was only when the food was brought –
a wholewheat crust on which rice was spread and then
boiled lamb, head, bones and all – that Ghashmi turned to
matters of more immediate concern.

Using his right hand – the left never touched food –
Ghashmi took a moist ball of rice and lamb. 'I was alarmed
to hear of Conrad's arrest,' he said. 'How is he holding up?
With fortitude I hope. But then it can only be a temporary
setback. For politicians like myself and international finan-
ciers too, jail is an occupational hazard.' He laughed,
pleased with his joke. Aurelius laughed with him but it was
as thin as water. 'So what brings you to Yemen this time,
Edgar? Your message sounded so foreboding. Urgent
matter to discuss, in person only – don't tell me we're about
to be invaded?' And he laughed again.

Aurelius steeled himself. 'I have been sent by Conrad on a
confidential basis to ask a great personal favour, Minister.'

Ghashmi's eyes narrowed but he remained smiling. 'If it
is within my powers, then of course.'

'You must have read of these absurd accusations against
him, making him out to be a terrorist, in league with the
Japanese Red Army or something equally asinine.'

'He denies these accusations?'

'Vehemently.'

'Then why doesn't he fly back to Hong Kong? He is
Chinese, they are Chinese. Justice will prevail. Isn't that the
shortest route to the end?'

'Why doesn't he go back? Because there is a conspiracy
against him, Minister. Yes, that's the truth of it, a web of
lies fashioned by the Hong Kong Police. They have
managed to extract false confessions out of a couple of embittered malcontents and they form the case against him. It's
nothing more than that.'

'But what can I do? If you wish, I can speak to the British
Ambassador in Sana expressing concern. But apart from
that . . .'

'Thank you, Minister. While your concern will be much
appreciated, I doubt what practical good it will do. The
Governor of Hong Kong will despatch some insipid

181

diplomatic note assuring you that everything is being done according to the rules of British justice, and everything will go on as before. No, I'm afraid Conrad realises that there is only one way to survive. He must find a good friend, a friend who can help him,' Aurelius searched desperately for the right words. 'As you know, Minister, the Vienna Convention ensures that a person who has diplomatic status can never be the subject of extradition proceedings.'

Ghashmi's brow furrowed with suspicion. 'Yes,' he said with menacing softness, 'go on . . .'

'Conrad is not at this moment a diplomat but if he could just secure—'

Ghashmi cut him short. 'Diplomatic immunity, is that Conrad's way out? Is he seeking some kind of diplomatic appointment?'

'Yes, Minister, an appointment.'

'Who does he wish to give him this appointment?'

'Conrad had been a good friend to you, Minister.'

'He wants it from the Yemen?'

'If a way could possibly be found . . .'

There was an abrupt, stunned silence. Ghashmi stared at Aurelius, a look of furious incredulity in his eyes. 'From the Yemen?' he repeated. 'No, no . . .' Then suddenly, like a man who has belatedly caught on to a joke, he burst out laughing. 'You cannot be serious. Conrad has as much connection to the Yemen as a Siberian fur trapper! He is not a citizen, he is not Arab, Muslim, nothing!'

'I can accept that, at first appearance, it may seem unusual, Minister. But ways can be found. You could perhaps appoint him as an ambassador-at-large to represent the Yemen's economic interests. There is precedent for such a course.'

'No, no, I am sorry, it is impossible.' Ghashmi was still laughing. 'I owe Conrad a great deal. But I cannot possibly help him, not in the way you suggest. Apart from anything, the Americans must first accept his diplomatic credentials. It is not automatic.'

'The Americans would never doubt your word, Minister, be assured of that.'

'Never doubt my word? Of course not, they would think it was a joke! How can I make a man who is sitting in jail be an ambassador from the Republic of Yemen? You must admit, Edgar, it is preposterous.'

'If the appointment was backdated to a time before Conrad's arrest, that would deal with the problem.'

Ghashmi glared at him, jaw hard set, any vestige of humour gone. 'Are you asking me – are you asking the Yemen – to deceive the United States Government?'

'Making an appointment retroactive is not necessarily a deceit,' argued Aurelius, attempting to push home the twisted logic. 'Far from it, Minister. It is often done.'

'Openly, yes, openly!'

'I agree, certain matters will have to be left unsaid but that is all. No great harm caused. In matters of state, Minister—'

'Matters of state! How will I explain such a ludicrous appointment to my Government? Tell me that.'

'For trade benefits, Minister, for trade.'

'No Edgar, I will not hear any more of this. It is outrageous! You do me dishonour, you do yourself dishonour.'

Aurelius took a deep breath. He had gone too far to pull back. 'Conrad is in the most desperate situation, Minister. Can you imagine what it is like to be an innocent man in his predicament?'

'Innocent? Come, Edgar, you're talking to me, Ibrahim al-Ghashmi. I know the man!'

Aurelius slogged on. 'Innocent or not, men in such situations think of only one thing – survival. They have just one loyalty – to themselves. Conrad cherishes your friendship Minister but if he feels he has been deserted in his hour of need . . .'

Ghashmi's voice went suddenly very soft. 'What are you trying to say?'

Aurelius was careful with his words. 'As you know, Conrad possesses certain information.'

'Yes, information about my personal affairs, my external assets. Are you saying he would use that information against me? Is that what you are saying?'

183

'Conrad is under great pressure, Minister, he is a drowning man. You and I can talk reason but at the moment you cannot talk reason to him.'

Ghashmi glared at him, speechless for a moment, then he hissed. 'This is blackmail. That is why you have come here, to blackmail me.'

'No, not blackmail – a bargain to our mutual benefit, no more than that,' said Aurelius, trying desperately to win back the initiative. 'Try and see reason, Minister. One appointment, that is all – for trade. It is done all the time.'

Ghashmi whirled on him. 'And if I don't?'

And Aurelius committed himself. He had no other choice. 'Then the volcano bursts,' he said with an air of finality, 'and only God knows who drowns in the lava.'

He had hoped that the words, allegorical and yet blunt as a hammer, would have made Ghashmi at least sit back and think. But the reaction was just the opposite – a cataclysmic eruption as fierce as the volcano he had alluded to.

'I knew it, you're common thieves, the two of you, just gangsters!' shouted Ghashmi, jumping to his feet. 'But this is not America, this is the Yemen, this is my country! Nobody threatens me like this, not in my own country – nobody!'

Aurelius watched him barge out of the tent in a fury, hoping to God he was going to storm off into the desert until his rage was spent. He heard him shouting outside in Arabic, unintelligible words, praying that he was calling for his horse and falcon or whatever it was he used for hunting up here. Ghashmi was as shrewd as a fox, he knew what he was up against. All he needed was time to cool down. The seconds passed. He heard no more. He began to relax.

They burst into the tent so fast he barely had time to react before they grabbed him. They were soldiers. God, where had they come from? They kicked him when he was still down. He tried to roll away and they were screaming and kicking and pulling him at the same time, dragging him out of the tent into the stones and the dust outside. One of them punched him in the face and Aurelius felt the cartilage of his nose give under the blow, blood spraying from his nostrils.

They were dragging him towards an open jeep, dragging him through stones that tore at his clothing. His glasses were lost, trampled underfoot, making him half-blind. Everything was a blur. They yanked him up and into the back of the jeep, somebody tied his feet and his hands. Oh Christ, what was happening? What were they going to do to him? Where was Ghashmi? Aurelius called out his name, spitting out his own blood. 'For God's sake, please, I didn't come to threaten you!'

But Ghashmi was beyond reason, beyond listening. Somewhere out there in the blur that now made up the world, Aurelius heard his voice. 'Now you will see how we deal with gangsters in the Yemen,' Ghashmi shouted. 'Now you will see!'

The time had come for the preparation of Wong Kam-kiu's extradition affidavit. In the late afternoon, after Wong had slept, Dave sat down with him in the apartment he occupied on the twentieth floor of Benevolence Villas and began patiently to try and coax the information out of him. The psychiatrist had advised him to take it slowly, day by day. Wong was suffering from manic depression, he was too heavily drugged, too deeply introspective, to concentrate for any longer period of time in the sequential, logical manner Dave demanded.

But a beginning was made and Wong, in his own tearful, torpid way, responded. Over the past couple of weeks, a tentative trust had grown between them. It was nothing like the jovial camaraderie that had developed between Dave and Tselentis, but it was an understanding at least, some kind of reaching out. In his own pitiful way, Wong Kam-kiu summed it up. 'Our sons are linked in heaven,' he said. 'We are linked on earth.'

Dave could only shake his head. What did the man have left in life? Nothing. He had killed his wife and child. He had destroyed himself.

Around five-thirty, when the first session finished, he was happy to get away, to escape across the lobby to 20B and a little of Tselentis's rough-edged sanity.

Tselentis was lying on the sofa in a dressing gown and socks leafing through a pile of old *Playboys*. 'If you don't get me access to a woman soon, I'm going to go blind – and not just from reading these magazines,' he said with an unshaven grin. 'How did it go in there?'

'At a snail's pace but I didn't expect much more. I can't seem to get him past the compulsion to dwell on the death of his wife and son all the time. He must have told me half a dozen times how he suffocated them both.'

'What motivates a man to kill his own family like that? That's what I want to know. Jesus, can you imagine?'

Dave went through to the kitchen, taking two cans of beer from the fridge. 'I suppose the pressures just build,' he said ruefully. 'I don't think any of us know how we're going to react until the spring actually snaps.'

'But your wife, your only child, suffocating them like that, one after the other, shit – I mean, you might as well tear your own heart out.'

Dave cracked open the first beer, handing it to Tselentis. 'Family obviously means a lot to you.'

'Family? Of course. Family is *everything*. In the end what else have you got?' Tselentis's standard glibness had been replaced by a sudden, surprising conviction. 'Ask any Greek, any Jew, ask any Cantonese or Italian. Without family you're nowhere, just floating in a vacuum.' Then he laughed. 'Not that I'm an expert. I mean, Christ, I screwed up on my own marriage pretty bad. Don't let that happen to you. You've got a great wife from what you tell me, going places too. Hang on to her.'

'I intend to,' said Dave, smiling.

'Is she still working every hour God gave her?'

'I'm afraid so. Up to her neck in production schedules. How long did your own marriage last?'

'Five years – to the best woman in the world. Of course I didn't realise it at the time. My fault. Spent my life travelling, hustling, being the big deal. Melina was an old-fashioned Greek girl. She never liked Hong Kong, too brash for her. In the end she couldn't take it any more. It brought me to my senses pretty quick but by then it was too late –

186

the story of my life up to this moment. We still see each other though. That's the crazy thing . . . now that we're divorced we've got the perfect relationship. She's back home on the island of Kos. I see her a couple of times a year. We confide in each other, never argue. Even the sex is better!'

Dave sat down at the table. 'What do you think you'll do when all this is over? Stay in Hong Kong?'

'Hong Kong? You've got to be crazy!'

'Where then?'

'One thing about us Greeks, we're the world's greatest emigrants. I've got family most places. The US, Australia, Africa, apparently even a few second cousins down in Papua New Guinea doing a great business in shrunken heads. Don't worry, I'll find somewhere.'

'What about Kos, where your ex-wife lives?'

'Serving dolmades and ouzo to German tourists, getting fat in the sun . . . sure, why not?' said Tselentis. 'When we got divorced, I bought Melina a restaurant there, just back from Marmari Beach. Taverna Melina, she calls it. A gold mine too. It might not be Madison Avenue but there's a lot worse ways to live. I'll tell you one thing, whichever way this thing with Fung works out, I've had a bellyfull of city-hopping, laundering dough and bribing government officials. Fancy hotels, whores on tap – as a life style it sucks.'

Dave placed a sheath of papers on the table. 'This is the final draft of your extradition affidavit.'

'Oh Christ, not that thing again.'

'Read it overnight, double-check for factual errors and I'll collect it in the morning.'

Tselentis walked with him to the door. 'How's my mother?' he asked.

'She's doing fine. Getting stronger every day. I visit her most mornings.'

'I'd like to see her.'

'We've spoken about that before. Right at the moment there's the security problem. You know it's difficult.'

'One ride to the hospital, that's all I'm asking. She's my mother, she's sick, I want a chance to be with her a little

187

'while, that's all. How difficult can it be?'

'Okay, I'll see what I can do.'

'Thanks,' said Tselentis. 'It means a lot to me.'

Charity Choi, dressed in her favourite *cheong sam*, the scarlet satin one with lotus flowers embroidered in gold, was enjoying herself that night. Invariably, because she spoke a few words of the language, she was allocated tables of Japanese businessmen, phalanxes of incomprehensible chauvinists who spent the night leering at her between bouts of Chivas Regal. But this man, Ah Shing, was different. He was Cantonese, which meant they shared a common language and, in a rough kind of way, she found him attractive.

The Jade Palace in Tsim Sha Tsui where Charity worked employed over one hundred hostesses: Chinese, Thai, Korean, Filipino. Their job was to be alluring and attentive and, as their manager put it, to ensure the customers spent enough to make their gold cards melt. Whether at the end of the night the hostesses slept with the customers was absolutely a matter for them. Charity invariably did.

That was why, around one in the morning, when Ah Shing suggested they spend the night together and did not try to bargain down the price, she readily agreed. She took him to an apartment house near the nightclub where rooms were rented by the hour. Her favourite room had a heart-shaped bed and red satin sheets, even a telephone that resembled pouting lips. Condoms were available at reception and there were blue movies on the television twenty-four hours a day.

Ah Shing stripped naked. There were tattoos on his chest, sure signs of a Triad background. He lit himself a cigarette, lay on the bed and watched Charity as she began to undress. 'I heard that a couple of weeks back you went with a customer who was picked up by the cops, something to do with the Kai Tak bombing.'

'Who told you that?'

'It's no secret. You've told enough people yourself, all the girls at the club.'

'Only my closest friends.'

'So your closest friends told other friends.'

Charity gave a dismissive shrug. Telling her companions was one thing, even if word did get around, but confiding in a customer was another. There was a thing called ethics. 'Some nights are better than others,' she said.

'This customer was assaulted by the cops, isn't that right? That's what you told your friends, that there was some kind of fight.'

'I don't remember. Why are you asking all these questions?' She smiled at him, part irritation, part enticement. 'Is that how you like to do it, asking questions?'

Ah Shing sucked deep on his cigarette. 'I know people who would be willing to pay a lot for the right story.'

'You're a reporter, is that it?'

'Do I look like a reporter?'

'Then what's this all about?'

'It's to help somebody.'

Charity took off her bra, admiring her breasts in the mirror; firm and high set, the nipples pink like a baby's cheeks. She had been looking forward to Ah Shing. He was strong and slim, no fat on his belly. But now it was all turning sour. 'To help who?' she asked.

'Somebody who is in trouble with the law.'

'Oh no, forget it. I don't want to get involved with the law.'

'I'm talking about big money.'

That made Charity stop and think. 'How much money?'

'If the story is good, one hundred thousand.'

One hundred thousand! For a girl raised in a squatter camp it was a fortune. 'Will I have to appear in court, give evidence, things like that? I don't want to appear in court.'

'Just swear an affidavit.'

'That's all, are you sure?'

'Your signature, that's all we need.'

'When do I get paid?'

'The minute you sign the paper.'

Charity smiled, her almond eyes full of satisfaction. 'You're right,' she said, 'I did see it all. I thought this

189

European cop was going to kill the poor guy.'

For five days they had kept him in the cell on the condemned row. In the evening, twice, Aurelius had heard them testing the gallows in the chamber next door, the terrifying boom of the trap doors followed by the sudden dumping sound of the sack straining at rope's end. Two mornings Aurelius had heard them taking the condemned man to be hanged. One, a Pakistani, a migrant, wailed and whimpered all the way.

Why in God's name were they keeping him here? Nobody had come to see him, to question him, nothing. He had been left in total isolation. And why this place, why the condemned row? Was it some kind of insane torture or was it worse, an indication of Ghashmi's intent?

The food had been inedible – congealed rice, little else – the heat beyond endurance and precious little water. Without his glasses Aurelius was nearly blind. Only the guards had spoken to him, one from Aden had a smattering of English. The guard had told him he was known as Camelback because of his deformity and the rumour was that he was going to die. 'Why?' Aurelius had demanded. There must be some reason, some judgement of a court! But the guard had no reason. The hanging would be quick, he had said, it never failed, as if that should console him.

Aurelius had barely slept, all he could manage were fitful dozes. Dear God, he kept praying, let them not decide to kill me, not yet, not yet. . . .

It was a little before dawn, the darkest, bleakest hour. The night before they had tested the gallows for the third time. The echoing boom of the trap doors rang in his muddled dreams. Aurelius was so lost in his exhausted misery that he did not hear the cell door open or the guards enter. He was aware of nothing until they seized his arms and dragged him to his feet. They pinioned his arms behind him with leather straps. Oh God, he thought, execution straps! 'What are you doing?' he kept asking. 'I must speak to Ghashmi, to General Ghashmi. You're making a terrible mistake. Please!' But nobody spoke English, nobody replied. Two soldiers appeared in the doorway of the cell, both wearing keffiyehs, the headdress of the bedouin arabs. They took his arms and led him out. Oh God, they were going to hang him. Oh no, no, how could this be happening to him? He began to sob.

But instead of taking him to the left, the soldiers swung him to the right, away from the gallows room. In his relief, Aurelius's legs buckled under him and they had to drag him along the passage. 'Where are you taking me? What are you doing with me?' Aurelius asked. But still there was no answer.

They took him outside into the cool, dry air of the desert highlands and there was an army truck waiting in the prison courtyard. A sergeant was waiting by the truck, more soldiers were seated in the back. And suddenly there was a new fear. Why all these soldiers, why at this time, at the break of dawn?

'Where are you taking me? I must speak to General Ghashmi. It's vital I speak to him,' said Aurelius.

The sergeant spoke English in a malicious singsong accent. 'Maybe we drive you into desert and arrange accident. What do you say?' He smiled wickedly. 'Stupid American businessman gets lost. Too bad. US Embassy writes letters. We send men looking. Find nothing. Happens all the time. Goatherd finds your bones in twenty years.'

'I must speak to the general, you don't understand!' Aurelius repeated, begging now.

But the sergeant motioned to the other guards and, before Aurelius could say more, they hauled him up into the back of the truck. Four men sat in the back with him, all armed with rifles. Aurelius pleaded with them, he had to speak to Ibrahim al-Ghashmi but they stared at him blankly. None spoke English, none of them understood a word he said.

The truck passed through the prison gates. It turned on to a dirt road and began to wind its way through the eastern section of Sana, the old city. They were driving through a biblical landscape . . . Sodom or Gomorrah . . . mud walls and narrow alleys, ancient flat-roofed buildings, donkeys

191

loaded down and women peering from behind the black veils of their yashmaks. Aurelius saw it all pass in a half-blind blur. Then they hit the open road, the road into the mountains.

None of the guards spoke. They did not joke with each other, none even looked at him. They sat as grim-faced as executioners. Aurelius couldn't believe this was happening. It was too fantastic, too unreal.

For thirty minutes they drove along the empty road until, without warning, the truck pulled off and rattled down into a rock-strewn depression. Aurelius let out a small dry gasp of shock. He heard the cab door open and the sergeant got out. He said something in Arabic and two of the guards jumped down from the back of the truck. Neither of them looked at him.

Despairingly, Aurelius looked around. He could see no sign of habitation, just a blurred, ochre-brown wilderness that stretched out into eternity, a vast forbidding graveyard where he would never be found. Hanging him in the prison made no sense but dumping him with a bullet in his head, leaving him here for the dogs . . .

He was so swamped with fear he felt as if he had been drugged. He didn't think he could walk a step. His legs were jelly. They would have to carry him to his death.

Incongruously, he heard one of the guards laugh. And another sound followed, a hissing that was at once familiar and strange. Aurelius sat there, breathless. Then, through the numbing paralysis of his fear, he realised what it was and, half hysterical with relief, slumped back. He began to giggle like a fool. He thought they had stopped to execute him and all it had been was a piss at the side of the road!

Ten minutes later the airport came into view. The truck drew up near one of the hangars. Two officials were waiting. Aurelius was helped down from the truck and his leather pinions unstrapped. The sergeant smiled at him, the same mocking malice in his eyes. 'Goodbye Yankee man. Next time shoot you, huh, next time.'

The two officials escorted Aurelius into a nearby building. He followed them down a long passage to a changing area where there was a toilet and a shower. His clothes – the ones that had been taken from him at the prison – were hanging on hooks, freshly ironed. One of the officials handed him his wallet and mercifully his glasses. 'You may shower and change,' said the one official. 'Do not take too long. You are being deported. Your flight leaves for Paris in an hour.'

Aurelius stepped into the shower like a man in a dream. The sting of the cold water on his body was the most beautiful sensation he could remember. The indescribable filth of the past five days, the dried blood from his broken nose, the ingrained dirt and the dust, all of it was washed away and he started to feel alive again.

When he was dressed, the officials took him out on to the tarmac. The sun, still low in the sky, sat like a golden ball on the brown-burnt horizon. He was handed his passport and a boarding card. The Air France Boeing 747 stood in front of him. Aurelius climbed the steps like an old man but with every step his heart was singing.

At the entrance to the aircraft a stewardess smiled at him. *'Bonjour monsieur, bienvenu.'* And, with one small step, the metamorphosis was complete. Prison was behind him, the terrible sound of the trap door was gone. He sat in a deep-cushioned chair in the first-class cabin and was offered champagne.

'Monsieur Aurelius?'

Aurelius looked up, eyes wide, terrified that, in some hideous twist of fate, Ghashmi had arranged for him to be dragged back off the plane. But it was only one of the stewards.

'I was asked to give you this by an official in the airport,' said the steward. 'I am sure you must know what it is.'

Aurelius sat for a time, staring down at the large white envelope. His fingers trembled, he was afraid to open it. Only when the aircraft lifted into the air did he summon the courage to tear it open and remove the contents. The top document was in Arabic but there was an English translation beneath which bore the full seal of the Republic of Yemen and it began, printed black and bold—

193

TO ALL TO WHOM THESE PRESENTS SHALL COME,
GREETINGS.

Know ye, that reposing special trust and confidence in both the ability and integrity of Fung Chi-man, also called Conrad Fung, I, Ibrahim al-Ghashmi, Member of the Presidential Council of the Republic of Yemen and Minister of State for External Affairs, have invested in the said Conrad Fung full power and authority as Economic Consultant and Ambassador-at-large . . .

Ibrahim al-Ghashmi stepped out of his official car, a black Mercedes, and stood watching the Boeing as it climbed into the morning sky. It banked, the sun glinting off its huge silver wings, and headed west out towards the Red Sea. If all had gone according to plan, Aurelius would have been dead by now, buried in a wadi somewhere. Aurelius was a lucky man. So perhaps were they both.

Yesterday evening, he had received a letter which bore the endorsement: 'For the exclusive attention of the Minister.' It had been despatched from New York and it had read—

Minister,

This letter is written prior to my departure to your country. I know that my request concerning diplomatic appointment may provoke a hostile reaction and, in the event of that reaction being extreme, I have had to take certain precautions.

Should I not contact my office by telephone within four days, I have instructed this letter to be despatched to you by courier. Forty-eight hours thereafter, should my office still not be assured of my safety, dossiers of material are to be sent to each member of the Presidential Council, to the commanders of the Yemen armed forces and to the editors of the two principal newspapers in your country. Further dossiers are to be sent to leading newspapers in New York, Cairo, Riyadh and Hong Kong.

The dossiers will detail how you and Conrad Fung first dealt in heroin shipments to Europe carried by Filipino seamen through the port of Aden, and how, since that time, we have moved several million dollars of corruptly obtained funds for you, laundering them through off-shore companies and investing them in European real estate. As you are aware, in a strict Islamic country, drug trafficking and corruption are both punishable by death.

I appreciate this is a doomsday option. In destroying you, we destroy ourselves. But with Conrad Fung facing multiple murder charges and myself either dead or on the edge of eternity, it is not a difficult option to take. If I am still alive, you can defuse the bomb or you can destroy us all. It is your choice.

Edgar Aurelius.

Ghashmi had read the letter twice, burnt it and then taken immediate steps, first to notify Aurelius's New York office that he was returning and then to implement Conrad Fung's appointment as an ambassador-at-large.

Fung and Aurelius had betrayed their trust. They deserved nothing. It was a defeat and a bad one. But the affair was not ended yet. He could bide his time. There was an English saying that Ibrahim al-Ghashmi found particularly appropriate – revenge is a dish best eaten cold.

Edgar Aurelius landed back in Miami late the following day, taking a limousine service to the Inter-Continental on Chopin Plaza. He had stayed there since the day of Fung's arrest, using his room as part bedroom, part office. But, when he entered the lobby, not a soul at reception recognised him. His nose had been broken, he had shed ten pounds in weight, gone distinctly greyer, was haggard and tired. He had aged ten years in a matter of days. But he was alive, that was all that mattered to him. The air had never smelt sweeter.

The following morning, rested, before he saw Conrad Fung, he drove up to Palm Beach, that little pocket of poverty on the east coast of Florida. His destination was the law offices of Zachary Hedgewood at 1400 Centrepark Boulevard. It was a fine day, the sky a dazzling cloudless blue, perfect for the month of June, the kind of day that made Florida the retirement capital of North America.

As he took the elevator up to suite 808, Aurelius couldn't hold down a feeling of tense anticipation. After the hell he had experienced, the tide at last was turning. That morning a ten-page fax from Hong Kong had been delivered to his room at the hotel. The covering note was from Hector Chan and accompanying it was the copy of an affidavit which began with the words: 'My name is Charity Choi. By profession I am a hostess . . .'

Chapter Fourteen

Pang Wai-ping – Flat Nose, as he was known – had agonised long and hard over his decision. He did not know why he was so worried. Was it instinct, a bad smell about the deal, Fung's shadow over it? Or was he just getting too long in the tooth?

But the amount of merchandise was huge. Twenty-five units to start followed by a shipment of fifty, then two shipments of one hundred units each – a total of two hundred and seventy-five units of top grade Number Four, the finest quality heroin the Golden Triangle produced. Payment in advance for each shipment was agreed, the whole deal was to be completed within six months and, best of all, Khalil Khayat would take the risk of getting the stuff into the States himself.

If prices held steady, Khalil stood to clear fifteen million on the deal. But then he took the greater risk. Pang Wai-ping calculated that his own net profit would be in the region of one million US dollars, the largest single payment of his life.

That much money could not be ignored. The gambler always looked to what he could win, not what he stood to lose and Pang Wai-ping had always been a gambling man. He made the call to Khalil's private number late at night from a room in Kowloon where he had been playing mahjong with friends.

When Khalil answered, recognising Pang's voice, he asked on the turn. 'Have you reached a decision?'

'Yes,' said Pang, 'I can do the deal.'

'Is the price acceptable?'

'Acceptable, yes.'
'What about the first twenty-five units?'
'Stored here in Hong Kong. No problem.'
'The quality?'
'Best quality, top grade. No problem.'
'I must be guaranteed the best,' said Khalil.
'Sure, sure. Quality is A1, guaranteed.'
'Good,' said Khalil. 'So we can begin.'
'Sure,' answered Pang. 'No problem with me.'

It was late afternoon and the sun was low in the sky. But the light it shed was a luminous apricot-gold in colour. It fell through the window on to her scattered sheath of sketches and Hannah stopped, marker in hand, entranced by the effect.

She imagined a young boy, a boy like Danny, all freckles and fringe, playing in a garden on a summer's eve. For a brief moment he was caught in a shaft of sunlight exactly the same as this and his clothes – cottons in sunflower yellow, denims in strong indigo blue – were rendered just as vibrant, just as richly hued as the sketches on her desk. She must tell Joel Grossman, she thought. Oh yes, this was how her summer collection had to be seen, in this glowing sunlight: the perfect distillation of the rich summer colours she had been striving to achieve. In this honey-sweet halo of light they would be just irresistible!

Over the past days, fired with renewed energy, Hannah had run off fifty sketches or more for her summer collection of Danny's Rags. The first sketches had been little more than an outpouring of visual consciousness, pure line and form squared in with bold marker colours; her colours for summer: ochre browns, yellows, rich full-bloomed reds and lush riverside greens. She had worked furiously, refusing to be interrupted, locked in her office for stretches of eight or nine hours, barely pausing to think, letting her instincts run until all the creative sap was gone, until it was all there, laid out before her in a chaos of line and colour and scribbled notes.

Scott, as always had been the first to see them and his

reaction had been ecstatic. They were brilliant, he had said, as good as anything in the original spring collection. He loved the colours, adored the cheeky innovations. And yet they were so wonderfully knockabout and tough, perfect clothes for climbing trees, boating on a lake or queueing at Disneyworld. How did she do it? How did the designs pour out of her like this?

Hannah had said nothing but inwardly she had been ecstatic too. The inspiration hadn't dried up, that's all that mattered. Danny's spirit, as impish as ever, was still skipping by her side.

The rough sketches were only the beginning, of course. Scott would spend weeks on the spec sheets, the precise drawings that would detail every aspect of each design, handing them to the pattern maker to cut out the first fits or muslins. When the muslins were ready, the painstaking work of fittings would begin. Every muslin would have to be fitted on to a live model, a young boy or girl supplied by a local Hong Kong modelling agency.

Hannah seemed to spend half her life doing fittings, trying to make the reality of cloth fit her original concept, dictating to Scott at five hundred words a minute – 'Make the neck smaller, I want more give around the shoulders' – while he frantically scribbled the corrections that would be incorporated into the final garments.

Hannah was scheduled to fly back to the States in a couple of weeks. She disliked business travel: the 'glamour' of jet lag, the 'sex appeal' of staggering off flights with swollen ankles. But there were sales promotions to attend, more interviews to give, and Joel Grossman said her presence was essential. Before she flew out, however, the summer collection would be well on its way.

Hannah started on a new sketch for Joel Grossman, one of the larger, finished ones that would be used for promotions. She had been working since ten that morning without a break, fuelled with black coffee and croissants. The telephone on her desk began to ring but she ignored it. Right now, answering calls was Scott's chore.

She heard him take the call in his cubbyhole of an office

199

next to hers. There was some brief mumbled conversation then Scott shouted through. 'Hannah, it's for you.'

'Take a message. I'm working.'

'It's Sam Ephram on the line!'

'Sam? Oh, okay, of course. Put him through.'

Hannah heard his voice, the distinct soft timbre in each word. 'Where are you?' she asked, laughing with excitement. 'You sound so close.'

'I am close.'

'Where?'

'Here in Hong Kong.'

'That's fantastic! But why didn't you give me some warning?'

'I wanted to surprise you,' said Ephram in that mellow, deliciously offhand way he used as a counterpoint to her excitement.

'Where are you staying?'

'The Regent.'

'That's just five minutes away!'

'Then why don't you come over?' he said. 'There are things we need to talk about.'

'I'm on my way now.'

'I'm in one of the suites on the fifth floor, room 521. Come directly up. I'll have an aperitif waiting.' He paused a moment then he said very softly. 'I missed you.'

Hannah got up from her desk. She was delighted Sam was here in Hong Kong, over the moon. But she was suddenly very nervous too. Because now she had to wrestle with it all over again, the impossible attraction she felt for him, the unbearable guilt she felt for Dave.

His room at the Regent Hotel, like all the de luxe suites, had a view out over the harbour. The suite was quietly luxurious, cool and elegant. The Regent, many said, was the best hotel in the world.

Sam Ephram met her at the door. He was dressed in a white towelling robe. 'Forgive me,' he said, 'I have only just got out of the shower.' He kissed her gently, almost hesitantly, on the lips and Hannah could smell the warm masculinity of him. It was crazy but her head was already spinning.

200

He had vintage champagne waiting and the best black Beluga caviar. Everything he did, he did with style. He poured the champagne into two tall, tulip-shaped glasses, handing her one. 'To life,' he said, using the Hebrew toast. The champagne was pale lemon in colour with a wonderful fruity bouquet. Hannah sipped it and the bubbles danced on her tongue. What was it that made just being with him so hopelessly seductive?

He gazed very solemnly into her eyes. 'You look tired,' he said.

'The summer collection.' she explained.

'Ah yes.' And in the smile there was a total understanding. 'It must be a great stress working so hard on something new,' he said, 'worrying all the time that you will not be able to repeat the success of the first occasion, to find the same magic.'

Hannah smiled. 'The worry – for the time being at least – is over. I finished the sketches today.'

'What do you think of them?' he asked. 'Are they good?'

'Good?' She gave a nervous laugh. 'I don't know! I'm still too close to them. Scott likes them though, yes – and he's my best judge.'

He smiled at her, that same tanned, courteous smile that had so flustered her the first time they met. 'That's all I needed to hear,' he said. 'Now I can tell Joel Grossman that the summer collection will be a wonderful success.' He refilled her glass. 'But before you forget the spring collection entirely, we are going to need many more samples. I think Joel faxed you, yes? Your collection has aroused great interest in Britain, in France and Germany and even the Russians would love to sell it – provided they can raise the hard currency of course!' He laughed. 'This is only the beginning, Hannah, I promise you, still the dawn rising.'

Hannah looked up at him, at his square-cut tanned face, at his black hair, cut short, frosted white at the tips and running to a devil's point at the centre of his forehead. It was a strong face, beguiling, the perfect good looks for her genie of the lamp. Where would she be without him?

Sam Ephram put down his champagne glass and came very close to her. 'But I must be truthful and say that I did not come to Hong Kong just for business. I missed you very much. You have been in my thoughts all the time.'

'No,' she said, her voice just a whisper, 'please Sam, this is wrong.'

'Why is it wrong? It was not wrong last time. It was wonderful, wonderful for us both.'

'What about Dave? Every time I'm with you, I'm betraying him.'

'Dave need never know. This is your secret and mine, locked in our hearts.' He slipped one arm around her waist and reached down to kiss the softest, most sensitive part of her neck. 'This is our own special, very secret world.'

Hannah gave a delicious shudder. Oh God, she thought, how do I resist him? She had resolved a thousand times that their affair must end, that it was impossible for her to love two men at once. But standing there in his arms, her head spinning from the champagne, overwhelmed by everything he was and everything he stood for, her resolve evaporated. Whatever he wished, whatever he asked for, she would do.

He led her through to the bedroom. Somewhere back in the lounge, Hannah realised, she must have kicked off her shoes. The carpet felt thick and luxurious beneath her feet. The room was cool and hushed. It looked on to the harbour which was bathed in the colours of sunset. The waters were black and maroon and silver.

Sam Ephram brought her close again, kissing her neck, biting into her shoulder so that she groaned out loud with the sharp pleasure of it. His fingers peeled the blouse from her shoulders, dropping it on to the carpet. Deftly, he undid her bra and let that too slip down to the carpet. He gazed down at her naked breasts, small, plump, perfect, her nipples dark as the water outside. 'You are so petite, so beautiful,' he whispered. He leant down to kiss her breasts and Hannah pushed herself into him, arching her back. Every nerve in her body seemed suddenly to be alive. Her fingers fumbled to undo the belt of his bath robe. The robe fell open and she felt the hard, thrust of him, so smooth, like sun-kissed marble.

He stripped her then – quick, brusque movements – and,

as her dress fell around her ankles, he ran his hands over her soft, flat stomach, gasping at the perfect roundness of her hips. He eased off her panties and he knelt. She was already aching for him but when she felt his tongue, the sensation was so incredible that she could barely stand. Her legs were shivering. 'Please, please,' she uttered in an urgent whisper. 'Please, oh yes, take me on to the bed now.'

He gave his assent with a deep-throated murmur, lifting her into his arms. He carried her as a bridegroom would carry a bride across the threshold and laid her on the bed. He let the bathrobe fall from his shoulders and then he was upon her, so heavy, so hard, yet his skin as smooth as silk. Deep down in the subjugated cells of her conscience Hannah knew she shouldn't be doing this, that it could only lead to disaster. But it was too late now, too late to stop and, oh God, she wanted him more than anything in the world.

When it was done, when they were both satiated, he went through to the lounge, bringing back the champagne and caviar. The lovemaking had heightened their appetites and they sat together, naked still, drinking the champagne and devouring the salted roe.

Hannah was dazzled by Sam Ephram, she made no pretence about it, by everything he was and everything he stood for. The physical side was breathtaking but that was just part of the inexplicable fascination. Sam was the entrepreneurial power behind her success, the financial bedrock that ensured it would last. The guilt she felt when she thought of Dave tore her apart. Dave could never be replaced. If Sam Ephram had represented nothing more than sexual desire, she would have been able to walk away from him without a qualm. But he wasn't simply a lover, he was more than that.

When her collections began to sell in the shops, Danny's memory would be enshrined . . . enshrined in the delight of children wearing his clothes, in their laughter when they played in them, in their tears when they fell and cried. Danny would live in all those incalculable moments, and without Sam Ephram it would never have happened. Sam was her lifeline to Danny, it was as simple as that. How could she cast him aside? How could she turn her back on the spirit of her son?

Later, after they had showered together, laughing and kissing under the hot water, Sam Ephram removed a thick wadge of papers from his briefcase and tossed them on to the rosewood desk next to the bed. 'A little light reading for you,' he said.

Hannah grimaced. 'What are they?'

'The draft legal papers for our corporate partnership.'

'So much?'

'I'm afraid so, the central agreement, royalty contracts, incorporation documents – two hundred pages of it.'

Hannah laughed. 'You don't seriously expect me to read all that, do you?'

'It is necessary,' he answered solemnly.

'Two hundred pages of legal documents – can't I take the easy option and just have my fingernails ripped out?'

Sam Ephram laughed.

'Give me an outline,' she said, 'the *Reader's Digest* condensed version.'

Sam Ephram smiled. 'I have structured it so that there are a number of interlocking operating companies. In the event of one failing, the others are not hurt. But they are all effectively owned by a single holding company – Liechtenstein based – called China Girl International. You will hold fifty-one percent of the issued shares. Scott, as you requested, will hold fifteen percent. I have negotiated a deal with Joel Grossman in terms of which he will acquire a nominal four percent and the balance of thirty percent will be in my name.'

Hannah shrugged as she put on her earrings. It seemed perfectly fair to her.

'You will see that there are certain royalty and marketing agreements, effectively agreements between you as an individual and the operating companies,' said Sam Ephram. 'They have been drafted to give you some extra benefit for your creative talents. In financial terms, they should boost your share of profits anywhere between five and seven percent.'

Hannah was satisfied. 'It's what you outlined to me in New York, what we agreed there.'

'Yes it is,' he replied. 'Even so, I want you to have your own lawyers study the papers. Don't worry, we'll capitalise the legal costs as part of the incorporation expenses so the fees won't come out of your own pocket, not directly, that is.'

'Didn't you get Wall Street attorneys to draw up the papers?'

'Of course,' he said with a dry smile. 'The best.'

'Then why double the expenses? I trust you, I trust them. Isn't that good enough?'

'Your trust is what matters to me most,' he said, reaching down to kiss her neck. 'But I don't want any misunderstandings in the future. Trust survives better when it is clearly defined. I'm happy in myself that it is a fair agreement – exactly as we agreed – but that is not good enough. You must have independent advice first, if only to make me happy.'

Hannah smiled at him. 'Very well,' she said, 'To make you happy.'

'Good,' he said in a brisk, businesslike fashion. 'And now, if you're ready, I would like to visit your factory. After all' – and his dark eyes were twinkling – 'I am about to become a part owner.'

For five days, in short spells of half an hour at a time, Dave had been closeted with Wong Kam-kiu attempting slowly and patiently to coax out of him the necessary evidence for his affidavit.

The psychiatrist had warned that it would be like interviewing a zombie and the analogy was apt. Most of the time Wong sat, dull-eyed and baleful, ignoring the questions, lost in his own bleak landscape of depression. All he seemed capable of doing, without a monumental effort, was drinking endless cups of jasmine tea or talking about his wife and son, which he would do in long, tear-filled monologues. There were times when Dave thought he was going to tear his hair out. But slowly, with the mind-blurred endless agony of a Chinese water torture, the affidavit began to take form.

Wong Kam-kiu had never dealt with Conrad Fung, he had never met the man. All his dealings had been with Tselentis. He was unable, therefore, to give direct, damning evidence against Fung.

But Wong's evidence, although not crucial, was still of great worth. Wong was able to give day-to-day details of the Peruvian immigration fraud and, most important of all, to supply the motive for the killing of Geraldo Gomez – that single phone call when Gomez had said he was being recalled and was going to confess everything he knew. That was why Dave had persevered and by six that evening he had a handwritten draft sixteen pages long.

'I'll type out the draft,' he said to Wong in slow, pedantic Cantonese. 'Then it must go to the lawyer who is in charge of Fung's extradition. Once he has said it is okay, I will arrange to take you before a magistrate to sign.'

Wong looked at him. 'Magistrate?'

'We have to send your evidence to America, so your statement has to be on oath, sworn before a magistrate. Do you understand?'

Wong nodded. He looked like a tired, sulphur-faced bloodhound.

'Don't worry,' said Dave, 'it won't be a problem. We'll drive you there and drive you back. You'll meet the magistrate in a private office. You won't be under any pressure. You can take as long as you like. All you have to do is confirm that the contents of the affidavit are true and correct. You can do that can't you?'

Wong nodded again, sipping jasmine tea. 'I understand everything,' he said in a slow, drugged voice. 'I know what to do.'

The telephone in the apartment rang. One of the police guards picked up the receiver. He acknowledged the message and turned to Dave. 'It's our *foki* downstairs in the lobby.'

'What is it?' asked Dave.

'He says that the ambulance for Tselentis has arrived – so he can see his mother.'

★

206

When his mobile telephone rang, Bruce Rexford was reading a novel by the French Author, Albert Camus. In English it was called *The Plague*, a story of personal courage in the face of the futility of life. Bruce Rexford read a great deal of Camus.

It was Fat Kwok on the line. 'An ambulance has driven into the block,' he said.

'Are there any markings on it?'

'It says Adventist Hospital along the side.'

Rexford did not hesitate. 'I'm on my way,' he said.

It took him less than a minute to reach the auto repair shop: down two flights of stairs at a full run, across the street, down an alley and in through the back door of the shop. It was a thick, muggy evening and even in that short space of time he was beginning to sweat.

'Is the ambulance still there?'

'It has backed up against the entrance.'

Kneeling in the corner of the shop, Rexford pulled aside a greasy piece of tarpaulin. A long box lay underneath. He opened it. The rifle he had brought into Hong Kong – now fully assembled – lay inside. It was of Soviet design, a 7.62mm Dragunov sniper's rifle semi-automatic, purpose-designed with an optical telescope, integral rangefinder and infrared sighting for use at night. It carried a magazine of twenty rounds, each one soft-nosed. But just one round would be enough.

Rexford's pulse was racing but he felt very calm, very much in control. He wiped the sheen of sweat off his forehead and stepped towards the open front of the shop.

The instructions he had received in Manila said that if he had to kill just one witness, Tselentis had to be that one. Wong could not identify Fung, Tselentis could; Wong had never dealt direct with Fung while Tselentis had become one of his closest aides. Both witnesses dead would be the optimum result. But Tselentis alone would be enough. Without his evidence, the case could collapse.

Rexford tucked himself down behind the car Fat Kwok was pretending to repair and looked across Po Man Street towards Benevolence Villas. As Kwok had said, the ambulance had backed right up to the entrance of the building. But it had not completely blocked it. There was still a space, four foot or so in width, to enable people to walk in and out, and that gave him a small but critically important view into the lobby – his killing ground.

The sky was quickly darkening, visibility was poor, but the lights were shining in the lobby making it as bright as a floodlit tennis court.

Rexford looked back at the ambulance. He could just make out the wording down the side. Tselentis's mother was in the Adventist Hospital recovering from a major heart attack. The ambulance had to be there to take Tselentis to her. For some people – people like Tselentis – the desire to see family was overwhelming.

Rexford tucked the Dragunov into his shoulder, focusing the optical telescope. The interior of the lobby zoomed in, seemingly just inches away, large and bright. He smiled to himself, a smile of professional satisfaction. The moment Tselentis stepped into that lobby, it would all be over. Conrad Fung would be a free man. But, infinitely more important, so would he.

Dave found Tselentis in 20B watching the early news on television. He was dressed in a crumpled shirt and old slacks and hadn't bothered to shave. 'Better get yourself spruced up,' he said.

'Why, what's up?'

'You wanted to see your mother, didn't you?'

Tselentis jumped up from his chair. 'Yes, of course. That's great. What have you managed to arrange?'

'It's all set. She's still in hospital but you can see her tonight.'

Tselentis switched off the television. He was beaming. 'You're a star,' he said, 'a friend for life. You don't know what this means to me. Have I got time for a quick shave?'

'Sorry, the ambulance is downstairs now.'

'Can't it wait a couple of minutes?'

'I don't think you understand.'

'What do you mean?'

Dave smiled. 'The ambulance isn't for you, it's for your mother. She's on her way up right now with a nurse.'

After twenty minutes had passed, Rexford knew it had been a false alarm. But he remained there waiting all the same. A full hour passed before he saw the elevator doors open. He brought the telescopic sight to his eye and in the ringed magnification saw a small, frail Chinese woman escorted by a nurse walk slowly to the ambulance. So that's the way the cops had played it. They had brought the sick mother to visit the healthy son. If they were that careful about security, it was going to be a long, long wait.

Dave got back to the offices of OCTG at seven-thirty that night. Everybody had gone home except for Kit Lampton and one of his sergeants who were putting together the final forensic affidavits, the evidence of the bomb experts and the pathologists, for the extradition bundle.

'How did it go?' asked Kit. 'Did Madam Ma get to see her dutiful son, little Dimitri?'

'Went like clockwork,' said Dave.

'And what about our friend, Wong, the resident psychotic?'

'Hard going. But all's well that ends well.'

'Don't tell me you got something halfway coherent?'

'Sixteen pages of it.'

'Bloody hell! I don't know where you get the patience from. You're a saint, my lad, a saint. Oh, by the way, Hannah phoned ten minutes back. She's sorry, she says, but she's going to be late tonight. That guy from New York, the financier—'

'Ephram?'

'Yeah, apparently he flew into Hong Kong today. It was all a great surprise. They obviously have a million and one business matters to discuss so he's treating Hannah and Scott to dinner – some fancy frog restaurant no doubt, ten crossed forks on the Michelin guide and fifty bucks for an anchovy. I regret to say, old buddy, that you are not invited – far too classy for a down-market cop. On the other hand, once I've finished this last affidavit, I'm thinking of trekking into the nether regions of the Wanch' for a couple of beers and a plate of Singapore noodles. What do you say?'

'Thanks, maybe another night,' said Dave. 'I want to put Wong's affidavit on to the word processor.'

'I'm going in about five minutes if you change your mind.'

Dave went through to his office, sat at his desk and booted up his computer. He spread out the handwritten notes for Wong's affidavit, began to type the heading – and got no further. It was crazy, he knew it, any adjective you'd care to use, inane, groundless, self-destructive . . . but just the mention of Ephram's name had knotted his gut so badly he couldn't think of anything else.

He sat there in front of the monitor trying to talk himself out of it. Ephram was a business partner, that's all. Sooner or later he had to come to Hong Kong. There was nothing suspicious about that. Nothing suspicious either about the fact that he was treating Hannah to dinner. Scott was there too. Nothing was hidden, everything was above board. He had no reason to be suspicious of Ephram and no cause at all to doubt Hannah. So what in the hell was he getting so steamed up about? But rationalising it did no good. This wasn't a question of logic, it was a matter of emotion: personal inadequacy, jealousy, fear. He didn't particularly like himself for it but there was nothing he could do to prevent it. The French had a saying – the heart has its reasons which the reason does not know of. Yes, he thought ruefully, that just about summed it up.

He sat, staring at the monitor for another couple of minutes trying to concentrate. But it was no good. Stuff it, he thought. He shoved the notes into his desk, switched off the computer and returned to Kit's office. 'Okay,' he said, 'what about these beers you were promising?'

He didn't get home until midnight. The bedroom was in darkness but in the pale silvery sheen of the moonlight he could see the corn-coloured flow of Hannah's hair on the pillow. He undressed in silence, not wishing to wake her.

210

But when he came across to the bed, he saw that she was smiling up at him.

'I must have dozed off for a minute or two,' she said sleepily. 'I've been waiting for you.'

He climbed between the sheets next to her, acutely aware of the soft, toasted warmth of her body. 'How was your dinner with Sam Ephram?' he asked.

'All contracts and finance,' she said, cuddling up against him. 'And you?'

'Kit and I had a few beers.'

With a small purr, she brought her lips to his. 'All night I've been thinking about you.'

Dave could never resist her, not that he wanted to, he was surprised, that was all. He began to caress her. Hannah's nipples grew erect and, as his hand came down over the silky flatness of her stomach, he felt the rich wetness between her legs. There – physically – was all the proof he needed. He had spent the night screwed up with jealousy, thinking that she was besotted with another man, and yet she wanted him as much as he ever wanted her. How could he ever have doubted her? he thought. What kind of fool was he?

After their lovemaking, long after Dave had fallen into a deep, contented sleep, Hannah lay awake. For the first time in her life, in the span of one evening, she had made love to two different men. If that had been suggested to her six months ago, she would have scoffed in disbelief. And yet it had happened.

She had waited for Dave tonight, intending to make love to him, wanting him to know how much she loved him, knowing too that it was the surest way of assuaging any doubts he might have about her and Sam Ephram. It had been a deliberate, premeditated decision.

She didn't think it would be possible, after the total saturation of feeling she had experienced with Sam, to experience anything like it with Dave. And yet, lying there in the bed, listening to him undress, catching glimpses of his tall lean body, all sinew and steel, knowing that soon they would be making love, had made her want him more than she thought possible.

How could it be? How could she want two men so much? What kind of whore was she? And she had to laugh inside. God, what a chauvinistic, medieval thought. A man could want twenty women and he was a stud, some kind of hero. She wanted two men and instantly she was a whore. No there was nothing whorish about it. Both men, in their totally opposite ways, entranced her, enchanted her. Both, in their own ways, were strong, sensual, masculine. It was an impossible predicament. How did she ever rid herself of it? It was impossible. She just didn't have the strength. Because, as much as she needed Dave's love and fortitude, at that moment, she needed the glittering promises of Sam Ephram more.

When Dave awoke in the morning, Hannah lay close to him. Her body was so warm and soft that for a time he couldn't bring himself to move and just lay there delighting in the feel of her breasts against his side and the way her legs were entwined with his. Eventually he crept reluctantly from bed, put on his running kit and took the elevator down to the ground.

It was a grey morning, humid, blood warm, with inky clouds scudding in over the Lamma Channel. A merchant vessel, caught in the first dark tendrils of rain, passed silently, its decks jammed high with containers: more Hong Kong goods being exported to the world . . . clothing, electronics, toys, porcelain.

Even after all these years it never ceased to amaze him that this small, overcrowded patch of land, no bigger than a Texas ranch and twice as barren, possessed one of the world's most vibrant economies. People, that's all Hong Kong had ever had, people squeezed together in din and bustle, misery and joy. But people fired like nowhere else on earth.

He ran for an hour, a good hard run through the warm China rain, before he returned to the apartment. Hannah was still asleep. He showered, had a quick breakfast and got to the office a little after eight.

Booting up the computer, he worked on Wong's affidavit until mid-morning, ran off a hard copy and then, just as he had done two days earlier with Tselentis's affidavit, faxed it over to Mike La Fleur in the AG's Chambers. Just before lunch he received Mike's faxed reply –

Affidavits great Dave. They blow Fung out of the water. No amendments needed. Arrange for them to be sworn as soon as possible. Let's get the show on the road.

As soon as Dave received Mike's fax, he rode up to the Supreme Court to see how safely he could get Tselentis and Wong in and out and back to Benevolence Villas.

The Supreme Court stood on high ground above Queensway, one of the major roads into the central business district. The public entrance to the court led through dark-tinted glass doors into a huge, beige-marbled foyer. There was no security check at the entrance. People came and went as they pleased, witnesses, jurors, law clerks, members of the public. The elevators that led to the Chief Magistrate's office were off to the right of the foyer. But they were notoriously slow and invariably crowded. Bringing Tselentis and Wong to the entrance by vehicle was easy enough, but, once they were in the foyer, they would be milling in the crowd for two or three minutes, maybe longer. They would be too vulnerable.

That left just one option – the prisoners' entrance. Prisoners arriving at the court came along Queensway itself below the court and swung directly through iron gates into the bowels of the building. The entrance was always kept clear and prison staff patrolled there. Tselentis and Wong wouldn't have to step out of their vehicle until they were deep inside the building.

When he got back to OCTG, Dave telephoned the offices of the Chief Magistrate, making an appointment for twelve noon the following day. He gave no names to the secretary, he said only that he had some documents to be sworn. After that he telephoned the senior prison officer at the Supreme Court to clear it with him for the prison entrance to be used.

Again, no details were given; he had some prisoners to bring in for a short hearing, that's all he said.

That only left the vehicles to be organised. Dave had planned on a commercial van to take Tselentis and Wong with their guards to the court. An unmarked police car would go in front to clear the way, another would follow behind. There would be no flashing lights, no sirens, nothing to attract unnecessary attention. The van would be just another vehicle travelling the roads. Tselentis and Wong would be out of sight all the way.

As expected, the motor pool officer squealed. 'Three vehicles for one escort duty! Who's coming to town, the Queen Mother? Sorry chum, no ways.' But in the end Dave got the vehicles, all three.

Everything was ready to roll. Wong and Tselentis's affidavits nailed Fung to the wall. Once they were signed, half the battle was won. Satisfied, Dave poured himself a cup of coffee and put his feet up on the desk. Time to take it easy.

It was three-thirty when Mike Le Fleur telephoned from the AG's Chambers. 'Can you come across now?' he asked. There was none of his normal Canadian bonhomie. He sounded grim. 'It's important.'

'What's the problem?' asked Dave.

'We've received some papers from Washington.'

'What kind of papers?'

'We'll talk about it when you get here.'

'What about Tom Mackay, do you want him along?'

'Tom and Kit Lampton are already with me.'

By now Dave was thoroughly alarmed. 'What in the hell is this all about?'

The reply was curt. 'The shit has hit the fan Dave – that's what it's about.'

Chapter Fifteen

The Attorney General's Chambers stood directly across from the Supreme Court, separated from it by a garish brick-tiled piazza with a fountain in the middle resembling a large, flat marzipan cake. The Chambers occupied the bottom nine floors of a towering, forty-seven storey government block.

It took Dave less than five minutes to get there. He parked his motorbike at the back of the building and made his way up to the seventh floor. His heart was thudding hard in his chest, mouth bone dry. When he entered Mike Le Fleur's office, the atmosphere was funereal. Tom Mackay and Kit Lampton sat unsmiling. They nodded in Dave's direction but said nothing. It was obvious they had already been given the news.

Mike La Fleur sat behind his desk. The Fung extradition file lay open in front of him. He got up, smiling, but it was a tight lawyer's smile. 'Care for a cup of coffee?' he asked.

Dave pulled up a chair. 'Maybe later. First, I want to find out what all this is about.'

'I received notification from Washington this morning that Conrad Fung's lawyers have filed certain papers with the State Department.'

'What sort of papers?'

Mike La Fleur looked down at his file. Then he said in a flat, businesslike voice. 'It seems, Dave, that Conrad Fung is alleging he is entitled to diplomatic immunity.'

'What?' It was so absurd that Dave thought he must have misunderstood.

'He's alleging he's an ambassador-at-large.'

215

'Who for?'

'The Republic of Yemen.'

'The Yemen? What possible connection could Fung ever have with the Yemen?'

'He has the papers apparently, all sealed and signed. Accordingly – so his lawyers say – he's entitled to full immunity from arrest in terms of the Vienna Convention.'

Dave couldn't believe it. 'Don't tell me the Americans are buying this shit? Fung is as much an ambassador as I am!'

'The State Department can't ignore it, Dave. The Embassy of the Yemen in Washington is demanding Fung's immediate release. They confirm that at the time of his arrest, he was a duly appointed ambassador-at-large – entrusted, as they put it, with the economic interests of the country.'

Dave was amazed that such a preposterous con could be given even ten seconds serious consideration. 'I just don't believe this, I mean, it's staring us in the face. Fung has bought the appointment. He's bribed some minister. The whole thing is ludicrous, Mike! If he was a genuine diplomat, why didn't he say so the moment he was arrested? And what about the Yemeni Government, why didn't it lodge an immediate protest? Why only now?'

'According to the Embassy, the relevant papers were lost in transit.'

'A diplomatic bag gone AWOL – that's crap!'

'Of course it is.'

'Diplomats have to be accredited, don't they? They have to go through some sort of acceptance procedure . . .'

'Yes, they do,' said Mike.

'Was Fung ever accredited by the Americans?'

'No.'

'Then why are we all sitting here with faces around our ankles? Why aren't we treating this thing with the contempt it deserves? The US isn't some ninny banana republic frightened of its own shadow. It's not going to kowtow to corrupt bullshit like this.'

'I agree,' said Mike. 'The State Department will look at it long and hard.'

'Then what's the problem?' Dave demanded, perplexed. 'We all knew Fung was going to come up with something. But if this is the best he can manage—'

'The problem,' said Mike grimly, 'is that it doesn't end there Dave.'

Dave sat back in his chair, on his guard again. 'What else is he alleging?'

Mike Le Fleur did not answer immediately. Again he was searching for the right words and when he spoke it was with reluctance. 'Conrad Fung is making certain allegations that affect you personally, Dave.'

'What sort of allegations?'

'Allegations that you are conducting a campaign of revenge against him – a blood vendetta is the way his Miami attorneys describe it.'

Dave shrugged. 'So what? I still have to satisfy a magistrate in the US that we have a *prima facie* case on the evidence, I still have to get the papers in order. My personal feelings don't come into it.'

Then, for the first time, Tom Mackay spoke. 'They do, Dave, when you interfere with witnesses.'

Dave swung his head to face him. 'What are you talking about, Tom, what witnesses?'

Tom Mackay glared at him, clearly boiling inside. 'Fung's lawyers say that Tselentis's evidence isn't worth the paper it's written on. That it's all a tissue of lies.'

'Of course they'll say that – the evidence crucifies them. What do you expect them to say?'

'They say they have evidence to back up their allegations, hard evidence, Dave. Fung has a witness, a nightclub hostess by the name of Charity Choi. She says she was there when Tselentis was arrested. She says that you were out of your brain with rage – that you threatened to kill him unless he lied for you.'

Dave felt the blood drain from his face. The woman, the hostess . . . oh Jesus, he thought, how in the hell had they got to her?

Mike La Fleur spoke again, more conciliatory than Tom Mackay. 'This woman Choi has sworn an affidavit that she was present in Tselentis's apartment the night you arrested him. Do you remember such a woman?'

Dave nodded. 'Yes,' he said, feeling sick to his stomach. 'There was a woman there. Tselentis had picked her up in some club in Tsim Sha Tsui.'

She alleges that she saw you and Tselentis on the balcony,' said Mike. 'She says she heard you arguing. She says you were threatening Tselentis, threatening to throw him over.'

Dave chose his words carefully. 'I had to grapple with him at one stage, yes, that's true.'

'Why?' demanded Tom Mackay.

'Because at one stage he became violent . . . hysterical.'

'You didn't mention it in your arrest report.'

'I didn't think it was important. Tselentis is a cooperating witness. He's on our side now for Chrissake. Anyway, the woman wasn't even there. I had her taken to another room.'

'Yes, so she says,' said Tom Mackay, unable to conceal his anger. 'A bedroom – with a view straight on to the balcony. That's where she saw you threaten to throw him over.'

'It was nothing like that,' said Dave, thinking all the time, Christ, how could I have been so stupid to leave her there? 'When I informed Tselentis he was going to be arrested in respect of the Kai Tak bombings, he became hysterical. We struggled briefly. That's it.'

But Tom Mackay wasn't buying any of it. 'What in the hell were you doing on the balcony in the first place?'

'The balcony doors were open,' said Dave, hating having to lie like this, humiliated by it. 'Tselentis walked in that direction. I followed. Do you think I would have threatened him in the presence of a witness? Please, Tom, credit me with a bit more sense.'

Tom Mackay gave a sardonic smile. 'But there was no witness, Dave, not according to you. You'd had her taken to the bedroom.'

Dave knew he was boxing himself into a corner, a corner he had to get out of fast. 'I'm sorry, I don't see where all this is leading,' he said angrily. 'It's a diversion, a red herring.

There's only one point at issue now – is Tselentis telling the truth or not? And tomorrow he appears before the Chief Magistrate to swear an oath that he is. That ends it, surely. If you want extra boiler plating Mike, then okay, we'll get Tselentis to swear that he has never been threatened into giving his evidence by myself or anybody else for that matter.'

Mike Le Fleur nodded, neither agreeing nor disagreeing, simply acknowledging what Dave had said.

'Anyway,' said Dave, 'I didn't think issues of credibility were relevant in extradition hearings. If Fung wants to destroy Tselentis's testimony on the basis that he's reciting a bunch of lies under duress, let him do so at his trial back here in Hong Kong. Whether this woman Choi is believed or not is a matter for a jury, not for some extradition magistrate in the US.'

'In many respects you're right,' said Mike. 'The magistrate in Florida doesn't make findings of credibility. How can he on affidavits alone? He doesn't see the witnesses, he doesn't hear them testify.'

'So why are we panicking? What Fung is raising is all stuff for trial, not the extradition.'

'The problem,' said Mike, 'is that Fung's attorneys haven't kept this to the court arena. They've politicised it. They've gone straight to the State Department.'

'Then the State Department must kick it back into court where it belongs.'

'Not that easy. Extradition always has an executive element. Not that easy either with the Government of Yemen making all kinds of threats about breach of the Vienna Convention – and no doubt a few US Congressmen being lobbied to raise the issue.'

'What issue?' said Dave in angry frustration. 'From where I'm sitting, shove the bullshit aside and the issue disappears.'

'Okay,' said Mike, 'let me be the devil's advocate a minute, argue it the way Fung's counsel are arguing it . . . our client is a bona fide diplomat, that's the first thing they're saying, he's entitled to immunity from criminal

219

proceedings in the United States. On that basis alone, he should be set free. But in addition, there's clear evidence that the investigation into his involvement in the Kai Tak bombing has been tainted – poisoned – from the outset.'

'How?' demanded Dave.

'I'll tell you how . . . Hong Kong has allowed the father of one of the victims, a police officer who should never have been given an active role in the investigation, not only to participate in it but to effectively take over the running of it. Worse – to be the officer who arrested the so-called star witness, the only witness who directly implicates our client.'

'This is all bullshit.'

'But they go further, Dave. That on its own would be a matter for censure, they say. But there is now evidence from an independent party, a woman who has no reason to show bias, that this officer, half out of his mind at the death of his son, threatened to kill Tselentis unless the man gave false testimony. And that same officer – clearly obsessed with his vendetta – has, since the date of the arrest, had daily access to Tselentis . . . ample time within which to invent and teach a web of lies. In the circumstances – and this is the central thrust of their argument – no reliance whatsoever could be placed on Tselentis's testimony at a trial fairly conducted and none can therefore be placed on it in the extradition proceedings in the United States. In fact, they say, the whole investigation has been so tainted that to order Fung's surrender to Hong Kong would be unjust and oppressive – a flagrant abuse of the system.'

Dave shook his head, stunned by the threat of it. 'Is that what Fung's lawyers are asking for, that Fung be allowed to walk free?'

'Yes, Dave, they're asking the US Secretary of State to exercise his executive discretion and order his immediate release.'

Dave was lost for words. All he could do was slowly shake his head in nauseated bewilderment. 'I don't believe this,' he muttered. 'I mean it's all such unadulterated shit. The man is a callous, cold-blooded murderer.'

'I agree,' said Mike. 'Of course it's shit. Well fashioned

220

and finely sculptured but shit all the same. The Americans know it too. They know what sort of man Fung is. Nobody across in the State Department has stars in their eyes. They want to nail the bastard as much as we do. But the way things stand, they find themselves in a difficult position.'

Dave waited, not sure what was coming next.

Then Tom Mackay spoke: 'You have to face hard facts, Dave.'

'What hard facts?'

'Your continued association with Tselentis is playing into Fung's hands. Washington have made their attitude plain – they want you removed from the case.'

Dave sat, incredulous. They knew how much this case meant to him. It was the centre of his life. How could they pull him off it now? He stared at Tom Mackay, struggling through his diminishing disbelief to find words. 'And how do you feel, Tom? What's your opinion in this matter?'

'I want to see Fung convicted in a Hong Kong court, that's my opinion.'

'Why jeopardise the result now?' said Mike Le Fleur. 'We're almost home, Dave. Ninety percent of the work is done. If the Americans reckon that your continued presence on the case will hurt our chances of extraditing Fung, what choice do we have?'

For the very first time in the meeting, Kit Lampton spoke. 'You've done a great job, Dave. But, as Mike says, ninety percent of the work is done. From now on it's just politics and law – and baby-sitting witnesses. Why give that shitbag Fung even one bloody fingerhold to cling to?'

Dave nodded. Inside, his emotions were raging but the rational side of him knew that what all three of them said made sense. At best, his continued presence on the case would be an embarrassment, at worse, fatal. He was in a cold, humiliated fury, hurt and angry. But the anger was reserved for himself. How could he have been so stupid? In his blind rage that night when Tselentis had been arrested – just as Fung's lawyers said, demented, obsessed – he had left himself wide open . . . and now he was paying the price. He sat for a time in silence. They were waiting for him to speak, all eyes on him. He looked up, gave a raw, wintry smile and said, 'Okay, I'll do what you suggest.'

The three of them left the building in preoccupied silence, each caught up in his own thoughts. There was nothing left to say. Post mortems wouldn't help.

Tom Mackay, the big sandy-haired Scot, the man who had made the decision in the first place to bring Dave on to the investigation, stood in the elevator, hands thrust deep into his trouser pockets, glowering at the floor. Dave's protestations hadn't fooled him for a second. Of course he had threatened Tselentis. He had probably half throttled the dumpy little turd. But that wasn't what angered him. In the same circumstances he might well have done the same thing. Every cop knew that occasions arose when a criminal's right to silence was so much horseshit. What made him boil inside was the lunatic stupidity of allowing a witness to be anywhere near when the violence was done.

Dave knew it too. All the way down in the elevator he attempted to reconstruct what had happened that night in Tselentis's apartment, trying to find some rational explanation for his sloppy handling of the woman. But there was none. He had allowed his emotions, all the grief, the hurt and pain, to blind him, that was the truth of it. He had no excuses.

They reached the deck level of the building, making their way to the harbour entrance across a vast foyer carpeted in black rubber, the standard KGB-style decor of Hong Kong's public buildings.

Kit was the first to break the silence, thankfully on a plain, practical note: 'You said something in the meeting about Tselentis and Wong signing their affidavits before the Chief Magistrate tomorrow. What have you arranged?'

'They'll be signing them tomorrow at twelve,' said Dave. 'I'll explain the arrangements back at the office.'

Kit turned to Tom Mackay. 'When do you want Dave to drop out? It seems to me that if he has already set up this thing for tomorrow—'

'Forget it,' said Tom Mackay. 'Dave, I don't want you

anywhere near that signing tomorrow. We're in enough trouble as it is. I don't want Fung's lawyers making further allegations of duress on the basis you were standing over Tselentis's shoulder when he signed.'

Dave didn't contest the point. 'I'd just like a chance to speak to them beforehand, a couple of minutes, that's all.'

Tom Mackay shook his head, his ruddy cheeks still flushed with anger. 'A clean break, Dave, that's what's been agreed. You bail out now.'

Dave tried to explain his position: 'They're my witnesses, Tom. I'm the one who's closest to them. Right or wrong, they trust me. If I'm whipped away from this thing without a word of explanation, how do you think it's going to affect their morale? They're under enough pressure as it is.'

Kit supported him. 'Dave is right,' he said. 'He has a relationship with them that I just don't have. If he disappears without a word – even if I try and sell them a bunch of excuses – it'll be like pulling the rug from under their feet. You know what it's like with accomplice witnesses, Tom, you've had to nurse enough of them yourself. They can be real prima donnas, edgy as hell, especially ones holed up month after month in the miserable little apartments we put them in.'

The three of them left the building, taking the open-air escalator down to the piazza that led across to the Supreme Court. It was a hot, muggy afternoon with humidity in the mid-nineties.

Tom Mackay said nothing for a time, turning the matter over in his mind. At last, he said unwillingly. 'Okay, the two of you have made your point. You can see them tomorrow morning, Dave, before they go to court. Explain whatever you have to in order to grease the wheels for Kit's takeover. But once you've finished with them, that's it. As I said, a clean break. I'm sorry, Dave, but from that moment on, as far as the Fung matter is concerned, you're nothing more than a bystander.'

Back at the office, still struggling with the shock of what had happened, Dave explained to Kit what had been arranged to get Wong and Tselentis to court the following day.

.'You're well rid of it all,' said Kit, trying to make light of it. 'What's left? Baby-sitting, boring bloody months of it. Let's face it, Wong has the personality of your average tree stump and as for our little Greek humpty-dumpty, all beer bop and garlic, I know you like him but he's going to cause me tons of grief, I can feel it.'

Dave gave a weak smile. Kit was a good friend. It was obvious that he felt wretched about taking over full management. It was an awkward time for the both of them. 'You've still got to organise the personnel for tomorrow,' he said. 'I'll leave you to get on with it.' He went through to his own office and, dazed, put his feet up on the desk, staring out over the darkening waters of the harbour.

Kit was right, of course. What was there left to do? Witnesses had been found, immunities given. The evidence was all there, affidavits had been drafted and exhibits prepared. The extradition was ready to roll. Keeping their two accomplice witnesses sweet, that's all that remained. But if that was the case, if there was so little left to do, why did he feel so devastated, so completely scoured of purpose?

He had been stupid, yes, stupid and careless and out of his head and it would be necessary later, at trial, to admit to an 'excess of zeal' in effecting Tselentis's arrest. That would cause him professional embarrassment – it might hold back future promotions. But he could live with that – so long as Fung was convicted.

What about Tselentis and Wong, could their positions be jeopardised? Tselentis would take it hardest. He was terrified of Fung. But in the end Dave was certain he would come through. He would give his evidence at trial and give it well. He would swear that whatever had happened at the time of his arrest had no bearing on the truthfulness of his testimony. And he would be believed. If Washington could get its act together – squash this absurd con about diplomatic status – there was no reason why the extradition shouldn't remain firmly on the rails; no reason why Fung shouldn't be returned to Hong Kong, tried and convicted.

No, the real reason, he knew, why he felt so sick inside,

224

so angry with himself, lay in something far more fundamental . . .

At the very beginning of this thing, kneeling in Danny's room with his heart close to bursting, he had sworn a covenant with his dead son, a silent promise that justice would be done. That promise had become the driving force of his life. But from this time on he would have to stand to one side and watch others do what he had sworn to do. Tom Mackay had said it – a bystander, that's what he had been reduced to, just another blank face in the crowd.

He had always prided himself on being a self-contained individual, one capable of carrying his own hurts. But this time Dave found it impossible to store away his feelings in some cold cavern of his conscience. This was one hurt he had to share.

It was Scott Defoe who answered the phone. 'She's here somewhere,' he said, 'running around like a headless chicken as usual. Hang on, I'll call her.' Dave heard him scream. 'Hannah, it's Dave, he's on line two!'

When she came to the phone, Hannah was panting from running. 'Hi,' she said, her voice full of breathless exuberance.

'Hi,' he answered, his voice sounding flat in his own ears. 'How are things going?'

'I could do with a hundred hands. Otherwise great.'

'You should get more staff.'

'That's what Sam Ephram said.'

'So?'

'So I don't have time!'

They both laughed.

'I know you've got work coming out of your ears,' said Dave, 'but I was wondering if you could get away a little earlier tonight. I thought we might have dinner in town.'

'I'd love to,' she said, the disappointment clear in the tone of her voice. 'I could think of nothing better—'

'But?'

'But I'm just so snowed under, darling. I've got an appointment with the lawyers at six and drinks with the advertising people an hour after that, a whole promotional campaign to discuss. How about tomorrow? God, it sounds terrible, doesn't it, having to book an appointment with your own husband!'

'It's okay, tomorrow sounds good,' said Dave, knowing how lame he sounded.

'What's the matter?' asked Hannah. 'You sound so down.'

'We've run into a few problems with the extradition, that's all.'

'What kind of problems?

'Some legal gobbledegook Fung's lawyers have boiled up. They're alleging that Fung is a diplomat. Would you believe it? An ambassador-at-large.'

'What does that mean?' she asked, an edge of anxiety in her voice.

'That he's entitled to diplomatic immunity – so he says. But the US State Department aren't going to buy it. He's never been accredited in the US – nor anywhere else that I know of. He's obviously bribed a couple of government ministers.'

'But it obviously doesn't end there?'

'No,' he said.

'What else have they come up with?'

Dave was silent for a moment. Then he answered, almost reluctantly. 'Fung is making certain allegations against me personally.'

'What kind of allegations?'

'That I'm waging a vendetta against him.'

'Too damn right,' she said.

Dave had to smile. 'Yeah. But he's also alleging that I've forced Tselentis to invent his testimony. That I beat him up, threatened to kill him unless he lied.'

Hannah didn't sound in the least perturbed. 'Surely you had to expect something like that? You've had it before, every cop has. It's part of the job. Men like Fung will say anything to get off the hook.'

'Except this time,' said Dave – this was the hardest part of it all – 'there is some small grain of truth in it.'

He expected an immediate reaction, some indication of

shock. But Hannah remained silent, patiently waiting for him to explain.

Dave continued, searching for the right words. There had never been any secrets between himself and Hannah in the past and there would be none now. 'When I arrested Tselentis in his apartment, he started with the standard spiel about lawyers and legal rights and I don't know what happened but I saw red, I suppose, just exploded inside. There was a struggle out on his balcony. The truth is – and I'm not proud of it – I threatened to throw the little bastard over the edge unless he told me the truth.'

'What happened then?'

'He came around and began cooperating.'

'Has he been cooperating ever since?'

'One hundred percent.'

'The full truth?' she asked.

'There was never any question of false testimony – never. I lost my temper for a couple of minutes, that's it. We're both on the same side now. He trusts me, I trust him.'

'Then how did Fung find out?'

'There was a woman in the apartment at the time, some hostess Tselentis had brought back with him from a night-club. It seems she's given an affidavit. Pretty wild stuff most of it but, as I said, there is a grain of truth.'

'Tselentis will support your story, though?'

'Yes, I'm sure he will. But it's gone further than simple issues of credibility now, it's moved into the realm of the quasi-political,' said Dave. 'Fung's attorneys have gone straight to the State Department making all kinds of allegations about abuse of process, a bereaved father running amuck, perverting the course of justice.'

'Bullshit!' said Hannah. 'A moment's justifiable anger, that's all. I'm sorry but I still don't understand. Surely, all we have to do is put it into context – tell the truth – and that ends it all? You want my opinion, I think you acted with admirable restraint!'

Hannah's sudden flare of protective anger surprised Dave – and pleased him too. 'We can handle it,' he said. 'I'm sure of that. Fung won't walk. But there are, well . . . certain tactical considerations that affect me personally. While I stay on the case, there could apparently be difficulties.'

'What are you saying, that they've taken you off it?'

'Yes,' said Dave, 'as of now.'

'But that's ridiculous! This is your case, Dave, you were the one who made it!'

'Tactically, it's the right move. I hate to admit it but, if I was in Tom Mackay's shoes, I would do the same thing.'

'But aren't there matters which you have to handle personally? What about the two witnesses? What about their evidence for the extradition? You're the one they trust, the one they look to.'

'I've done all the work with the witnesses,' said Dave. 'Their affidavits are finished. They sign them tomorrow morning at the Supreme Court. Once that's done, it's just a case of sitting back and waiting for Fung's return. I'll get a chance to see them both before they go to court, just a few minutes to explain the situation, and after that it's over to Kit. He's a good operator, he'll handle them fine.'

'But that's not the point, is it?' said Hannah.

'No,' said Dave, 'not really.'

'The point is that you wanted to see this thing through to the end.'

He tried unsuccessfully to laugh it off. 'I feel a bit like a beached whale, yeah . . . like I've let Danny down.'

Hannah could sense the pain in his voice. 'Look,' she said, 'to hell with the lawyers and the advertising people. There's nothing that urgent. The appointments can be rescheduled. Why don't we have that dinner together, just the two of us?'

'I don't want to mess up your schedule.'

'You're not messing up anything,' she said.

'Okay, great.' The relief in his voice was palpable. 'I'll come across to your office about seven-thirty, how does that sound?'

'That sounds fine.' Hannah fell silent for a moment then, in a voice filled with a sudden sadness, she said. 'Believe me, you haven't let Danny down, Dave. You've done him proud.'

★

It was too late to catch Sam Ephram at the Regent. He was already on the way to her office. When he arrived, they sat. in her office. Hannah poured coffee and did her best to explain why she would have to cancel the appointments.

Sam Ephram listened quietly, without interrupting, and then, as she had expected, he gave that soft, solemn smile of his. 'Yes, of course, you have to be with him tonight,' he said. 'It would be callous to do anything else. Leave it to me, I'll speak to the lawyers and the advertising agency. It must be a crushing disappointment for him.'

'He's trying his best to hide it,' said Hannah. 'But yes, it must be. You know how much this case meant to him.'

Sam Ephram sipped his coffee. 'I don't pretend to be an expert but it seems mad to me to take him off it now. He knows more about it than anybody, he is more committed. You don't retreat in matters like this, you stand firm. What about the two witnesses, how are they going to react?'

'Dave is seeing them tomorrow morning to explain the situation. Their extradition affidavits have been prepared. He tells me that they're signing them tomorrow morning at the Supreme Court. So there's not much work to be done. It's not the operational necessity, Dave admits that, it's the fact that he had his heart so set on seeing this case through to the end.'

Sam Ephram smiled. 'The English poet, Milton, said it: "They also serve who only stand and wait." Just because Dave is out of the case, it doesn't mean he has to abandon it. There's still the assassin himself to be found. I'm sure he'll find a way to stay involved.' He finished his coffee and rose up from his chair. He kissed Hannah once, not so much as a lover this time, more as a sympathetic friend. He walked to the door. Then he turned and said. 'It must be a terrible burden, being loved by two men.'

Sam Ephram caught a taxi back to the Regent Hotel. The distance was not great and the traffic, mercifully, not too congested. He went up to his suite, taking off his jacket and tie, throwing them over the back of the sofa. There was one small bottle of champagne in the fridge of the mini bar which he opened and drank from a tall-stemmed glass.

He knew what would happen tonight. Hannah and her husband would have dinner. He would pour his heart out to her. They would return to their apartment and they would make love. The thought of it, her legs open to him, her cries of pleasure, as soft as a cat's purring, made his stomach churn. But balanced against that was another feeling entirely . . . a feeling as effervescent as the champagne in his hand, the heady sensation of success.

He went to the telephone, dialling a local Hong Kong number. It was an unlisted number that avoided the standard phalanx of receptionists and secretaries. The telephone rang but nobody answered. He began to worry. Time was critical.

Then he heard the receiver lifted at the other end and a voice answered in slow, dry tones. 'Hector Chan speaking.'

Sam Ephram smiled, a smile of self-satisfied triumph. 'Hullo, Hector,' he said, 'it's me – Khalil.'

Chapter Sixteen

Bruce Rexford sat up sharply, wrenched from his dreams. His green eyes darted around the unfurnished room. What was the time? His heart was pounding. He looked at his watch. Six-fifteen. Early yet. No need for panic.

He sat on his sleeping bag, breathing deeply. He was naked, a thick mat of ginger hair on his chest, ginger freckles covering much of his body. He turned on to his belly, executing a dozen quick press-ups. His shoulders and arms were strong but around his waist was a bulge of excess flesh. Fifteen years ago physical fitness used to bring him through these things. These days he had to rely on the adrenaline. He rose to his feet, pulling on a pair of briefs and padded through to the tiny kitchen to boil water for his coffee. There were some bread going mouldy in the humidity, some canned asparagus, some shortbread biscuits and an apple. But he was too keyed up for food.

Last night, after Hector Chan and he had spoken, he had planned the hit. It was not going to be easy . . . two witnesses, both guarded by police, both moving quickly. He had never undertaken a task so difficult before, so fraught with risk. Surprise, that had to be the key, surprise and speed of execution.

While he waited for the kettle to boil, he walked to the window, looking down to the street below. A thin sea mist hung in the air and in the lavender-grey light he could see two old men, as ethereal as ghosts, practising *Tai-Chi*, the ancient Chinese art of sublime movement, the harmonising of body and soul in the graceful turn of the head or the fluid, breathless wing sweep of an arm. The concentration of the

231

two old men was absolute. Not even an early morning truck rattling by, spewing out black exhaust, disturbed the polished tranquility of their movements.

So it had to be with him, thought Rexford. No more guilt, no more inward anguish, just a clear mind and a firm resolve.

Dave ran at five-thirty that morning. He ran hard and fast, high up into the hills. He was still burning with disappointment but the time spent with Hannah the previous night, the talking and consoling, had eased much of the pain. He could face it now, deal with it rationally. What counted was bringing Conrad Fung to justice and if, to do that, he had to wait in the wings, so be it.

Back at the apartment Hannah was still sleeping. He showered and dressed, read the morning paper and then rode out to Benevolence Villas. He didn't relish what lay ahead.

He went first to 20A where Wong Kam-kiu sat mournfully eating a bowl of rice congee for his breakfast. His prescribed daily dose of sedatives had been curtailed that morning so that he would be alert enough to swear his affidavit and his normal dull torpor was replaced by a high state of tension. He took the news badly.

'You are the only one I trust,' he said in Cantonese. 'That other one, Lampton, what does he know? What does he care? But you and I, we share a bond. Both our sons are dead because of Fung. Why are you abandoning me?' His lower lip began to tremble; tears swam in his eyes.

Dave tried to explain that nobody was abandoning him. When the time came for the trial, they would be there together, shoulder to shoulder. But right now, until Fung was brought back from Florida, the legal imperatives dictated that he must bow out. Wong would still be well guarded, however, given all the care he needed.

Wong listened but he didn't believe it. That was clear from the melancholy droop of his mouth and the cynical shake of his head. It wasn't simply a matter of Dave abandoning him, a breach of trust, it was proof that even at this early stage, even from his cell in Miami, Conrad Fung's power was able to plough its own unstoppable furrow.

Dimitri Tselentis felt no different. He took the news with a greater show of outward resignation but his disappointment was just as profound. He walked across to the sideboard, took out a bottle of cognac and poured himself a double tot.

'A bit early for drinking, isn't it?' said Dave.

Tselentis gave a disconsolate shrug. 'What else is there to do in this air-conditioned rabbit hutch? Eat, drink, masturbate, watch videos . . . and wait for Fung to stuff us all.'

'He's come up with a few cheap points,' said Dave. 'We all expected that. It's no big deal.'

'Oh yeah, then why are you being pulled off the case? You want me to give a statement saying that whore I picked up in the nightclub is lying? Okay, I'll give it. Isn't that enough? Fung growls once and we all fall down.'

'Ninety percent of the work has been done,' said Dave, 'You don't need me any more, not until trial.'

Tselentis swilled back his cognac, his cheeks flushing purple. 'Maybe you've done ninety percent of the work, but Fung has only just begun.'

'The law might grind a little slowly—'

'The law? Christ! Don't feed me that bull. Fung bought the law in this town years ago. He owns more cops in Hong Kong than the Commissioner of Police. What garbage are you going to feed me next? Truth, justice? Truth is what some smart-assed lawyer tells you it is and Fung owns the best. Justice? Justice is a bloody myth – you know it and I know it. I warned you about Fung. I told you his real power lay in his ability to corrupt people. How do you think he got that diplomatic immunity? How do you think he secured the affidavit from the nightclub whore? He makes his first counter punch – his first! – and suddenly, wham bam, thank you mam, he's an ambassador-at-large with a whole damn government supporting his cause! What's he going to come up with next, an H-bomb in the basement?'

'So what are you going to do?' said Dave, unable to

restrain his anger. 'Give up on yourself, crawl into a hole and let him get away with it, is that it?'

Tselentis stared at him, his voice husky. 'What I care about is surviving. That's the only reason I agreed to co-operate, that's the only reason I'm here. I'm not interested in high moral causes.'

'Great,' said Dave contemptuously, 'so go join the rest of the world's top survivors – the rats, ragweed and cockroaches. But I'll tell you one thing, you renege on our deal and you'll be an old man before you see the light of day.'

Tselentis gave a snort of anger. 'So what are you going to pin on me, the Kai Tak bombing? You know I wasn't involved in that.'

'I don't need Kai Tak,' said Dave. 'Your whole life has been a long list of offences: money laundering, bribery, theft. The Americans would love to get their hands on you. At the moment, because we've got a deal sanctioned by the Attorney General, because there are some bigger issues at stake – like justice for those people killed at Kai Tak – you're protected. But renege on the undertaking to cooperate against Fung and all deals are off. Nobody said getting Fung was going to be easy.'

'Christ, that's a cliché if ever I heard one!'

'Cliché or not, it can be done. All we have to do is persevere.'

'Rah rah! Bring out the band.'

Dave ignored the sarcasm. 'It's your choice. Either sign the affidavit this morning or pull out of our cooperation deal and live with the consequences.'

'Great choice, thanks. Either sink with this ship or go drown on another.'

'This ship isn't going to sink.'

'It's not looking too bloody seaworthy at the moment, is it?'

Dave left it. An emotional slanging match wasn't going to get them anywhere. He let the silence hang in the air, giving Tselentis time to calm down. Then he asked. 'So what's it going to be?'

Tselentis didn't look at him. He felt fearful, he felt

betrayed. It was etched on his face. 'What choice do I have?' he said bitterly. 'I'll sign.'

Kit Lampton arrived at the appointed time, forty minutes before the noonday appointment at the Supreme Court. He and Dave spoke in the lobby outside the two apartments. 'What was the reaction?' he asked. 'No sudden changes of heart? No prima donna tantrums?'

Dave answered with a resigned shrug. 'Neither of them were too happy. Wong has got himself into an emotional state, Tselentis is running scared. But they'll live with it. Give them a little time, that's all.'

'No hassles about signing their affidavits this morning?'

'Don't worry, they'll sign.'

'I've got to tell you Dave, I need this job like a hole in the head. I don't have your innate talent for wet-nursing miscreant little shitbags. But if you say everything is fine, great, let's put on our Mary Poppins faces and get it done. I've got the vehicles waiting downstairs.'

'I'll come down with you,' said Dave. 'Sign off in the lobby.'

Early that morning, Fat Kwok had brought a vehicle to the repair shop. But it needed no repair. It was a Volvo 740, a solid, square tank of a car with a powerful engine. He had backed it into the auto repair shop opposite Benevolence Villas and that's where it waited now, looking into the street, keys in the ignition, ready to go.

Fat Kwok sat back in the dark shadows of the repair shop, waiting. Bruce Rexford waited with him.

Five minutes earlier – after a three hour wait – they had seen three vehicles arrive at Benevolence Villas. One, a white sedan, a Ford, had parked out on the street. The other two had driven through the iron gates and up to the entrance. The first of the two was a commercial van, a goods vehicle. It stood in front of the entrance blocking the lobby from view. It was painted green and had orange lettering down the side in English and Chinese characters: Pak Wu Fruiterers. There was even a logo under the lettering, an apple with a smiling face. The second vehicle was a Japanese sedan, red in colour. Each vehicle had a driver and one front-seat passenger, all men. They wore an assortment of open-neck shirts and jackets. A couple smoked. One, wearing dark glasses, read a newspaper. They were all unmistakably cops.

It wasn't difficult to anticipate the strategy. When the two witnesses were brought down, they would be placed out of sight in the back of the commercial van. Then the small convoy would set off, the van squeezed in the middle like a book between two bookends. The tactics were sound, straight out of the manual. But if he hit hard enough, if it was done with timing and speed – lightning speed – it could be accomplished. He would have preferred something cleaner, more clinical, quiet deaths relegated to the back page of a newspaper. But he had no choice in the matter. This was the only way.

Rexford looked at Fat Kwok. 'We can expect them down any second now. Get into the Volvo, start it up. But don't move, not until I say so. When the hit is made, when it happens there'll be a lot of noise, a lot of shouting. Don't panic. Keep your head, follow my instructions and we'll both get out of this alive.'

Fat Kwok nodded. He lit himself a cigarette, sucking the smoke deep into his lungs then exhaling it in an acrid blue stream. Dribbles of sweat ran down the back of his neck. He was a nervous man. But so were they both . . .

Rexford's chest was so tight that breathing was a conscious effort. It was always this way in the moments before a hit. These were the worst moments of all, the moments of doubt. Every muscle seemed saturated, his limbs made of lead. He took a deep breath, willing himself to relax. He got up, stretching, shaking his fingers, limbering up like an athlete before a race.

He walked to the front of the shop and looked down the street. It was a hot, hazy morning, grey and muggy. Forty yards down the street, two men were waiting. They were dressed as labourers, everyday coolies, in grimy cotton shorts and cheap cotton vests. They stood talking by a cart

236

that was piled high with boxes and buckets. They were smoking too, sucking on their cigarettes with an intense fervour that betrayed their tension. Their part in the plan was crucial. They looked to be ready . . . as ready at least as they were ever going to be.

When he stepped out into the open, Dimitri Tselentis had to shield his eyes from the glare. It seemed like months since he had last been out in the sun. He looked at the van with an air of disdain. 'Pak Wu Fruiterers – so this is the way we're being taken to court, is it, like a bunch of bananas?'

Kit Lampton slid back the door of the van. There was a single bench seat in the back, no windows. 'The Rolls is being serviced,' he said with a smile. 'Maybe next time.'

Tselentis turned to Dave, the angry resentment still in his voice. 'When will I see you again?' he asked. 'If ever?'

'At the trial probably.'

'The trial – huh! – we could both be old men by then.'

'Not if we can help it.' Dave gave him a brief, encouraging nod. 'Good luck,' he said. 'And thanks.'

Tselentis was taken aback, flustered by the show of gratitude. 'Yeah, well,' he muttered. It was impossible to articulate a response. He climbed into the van, edging along to the far end of the bench seat.

Wong Kam-kiu climbed in after him. He sat next to Tselentis, refusing to look at him, staring glumly down at the floor, his lips moving as if talking to himself. Dave said goodbye but he didn't acknowledge it.

Kit Lampton was the last to climb in, sitting on the bench seat next to Wong. He gave Dave a friendly grin. 'See you later,' he said.

The door of the van was pulled shut. Outside, on Po Man Street, the white Ford sedan, which would lead the way to court, began to pull away from the kerb. The van's engine coughed into life and it made its way down the drive towards the iron gates. The third vehicle, the red sedan, followed close behind.

Dave stood at the entrance of the apartment block, hands

in his pockets, watching them depart. So that's it, he thought, now I'm well and truly redundant.

'Okay now, begin to edge out into the street,' said Rexford, sitting in the back seat of the Volvo. 'But slowly, slowly. No rush. Take it easy.'

Lying next to him on the back seat was the Dragunov sniper's rifle and next to that, just eight inches in diameter, was a squat brown pudding of an object, a limpet mine. The timing mechanism had been set to just ten seconds. The moment its magnetic clamps attached themselves, the countdown would begin.

Slowly Fat Kwok eased the Volvo out of the repair shop and into the street. Sweat was now pouring down the back of his neck. He was gripping the wheel so tight that his knuckles were white.

Rexford's eyes were on the van all the time, the van emerging from the gates of Benevolence Villas. He saw the driver stop, look each way, then slowly pull out. Fat Kwok swung the Volvo into the street, moving in the same direction but giving way to the van. 'That's good, yes, just like that. Slowly now,' said Rexford.

He had choreographed each step and now was when it had to happen, now, before the van increased speed. Come on, do it, now, now!

And at that moment it happened. The two coolies pushing their cart, heads down, bulldozing along, swung across the street directly into the path of the van. The driver of the van slammed on the brakes. There was a screech of tyres. The two coolies looked up, feigning horror. They tried to swerve their cart out of the way and, exactly as planned, everything fell . . . boxes of stinking fish, buckets of brine, green crabs, jellyfish, ropes and tarpaulin. It all went spilling and crashing, slithering across the tarmac. And pandemonium ensued.

The one coolie shook his fist at the driver. '*Du lai lo mo!*' he shouted, using the time-honoured Cantonese obscenity – fuck your mother!

Then the second coolie joined the melee, banging on the

238

windscreen of the van in a burst of theatrical rage. '*Lai do chi sin ge!*' he shouted – you're a crazy man, look what you've done!

Rexford spoke to Fat Kwok. 'Drive closer, get as close as you can. That's it. Yes, yes, – now stop!' As he pushed open the door, the limpet mine felt as heavy and solid as a shotput in his hands.

This was the perfect moment, just as he had planned. The driver of the van was still confused, uncertain what to do, blocked by the overturned cart and, in his turn, blocking the third vehicle behind.

A few moments of chaos, that's all Rexford had needed. With the limpet mine tucked into his belly, he covered the five paces to the van and bent down next to it on his knees.

It was the shouting that alerted Dave, the sudden high-pitched burst of Cantonese obscenities. He could still see the van out on the street, half turned, but he couldn't see what had happened. The shouts though were enough to galvanise him. Wrenching his service revolver from its holster in the small of his back, he began to sprint down the driveway.

The two policemen in the rear vehicle were jumping out, reaching for their revolvers too. One of them turned to Dave as he ran up. 'Seems like an accident,' he said. 'Some bloody cart in front of the van.'

Then Dave saw it . . . the overturned cart, the boxes and buckets all over the tarmac, the two Chinese bellowing with rage. It looked like an accident, nothing more than that, so typically – chaotically – Hong Kong. But every instinct was shrieking inside: no, no, it can't be, it's too pat, too convenient. There has to be more to it. But what, for God's sake, what?

He turned to the two officers next to him. 'Get that cart out of the way. I want the van to go through. Hurry, hurry!'

The two of them ran forward. One managed to grab the cart, hauling it to one side, while the other, wading in among the flotsam of jellyfish and broken boxes, tried to push the two hawkers out of the van's path. But they resisted him, waving their arms, demanding compensation for their spoilt goods. 'Fuck your mother!' they were shouting. 'Don't push us!'

Dave knew he was going to have to intervene. He pulled his warrant card from his wallet – and it was then that he glimpsed the European.

The man was moving away from the van, bent low, head down. Dave didn't see anything in his hands but it was the way he was moving – the stealth, the purpose. Oh God no, he thought – and he knew. 'It's a bomb!' he shouted. 'It's a bomb!' He rushed forward, vaulting around the van to the far side, hammering all the time on the side. 'Get out, get out! It's a bomb!'

He saw the European climbing into the back of a Volvo and he screamed at the two nearest officers. 'Stop that man! Stop him!' His own attention though was focused on the bomb and the carnage it could cause. He threw himself flat on the tarmac, looking under the vehicle. No sign of it. Nothing. But it had to be a bomb. Nothing else made sense. The van door was pulled back. Kit Lampton appeared, face white with apprehension. 'What in the hell—'

And the first bullets punctured the van before Dave even heard them.

In one fluid movement, Rexford brought the Dragunov up to his shoulder. He had been seen but it didn't matter. Nobody would get the limpet mine out from where it was clamped behind the rear wheel, not in the brief seconds that remained. All he had to do was keep the targets pinned inside. He pushed the rifle through the window, his fingers resting on the trigger. The Volvo began to pull away. He saw the door of the van slide open, saw a European appear: it was Whitman's friend, the other cop. Their eyes met, the man saw the black lethal nozzle of the rifle and hurled himself out on to the road. But he didn't matter, the witnesses – they were the only ones that concerned him. Rexford concentrated on the open door, that dark well where he knew the two witnesses would be seated. And he fired.

As the Volvo roared past the van, above the concussive

240

backwash of the shots, dimly, he heard a gagging cry of pain. He fired one more burst, his mind totally concentrated, aware of nothing except the tight oblique pattern of the bullets as they shredded the side of the van.

But at the wheel Fat Kwok suddenly grunted. 'Fuck, I'm hit! I'm hit in the leg!'

Rexford saw that Whitman was firing his .38 service revolver, both he and that other cop, the one who had thrown himself from the van. They were firing at the Volvo. A shot punctured the rear window, shattering the glass around him like an explosion of ice. Rexford fired back at them, one last shuddering burst that ploughed up the tarmac around their feet. His magazine was exhausted. 'Go, go!' he shouted to Fat Kwok. 'Get the hell out of here!'

As the Volvo sped away, Dave was on one knee. He brought up his revolver. He saw the muzzle flashes of the shots being fired at him from the car but he was oblivious of them. He fired himself once, twice, both shots an instant too early. He took aim again, all his concentration on that man in the back seat. The man half turned to get in a final burst. For a moment his head was lifted – and Dave found himself staring into the eyes of his son's killer.

Tselentis remembered so little. It all fell within the compass of five or six seconds, barely enough time to breathe, yet it seemed to last a lifetime.

The van suddenly jolted to a halt. He heard the shouts outside but he had no idea what was going on. Then further shouts and loud banging, at first incomprehensible. But he recognised Whitman's voice and suddenly the words were distinct. 'Get out! It's a bomb!' Lampton was fumbling with the door handle. 'Oh shit,' he was muttering. The door was thrown open, light flooded in, light so brilliantly glaring white that it blinded him. He half rose, heart pounding against his chest, and then, in a terrifying banshee scream, the rifle fire poured in. The noise alone reverberating around the inside of the van seemed enough to burst his skull.

He remembered screaming and falling to the floor with

241

Wong's writhing body on top of him. Wong was making terrible sucking sounds like a man suffocating, twitching and kicking, spitting out blood. When he looked up at him, half his jaw had been shot away. He remembered Whitman reaching into the van then, grabbing Wong and heaving him up into his arms. He remembered Whitman shouting at him. 'Get out, there may be a bomb! Get away from the van!' How he got out he didn't know but he remembered stumbling out after him, his hands wet with Wong's blood. He remembered staggering up and running and sobbing all the time: oh God, don't let me die.

Then came the explosion.

There was a monstrous black convulsion, no light, no flash, just that invisible, unstoppable energy smashing everything before it, catching him and slamming him down as if he was made of straw. He fell hard, bruised to the bone. He lay in among the fish and the slime and when he turned his head back, great chunks of the van were cartwheeling through the air. He didn't see what had happened to Whitman. Everybody was down, flat on the ground, he saw nothing except the debris of the vehicle and then, in the eye of the storm, a sudden spurt of orange flame as the gas tank caught.

Climbing to his feet seemed to take an eternity, like scaling the highest, icy peaks of Everest without oxygen, but he had to get away, away from those flames. He stood for a moment, tottering uncertainly. He expected arms to grab him but everybody had been turned to pillars of stone.

He began to run, he didn't know where, he just ran. He stumbled and fell, he staggered past onlookers still flat on their bellies. He found a side street and fled down it. His hands were sticky-wet with blood, Wong's blood. He didn't think ahead, he had no destination. At that moment, he was driven by one thing only, a wild-eyed, unspeakable terror.

Dave was twenty feet from the van when it exploded. He had seen Tselentis scramble away and had Wong in his arms when the blast hit him. He remembered nothing, just his back arching, just a searing gale catching him and the sensation of going down.

242

When sense came back again – it could have been minutes, seconds, he didn't know – when he was able to focus, he was lying on the street surrounded by twisted debris from the van. One of his men was dragging Wong clear, another two had Kit Lampton by the arms trying to lift his inert body. Dave watched them, possessed by a terrible, dull lethargy that made it impossible to move. He saw them lay both men down, he saw them shouting into their radios calling for help. He saw them trying to push back the crowds, the morbid, milling onlookers who seemed to have been conjured out of the smoke of the explosion.

Slowly, with great effort, Dave climbed to his feet. There was no blood, no pain. In a daze, he walked across to where Wong and Kit Lampton lay. One of his men, a young constable, was repeating over and over again into his beat radio. 'We have men down, we must have ambulances. The address is . . .' And there were tears streaming down his face.

Dave looked at Kit. His eyes were closed, he lay still, face grey, jaw slack. A small puddle of blood was spilling out from under his body across the tarmac. There was a terrible gash to his hip which must have been caused by shrapnel from the van. There was bleeding from his chest too but he couldn't see how that had been caused. Dave knelt next to him, still dragging himself through the impossible, glue-thick viscosity of his concussion and thinking all the time, oh God, how could this have happened? He looked up at one of his men, a sergeant, one of his best. 'What's this wound to the chest?' he asked. 'Why is there so much blood?'

The sergeant, a tough man with twenty years on the force, had to steel himself visibly before he spoke. 'Mr Lampton has been shot, sir,' he said. 'He has been shot through the chest.'

Dave nodded, still too concussed to fully comprehend. The chest . . . oh Christ. 'Are there ambulances on the way?'

'Yes, they're coming.'

'What about roadblocks? I want roadblocks set up.'

243

'That's being arranged sir,'

'Have you passed on the registration number of the Volvo? It's EK—'

'Yes we have, sir, EK5658.'

Dave seemed to be speaking from within an airless chamber. 'The man I want is European. Have you passed on the description?'

'We didn't get a chance to see him sir. It all happened so fast.'

'Mid-forties, thick-set, a big man. He's wearing a windcheater, some shiny nylon sort of material – and he has red hair. The red hair, that's how they'll recognise him.'

'Good, thank you sir.' The sergeant ran over to one of the police cars to relay the message.

Dave remained there, slumped next to Kit. Slowly, his head was beginning to clear. He heard a soft voice speaking to him, barely a whisper. 'Typical of us expats, leave all the leg work to the locals . . .' He looked down and Kit was smiling up at him, a ludicrous smile, all bullshit and shock and heart-wrenching courage.

Dave smiled down at him, lost for words.

'How are our two witnesses?'

'Fine, fine.'

'What about Wong? You were carrying him.'

'He'll be okay.'

Wong's body lay so close that Dave could reach out and touch it. The man's jaw was shattered, half the back of his head was gone, a terrible mess of blood and matted hair. Wong was dead, beyond all help. But how did he tell Kit that?

Kit was beginning to shiver. It was the loss of blood and the shock. 'Bloody silly, isn't it?' he murmured. 'You could fry an egg on the pavement and I can't stop shivering.'

'You're going to be fine,' Dave urged him. 'Just hang in there, Kit, hang in.'

'That's what you used to tell me back in training . . . those awful bloody long-distance runs, remember? Hang in there, Kit. Could have kicked you every time you said it. Always hated running. Senseless bloody sport. What about

Tselentis? Is he okay? Are you sure he got clear?'

'He's okay. Don't worry, he got clear.'

Tselentis – where was he? Dave looked around but all he could see were the throngs of onlookers. He saw the sergeant coming back and pulled him to one side. 'Where's Tselentis?' he asked in an urgent whisper.

The sergeant's mouth fell open.

'Find him,' Dave hissed. 'Find him before they do.'

The Volvo, using all its massive bulk and power, had smashed its way clear, bulldozing the white Ford aside as it tried to cut it off. It had taken a dozen bullet shots, one into a tyre, but none that was capable of stopping it. And now, half a mile from Benevolence Villas, up into the hills, it turned up a narrow street behind a school and into a deserted building site.

The building had risen six levels when a dispute between the owner and the building contractor brought work to a halt. The only man there now was a sun-wizened old watchman whom Fat Kwok had paid a good price to turn a blind eye. Even so, when the watchman saw the Volvo, one side gouged, two windows smashed, he gawked in alarm. Fat Kwok had to say a couple of sharp words to him in Cantonese before the old man slunk deeper into his tin box at the entrance.

There was a prearranged spot behind a high screen of bamboo scaffolding where the Volvo could not be seen from the road. Fat Kwok parked it there, switched off the ignition and slumped back with a groan.

'You've got to look at my leg,' he said. 'The fucking cop shot me.'

Rexford stepped out of the vehicle. Broken glass fell from his shoulders like crystal confetti. Fat Kwok opened the driver's door, easing his leg out for Rexford to see. Rexford looked closely and a thin smile settled on his face. The bullet had hit the bodywork of the Volvo which had diverted it, blunting ninety percent of its impact. But the bullet had still carried enough velocity to plough through the metal and strike Kwok in the thigh . . . just enough to imbed itself like a twisted copper-coated leech into the surface of his skin. Rexford plucked the bullet out and handed it to Kwok. 'You're a lucky man,' he said. 'Keep it as a souvenir. Now hurry, there's work to be done.'

Picking his way through the builder's rubble, Rexford made his way over to their second vehicle, a white Toyota. He was carrying an aluminium case, the Dragunov locked inside. He turned back to Fat Kwok. 'Hurry, man, I need the keys to the boot.'

Fat Kwok climbed out of the Volvo. Now that his wound was something purely superficial, a look of primitive triumph lit up his face. He shook his fist in the air. 'Did you see that van go up? Fuck your mother, it was incredible! I never thought we were going to make it. There were cops everywhere. It was just like you said – we hit them fast, as fast as a fucking train!'

Rexford was experiencing the same emotions, the emotions of a fighter pilot when he had successfully run a gamut of surface-to-air missiles to deliver his payload – that unbelievable release of tension, the pure exhilaration of survival.

He took the Toyota keys from Fat Kwok and opened the boot. A suitcase lay inside, a standard travel case peppered with airline stickers. He removed it from the boot, replacing it with the metal case. He closed the boot and said to Fat Kwok. 'Fetch me a bucket of water.'

Fat Kwok gave him a look of incredulity. 'A bucket of water, what are you talking about? We have to go. Can't you hear the sirens?'

'Do as I say,' said Rexford. 'I'm trying to get us both out of this thing alive. Speak to the watchman, there must be a tap somewhere. I'll be inside the building. Bring the water to me there.'

Suitcase in hand, Rexford made his way through the bamboo scaffolding and the piles of building debris into the concrete skeleton of the building. He found a shaded spot where he could look back into the yard, set down his suitcase and opened it.

The hit on the two witnesses had been a high-risk venture, he had known that from the beginning. But he had

had no choice, not in the limited time and restricted circumstances. He had relied on speed to get him clear and it had
worked – but not one hundred percent. What he hadn't
counted on was that cop, Whitman, reacting so quick.
Whitman had seen him, he knew it. For one critical
moment their eyes had met. That meant that by now his
description would have been relayed to every cop in Hong
Kong.

Fat Kwok came staggering into the building with a
bucket of cold water. The crude glow of tribal triumph was
gone, replaced now by a steadily mounting panic. 'Listen to
those sirens,' he said. 'They're all over the place.'

'Wait by the Toyota,' Rexford instructed him. 'I'll be out
in a few minutes. And don't think of running. I'll be
watching you.'

Fat Kwok returned to the Toyota. He climbed inside and
started the engine, keeping it idling. The wail of police
sirens filled the air. Every few seconds he kept peering back
towards the entrance to the building site, expecting to see a
regiment of cops come charging in. If the cops caught him
for this, he would get life for sure, die in prison. What was
that crazy *gweilo* doing with a bucket of water?

Ten minutes passed. The waiting had become unbearable. A police car cruised slowly past the entrance to the
building site. Fat Kwok almost threw up with terror. He
couldn't wait any longer. This was suicide. Another minute,
he promised himself, just sixty seconds . . .

He looked towards the building. He saw movement and
at last Rexford appeared. Fat Kwok blinked. After the blue
jeans and black windcheater, Rexford was now dressed in a
navy blue business suit with a white shirt and striped tie. He
looked like a banker. He was wearing metal-rimmed glasses
too. But there was one amazing transformation that changed
his entire appearance – Rexford was now totally bald.

Dimitri Tselentis couldn't run any more. He had reached
the limits of his stamina. The blood was rushing in his head,
his legs had turned to jelly. He found an alley that led off
the street and turned up it.

A few yards up the alley, he could see an open door.

Plastic bags full of rubbish lay sprawled outside. Potato peelings and rotted cabbage lay thick on the ground. It was the kitchen entrance to an eating house. He saw two wooden chairs and, lying over the back of one, put out to dry, was a white waiter's tunic. Tselentis hurried past the chair, grabbing the tunic as he went. He continued to the end of the alley then pulled it on. It was several sizes too small, there was no way he could button it up, but at least it covered most of the blood splashes on his shirt, at least he didn't look like an abattoir worker.

He tried to think. What now? Where to? He had no money, no credit cards. All he knew was that somehow he had to find a way to get out of Hong Kong. If he didn't, he was a dead man.

He walked to the end of the alley, peering out into the street. He saw a taxi a little way up the street. It was dropping a passenger. On impulse, he walked towards it, waving his hand. The taxi driver gave him a suspicious look, but a fare was a fare and he waited. Tselentis climbed into the back, speaking to the driver in rapid Cantonese: 'The south side of the island – Aberdeen.'

Dave wouldn't leave him, he insisted on staying with Kit in the ambulance all the way to hospital. Kit was his best friend. There was no way on earth he would leave him, not now. He sat next to the narrow stretcher on which Kit lay. The paramedics did their best. They dressed the two wounds but Kit was sinking fast. His pulse was erratic, he was coughing blood. All the time Dave's hand was there on Kit's arm, reassuring him. 'Not much longer now, a few minutes, that's all.' God, he felt so helpless.

Kit grinned, that same brave, stupid grin. 'Knowing my luck, there'll be a traffic jam.'

'Feel any pain?'

'An ache here and there.'

'They'll dope you up soon enough.'

Kit closed his eyes. His breathing became faint.

Dave gently shook him. 'Come on Kit, wake up.'

The eyes opened but they were barely focusing. The grin

remained, though. 'Always fell asleep in cars, ever since I was a kid. Can't help it.'

'Just a few more minutes. We're almost there.'

'Where's Wong?'

'He's in another ambulance.'

'Is he okay?'

'Yes, I'm sure,' Dave lied.

'And Tselentis?'

'He's fine.'

'So the bastards didn't succeed?'

'No, they didn't.'

'Good, good, that's what counts . . .' Kit closed his eyes. 'I feel so tired,' he said. 'Sorry old buddy, anti-social I know, just going to drift off for a while . . .'

After that he said no more. His eyes were shut, he lay very still. His mouth was slightly open and at the corners remained the faintest shadow of that infuriating, cocky grin. Dave took his hand, holding it firmly. They were still a mile or more from the hospital but he knew it was already too late. First his son and now his best friend. Oh dear God in heaven, how much more could he take?

Chapter Seventeen

They hit the first roadblock less than three hundred yards from the building site. It was manned by police officers in blue berets, the Police Tactical Unit. They were ordered to pull to the side of the road, switch off the engine and climb out.

Rexford had learnt a long time back that stoicism was the greatest ally to flight. What will be will be. Don't fight it, accept it. Show any fear, display even the smallest sign of tension and you are finished. So he obliged with a smile. 'What's the problem?' he asked. 'I heard all the sirens. Has there been a robbery or something?'

The officer, a short, stocky Chinese in his early twenties, did not answer. There was a grim, hard-set look on his face. He looked Rexford up and down then demanded. 'ID card.'

'I am a visitor to Hong Kong. I don't carry a local identification card.'

'Passport.'

'Certainly.' Rexford removed the document from his jacket pocket. It was an Irish passport in the name of Philip O'Brien. Date of birth, 24th July, 1948. It was the passport he always carried in anticipation of exactly these circumstances. He handed it to the police officer.

The officer opened the passport, studying the black and white photograph with a ferocious glare. He looked at Rexford and then back at the photograph. It showed the same man: glasses, bald head, solid, well-worn face. But the officer was suspicious. He stepped closer. 'You have a cut,' he said, 'up there on your head, above your ear.'

'I did it shaving this morning,' Rexford answered.

'You shave your head?'

'Sometimes small hairs grow. They don't look nice. Yes, when necessary, I shave my head.'

But the officer's suspicions remained. This *gweilo* was the right age, the right size. Admittedly he was dressed in a business suit and he was bald but there was something about him, the freshness of the aftershave, the creases in the suit that looked like it had only just been unfolded. 'Why are you in the area? What is your business here?' he asked.

'I have been visiting a building site,' Rexford explained calmly. 'I am an engineer by profession. There has been a dispute between the owner and the contractor. I have been brought in to arbitrate.'

'Where is this building site?'

'It is a little way back along the road. I can take you there if you wish. But I don't think you'll find it very interesting.' He smiled. 'Just a lot of bricks and bags of cement.'

The officer looked down at the photograph again. Then he glanced at Fat Kwok. He frowned. 'What's that blood on his leg?'

'He caught his leg on a nail,' said Rexford with an easy smile. 'Those things happen on building sites. It's only a scratch. Have a look.'

The officer stepped over to where Fat Kwok stood, peering down at the wound. He went to touch it but then held back. Everybody, even police officers, had to consider AIDS these days. He said something in Cantonese to Fat Kwok. It must have been an instruction to walk because Fat Kwok turned and took three or four steps – mercifully without limping.

The officer stood for a moment, the passport still in his hand. He was clearly undecided. Should he take this matter further, should he let it go?

Rexford waited, one hand in his pocket. *Que sera sera* . . . don't fight it, let it go. He began to whistle a slow tune.

There were six or seven vehicles queuing at the road block, goods vans, lorries, Chinese housewives in little Japanese cars bringing their children home from school.

252

The police constable stared intently at Rexford, his eyes narrowing. He made no attempt to disguise his suspicion. He smelt something wrong but he didn't know what. He glanced across at the queue of cars and then brought his attention back to the passport.

So this is how it ends, thought Rexford. Amazing. After all the years, all the assignments, it's going to end here in the back streets of Hong Kong with a young cop whose mother still probably makes his bed.

The policeman looked up from his passport, his eyes boring into Rexford's as if by sheer willpower he could read his mind.

Rexford knew he was finished. The sum total of the suspicions were just too much. But instinct, pure grit, wouldn't let him give the game away and he smiled back, a bland curtain of affability that admitted nothing.

The police officer grunted, snapping the passport shut. He had made his decision. 'Okay,' he said. 'You can go.'

It took twenty minutes for Tselentis to reach his mother's shop in Aberdeen. All the way there he was terrified of being stopped at a roadblock, terrified that, with his mother in hospital, the shop would be shut. But there were no roadblocks, he had outrun them before climbing into the taxi, and when he reached the shop he saw his mother's assistant behind the counter. 'Wait here,' he said to the taxi driver. 'I have to get the fare.'

His mother's assistant was named Lau Wai-hing but he had called her Hing Yee – Auntie Hing – since he had been a boy. When he entered the shop, she stared at him in amazement. 'What are you doing here alone? Aren't you meant to be with the police?'

'I'll explain everything,' Tselentis told her. 'But first, please, Hing Yee, can you pay the taxi outside? Don't say anything, just pay him and come back into the shop.'

Lau Wai-hing, who was into her seventies, a tiny, nervous woman, fumbled for her purse, muttering to herself in shock. But she did as he requested, scampering outside, paying the fare and then scampering back into the shop.

253

Tselentis locked the shop door, sat her down behind the counter and, still in a state of shock himself, did his best to explain. 'There's been a lot of trouble,' he said. 'Very soon you'll hear about it on the radio. The people I've agreed to testify against have tried to kill me.'

'I can see blood on your hands. Are you hurt?'

'No, I'm not hurt. It's blood from another man, another witness who was sitting next to me. But you can see how lucky I was to escape. You have to help me, Hing Yee. I can't go back to the police. I have to get away. Can I trust you?'

'I've worked for your mother for over thirty years. I remember you as a boy. Of course you can trust me. What must I do?'

'I have to see my uncle. He's the only one who can get me out of Hong Kong. Is he here, is he in port?'

Lau Wai-hing nodded. 'He returned yesterday from a fishing trip.'

Tselentis leant back against the counter, weak with relief. 'Is his junk at its usual mooring?'

'I think so, yes, but I'm not sure.'

'I need a little money, just sufficient for the sampan to get me to the junk.'

'Take as much as you need.'

'I need to wash too, to get some of this blood off my hands.'

'There's a sink at the back,' she said. 'Use that.'

A couple of minutes later, his hands washed, Tselentis made his way down to the water's edge. This was where he had been raised. He knew every inch of it. Despite all the years of high living, the international hotels and vintage wines, despite all the gloss and glitter, coming back here was coming back home.

The water was a deep oily green in colour, so fetid and thick he could smell it. Along the far shoreline, in the shadow of the forty-storey housing tenements, there were painters and masons and carpenters at work. The harbour itself was so jam-packed with fishing junks moored side by side in endless rows that there seemed to be no room left. Yet in the few open channels, hundreds of vessels of every kind chugged through the waters . . . pleasure boats, flat boats, sampans.

Tselentis hailed a water taxi, a brine-encrusted sampan with an old Hakka woman at the rudder. He gave instructions and they set off through the pungent waters, under the bows of the deep-sea junks.

Children were playing on board the vessels, women were hanging out laundry. The occasional piebald dog slept in the bow. Nothing had changed. Nothing ever would. The engines would get bigger and better, the fish would become harder to find. But the life of these people would go on as it always had. At that moment, scared out of his mind, lost, not knowing what was for the best, Tselentis was returning to his roots. In that, he believed, lay his only hope.

He recognised his uncle's green-hulled junk moored at the end of the line. It bore no name, just a registration number. Chinese fishing folk were thrifty, pragmatic people. A boat was a piece of machinery, not an object of sentimentality. The little sampan, bobbing in the water, drew alongside. Tselentis paid the Hakka woman and climbed aboard. So far there had been no sign of police.

He found his uncle in the wheelhouse. The old man was surprised, there was no hiding the fact. But he had seen too much in life to let it be more than a passing emotion. 'You've escaped,' he said, almost matter-of-fact.

Tselentis, shivering with the aftershock of events, fighting desperately to keep control of his emotions, replied, 'It's a complicated story, Uncle. Half an hour ago Fung's people tried to have me killed. I have to get out of Hong Kong, I have to get away.'

'What about the police? Do you wish to get away from them too?'

'The police can't protect me, not against Fung. The other witness – Wong – I'm sure he's dead. We were ambushed driving out of the apartment block. Wong was shot to pieces, I mean, right there in front of my eyes. It was a massacre. I don't know how I got away.'

His uncle tried to calm him. 'So you wish to get away, is that it?'

'I have no choice. Can't you see that?'

His uncle nodded gravely. 'Very well,' he said. 'If that is what you wish, we must find a way.'

When the air force helicopter landed in the grounds of Queen Mary Hospital, Dave was there waiting for it, ready to be ferried across the harbour to Kai Tak Airport.

There was no way that every red-haired European male could be prevented from leaving the Territory. Hong Kong had six million visitors a year. Logistically it was impossible, the immigration authorities would never agree to it. But at least if he was at the airport, strategically positioned, he might be able to spot the killer. He knew it was an outside chance. There were other exit points, Lo Wu up on the Chinese border, the Macau Ferry Terminal. He couldn't cover them all. But if the killer was a European imported specifically for the hit, Kai Tak was his most likely way out.

Dave had been the one to suggest it. The odds against success didn't matter. It was a logical move, the one place where he could best be deployed. When he climbed into the belly of the chopper, Tom MacKay was waiting for him. They nodded to each other, unable to find words to express their feelings.

Tom MacKay was the first to speak, shouting above the clatter of the rotors. 'Is it true, is Kit dead?'

Dave nodded, a slow and solemn nod. 'Yes, he's dead.'

Tom MacKay put his head back, screwing his eyes shut. 'Oh sweet Jesus,' he murmured.

The chopper lifted off, heading out over the Lamma Channel, in sight of the apartment block where Dave lived, out over the water towards Kai Tak.

'What about yourself?' asked Tom MacKay. 'Are you okay? Not injured in any way?'

'I'm okay . . . functioning at least.'

'We've started questioning the two hawkers, the ones who pushed their cart out in front of the van.'

'Got anything from them?'

'No admissions, not yet,' Tom MacKay shouted above the increasing noise.

256

Dave shouted back. 'They're in it up to their necks. I saw one of them move his bloody cart out of the way to let the Volvo through.'

'Didn't want his cart damaged, that's what he says.'

'Bullshit! They're both accessories to murder. I saw what I saw, Tom. There's no way that was an accident, no way on earth!'

'There is one thing – both men have tattoos on their arms.'

'The dragon flying through the circle of flame?'

'Both identical.'

'They have to be Fung's men.'

'They deny any knowledge of Conrad Fung. Never heard of him, that's what they say.'

'What about Tselentis, has he been located yet?'

'No sign of him.'

'His mother runs a shop in Aberdeen,' Dave shouted. 'He has an uncle too, Ma Chi-wan is his name. He's a fisherman. He has his own deep-sea junk. If Tselentis is going to try and get out of Hong Kong, that's probably the way he'll try to do it.'

Tom MacKay went forward to the cockpit, radioing information through to Police Headquarters. He asked for a progress report and then returned to the belly of the chopper.

'Any developments?' asked Dave. 'Anything on the killer?'

Tom MacKay shook his head. 'We're doing everything we can, Dave, stopping every car, searching every building. We've got police at every exit point. We've broadcast his description, asking people to give us any information they can. All the stops are out. The bastard isn't going to get away, not if I can help it.'

Dave turned to face him. 'I hope not, Tom,' he said, barely able to contain his emotions. 'You see, he's the same man I saw at Kai Tak . . . the man who killed my son.'

Without warning, marine-police stormed aboard the junk. They isolated the crew in the wheelhouse and began a systematic search of the vessel. More police officers stormed into the shop on the shore. They searched every room, they searched the streets and alleys nearby. But they found nothing.

In the shop, Lau Wai-hing, despite her nervousness, kept her bond of trust. She told the police that she had no idea where Tselentis was. She thought he was still in custody. When the police found spots of watery blood on the basin at the back of the shop, she explained that a delivery man had cut his finger.

On the fishing junk itself, Uncle Ma remained stubbornly tight-lipped. He refused to say whether he had seen his nephew or not. This was Hong Kong, he said, a free society, at least for the next few years. He had a right to silence and he intended to exercise that right.

Police did manage to find the old Hakka woman, the one who had brought Tselentis to the junk in her sampan. Did she remember the journey? Yes of course, she answered, it had been just half an hour earlier. She wasn't senile. Anyway, she had seen the man many times before. He was short and round with black hair. He spoke Cantonese fluently.

When the police looked pleased, the old woman knew that somehow she had said too much and her memory immediately began to fade. She didn't want to cause trouble for the fishing junk families who were her main customers. She couldn't remember the exact junk of course, she said. It was somewhere along that line . . . or maybe it was the next line, she couldn't be sure. The marine police extended their search to the neighbouring junks. But they still had no success.

The head of the search party, a young Chinese inspector, took Uncle Ma to one side. 'We know he was here,' he said. 'The old sampan lady confirms it. I don't think you understand. Nobody wants to hurt him. He was cooperating with the police. After what happened, it's understandable that he's frightened. But you're not helping him, not by hiding him. Please, listen to some reason, tell me where he is.'

But Uncle Ma clung to his right of silence. He merely shrugged, staring out of the wheelhouse through the crowded masts and rigging of the fishing junks.

'You may well be committing a criminal offence,' said the inspector. 'Why get yourself into trouble for nothing? Tell me, where is he?'

'I do not know,' Uncle Ma replied. But of course he did know, he knew only too well. As he stared out of the wheelhouse, he could see a lone fishing junk making its way down the crowded central channel heading for the open sea. The junk was owned by an old friend in his debt, and, in repayment of that debt, Dimitri Tselentis was hidden aboard.

Rexford's intention was to drive direct to the airport. He had a ticket booked on a flight to Jakarta departing early that afternoon. Fat Kwok took the Eastern Island Tunnel under the harbour coming up in the industrial area of Kwun Tong. It was the longer route to the airport but normally less congested. That day, however, the road to Kai Tak was a turgid groan of vehicles, bumper to bumper all the way.

If he had reached the airport on schedule fifteen minutes earlier, Rexford would not have heard the newsflash on the car radio. He would have entered the terminal unawares. But when it came through, it spun everything on its head.

There had been a fatal gun battle in Shau Ki Wan, it said. Details were sparse but it appeared that police, escorting two witnesses to court, had been attacked by an unknown number of assailants using automatic weapons. The vehicle in which the witnesses were travelling had been destroyed with an explosive device. A territory-wide hunt was underway for one of the alleged attackers, described as a European male in his mid-forties, about five foot eleven, strong build, red hair. Initial reports indicated that two men had been killed in the gun battle. The first was one of the witnesses, a Chinese male. The second was a police officer. The fate of the second witness was not yet known but police sources indicated that, in the confusion of the gun battle, the witness had fled.

'Stop the car!' said Rexford. 'Stop now, pull into the side!'

Fat Kwok did as he was instructed. His English was not good enough to absorb all the details of the newsflash. 'What is it?' he asked anxiously. 'What did it say?'

Rexford did not reply, not immediately. He sat very still, only his jaw muscles working, staring stonily ahead. 'One of the witnesses got away,' he said at last. 'Tselentis is still alive.'

The police found the Volvo late that afternoon. It remained where it had been abandoned behind its screen of bamboo scaffolding on the building site. Tyre treads in the dirt revealed that a second vehicle had been waiting. It was obvious that everything, including the method of escape, had been carefully preplanned.

The watchman at the building site was questioned. He admitted seeing the Volvo drive in and seeing the two occupants depart in the second car, a white sedan of some sort but he could not remember the make. He said he had allowed the vehicles on to the site because they had stickers on their windshields. How they had obtained those stickers he did not know. He wasn't management, only a watchman. He admitted he was under a duty to record the registration number of every vehicle that came on to the site but that only applied he insisted, to vehicles delivering things, bricks and piping and the like. No, he had no idea of the registration number of the second vehicle, no idea at all.

A search of the site was carried out, of course. But by then the watchman had recovered his bucket. He had emptied it into the dirt so that the scum of the shaving cream and the fine peppery flecks of hair were lost. As for the hair that had been cut off in bigger chunks with scissors, Rexford had scuffed dust and rubble over the area where it lay. So the search continued for a red-haired man . . . the red hair, that remained the key.

Dave remained at the airport that night until the last flight had taxied out on to the runway and there was no chance –

no matter how remote – of a final passenger boarding. He had been there ten hours, knowing in his heart it was futile, but doggedly hoping against hope, watching the endless stream of passengers pass through the checkpoints into the departure lounge. In all that time he had seen only two dozen passengers, men in their thirties or older, who had reddish or ginger hair. None had resembled the murderer of his son, the murderer of his best friend.

Eventually, around midnight, he left. It had started raining, warm thick Asian rain that scoured the pavements. His mind was so pummelled that it took him time to work out that his motorbike was still at Benevolence Villas. He caught a taxi, too exhausted to worry about the cost.

The rain came down harder, beating against the roof. Dave sat in the back, cocooned in the darkness, and all the questions that he had managed to shut out until now came at him as hard as the rain. How had they been caught so flat-footed? What in the hell had happened? Had he inadvertently done something wrong, spoken out of turn, advertised himself in some way? Was he somehow to blame? Because there was only one way the killer could have known the exact spot and the exact time – somebody must have passed him the information. But who, for God's sake, who? So few knew the details and those who did he would trust with his life, every last one of them.

When he got up to the apartment, the lights were on. Hannah was waiting for him. Her eyes were swollen, she had been crying. The news of Kit's death had crushed her. She and Kit had been close friends for so long. Kit had been the best man at their wedding – he had been Danny's godfather.

'I'm so sorry,' said Hannah, fighting back the tears. 'I'm so, so sorry.'

Dave could only nod. He had no words.

'Are you okay?' she asked.

'I'm fine.'

'You weren't hurt in any way?'

'No.'

'Tom MacKay said you were at the airport. I phoned and

phoned but they didn't know where you were. I was so worried.'

'I'm sorry, I should have phoned myself.' The ghost of a smile, part apology, mostly love, lay on the gaunt, harrowed creases of his face.

'I'll make you coffee,' she said.

'If you don't mind, I'm going to have a shower.'

He stood under the water for a long time watching Kit's dried blood wash away in a thin stream of crimson. He had hoped the water would wake him, let him think a little clearer. But he remained in a functional trance.

After they had drunk their coffee, he and Hannah lay together in the darkness. In silence they shared their grief. After a long time, in the early hours of the morning, Hannah fell asleep. But for Dave sleep was impossible. He was beyond exhaustion. He lay staring at the ceiling, at the fan endlessly churning the damp air, and the one question kept pounding at him with the same relentless rhythm. Who had leaked the information? Who could it have been? Who? Who?

Chapter Eighteen

It had rained all night, hard monsoonal rains that swept across the South China Sea. The rain blanketed the Pearl River Estuary, that great expanse of mud flats and rocky islands that the Chinese used to call the Peninsula of the Water Lily. With the encroachment of dawn, however, the rain ceased. The sky lightened a little but remained a dull, water-washed grey. The air was thick, every sound suffocating in the humidity. The water was still, the silence immense.

The fishing junk heaved to three hundred yards off Hak Sa beach and waited. The island of Coloane, the most southerly of the three islands that made up the tiny Portuguese enclave of Macau, was shrouded in mist. Only Hak Sa beach, named for its black sand, stood clear, a long charcoal strip against the soft lapping of the tide.

Dimitri Tselentis came up on deck, unshaven, eyes red, having barely slept. He was offered tea and sat waiting with the rest of the crew. A few of them smoked but there was no talk, only the tense, silent waiting.

They heard the small boat before they saw it, the growl of its outboard motor cutting through that great grey blanket of silence. The motorboat came alongside.

The captain of the junk shook Tselentis's hand. 'You must go now,' he said in rough, colloquial Cantonese. 'This man is a fisherman like us. He will take you to an apartment in town. Don't worry, everything has been arranged. You must wait there until your uncle comes. He has things to arrange. It may be a few days, perhaps a week or longer. Do not leave the apartment. He will come to you when he is ready.'

263

Tselentis climbed down into the motorboat. He waved to the captain and sat in the stern as it headed back to shore. The boat moored just north of Hak Sa beach at a jetty in among the rocks. The fisherman led him up through the trees to the road. There was a car waiting, a small blue Fiat, wet with mist. 'Climb in,' said the fisherman.

They left Coloane, crossing the causeway to the island of Taipa and from there across the long, curved bridge to Macau itself. They were never stopped, never once saw a policeman. It was the first time that Tselentis had appreciated the contented, Latin indolence of the place.

Macau had been a Portuguese possession since 1556. Centuries ago it had possessed a monopoly on trade between China and Europe. Under the influence of the Jesuits it had been a centre of Asian studies. The museum still contained wonderful old maps and journals. But those days of wealth and academic stature were long gone. The inner harbour had silted. Macau was now a sleepy backwater, a place where the Hong Kong fat cats came to gamble in the casinos and the tourists came over at weekends to wash down curried crab with cheap rosé wine.

It was early still, just six. Even on Macau the traffic was light. They swung into the narrow back streets past the tea houses, the early morning meeting places for the old men and their song birds. Somewhere along the Rua do Pagoda, the Fiat pulled up on the pavement next to an old, colonial-style building. A short walk north through the streets would take them to the border with China. But of course Tselentis had no passport, no travel document of any kind – not yet at least.

'Go upstairs to the first floor,' said the fisherman. 'Go into apartment five. The door is open.' He waited for Tselentis to climb out and, without a further word, drove off.

Nervously, Tselentis entered the building, climbing the stairs. The place smelt musty, of joss sticks and damp paint. He could hear a baby cying in one of the ground-floor apartments. He opened the door to apartment five. It was small, even smaller than the apartment in Benevolence Villas: a tiny lounge, kitchenette, bedroom with shower. The windows had wooden shutters through which the light filtered in soft, translucent bars. The floors were of pinkish marble in the Portuguese style, the furnishings were sparse. Tselentis checked the fridge. It was full, a week's supply at least. But there was no television, no radio, just a couple of paperbacks, some back issues of *Time* and a Scrabble set.

It was going to be a long, hard wait.

In Hong Kong that morning, out in the New Territories, everything was green and slippery and wet. The back roads into the villages had turned to mud. Water dripped from the leaves of the mango trees. Mist, like gauze, lay on the hills and the air was blood-warm.

Sam Ephram had never been into the New Territories before, the lungs of Hong Kong, the land beyond the nine hills of Kowloon. He was collected from the Regent and driven out in the air-conditioned comfort of a Mercedes. The journey took an hour along congested roads past duck farms and housing estates and finally along a dirt track to an old brick building in the hills above Tai Po. This was where his meeting was to take place, his meeting with Pang Wai-ping – Flat Nose, as the Cantonese called him.

The building was a small factory, a gloomy Dickensian place where kapok was stuffed into cheap mattresses. The cotton-like mulch lay everywhere, coating the walls with a grey-textured, slimy fungus. There was no air-conditioning, no semblance of comfort. Six or so workers toiled bare-chested in the wet heat, old men before their time.

There was a room at the back, a small room with a desk. A mildewed calender hung on the wall, some Taiwanese beauty, Miss June, advertising compatible software. There was no air-conditioning here either but there was a fan at least which moved the air. A table had been set up in the room with two chairs. A pot of tea stood on the table and two thimble cups had been set out, Chiu Chow style.

'Ah my friend, it is good to see you.' Pang Wai-ping entered through a side door. 'My apologies for the surroundings,' he said. 'But at least we are secure here.'

Ephram answered with a fixed smile. He took out a

handkerchief, mopping his brow. 'I take it that you own this factory?'

'A modest business but profitable.' Pang gave a self-conscious smile, a small puckering of his lips beneath the rubbery mush of his nose. 'I have a contract to supply mattresses to the Hong Kong Prison Service.'

'Then may you never have to sleep on your own mattress,' said Ephram and they both laughed, appreciating the irony.

'Would you like tea?'

'Thank you.'

Ephram waited while Pang poured the scented tea, setting one of the thimble cups in front of him. He felt dizzy. He wasn't used to the stifling heat. Specks of kapok, like pollen, floated in the air.

They both sipped the tea: the etiquette of Asian crime. Then Pang removed a small transparent packet from the breast pocket of his shirt which he placed on the table. 'A sample,' he said. 'Excellent, ninety percent pure. Double Uoglobal brand, grown in Burma. Best Number Four on the market. I know you were anxious about quality. I have the first twenty-five units waiting. Take them any time you wish, Khalil.'

Pang had always known Ephram by that name, the name of Ephram's birth, Khalil Khayat. Pang had no idea that a man called Ephram existed. It was one of the benefits of having two names, two totally different personalities.

Ephram took up the sample, looked at it and, with a thin smile, handed it back. 'We have done business for many years. I purchased from you when I was still in Istanbul. We have never had problems in the past. By now I think we can trust each other.'

Pang smiled, accepting the compliment.

'How must I pay for the first twenty-five units?' asked Ephram. 'Cash?'

Pang nodded. 'I will send a man to your hotel tomorrow. Say, four in the afternoon?'

'I will have the money waiting.'

'What about collection of the merchandise, Khalil? How do you wish that to be done?'

'As far as collection is concerned – and shipping too – I must seek your assistance,' said Ephram. 'I will need a couple of people, people who can be trusted.'

Pang poured tea. 'You wish them to handle the merchandise, transport it for you? I see no problem in that.'

'Except they must have experience in the garment industry – shipping, quality control . . .'

Pang sipped his tea. 'That is a little more difficult. You wish them to be employed in a garment company, is that it?'

Ephram nodded.

'For how long?'

'Several months.'

Pang considered the proposition. Then, diffidently, he said. 'I do have certain connections.'

Ephram smiled to himself. He knew all about those connections. Pang was Chiu Chow, and the Chiu Chow were notorious heroin dealers. They had connections that ran all the way from the poppy fields of the Golden Triangle to New York's Chinatown. The Chiu Chow also dominated one of Asia's strongest triads, the Sun Yee On. Every Chiu Chow in the drug trade owed some kind of allegiance to it. It was the common pool into which they could all dip when the need arose.

'Hong Kong was built on garments,' said Pang. 'It cannot be too difficult to find these people you want. They will require commission, say, a thousand each, two thousand US dollars per unit. That, I think, is reasonable.'

Ephram nodded his agreement. 'It is understood, of course, that they will handle everything, the collection of the merchandise, the packing, the shipping.'

Pang gave a knowing smile. 'Why buy a dog and bark yourself? If you wish, you need have no connection with them at all. It can be done through middle men.'

'No, I must maintain control, even if there is some risk involved. Once they are recruited, let me know. I will brief them.'

'Do the owners of this garment company know anything?'

'Nothing.'

'How happy will they be about the employment of two extra people?'

'That's covered,' said Ephram. 'I have a connection to the company . . . financial, directorial. We're expanding rapidly, we need the extra personnel. The labour market is tight in Hong Kong. I will say they were recommended to me. I took it upon myself to hire them before they were snapped up elsewhere. Simple enough. Provided of course they are experienced.'

'They will know their job,' Pang assured him.

'Good. How long do you think it will take to find them? Time, as you know, is important.'

Pang shrugged. 'A few days,' he said, 'no more.'

A small group of journalists and television people were clustered at the gate of the Metropolitan Correctional Centre in South Dade County. The moment Edgar Aurelius saw them, he felt his stomach knot. He knew exactly why they were there and they clearly knew who he was – somebody had tipped them off – because, as his car drew up, they swarmed around it.

Aurelius was not good with people. He was too acerbic, too defensive, too quick to resort to sarcasm. But in the United States, a refusal to speak to the Press was as good as an admission of guilt. With trepidation, he rolled down the window.

'Mr Aurelius, what does your client have to say about the Hong Kong attack?'

'My client knows nothing about the attack. I am on my way to tell him now.'

'What do you think his reaction will be?'

'The same as mine, I am sure. Shock, outrage. Mr Fung abhors violence.'

'Except this violence may just have destroyed the case against him?'

'My client always wished to prove his innocence in the courts of law, the way an honourable man does it.'

'What about his claim to be a diplomat?'

'Yes, that's true, my client does have diplomatic status.'

268

'Tell us, how does a Chinese man from the Philippines get to represent a Middle Eastern country like the Yemen?'

'Mr Fung is an economist and businessman of great skill.'

'What's happening on the diplomatic front? Any comment there?'

'We are negotiating with the State Department at this moment, lobbying in Congress too. The case against my client is nothing more than a poisonous crusade hatched by a single police officer. In his own wretched way he may believe in the justice of his cause. But the fact is, he has the wrong man. It's an outrage that Mr Fung is still in custody, an affront to the Republic of the Yemen and its people, an affront to international standards of justice – print that with pleasure.'

The gates swung open and Aurelius drove through. He was flushed but happy with the brief exchange. The last few words had been a bit aggressive, a little overblown perhaps. But why not? They had the tools at last and they were getting the job done. They were entitled to a little rhetoric.

Conrad Fung was waiting for him in the small beige box of a room where their meetings were conducted.

Aurelius sat opposite him, a dry smirk on his lips. 'I remember you telling me a little while back, Conrad, that I shouldn't concern myself with the witnesses in Hong Kong. They would be dealt with, you said. Well, it seems you were right. There were developments in Hong Kong yesterday – fairly dramatic developments.'

Fung said nothing but Aurelius saw the way he clenched his fists, the sudden lifting of the chin in anticipation.

'Wong and Tselentis were being taken to court to sign their affidavits when they were attacked,' said Aurelius. 'Wong was shot dead along with one police officer.'

'Whitman?'

'No, another European.'

There was a flicker of disappointment in Fung's eyes. 'What about Tselentis?' he asked.

'Tselentis fled. Nobody know where he is. Hector Chan spoke to some of his police contacts. They believe he has found a way out of Hong Kong and has gone to ground.'

'Did he sign his affidavit?'

'No, the attack took place on the way to court, before the signing.' With a self-satisfied grin, Aurelius removed his glasses, polishing them with his handkerchief. 'The State Department is in disarray Conrad. Zachary Hedgewood has done a brilliant job. You may just walk free on that basis alone. But even if the State Department filibusters, plays for time . . . well, with Tselentis missing – unless the Hong Kong police can find him and get his evidence across within the sixty days allowed by the extradition treaty – you still walk free.'

Fung smiled, cold and enigmatic. 'Don't worry, Edgar,' he said, 'they won't find him . . . not alive at least.'

Four days had passed and they had achieved nothing. The Hong Kong press had received further letters claiming that the Japanese Red Army had carried out the attack but nobody, except a few eccentrics in Special Branch, believed the Red Army claims anymore.

Tom Mackay, like everybody in the Organised Crime and Triad Group, had taken Kit Lampton's death badly. He was exasperated, he was angry, he was at a loss what to do for the best. 'Four days,' he said that evening as he and Dave sat in the mess, 'four days chasing our bloody tails. We don't know who the killer is, we don't know where he comes from. All we have is your description. But by now the bastard has probably dyed his hair black and grown a ponytail. You want my opinion, I think he's sitting on a beach in the Bahamas counting the goddamn money Fung paid him.'

'No,' said Dave, 'I think he's still here. He's not going to run scared, he's going to try and finish the job. He has to find a way of getting to Tselentis and the most obvious way is through the uncle or mother.'

'We have them both under surveillance,' said Tom Mackay. 'But they're free agents Dave. There's no way we can restrict their movements. About the only thing we can pin on the uncle is a misdemeanour for buggering around with the police. Technically, Tselentis was in voluntary custody, remember that. It's not a question of assisting a wanted fugitive.'

'Has anybody spoken to the uncle, explained the danger he could be in?'

'Sure, I did it personally.'

'And?'

'And, as Woody Allen says, he told me to increase and multiply – but not in those words exactly.'

'What about the mother?'

'Tight as a clam. Neither of them are going to say a word. Sonny boy is free and running. He's going to find himself a mud hut in Timbuktu and be happy the rest of his life.'

'Do you mind if I speak to the mother?' asked Dave. 'I don't want to make it official, just a personal visit. But in a strange kind of way Tselentis and I grew to trust each other. I think she knows that. Maybe she'll open up to me a little more.'

'Why not?' said Tom Mackay. 'At the moment we're getting nowhere fast. Just don't dangle her over the balcony.'

Ephram met them in a dim sum restaurant on Nathan Road, a large, noisy establishment decorated in red and gold with mirrors everywhere. At first sight, he was disappointed. He had been hoping for a more innocuous couple – Cantonese petit bourgeois, honest and dull. These two, however, gave off an air of hostility that was tangible fifty feet away. The two introduced themselves. Both spoke fluent, American-accented English. They had been living in Canada, they said. They had got married a couple of months back. Now they were back in Hong Kong looking for fast times and better money. The husband called himself Paco Lai. He had worked for Flat Nose Pang before, obviously Sun Yee On. He was thin, nervy, constantly picking at his food. But he was articulate and nobody's fool. His wife called herself Candy. In her dress sense she came close to the music hall image of a whore: tight clothing, bangles the size of grenades, face powder applied with the consistency of clay. But she was bright too, surprisingly so.

271

Ephram began to relax. All they needed, he thought, was a little polishing . . .

That evening, Ephram telephoned Hannah at the factory. 'I'm sorry but I have to fly out tomorrow,' he said. 'There are so many things happening in New York – the other, duller side of my business life. I have a day in Tokyo and then on to New York. I'm sorry I have to rush off like this but I was hoping we could spend tonight together, dinner perhaps.'

Hannah, however, was clearly reluctant. 'There's no way Scott and I can get away before nine tonight,' she said. 'And I promised Dave I would be home.'

'An hour, that's all, just a cocktail in my room at the hotel?'

She laughed. 'Your cocktails tend to last longer than an hour.' And she wouldn't be persuaded. 'I'll be in New York myself in a few days. We'll have time together then. I see Dave rarely enough as it is, Sam, and with Kit's death and everything . . .'

'Yes, of course, I understand,' he said, doing his best to stifle his frustration. 'These have been difficult times. I can see why you need to be with him.' Then, with barely a pause, he said. 'By the way, do you remember our discussion about the need for additional staff? Well, I had two people – a husband and wife team – recommended to me today by an old acquaintance in the clothing business. The husband is a shipping clerk, the wife a quality controller. They're back from Canada and looking for work. I tried to get through to you but your line was engaged. So I made the decision myself, I hope you don't mind, and offered them both a job. It's strictly on probation of course.'

Hannah was a little surprised but that was all. 'Fine,' she said. 'If you think they'll do the job. When do they start?'

'Tomorrow morning.'

She laughed. 'My God, no messing around! But you're right, we desperately need the extra staff, especially on the shipping side. With so many boxes of samples going out, we're soon going to be up to our necks in air freight.' She asked him. 'Will I see you tomorrow before you go?'

'Are you free for lunch?'

She gave a long moan of frustration. 'God, it's awful, isn't it? Where does all the time go? I'm sorry, Scott and I have an all-day meeting in the New Territories with one of the factories producing our collections.'

'What time will you be back?'

'In the early evening, by six at the latest. Is that too late for you?'

'No,' said Ephram, 'I can make it. Don't worry, I will see you then.'

Dimitri Tselentis's mother had a private room at the Adventist Hospital. Her son had seen to that. When Dave got to visit her the following afternoon, she was sitting up in bed, propped up with pillows, watching a Cantonese soap opera on television. Dave brought a modest bouquet of flowers with him, white and yellow roses.

Madam Ma cast him a stern look. She put on her glasses to see him better and said, in Cantonese, 'You needn't have brought flowers. I'm being discharged in a day or two. They'll only go to waste.'

Dave placed the roses into water. 'You're going home? That's good.'

'About time,' she said. 'I hate hospitals. I hate the smell and I hate the food.'

Smiling, Dave sat next to her bed. 'You must know why I've come.'

'Of course I know. But you're wasting your time. I've already told the others. I have no idea where my son is.'

'He could be in danger, you know that: very grave danger.'

'Of course I know that. Look what happened five days ago. It's a miracle he got out of that van alive. You promised you would protect him.'

'I can make no excuses,' said Dave. 'All I can tell you is that in future nobody will underestimate the threat. If your son comes back, if he agrees to continue his cooperation, I promise you, we'll do everything humanly possible to protect him.'

She gave a disdainful shrug. 'How do you protect him

against your own kind Mr Whitman, against police officers who sell secrets to Conrad Fung? I'm not blaming you or that poor friend of yours who died but how else would those murderers have known to be waiting on the street at that exact time?'

'Now that we know the full nature of the threat – including betrayal from inside the system – we can guard against it,' said Dave. 'If necessary we'll put him into protective custody outside of Hong Kong. It can be done, somewhere in America or Europe. But your son has to let us know where he is. He escaped Fung once. Do you think he will escape him a second time?'

Madam Ma lay back on her pillows. 'The greatest mistake my son ever made was to associate himself with that man. But at least he understands him, he knows how Fung's mind works and how he operates. Dimitri knows that the minute he is tied to one place, the minute he is in the custody of government officials, Fung will find a way of getting to him. The attack on the van proved it. You can hide Dimitri where you like Mr Whitman, put him on top of a mountain in Alaska. But you cannot keep it a secret. People will still have to make entries in files, people will still be willing to sell what they know. The ability to buy people – that is one of Fung's greatest skills. Policemen, immigration officials, prison warders, they are all underpaid and none of them are angels. Dimitri's only chance is to stay away from people like that. He must be free, he must be with the kind of people he can trust.'

Dave got up from his chair. 'I know that Dimitri will contact you,' he said. 'He's a good son. Let him know what I've said, that's all I ask. If he stays out there on his own, he'll be running for the rest of his life.'

Madam Ma looked up at him, her gaze steady, her resolve unbroken. 'You are a good man, Mr Whitman. But Dimitri is free now, free of you all. Why don't you leave him that way?'

Dave could understand why Tselentis's mother thought the way she did. It was always easiest to run away from problems, hide in a corner and pretend they didn't exist. But she was wrong, as wrong as could be.

Until Conrad Fung was convicted, until his power base was destroyed, Tselentis would remain a hunted man. But there was only one way for that conviction to be obtained – Tselentis had to return, he had to point his finger at Fung across a court of law and send the bastard down. Tselentis was the key, the key to everything. Somehow he had to be found and persuaded to come back. But how?

He wasn't a wanted murderer on the run, he was an unwilling witness, that's all. Foreign police agencies couldn't be expected to waste money and manpower trying to track him down. Even if they did, they couldn't hold him. Maybe the Americans could be persuaded to put out an Interpol Red Notice charging him with money-laundering offences. But how effective would that be? Many countries only recognised money laundering as a crime within very narrow limits. Many didn't recognise it as a crime at all. Tselentis could enter those countries without any fear of arrest. As for Hong Kong, it had no jurisdiction to send its police officers halfway around the world looking for him . . . *not officially anyway*.

Dave knew what he had to do. As soon as he got back to OCTG from the Adventist Hospital, he went through to Tom Mackay's office. 'I'd like to take some leave,' he said.

Tom Mackay leant back in his chair, put his hands behind his head and gave a broad, conspiratorial grin. 'Good idea. You've probably got about six months in the kitty. I'll recommend whatever you need. When are you thinking of leaving?'

'If I can get a ticket out, tomorrow night after Kit's funeral.'

'Where are you thinking of going?'

Dave grinned back at him. 'There's a little island in the Aegean Sea. I thought I might start there. It's called Kos.'

Dave hadn't much to go on, just snatches of conversation he and Tselentis had had over the past weeks, snatches that he now hoped would point the way.

At the hospital, when Madam Ma had been talking about her son's best chances of survival, she said he had to be with people he could trust. But, alone out there, running for his life, terrified of Fung's powers to corrupt, terrified even of the police who were on his side, whom could he trust? Family, that's who – only family.

Dave recalled a conversation he and Tselentis had had one evening. They had been talking about Wong Kam-kiu, how he had killed his wife and child. It had turned Tselentis's blood cold. He remembered Tselentis's words – suffocating them like that, one after the other, you might as well tear your heart out. They had moved on to the question of family generally and Tselentis had said that family was everything. Every Greek, every Jew, every Cantonese and Italian knew it, without family you were nowhere, just floating in a vacuum.

Family – yes, that had narrowed it down. But Tselentis had family all over the world. Then he had remembered another part of the same conversation he had had with Tselentis. The ex-wife, yes, Melina . . . *that's the crazy thing, now that we're divorced we've got the perfect relationship. She's back home on the island of Kos. I see her a couple of times a year. We confide in each other, we never argue. Even the sex is better!* So the ex-wife it had to be, she was the starting point.

By six that evening Dave's bookings had been confirmed; Swissair to Zurich departing the following night, a connection south to Athens and from there to the island of Kos.

He appreciated only too well that it was all being done in a rush, head first and head down, following his nose. But there were times when fancy plans were of no value at all, when the only way ahead was to start at the most likely point and see where the road took you.

He still had Hannah to tell, of course. He dialled her office number but it was engaged. Well, at least she was there. Provided she wasn't up to her neck in work, hopefully they could have one last dinner before he left; a few hours together.

He left his office and made his way downstairs. On his

motorbike, if he took the Cross Harbour Tunnel, he could be at her factory in Tsim Sha Tsui within quarter of an hour.

When Sam Ephram arrived to say goodbye, most of the staff had already left. Just a couple remained, packing up their things. Hannah and Scott Defoe were through in Hannah's office. After a full day in the New Territories, Hannah had a dozen or more calls to return and was at her work board, mug of coffee in one hand, telephone receiver in the other.

'Tell me, did those two new people show up today?' Sam Ephram asked Scott. 'The husband and wife.'

'Yeah. Here first thing.'

'How did they do?'

'Hannah and I were out most of the day but they seem to know what they're doing. They should be okay.'

'Apparently the husband did a lot of air freight work in Canada so you can get him on to that. It's the beginning of a long upward curve Scott. If things go the way I envisage, we'll need new offices, at least double the staff. There are some profound changes on the way.'

'I hope you're right,' said Scott. He glanced at his watch. 'I'd better be on my way. I've got a junk trip to Lamma tonight. Seafood and beer and a night on the water – it's hell in the East.'

Sam Ephram gave a polite smile. 'Have a good evening.'

'Thanks. And have a good trip back to the States. We'll be seeing you soon.' Scott left the office, grabbing his jacket. He checked that the last of the staff had gone and shouted through to Hannah. 'Okay, everybody has gone. There's just you. Can you lock up?'

'No problem,' Hannah called back. 'I'll see you tomorrow. Have a good time on the junk.'

She put down the telephone. 'The calls can wait,' she said. But Sam Ephram could see from the agitated way she kept glancing down at the list that she wanted to get on with them.

'You're driving yourself too hard,' he said. 'I don't want you burning yourself out on me. Other people should be

277

doing half of this work. You should be concentrating on the creative side.'

She got up from her desk with a tired smile. 'You're right. I live in chaos. I need a whole new system. I just don't have time to organise it. When you're back again, you can instal all kinds of fancy computers, even hire me an office manager. How's that?'

He put his arms around her. That solemn, mesmerising smile was on his lips. 'It's a deal,' he said.

They walked out of the office towards the main door that led into the elevator lobby. Ephram kept his arm around her shoulder. She smiled up at him, obviously tired, a little limp, but her body was soft and warm against him. Ephram stopped, leant down and kissed her on the lips. He turned her body fully into his, pressing his hips against her. Last night he had been denied her, he wouldn't be denied again.

Hannah smiled up at him. 'You'll miss your plane,' she said.

'There's no rush, I have all the time I need.' His mouth was on her neck. He began to unbutton her blouse.

She laughed softly. 'But I've got so much work to do.'

'The work can wait,' he whispered. Her bra came free. He caressed her breasts and she gave a sudden delighted moan.

There was no way Hannah could resist him. 'But we can't do it,' she murmured. 'There's nowhere . . .'

'Just wait,' he said and there was a smile on his lips. On the workbench next to where they stood lay rolls of cloth. He took hold of the first one, a denim material, and rolled it out along the bare concrete floor. Then he took a second and a third, unfurling each, one on top of the other, magenta on green, burgundy on blue. 'There,' he said. 'Not the softest bed in the world but a bed all the same.'

He removed his jacket, his eyes on her all the time. He placed the jacket on the workbench, undoing his tie. He undid his shirt, letting it drop to the floor. Then, slowly, carefully, he undressed her until she stood naked before him, her clothes around her feet. He kissed her, his tongue searching her mouth. She clung to him, her body very warm, and slowly, locked together, they sank down on to the carpet of cloth.

Dave arrived at the building, parked his motorbike and took the elevator up to the third floor. When he came out into the lobby, he saw that the iron grill securing the entrance to the factory was still open. Good, he thought, so he hadn't missed her. He knew that the main door would be locked but there was a bell that could be rung. Most of the offices in the building had closed. It was very quiet. He walked towards the door.

As he drew closer, he heard something, almost like a person in pain. Puzzled, he reached the door. The sound was coming from the other side of the door, from within the factory, growing in intensity. Then suddenly it hit him. He stood there transfixed, sickened and yet unable to tear himself away. He could hear a man's hard, punctuated grunts and fixing with that, in the same harsh rhythm, a woman moaning. He knew exactly what was happening. He could see it in his mind, the man plunging into her, each stroke a summons for her cries, her belly curved up against him. The rhythm was intensifying, faster, faster, but he could not move. He was frozen there, a voyeur of his own destruction.

The peak came in a brief, harsh duet of cries. An abrupt silence ensued. Dave stood trembling at the door. Then he heard the woman's voice: 'Oh God, that was wonderful.' And all doubt was gone.

Shock can be a friend. It keeps the pain at bay. For a few moments there exists only a sense of disbelief, a kind of confusion as if the world has lost its centre and everything is out of kilter. During that short time, before the drowning comes, you can swim with events, even think rationally, plan and act and, like an animal gnawing at its own wound, confirm what you already know to be true.

Dave stood on the street three doors away from the entrance. The neon lights were on, shoppers crowded the pavement. Hawkers were out with their barrows selling cheap ties and shirts; others were selling food, hot squid and tripe. Tsim Sha Tsui at night: all colour and smell and crush. But Dave saw none of that, his eyes were focused only on the building. He knew who would be coming down but he needed confirmation, he needed the proof of his own eyes.

Ten minutes passed. But time meant nothing. It happened as he knew it would. That was never in doubt. Sam Ephram came down, leaving the building and standing in the street. Before walking away, he turned towards a shop window, using the reflection of the glass to adjust his tie. He looked like a man at ease with the world, one of life's winners.

Dave was waiting in the apartment when Hannah got home. He sat in a chair that looked towards the entrance so that he could confront her the second she was through the door. He had a glass of whisky in his hand. It was his second or third . . . he couldn't remember.

When Hannah came in, she smiled and called out to him. But the moment she saw Dave's face, the moment her eyes fell on that raw, implacable stare, she knew that something was terribly wrong. 'What is it?' she asked, the blood draining from her face.

At first, gagging on his humiliation, Dave couldn't find the words to answer. How did he even begin to start? Then out it came in a string of outraged sarcasm, cruel and stupid, the opposite of the way he wanted it to be. 'Did you have a good time at work at this evening?'

Hannah stared at him.

'I understand Sam Ephram came to see you.'

That hit her hard, he could see it. 'That's right,' she answered. 'He flew out tonight. He came across to say goodbye. Why, what's the matter?'

'I heard . . .' he said, his voice croaking, almost inaudible.

She blinked. Her lips opened but no sound came.

'I said, I heard.' He spoke louder this time, with more pain, more definition. 'You're lovers, aren't you?'

280

For a moment she was stunned. Then, protesting too much; she blurted out. 'No, no!' She shook her head so violently that her golden hair flew across her face.

'For God's sake Hannah, it's enough! I heard you! Jesus Christ, I was standing outside the door and I wanted to be sick, I wanted to run, anything, but I couldn't move. I heard you, the two of you. Don't you understand what I'm saying? The pretence is over, all the lies, the shit. It's finished, Hannah! I heard you, the two of you, I heard you there on the floor!'

Hannah closed her eyes. She swayed uncertainly on her feet. Her head fell forward. She was too stunned to answer.

'What angers me most,' said Dave, his voice tight, his chest heaving, 'is that I knew it all the time. I could see it happening and I kept saying to myself, no, don't eat your-self up inside. It's a business relationship, that's all.' His words trailed away into a small involuntary moan. He couldn't even look at her. He swallowed his whisky. 'Why?' he asked. 'Just tell me that.'

At first all she could do was shake her head. But then, in a fractured, half-incoherent way, she answered. 'Oh God, I don't know. Don't you think I've been asking myself that same question for weeks, since it began. I just don't know. I met him in New York, he swept me off my feet. But I never stopped loving you Dave, you have to know that. I always knew how wrong it was.'

'But you have to have some kind of explanation,' he demanded. 'Do you love him or was it just ambition? Were you so determined to be successful you didn't care what you did or who you had to sleep with?'

But again, all she could do was shake her head.

Dave's fury was meeting a brick wall. 'You said you wanted to remember Danny, that's what it was supposed to be all about. Well, was it? Do you think that's the way to remember our son? By wrecking our marriage, do you? Do you think this would make Danny happy?'

Tears welled up in Hannah's blue eyes. 'I'm so sorry,' she said. 'I promise, it'll never happen again, never. Please Dave, I love you.'

281

But there was no way Dave could accept that, not after what he had heard, not after the betrayal he had earlier witnessed. 'You're sorry? God, do you think that's enough?' he shouted. 'You wanted everything, didn't you? You wanted me, you wanted him – you wanted the world!'

Hannah looked at him, her eyes wide. She didn't know what to say. All she knew was that everything was tearing apart inside her and that she was going to lose him.

Dave's heart was near to breaking. He wanted so much to reach out and take her and be able to say, let's start again, let's pretend it never happened. But the hurt drove him on in a remorseless, wheel-grinding advance to perdition. 'You say you love me . . . but no, Hannah, it's your ambition – that's what you love! It's the money, it's the fame. You always wanted it, I just never knew how much until now. Christ, I have to make a bloody appointment to see you! Okay, I'm just a cop. I couldn't help you get there. So you go off and screw another man. Well, good luck to you. Screw Ephram to your heart's content.'

Tears were streaming down Hannah's cheeks. She was standing there saying nothing, knowing she loved him, knowing she was wrong. In her muteness she was pleading with him to stay, to give her one more chance. But Dave's course was irreversibly set. He had already packed a suitcase. It was waiting by the kitchen door. He walked across to it, picked it up and turned towards the front door.

'Please no, Dave, please,' said Hannah, the tears streaming. 'I'll find a way to make it up to you, I promise.'

But at that moment he was made of stone. 'You can't have everything Hannah, none of us can. That's what you never understood. You wanted it all, didn't you. Well, you made your choice. You turned your back on me, you turned your back on our memories. Now – somehow – we both have to try and live with it.'

Dave slept that night in a hotel in Wanchai near Police Headquarters. The following morning, in full dress uniform, he attended the funeral of Kit Lampton. The sun beat down as they fired a volley over Kit's coffin. The psalm of

David that begins, 'Yea though I walk through the valley of death . . .' was read by the Commissioner. Kit's parents were there. They had flown out from England for the ceremony, a sad couple trying to maintain their dignity in the burning, muggy heat of the tropics. During the service Dave glimpsed Hannah in the crowd. Her eyes were very red. It looked as if she hadn't slept. As soon as the service was finished, she left. They never got a chance to speak. What was there left to say?

After the service Dave said goodbye to Tom Mackay. They had a drink together, Dave promised to keep in touch, to report each of his locations. He never said anything about the break-up with Hannah.

That night, alone, he caught a taxi out to Kai Tak Airport. His son had been taken from him, his best friend had been murdered at his side. Now his marriage was finished. When he walked on board the plane, he was a man who had entered the long dark season of the soul.

Chapter Nineteen

Dimitri Tselentis had been holed up in the apartment on the Rua do Pagode for a full week; seven days, each counted by the hour, and he was about to go mad.

The telephone had not rung once. He had not heard from anybody. He had been left there, marooned. No television, no radio; he was too frightened even to put on the air-conditioning in case the neighbours realised the apartment was occupied. About the only thing he had dared do was take a daily shower.

There were times when he regretted ever fleeing. What was he getting himself into? If only he had kept his nerve. But what was done was done. What mattered now was getting away to somewhere safe. It didn't matter where, a cellar in Bulgaria, a stone hut in the Andes, just so long as he could build a life for himself. A new name, a new identity, money in the bank: then at last he would be safe from Fung and rid also of Whitman's relentless – fatal – quest for justice.

It was four in the afternoon, hot and unbearably muggy behind the closed shutters, when he heard the sound of footsteps on the stairs. Instinctively, he retreated to the kitchen. Then, like a pistol crack, came the knock on the door. He waited, too frightened to respond. What if Fung's men had found him? He fumbled for a carving knife that lay next to the sink. But it was useless protection and he knew it. He was too sick with fear to put up any worthwhile resistance. But then from the hallway a muffled voice called in Cantonese and relief flooded through him. He limped out of the kitchen. 'Uncle Ma, is that you?' he called.

285

'Yes, it's me. I'm alone. Let me in.'

Tselentis unbolted the door. 'I've been going out of my mind waiting here. Why have you taken so long?'

Uncle Ma sniffed at the air. 'It stinks in here. Why didn't you put on the air-conditioner? It's like a sauna. Look at you, you're sweating like a pig.' He went across to the wall, flipped the switch and grunted with satisfaction as the unit growled into life, cold air whooshing into the room. He had a brown paper bag with him which he set down on the dining table. 'Fresh fruit,' he said. 'It will put some colour back into your face.'

For a week now Tselentis had been living on long-life milk and canned food. He took out a peach, wolfing it down, the juice dribbling through his fingers. 'What's been happening?' he asked. 'Have you been able to organise anything?'

His uncle lit a cigarette. Since boyhood he had smoked forty a day. 'What's been happening? Well, for a start, you've been on the front page of all the newspapers.' He grinned impishly at him. 'You're a celebrity, Dimitri.'

Tselentis rolled his eyes. 'A celebrity, that's all I need. All I want to do is get out of this place, be as anonymous as possible.'

'Everything is arranged. Your mother and I have spoken. There's been plenty to do in the week. And with the cops checking everything, we had to be careful.'

'How is mother?'

'She should get out of hospital tomorrow.'

'I worry about the stress, how it must be affecting her condition.'

His uncle chuckled. 'Don't worry about her, she's fit and strong. Knowing that you're free at last has given her a new lease on life.'

'Free? I feel about as free as a chicken in a cage on its way to market.'

His uncle sat down at the table. 'As I said, it's all arranged. You're leaving today, in a few minutes time . . . across the border into China and up to Guangzhou. You'll spend tonight there in the house of a friend and tomorrow morning fly up to Beijing to connect with an international flight.'

'Where to?' asked Tselentis. 'Where are you sending me?'

His uncle removed a buff envelope from the inside pocket of his jacket. He opened the envelope, taking out an airline ticket which he placed on the table. 'See for yourself,' he said. 'Your mother and I agreed that you needed to be as far away as possible, the other side of the world, somewhere you can lose yourself. But a place also where you have family, people you can trust.'

Tselentis examined the ticket and a slow smile settled on his face. 'It's the best, I agree. But what about travel documents? How am I going to get there?'

'I have a passport for you,' his uncle said. 'It's genuine too, except for the photograph of course. You are now a Portuguese national born here in Macau.' He removed it from the buff envelope and passed it across to his nephew.

Tselentis picked it up. It looked comfortably well-worn. The previous photograph had been expertly removed and his own photograph, an old one from an international driving licence, glued in its place. His new name, he noted, was Manuel da Silva, the same name that appeared on his airline ticket.

'I have cash for you too, five thousand United States dollars,' said his uncle. 'It will be enough to keep you going. When you need more, contact either your mother or me. Don't use your own resources. Money leaves a trail of paper, you should know that.' Stubbing out his cigarette, he glanced at his watch. 'Come,' he said, 'you must be going. There is a small door at the back of the building which leads into a yard. There is a carpenter's van there. It has backed up to the door. You will be able to step into it without being seen. The carpenter is an old friend, you can trust him. He will take you across the border and drive you to Guangzhou. Hurry now. Don't forget your ticket and the passport. I will remain here until you are gone.'

The two men hugged, the old man patting Tselentis on the back. 'You just be safe now, you hear me.'

'Thank you for everything,' said Tselentis. 'I'll make it up to you, I promise.'

The old man smiled benignly. 'Rubbish. You're my nephew. What are families for?'

After he had watched the van drive off, Uncle Ma found the most comfortable chair in the apartment and sat down to wait. The barrier gate into China was less than three kilometres north, on the far side of town. His nephew should be through it within twenty minutes. But in case there was trouble, just in case, he had agreed with his friend to remain by the telephone.

Half an hour passed. He ate fruit and smoked. He made himself tea. When the hour was up and the phone had not rung, he knew that everything must have gone according to plan. Dimitri was now in China on the road to Guangzhou. Uncle Ma sat back, contented, and lit another cigarette.

Earlier that day, he had come across from Hong Kong on the jetfoil. It was a great ugly thing, a giant red and white cockroach that rode out of the water on skis. As an old fisherman, he found it an insult to the sea. But it did the journey in fifty minutes, that's all that seemed to matter these days. He had known of course that he would have a policeman shadowing him even if he was leaving the colony. That's why, after he had arrived in Macau, he had gone through such an elaborate charade.

First, he had visited the casino at the Hotel Lisboa, the biggest, noisiest, most garish in town. He had lost a few hundred at fan tan, played the slot machines for a time – hungry tigers, the Chinese called them – and then, when the crowd was at its thickest, he had ducked out of the casino through a fire exit door. One of his crew members had been waiting for him in a Mini-Moke, a little rag-top car, and they had driven off together. Five minutes later, on the Rua da Medeira, he had jumped out of the vehicle and entered a restaurant. He had walked right through the kitchen, out the other side, along an alley, through a yard and on to the Rua do Pagode.

There was no need now, of course, for the same complex

fandango. Now he could return to the casino at his leisure. He might even win a little back at the fan tan tables, he thought.

Luck was with him too that night. When he returned to the Lisboa, he won at fan tan and he won at roulette. He won himself a good few thousand, enough almost to recoup the expenses he had laid out on Dimitri. Delighted with himself, he had an expensive meal washed down with glasses of cognac, took a front seat at the Crazy Paris strip-tease show and then returned to win some more in the noisy, anxious crush of the casino.

Around two in the morning, a little tipsy, he decided he should find himself a room for the night. He would take the ferry – the red and white cockroach – back to Hong Kong in the morning. Right now he needed a sleep. The Lisboa was full but there was another hotel along the esplanade. He stepped out into the night air. A queue of taxis stood waiting. It was humid but there was a breeze blowing in from the sea, a good strong breeze that cleaned all the smoke and the muck from the lungs. Uncle Ma enjoyed the night breeze. It was a good night for a walk.

He started along the esplanade; as always there was a cigarette in his hand. The pavement cafés were closed; no people on the street, just a couple of taxis cruising by. The breeze ruffled the palm trees. Back at the Lisboa a band was playing. He could hear distant laughter.

Dimitri would be asleep now in Guangzhou. Poor Dimitri, he thought, what a mess he had made of his life. All that talent, all that money and where had it got him? He would be happy now to live in a dog kennel if people would only leave him alone. He heard the car draw alongside but thought nothing of it – another taxi probably. He didn't even turn his head.

Before he could react, the hand, like a black shadow, was clamped over his mouth. He tried to resist, tried to fight back, but he was seventy years of age, as brittle as a twig, and the man dragging him was built like a bull. He tried to scream but the hand over his mouth was held so tight that the insides of his lips were impaled on his teeth. Feebly kicking, he was hauled into the back of the car. His face was forced down into the seat, one arm was jerked up behind his back. He couldn't utter a sound, he could barely breathe. He was certain he was going to black out.

The car drove off along the esplanade. He felt it swing left at the monument to Gorge Alvares, the first Portuguese to set foot on Chinese soil, and knew it would be crossing the bridge to Taipa Island, away from the city.

As they crossed the bridge, the hand over his mouth was taken away. He gasped for breath. His arm was released and he was able to sit up, cringing in a corner of the seat. 'Take my money,' he said. 'I won't report it to the police. Just take it and let me go.'

For the first time the man sitting next to him spoke. 'I don't want your money,' he said in English.

Uncle Ma peered at him in the darkness. The man was a European, a large man with a reddish complexion. And he was bald, as bald as a Buddhist monk.

The car was parked on Taipa Island in among a dark shelter of trees close to the race track. The man behind the wheel, a Chinese, kept the engine running. The car radio played a medley of songs from *The Sound of Music* sung in Portuguese.

The European man spoke quietly, gently, like a doctor who had to tell a patient he was very ill. 'Why did you leave the casino through the fire exit door?'

'I was not feeling well,' blurted Uncle Ma. 'I needed air.'

'There was a vehicle waiting for you. I saw you drive off in it. You drove off at speed. Where were you going in such a hurry?'

'Nowhere, I swear to you. For an early meal, that's all. He was a friend.'

'But you had a meal at the casino, a very expensive meal. Two meals in one night? No, I don't think so. I think you came across to see Tselentis. This is where you have hidden him, here in Macau. Tell me where he is. That's all I ask.'

'I don't know.'

'Oh yes you do, Mr Ma. You know where he is or you

know where he is headed. And I promise you one thing . . . before the night is out you will tell me.'

Kos lay a few miles from the Turkish coast north of the Island of Rhodes. It was a small, mountainous island devoted to the business of tourism.

Dave flew in from Athens, landing at midday. He made his way through immigration dressed in a red running singlet, shorts and white joggers, just another face among the hundreds of Germans and Scandinavians who arrived every day to drink ouzo and lap up the early summer sun. He caught a bus into Kos town, a small Byzantine fishing port at the northeastern extremity of the island. Tselentis had said that his ex-wife's restaurant was set back from a place called Marmari Beach. The restaurant was named after her, he had said: Taverna Melina. Dave purchased a map of the island and sat down at a pavement café with a glass of beer to orientate himself.

The island was small, the road network simple. There would be no problem finding the place. Dave hired a motor-bike, one of the thousands leased to tourists, and headed back out of town.

The road to Marmari led along the northern coastal plain. It was a warm, blue afternoon with a mauve haze hanging over the central mountains. The road was busy, mainly with young, sun-bronzed tourists on motorbikes like himself or older tourists chugging up into the mountains in convoys of Lambrettas, husbands and wives in swimming costumes and straw hats.

Ten minutes from town he found the Marmari turn-off. He drove towards the beach along a narrow avenue lined with plane trees. On either side of the road goats grazed amid the stubble of reaped sunflowers. A brisk, warm wind came in from the sea and the air was full of the dry crackle of cicadas.

He came across the taverna at a junction in the road. It was a large, square building painted in the ubiquitous sun-glared white of the islands. There was a shaded patio at the front where a dozen or so tourists sat eating lunch.

291

Dave parked his bike and found a table on the patio. On the far side of the junction stood a residential dwelling, a white handsome building fronted by a low concrete wall. A name plate was set into the wall near the gate: M. Tselentis. So she was still using her married name. Dave wondered if Tselentis himself could be across there in the house hiding behind locked doors. With a little patience he would find out soon enough.

The moment she stepped out of the taverna to take his order, Dave knew it had to be her. She was a small woman, a little stout now but handsome. Her black hair was streaked with silver, her eyes full of wit and sparkle. She took his order in perfect English and lingered at the table to talk. 'You look as if you've just arrived,' she said. 'No tan as yet.'

Dave grinned.

'Where are you staying?'

'I only arrived a couple of hours ago. I'm still looking for somewhere. Around here if possible. Any suggestions?'

She pointed across the open fields towards a white building two hundred metres away. 'Villa Dionisia. They have rooms to let. Very clean, very good. A swimming pool too.'

'Thanks. I'll try it.'

He had a lunch of Greek salad and white wine then rode across to the place she had recommended. He obtained a room on the top floor, a room with a view back over the fields towards the road junction where the taverna and the house stood in the speckled shade of the plane trees.

In the late afternoon he put a call through to Hong Kong. It was close to midnight there and he caught Tom Mackay getting ready for bed. He gave him the address and telephone number of the villa.

'How long are you going to be there?' asked Tom.

'If Tselentis is here on the island, he could be anywhere,' said Dave. 'I've met the ex-wife. She's the obvious link. I'll have to shadow her and see where she takes me.'

'And if that gets you nowhere?'

'Then I'll just have confront her, lay it on the line. What else can I do, Tom? At the end of the day, that's all we've

292

got, isn't it, persuasion? She seems like a sensible enough woman. Maybe she'll see it our way. How have things been going in Hong Kong, any developments?'

'No,' said Tom, dispirited. 'Quiet as a tomb.'

In the morning the June heat came up fast. That was why the two joggers from the Hyatt Hotel on Macau's Taipa Island were out so early pounding the pathways together. They were American businessmen, both in their early thirties, taking a break with their wives from the stresses of Hong Kong. While they ran, they talked about the yen and inflation and how they planned to be back in the States at Christmas skiing at Aspen.

They came near the race course and, in the thick brush down near the shore, saw a pack of pariah dogs. The dogs appeared to be feeding on something, carrion of some kind. It was pure luck that one of the joggers heard a ripping sound, the sound of cloth being torn. He looked, wiping the sweat from his eyes, and thought he saw a glimpse of colour, the blue and white stripes of a shirt. He stopped his companion. 'What in the hell are those dogs feeding on back there?'

His companion, his face bright scarlet from the running, wanted to jog on. 'Leave those things well alone,' he said. 'You get bitten and you'll end up with rabies.'

But the man who had heard the ripping sound was concerned. 'I tell you,' he said, 'I saw something there, something spooky. Grab a couple of stones, let's see if we can't frighten the dogs away.'

Tom Mackay took upon himself the unpleasant duty of breaking the news to the next of kin. The deceased had no wife or children. He had been a bachelor all of his life. The only surviving family member in Hong Kong was his sister, just out of hospital.

He found her in her shop close to the waters of Aberdeen Harbour. She had been out of hospital less than a day and, although it was well past closing time, was still behind her counter going diligently through the books of account. Tom

Mackay took her to one side, sat her down and, as gently as he could, told her of the death.

At first Madam Ma was surprisingly resilient. 'He had a good long life,' she said, her face very pale. 'He is in a new life now. I am sure he has no regrets. Where was he found?'

'In Macau, on the Island of Taipa.'

Her eyes widened. Somehow she sensed what was to come. 'How did he die?' she asked, fear in her voice.

Tom Mackay tried to find the easiest, kindest way of answering. But what bland euphemisms were there for a situation like this? 'An autopsy still has to be conducted,' he said. 'But I'm afraid, Madam Ma, that all the signs indicate your brother was murdered. An attempt was made to bury his body. It was only by fortune that it was found so soon. I'm afraid I also have to tell you that, well, you see, certain marks were found on your brother's body . . . marks that indicate torture.'

It was ten in the morning, Dave's third day on Kos. He was sitting outside by the pool, pretending to read, looking across the open fields towards the taverna, and thinking all the time of Hannah, wondering what she was doing, what she was thinking, what would become of them both.

'Mr Whitman,' the barman called. 'Call for you – Hong Kong!'

It was Tom Mackay on the line. He explained in brief, dry terms how the body of Ma Chi-man had been found, how it was certain he had been tortured and then murdered.

Dave didn't need him to explain further. There could only be one reason for that kind of treatment. While he was digesting the shock of the news, Tom said. 'I have somebody with me, Dave. She wants to speak to you.'

'Who is it?'

'It's Tselentis's mother. She says she may be able to help.'

Madam Ma spoke in Cantonese. She spoke haltingly, out of a great depth of sadness, each word spare and appropriate. 'My brother was a good man,' she said. 'But he was frightened of pain like all of us. I am told he was tortured, that terrible things were done to him. I am sure my brother would have tried his best. But a man can only stand so much. Then he says things, anything to make the pain stop. Do you follow what I am saying? I am saying that Fung's people must now know where my son is hiding. They will go there and they will kill him unless you can get him back, unless you can get him into the safe custody you promised.'

'Where is he?' asked Dave.

'He is in Africa,' she said. 'He is on a small gold mine deep in the African bush. It is in a country called Zimbabwe.'

'If we can flash a message through Interpol, we can have him alerted within a couple of hours.'

'No,' she said firmly. 'I don't want this to be public knowledge. Mr Mackay knows about Zimbabwe and now you, that is all. You must go, Mr Whitman. Dimitri trusts you. If the message reaches him through a government official, he'll only panic and run again. We spoke about this before. You know how Dimitri feels, you know how I feel too.'

'But it's a question of time,' said Dave. 'Whoever killed your brother has a good twenty-four hours start. Sometimes the risks are necessary.'

'No,' she said again, just as firmly. 'Please, I will meet all the costs, but you must go. If Dimitri is escorted out of Zimbabwe by some police officer, there will be messages sent to Hong Kong, telexes, faxes . . . the word will circulate. It can never be kept secret, you know that. Dimitri will have an accident, a car crash, something that can never be explained. But he'll never get back here alive. Don't worry about the delay, he is with a relative, a man who knows how to look after himself. I'm sure he'll be safe until you get there.'

'Is there any way we can contact him by telephone?'

'He is very far out in the bush,' she said. 'We thought that would be safest for him. But there is no telephone.'

Bloody hell, thought Dave. 'All right,' he said. 'If I can get a flight out of here, I'll leave immediately. Can you give me the name of this mine, where I can find it?'

295

'It's called Shamwari Mine,' said Madam Ma. 'I don't know where it is but there is somebody who can tell you. You are on Kos at the moment, isn't that right? You went there thinking Dimitri would go to Melina?'

'It seemed probable at the time, yes – obviously a wasted trip.'

'No, not wasted at all,' she said. 'You see, Mr Whitman, the man who owns Shamwari Mine is her brother, Dimitri's brother-in-law. All you have to do is ask Melina, she is the one who can tell how to get to the mine.'

Bruce Rexford needed twenty-four hours back in Manila, just time enough to make arrangements, to collect more cash and restock. The old man had given the name of the country: Zimbabwe. He had given him the name of the mine: Shamwari. He had given him the name of the mine owner too. But the old man had never been to Zimbabwe, he didn't know its location. That Rexford would have to find out when he got there.

The quickest routing to Zimbabwe was back through Hong Kong but he was not prepared to tempt fate. The most viable routing for him was via Bombay on Air India. The total flying time from the Philippines was just short of twenty-four hours.

Zimbabwe was in central Africa. It was bordered to the south by South Africa and to the north, across the Zambezi River, by Zambia. It was a landlocked country well south of the equator. The month of June there would be early winter, the dry season. The days would be warm, the nights cold and dry.

Malaria tablets would be necessary in the bush; he would need bush clothing too, strong shoes. The prospect excited him, it was like the old days again, those hard-slogging days on patrol with Johnny Dean in the boondocks of Vietnam.

He chose two weapons, the first an elephant gun, a Holland and Holland double-barrelled 500 Nitro Express, 1935 vintage but better than anything made since. The elephant gun was more for show, to prove his bona fides when he arrived in Zimbabwe. The second weapon – the one he would almost certainly use – was the Soviet-designed Dragunov sniper's rifle, the one that he had smuggled back from Hong Kong.

One good thing about Zimbabwe, he thought, was the fact that this time there would be no need to break down the weapons into machine tool parts. This time they would be able to accompany him clearly marked and identified. Because this time he would be flying in legitimately to hunt big game.

Melina Tselentis gave Dave all the help she could. She understood only too well the kind of danger her ex-husband was in. His association with Fung had been one of the reasons why she had left him in the first place, she said.

She knew where Shamwari Mine was located. She had been there five years back to visit her brother, Nikos. It was situated in the far north of Zimbabwe, she told him, far out in the bush in a range of hills they called the Matusadonas. It was very remote, very isolated. Her brother had mined in the area for over twenty years. He loved it out there.

The nearest town, she said, was a place called Kariba. It was positioned on the Zambezi River where they had built a dam, flooding the river valley and creating one of the world's largest man-made lakes. But the mine was a good six hours drive from Kariba.

Dave asked her if she had a map to help him pinpoint the exact location of the mine. She said she did have one somewhere among her things, one that she had brought back from Zimbabwe. She found it for him among some old papers in her bureau. It was falling apart along the fold lines, smudged with the red dust of Africa. She had circled the position of the mine in blue ink.

'You can see Kariba township here,' she said, 'here where the dam is situated. You must take the road from the township southwest along the southern shores of Lake Kariba until you come to the turn-off for Mangwende Mission. The mine is fifteen to twenty miles deeper into the hills.'

'Is there some way I can get there by air?' asked Dave, knowing this was a race against time.

'There is no airstrip,' she said. 'The hills are too rugged. Anyway, the mine is very small, just Nikos and twenty or so African workers.'

'Couldn't I get there across the lake? If I could charter a motorboat of some kind . . .'

She smiled at him. 'Don't think it is like a lake in Europe with jetties along the side and scenic paths. The lake there runs for hundreds of miles, ninety-nine percent of the shoreline is just bush where the elephants come to drink. The water is green, thick with lilies and weed, and there are crocodiles on the sandbanks. There is no road from the shore to the mine. You can see for yourself, there are only hills, twenty miles or more of hills. 'No,' she said, 'I am afraid there is only one way to reach Shamwari Mine, that is across land.'

Melina had a friend, a widow, who ran a small travel agency in Kos town. Confirming the international flights to get Dave down to Africa was easy enough. There was, however, one problem: no matter whom she begged, she couldn't get Dave on to a flight out of Kos until the following morning. Dave had no choice, he had to wait.

He barely slept that night. His mind was too crowded with thoughts of what lay ahead, whether he would be in time or too late, whether Tselentis would see sense, whether he would take courage in his hands or just dig himself deeper into an isolated hole. And all night, breaking into every thought, every emotion, still tearing him apart, were images of Hannah.

At four-thirty in the morning, when it was still dark, he went for a run into the central mountains, following the road up through silent olive groves. He ran through a small village where dogs barked at him, up past an Orthodox cemetery until, with the dawn, he had an eagle's view out over the sea, way out over the dark, lustrous purple of the Aegean. The sweat, the pain, the hard-earned satisfaction of the run, was making him think more clearly again, setting his priorities. After the emotional ravages of the past few days he was beginning to refocus his will.

*

Zimbabwe and the Greek Islands lie in the same time zone. At eleven that morning, while Dave waited for his flight out of Kos, Bruce Rexford landed in Harare, Zimbabwe's capital city.

It took time to clear his weapons through customs; there seemed to be a hundred forms in triplicate to complete. But it was all standard stuff. Safari hunters arrived every day. They didn't even question the Soviet-made 7.62mm Dragunov. Hunters used all sorts of guns. Provided it was declared, provided it used acceptable ammunition, it was allowed through.

Rexford caught a taxi into the city. At twelve-thirty he booked into a hotel in the centre called the Monomatapa. The Ministry of Mines, he was told at reception, was within walking distance and would be open again after lunch. Rexford ate nothing himself for lunch; twenty-four hours of aircraft food eaten in six different time zones was enough for his constitution, and at two that afternoon he was the first man through the doors.

The clerk in the registry was obliging. 'What details can you give me?' he asked.

'It is a gold mine,' said Rexford.

'Any idea where it is situated? We have gold mines all over the country.'

'I'm sorry, no. But I have the name, Shamwari. I have the name of the owner too. It is Pangalos, Nikos Pangalos.'

Ten minutes later the clerk had returned. Yes, there was such a mine and it was operational. The best way to explain its position was on a map of the area. Rexford purchased one over the counter and the clerk gave the mine's grid reference, marking its position with a cross.

'How do I get there?' asked Rexford.

'You could drive,' said the clerk. 'Do you have a car?'

'I can hire one.'

'You will need a four-wheel drive for the bush conditions. It will take you time to hire one. You will probably not be able to take delivery until tomorrow. Then it is a long drive up, six hours or more just to get to Kariba, another six hours to the mine. I think you would be better to fly in

299

the morning. There are companies in Kariba who hire out vehicles for the bush. You can arrange that in advance. The car will be at the airport to meet you.'

It seemed to make sense. Rexford was jet-lagged too. A good night's sleep in a hotel bed and an early morning flight to Kariba would put him on the ground fresh and with his wits about him.

Dave's flight out of Kos that day took him to Athens and from Athens east to the island of Cyprus where he landed at five in the evening at the international airport in Nicosia. He had to wait in Nicosia until midnight, kicking his heels in the airport lounge, drinking beer, trying to read a paperback book, until he was able to board a Zambian Airways flight.

That flight took him overnight down two thirds of the length of the African continent, down to the central African republic of Zambia, Zimbabwe's northern neighbour. He landed in the Zambian capital, Lusaka, at eight in the morning.

It was cold and crisp, the sky cobalt blue and not a cloud to be seen. The only luggage he possessed was a canvas backpack and within half an hour he had been cleared through customs and immigration and was with the car hire people completing his forms.

Lusaka lay just seventy miles north of the Zambezi River, an easy drive along a tarred road to the border with Zimbabwe. Dave calculated he could be across the border by mid-morning. If luck stayed with him, if he didn't lose his way, if the dirt road into the hills wasn't too badly potholed and if the battered Mazda truck he was hiring didn't give up the ghost, he might just make Shamwari Mine before dark.

At eight that morning Bruce Rexford was waiting in the domestic terminal of Harare Airport, a converted hangar, for his thirty-five minute flight to Kariba.

The flight was due to depart at eight-fifteen. He began to check his watch, worrying about the delay. Then the announcement came through the tannoy system. Air Zimbabwe offered its apologies. Due to a mechanical fault, the

300

flight would be delayed. There was, however, complimentary coffee.

Dave crossed the border into Zimbabwe at the Kariba crossing point. So far so good, he thought. He drove into Kariba township following the road along the lake shore past a few scattered hotels and sleepy boat yards. He found a garage and pulled in. It was eleven-thirty.

He had to ensure there was enough fuel for the journey to the mine. More important, however, was the need for clear instructions on how to get there without losing his way and ending up in some kraal fifty miles off course. Navigation with a five-year-old map in an area of the world that was totally alien was a risky business.

When the attendant came over, Dave showed him his map. He needed to get a place called Shamwari Mine, he said, it was in these hills past a place called Mangwende Mission. Where would be the best place to get directions?

'Mangwende, bossie? Ah, that's too far, too far from here.' The voice came from a young African sitting a little distance away drinking a Coca Cola.

'Do you know where it is?' Dave called to him.

'Sure, bossie. I come from Mangwende. That is my home.'

'Do you know the mine?'

'Sure thing, bossie. Shamwari Mine, no problem.'

'What do you do here, do you work in Kariba?'

'Too few jobs, bossie. I am visiting my uncle. Things very bad in Zimbabwe. Where are you from, bossie, England?'

Dave liked the look of him. He was obviously down on his luck but he wasn't complaining, just observing the fact. He was in his early twenties, tall, relaxed and direct. 'How would you like to take me to the mine?' he asked. 'I'm prepared to pay for your time.'

The man smiled. 'Sure thing.'

'How much do you want in Zimbabwe money?'

The man looked at Dave as if he was simple. 'Zimbabwe money?'

'US dollars then?'

301

The smile was transformed into a delighted grin.
'Twenty-five US dollars – I take you all the way. And some money for beer.'

Dave grinned at him. 'What's your name?'

'My name is Elias, bossie.'

'Pleased to meet you, Elias, my name is Dave. Jump in, from what you tell me, we've got a long way to go.'

The flight to Kariba eventually left Harare at twelve, four hours behind schedule. Other passengers complained but Bruce Rexford had matters on his mind more important than a few hours delay.

The flight to Kariba in a short-haul Boeing took just thirty-five minutes. When the aircraft made its approach run, it came in over the lake. Rexford glimpsed buffalo drinking in the green shallows. A small herd of impala skipped away through the bush and he could see baobab trees – big, fat and grey like bloated upturned roots – along the edge of the airstrip. This was the African bush as he had always imagined it, golden grass, thorn trees and iron-hard hills. In many ways, in the feel and spirit, it was similar to the outback of Australia as he remembered it as a boy.

It was an internal flight so there was no customs check. He collected his gun case and backpack and made his way out of the tiny terminal building into the warm wintry sunshine.

'Mr Rexford?' A large, blustery man dressed in a sky blue safari suit came marching across the car park towards him accompanied by an African in mechanic's overalls. 'Tommy Van Cleef,' said the man, 'Kudu Car Hire. Delighted to meet you. Pity about the delay. Hope it hasn't set your plans back. I have the vehicle you wanted, a little Suzuki jeep but with all the guts in the world. There she is. Tank full, spare jerry can in the back, machete for cutting your way out of trouble, tow rope and tackle, couple of water bottles, everything you need. And Philemon here has checked out the mechanics. She's in tiptop shape.'

'Thank you.' Rexford tossed his kit into the back of the vehicle, which was painted a dull desert buff.

'You were paying with American Express, I think.' The car hire man checked the wodge of papers he had with him. 'Yes, we've got your details here. If you could just sign these contract documents. Reams and reams of the stuff, I'm afraid. No wonder lawyers are so rich.' He chortled, his beer paunch wobbling under the jacket of his safari suit. He had the smell of a bush town about him: too much beer, too little work. 'Who are you hunting with by the way, any of the operators I know?'

Rexford shook his head. 'Strictly a private hunt. I have a friend who has organised it.'

'Who might that be? We're pretty much of a village up in this part of the world.'

'Pangalos is his name, Nikos Pangalos. He operates a gold mine in the hills to the west of here, somewhere along the lake – Shamwari Mine he calls it.'

Van Cleef gave a blank shrug. 'Sorry, don't know him. No disrespect, but these mining types tend to be loners.'

'I've agreed to meet him at the mine,' said Rexford. 'I've got it marked on a map but it's a question of finding the right road.' He spread out the map on the bonnet of the Suzuki, putting his finger on the inked cross that pinpointed it.

Van Cleef put on a pair of dusty spectacles. 'Ah yes, I see. So you're driving into the Matusadonas are you? No problem, I can point you in the right direction. It's a fair distance though. You're not going to get there until well after dark. Rough road too. Maybe you should think of spending the night over and set out in the morning.'

Rexford checked his watch. It was one o'clock. 'Thank you but with the flight delay I'm late as it is.'

Van Cleef chortled again. 'Okay. Just be careful with my jeep, that's all – it's rugged bloody country out there.'

303

Chapter Twenty

They almost missed the dirt turn-off. It was little more than an overgrown farm track shaded by mukwa trees. There were a couple of faded, hand-painted signs but they were lost in the thick profusion of scrub. Dave would never have seen them if Elias hadn't suddenly called out. 'Bossie, stop! There, on the right – you've missed it!'

Dave swung the Mazda around and pulled up next to the signs. The first sign read: Mangwende Mission. The second was so faded it was barely decipherable. But Dave could just make out the words –

SHAMWARI MINE
Nick Pangalos

That was it. They had found the road. Dave looked at his watch. It was close to two. They were making good time. 'What does Shamwari mean?' he asked. 'Does it have any special meaning?'

Elias grinned. 'That's Shona language. In Shona it means – friend.'

For the first four or five miles, the track ran along relatively flat ground through open bush kraals where dusty piccannies stood waving. They passed a couple of trading stores and at one Dave bought lukewarm Coca Colas. A mile or two on they caught a glimpse of Mangwende Mission set far back off the road in among giant marula trees. But as soon as the track began to climb up into the Matusadona Hills, any sign of human habitation quickly fell away.

They entered an area of wild bush country, all hills and

gullies and steel-grey thickets of thorn. The track – in parts nothing more than exposed rock and gravel – wound its way tortuously through the terrain. Some of the hills were so steep, the track so badly eroded, that the Mazda was unable to make the climb unless Elias jumped out and put his shoulder in to push.

For long stretches they progressed at little more than a walking pace. The shadows grew longer as the day wore on. The going had become a hard, frustrating grind relieved only occasionally by the odd pack of baboons that would cross the track ahead of them or the glimpse of a small buck high up in the flinty trees. Elias seemed happy enough. It was all in a day's work for him. But in the mounting frustration Dave's concern mounted too. What would he find when he reached the mine? Would Tselentis still be there or had he moved on? Was he still alive or was it already too late? At five-thirty that evening, both men now coated in a film of peppery red dust, they came at last across a second sign. There was a white arrow on it pointing to a dirt track that curved off to the left.

They followed the track for quarter of a mile until they came across a compound of traditional African huts built of mud and thatch. A kraal dog barked at them; a couple of women with babies strapped to their backs looked curiously up from their cooking fires.

They drove on, turning a bend in the track and there ahead of them, set on high ground, stood what was clearly the mine owner's house. It was a single-storey dwelling built of red farm brick; a basic box with an asbestos roof and a small lawn of tough kikuyu grass at the front.

A European man in his mid-thirties, dark with a jet black beard, stood at the front door watching them. He wore an open-neck khaki shirt and khaki shorts. A rifle was cradled in his arms. Dave noticed the hard set of his jaw, the black eyes filled with suspicion. That had to be Nick Pangalos.

Dave climbed from the Mazda, taking a pace or two towards the steps that led up to the house. 'Good evening,' he said with a smile.

'Who are you?' came the challenge in that gruff, flat

306

accent of Southern Africa. 'What do you want?'

'My name is Dave Whitman. I'm from Hong Kong.'

There was not so much as a blink of reaction.

'I'm here to speak to Dimitri.'

'How did you find this place?'

'Your sister, Melina, sent me here. I know that Dimitri is with you.'

Still no reaction, just that black-eyed, suspicious stare.

Dave walked closer. 'I'm here because Dimitri is in danger, very great danger.'

'Where did you speak to Melina?'

'On Kos, at the taverna she has there close to Marmari Beach. I left Kos yesterday morning. Please, just speak to Dimitri, he knows who I am. He knows I don't intend him any harm.'

For the first time there was a look of uncertainty; Nick Pangalos frowned. 'What did you say your name was again?'

'Whitman, Dave Whitman. I'm a Hong Kong cop.'

But a latent suspicion kept Pangalos rooted at the door, legs astride, like an ancient Spartan hoplite guarding the pass at Thermopylae. Dave waited. With a man like this too much talk would be misinterpreted. Let him take his time. Silence hung as heavy as the wood smoke that drifted up from the cooking fires of the compound.

Nick Pangalos's frown grew deeper. 'Whitman, you say. All right,' he said at last. 'Just wait—'

But, before he could complete the sentence, the shadow of a figure appeared behind him in the doorway. A hand came out, easing him to one side.

Dimitri Tselentis stepped out into the light. He was dramatically thinner, by twenty pounds at least, pale and hollow-eyed; a hunted, haunted man. Tselentis looked down at Dave and a wan smile came to those swarthy jowls. 'So it's you,' he said. 'I thought so. I knew my luck couldn't hold out forever.'

In the kitchen at the back of the house, they sat around a rough wooden table. Tselentis sat facing Dave across the table, a look of fear in his eyes. 'You might as well lay it on

307

the line,' he said. 'For my mother to tell you where I am, something bad must have happened.'

'Yes, I'm afraid it has,' said Dave. 'I'm sorry to tell you that your uncle is dead. His body was found on Taipa Island in Macau. He had been murdered.'

Tselentis went a shade paler. He momentarily closed his eyes, dropping his head. 'Fung?' he asked.

'It has to be, yes.'

'Why do you say that?'

'Your uncle had been tortured.'

'Oh God.'

'Your uncle knew you were coming here. Your mother tells me he arranged your passport, tickets, everything.'

'Torture? Oh dear Christ, was it bad?'

'Yes, it was,' said Dave, quietly but firmly, making sure the message got home.

Tselentis's chin began to quiver. 'It's all my fault,' he mumbled, barely comprehensible. 'I should never have got him involved. How could they have done that to him? He was an old man. He never harmed anybody.'

Dave said nothing. At that moment silence spoke with greater force. Let it sink home, let Tselentis realise the extent to which Fung and his people were prepared to go.

It was nearly dark outside, the sun a ball of molten maroon, had settled low over the Matusadona Hills. He could hear laughter coming from the compound where the mine workers were resting. Elias was down there with them, sharing their food. The dust had settled, work was done, the day was drawing to a close in the distant, mournful cry of a fish eagle.

The silence, heavy and oppressive, remained until Nick Pangalos, frowning grimly, said to Dave. 'With the uncle dead, we have to work on the basis that one or more of Fung's hired killers could be on the way to the mine right now, is that what you're saying – even in the vicinity already?'

'Either in the vicinity or on their way, yes.'

Nick Pangalos went to the fridge, an ancient machine powered by a gas cylinder. He took out three bottles of beer, snapped off the caps and sat them down on the table. 'Since Dimitri arrived, I've had patrols out all the time. I received a report that you were coming a good five miles back. That's why I had the gun. My workers know the bush, they know who's meant to be here and who's a stranger. There's been no reports of anybody unusual, no tracks, nothing: not yesterday, not today.'

'Good,' said Dave. 'So we may still be ahead of them. We may still have time.'

Nick Pangalos took a long swig from his beer. 'Time for what? You've obviously got some kind of scheme in mind.'

Tselentis gave a jittery snort. 'I know what his idea of a scheme is – go back to Hong Kong, give evidence, put myself in the firing line again.'

'Is that it?' Nick Pangalos asked him.

'Yes,' said Dave, 'it is.'

'Forget it!' Tselentis exclaimed in a flurry of panic. 'I'm not sitting in some miserable apartment in Hong Kong for the next two years waiting to get killed. Maybe you've got a short memory but we've tried that once before!'

'How much better off are you here?' Dave asked him. 'How much better is it on the run? Nick has patrols out scouring the bush, you're half a day's drive from anywhere with more than fifty people and you're still too frightened to show your face.'

'There are other places—'

'And they'll all be the same. Australia, Canada . . . every time you see a shadow, every time you hear a noise, you'll wonder if it's one of Fung's killers. What kind of life is that?'

'And what better life can you offer me? Sitting like a rat in a trap until Fung kills me.'

'This time there'll be no expense spared, no red tape, no lapses of security. We'll house you somewhere outside of Hong Kong,' said Dave. 'Europe maybe, a place in the British Isles, a place with a garden, a place where you can live like a person. It can be arranged. I promise you, the same mistakes won't be made twice.'

Tselentis retaliated sarcastically. 'So I sit on some moor in

309

the north of Scotland eating porridge and watching the rain. So what? How does that help? I'll still be missing a heart-beat every time I hear a twig snap. Do you think a few British bobbies are going to deter Fung? I'm just as well off here with Nick. At least he's family. What's the difference?'

'The difference,' Dave replied, 'is that if you decide to testify, all the discomfort, the guards, the living like a prisoner, will be finite. Once you've testified, once Fung is convicted, the threat against you will wither. We'll put you through a witness protection programme. You'll be able to start your life again. But on the run, the threat will never diminish. You'll be hunted until the end of your days. While Fung knows you're alive, still capable of testifying, he'll spend every last dollar he has to kill you. There's only one way of destroying the threat. Deep down you know it too – that's by meeting it head on.'

Tselentis gave a small, agitated grunt. 'You've missed your vocation, you should be selling insurance – except I know what's behind it all. You're not interested in me. It's your son, isn't it? I'm a means to an end, that's all.'

'You're right,' said Dave quietly. 'I do want to avenge my son. I don't make any bones about it. But without you, I don't even get to the door of the court. That's why I have to keep you alive. That's why my interests are your interests.'

Tselentis grunted, halfway to a sigh, aware that both men were watching him intently. The truth was he didn't know what to think. All he knew was that he was terrified. He wished to God he had never heard of Fung, never encountered Whitman, that all this was just a bad dream.

Then Nick Pangalos spoke. He addressed himself to his brother-in-law, speaking in his blunt, pragmatic way. 'Listen to him, Dimitri. There's sense in what he says. You can't stay here, not now that they know. So where do you run? Who do you go to? My brother, Steve, down in Australia? He's a storekeeper. He sells bread and cigarettes. How can he protect you? You're putting everybody's life in danger. If it was me I wouldn't give that bastard Fung the pleasure of chasing me. I'd testify.'

'But you don't understand the risks, Nick—'

'There's a risk – of course there is. Whichever way you choose, there's a risk you're going to get culled, you've got to accept that fact.'

'Thanks,' said Tselentis, looking sick.

'A fact is a fact, Dimitri. So, if the risk is there anyway, do the right thing. What have you got to lose?'

'Your uncle is dead,' said Dave. 'How many more people have to die?'

'Simple case of self-preservation,' Nick Pangalos added. 'You cull him, Dimitri, before he culls you. Fung is lower than snakeshit. You'd be doing the world a favour.'

'Fung has to be stopped,' Dave emphasised. 'You know it. And you're the one who can do it.'

Tselentis sat at the table, eyes cast down. He said nothing in reply. He was making what he knew – what all three of them knew – was the most momentous decision of his life. He drained his beer from the bottle. He looked at his brother-in-law first then at Dave. Then he said in a thin voice. 'All right, I'll testify.'

Thank God, was all Dave could think. So we're back on course again.

Nick Pangalos went to the fridge to take out more beers. As he stepped past Tselentis, he put a fraternal arm on his shoulder. 'The next question,' he said, 'is when do we move you?' He glanced back at Dave. 'What do you think? It seems to me the sooner, the better. There's only one thing we know for sure. The longer we stay here, the more vulnerable we become. I reckon we leave tomorrow morning at first light.'

Dave nodded. 'How do we get out?'

'Same way you came in. There's only one road.'

'What about the chances of ambush?'

'It's a possibility, sure.'

'Could we walk out, cut through the bush?'

'You and I together maybe, yeah. It would take a couple of days. But Dimitri wouldn't make it. His wheels would fall off long before then. No, we have to get out by road.'

'When we get to Kariba, what then?' asked Dave.

'Down to Harare and book a flight out for the two of you.'

311

'No, no!' said Tselentis, the fear showing in his bloodshot eyes. 'It's too obvious, too direct. Fung knows I'm here, he knows I'm in the country.'

'Okay, so we leave by a more indirect route,' said Nick Pangalos. 'Once we reach Kariba, instead of driving south to Harare, we cross the river north into Zambia. I have a friend who owns a cattle ranch a few miles outside of Lusaka. We can stay there until we can get you both booked on to a flight. He's a good guy, we can trust him . . . ex-army, does a lot of hunting. He has a lot of clout in the area too. Nobody bothers him.'

'What about air tickets?' asked Tselentis.

'He'll arrange those for us. That's no problem.'

'What about getting out of Zambia? What about the officials there, customs, immigration?'

Pangalos smiled. 'Fung isn't the only one knows how to slip a little money under the table. For a couple of hundred bucks in hard currency, the two of you will go through customs and immigration at Lusaka like invisible men.'

Darkness came quickly, too quickly for Rexford's liking. Low clouds scudded in from the north over Lake Kariba. He was still on the track, marooned in the hills. He had hoped at least for a clear night but the clouds blanketed out the moon. To continue, he would have to use the jeep's headlights. But, alone out there in the darkness, the headlights would be seen for miles. It was best, he decided, to pull off the track, hide the vehicle and wait for morning.

A little ahead of him, to the left of the track, rose a high, rocky hill crowned with scrub and balancing boulders. It was an ideal vantage point. He drove off the track, finding a way through the broken scrub around to the back of the hill and parked the Suzuki in a thicket of msasa. He would sleep at the top of the hill. But there was one matter that had to be attended to before he started his climb – a way to stop any passing vehicle long enough to check out the occupants.

From the back of the Suzuki, Rexford removed a sharp-edged machete and, stepping silently through the bush, made his way back to the track . . .

*

They ate a cold supper; salami, beans and a slice each of yellowish bread baked from maize flour. When they had finished the food, Nick Pangalos took a bottle of scotch out of the cupboard and three dusty glasses. They drank by the light of a hurricane lamp.

Nick Pangalos kept a fully stocked gun cupboard, chained and bolted. He took two rifles from it, handing one to Dave. 'Here,' he said. 'You're a cop, you should know how to use it.'

Dave weighed it in his hands. It was a military weapon, a Belgian FN. In his training days as a young cop, Dave had fired the SLR, the British version. The two rifles were almost identical. If he had to, he could use it efficiently enough.

'The magazine is full. It takes twenty rounds,' said Nick Pangalos. 'If you get into trouble, don't get clever and fire on automatic. The full twenty rounds will go in two bursts. The rifle will climb so fast with the recoil you'll end up shooting leaves out of the trees. Keep it on single shot – double-tap, you know what I mean? Two shots at a time, never any more.'

'You obviously have experience,' said Dave.

'Some, yeah. I've lived in this country close on twenty years. For five of them I fought a bush war against black guerrillas. I still do a bit of hunting, buck mainly for the pot. But I know my way around.' He placed the second rifle, a single-shot hunting weapon, on the table in front of his brother-in-law. 'Just to be on the safe side,' he said.

But Tselentis's instinctive reaction was to recoil from it like a rabbit from a cobra. 'Oh no, not me,' he said. 'I hate the bloody things.'

'If we get into a scrape, your views might change a bit.'

'Trust me, Nick, guns and I weren't meant for each other. It's all bullshit anyway.' He tried to make a joke of it. 'This hit man Dave talks about is probably still in Asia putting together his traveller's cheques.'

Nick Pangalos grinned. He picked up the hunting rifle, returning it to the gun cupboard. 'Knowing you, you'll just shoot yourself in the foot anyway.'

In the harsh, bloodless light of the hurricane lamp,

313

Tselentis looked gaunt and worried. He poured himself more whisky. He was drinking hard like a man digging deep for the last resources of his courage. Dave couldn't help feeling compassion for him. Despite everything, despite all his years of larceny and money laundering, at heart Tselentis was a good man, a man who took the world as he found it and wished no one evil.

Dave splashed more whisky into his glass. 'I've got a copy of your affidavit here with me,' he said, 'the one you never got to sign. Remember the days we spent working on it? Seems years ago.'

'Let's have a look at it,' said Tselentis.

Dave went to his bag. It was stuffed into a travel wallet with his passport, his international driving licence and the fast diminishing residue of his cash. Like everything else it seemed to be ingrained with red dust. He unfolded it and placed it on the table.

Tselentis picked it up, reading the opening paragraphs. 'Why did you bring it?' he asked.

'In case we got a chance to sign it.'

'In case I got written off before I got back to Hong Kong, is that what you mean?'

'In case of problems, yeah,' said Dave, making no attempt to hedge the realities. 'Your death, your disappearance, your refusal to return . . . a signed back-up for emergencies, that's all it is.'

Tselentis stared at the document for a time. 'What value would it have if I signed it now?'

Dave shrugged. 'I was thinking maybe in Zambia, if we could find a magistrate, a notary, somebody like that.'

'I'm a JP,' said Nick Pangalos, very matter-of-fact. 'If you want, Dimitri can sign it in front of me.'

'You're a justice of the peace?'

'Sure. No need to look so surprised. Before I started gold mining full time, I used to run a safari operation in Kariba. Even got elected on to the town council for a time. They made me a justice of the peace about ten years back.'

So it was done right there in the kitchen in the light of the hurricane lamp. Tselentis, with an embarrassed laugh, swore to his brother-in-law that the contents were true and correct and then, pushing the plates and glasses aside, they both signed the affidavit. Nick Pangalos, always to the point, gruff and practical, dated the document, initialled the bottom of each page and handed it back to Dave.

Tselentis looked on; he was getting drunk fast. There was a cynical smile on his face. 'Try to think of everything, don't you?'

A question like that was best not answered. Dave placed the affidavit back into his wallet.

'Tell me,' said Tselentis, 'I'm interested . . . I thought your bosses back in Hong Kong had kicked you off the Fung case. What happened, were you reinstated, put back on the team, or is this trip out here a private venture?'

'Some things you can't do officially.'

Tselentis gave a quick, drunken laugh. 'I'm surprised you could afford it on your cop's salary. What did you do, break open the piggy bank?' The drink was turning him belligerent. 'Oh no, of course, your wife, the designer. She must be making big bucks, ten times more than you'll ever see. What did you do, ask her for an advance?'

Dave knew it was just the whisky talking. Tselentis was being dragged back into a maelstrom, terrified of what lay ahead. He was hitting out at the nearest target. But the break-up with Hannah was too raw a wound and he snapped back in a voice full of resentment. 'If we're going to travel together, the first thing you do is keep your nose out of my personal affairs.'

Tselentis smirked. 'Hit a raw nerve, have I?'

Dave splashed more whisky into his glass. This wasn't the time or the place to talk about his marriage, not with these two men hunched down in some two-bit gold mine in the middle of Africa.

But Tselentis was too drunk, too screwed up inside, to know when to stop. 'If you want to keep your marriage on the tracks, you're going to have to come to terms with it, being married to a woman who is more successful than you, I mean. Not the most likely combination is it, the cop and the fashion queen.'

315

Dave drunk his whisky, hoping it would cauterise his emotions but it had no such effect. They continued to bleed inside him, a hopeless open wound of hurt. He looked across at Tselentis and, before he could check himself, the words were out. 'You want the true situation,' he said. 'My wife and I split up. She's gone her way, I've gone mine.'

Tselentis blinked; it took him a moment to react. 'Shit,' he muttered, 'I'm sorry, I didn't realise. I was kidding around, that's all. I'm sorry, me and my bloody mouth . . .'

Dave gave a dismal shrug, uncertain what to say. 'It was on the cards for some time, I suppose. I didn't see it, that's all. You're right, the cop and the fashion queen . . . not the most likely combination. Her success came overnight and I don't think either of us really knew how to handle it.'

'Could be a temporary thing,' said Tselentis, trying to make up for his crude bull-baiting. 'Sometimes you go through these patches.'

Dave shook his head, finishing the drink in his glass. He was getting maudlin. But what the hell. 'The truth is, I just got left behind. New success, new life – new man. She met this hotshot New York financier who made it all possible for her. There was no way I could compete with him. An Israeli guy called Ephram.'

Dave reached across for the whisky bottle. Why in the hell was he saying all these things? What did they care? He poured the dregs of the whisky into his glass. Nobody spoke. But suddenly Tselentis seemed to be looking at him in an odd kind of way, eyes wide, as if he had uttered a revelation.

'What is it?' asked Dave. 'What have I said?'

'That financier, the Israeli.'

'What about him?'

'What did you say his name was?'

'Ephram, Sam Ephram. Why?'

Tselentis was still staring at him across the table but the blood appeared to have drained entirely from his face. His mouth hung slack as if he was in deep shock. 'Jesus Christ,' he murmured, 'just as I said, the bastard comes at you from every direction.'

316

'What are you talking about?' Dave had suddenly sobered too, sensing something disastrous. 'You know this man, Ephram, obviously you do.'

'Yes, I do.'

'You've had dealings with him?'

'Yes.'

'What kind of dealings?'

'There's a company registered in the Cayman Islands. It's called Fate Incorporated. Fate is just the first letter of our surnames.'

'Whose surnames?'

'The T is mine, the E is Ephram. The A is Aurelius.'

'And the F?'

'The F is Fung.'

For a moment Dave found it impossible to react. It had to be a joke, some terrible, sick joke. 'Fung? Are you telling me that Ephram and he are close associates, that Ephram is one of his inner circle, the same man who has helped my wife? I don't believe it.'

'Not part of the inner circle, no,' said Tselentis. 'But an associate, yes, when opportunities arise.'

'What about this company, Fate?' Dave was asking the questions but it seemed to be another voice, another mind operating outside the shattered remnants of his own.

'We have hundreds of companies, a network of them all over the world. Fate is just one, one in which he's involved. We keep monies there, profits skimmed off deals.'

'What kind of deals?'

'With Ephram, you mean? Straight trade, import, export. Perfectly legitimate. Ephram has made us some good money. He's a shrewd man.'

'So it's all been legitimate?'

Tselentis shook his head. 'With myself and Aurelius, yeah. But with Fung? No, Khalil and Fung go back a long way, back to their early drug days.'

'Khalil? Who is he?'

'Khalil – that's the name Ephram was born with, the one Fung still calls him. Khalil Khayat. He was born Turkish, a Muslim.'

'But Ephram is Israeli, a Jew.'

'All assumed: name, nationality, religion.'

'Why, for God's sake? Why from a Muslim to a Jew?'

'He was on the run, that's why. It suited him. A Middle Eastern Muslim, a Middle Eastern Jew . . . totally the same, totally the opposite.'

Dave sat locked in silence, devastated by the news. 'But why didn't you ever tell me about this man?' he asked. 'All that time we had in Hong Kong and you never said a word.'

'If I had known, of course I would have done. But I had no reason. Khalil was never involved in the Kai Tak thing, never involved with Geraldo Gomez. Most of the time he stayed clear, operated his own businesses. Fung associates with half a dozen men like him. He was just never relevant.'

'How close are they, Fung and Ephram . . . Khalil or whatever the bastard calls himself?'

'When it suits them. When there's a profit to be made, especially in drugs, or when either of them is threatened, then yes, they're very close. They go back a fair way together.'

'Do you think it's possible that Ephram could have met my wife by accident, totally independently?'

Tselentis shook his head. 'Sorry, I don't believe in coincidences that great. Fung set it up somehow. It originated with him.'

'But why?' said Dave. 'It makes no sense, no sense at all. Ephram was my wife's guardian angel in New York. If it wasn't for him she'd still be out in the cold. Why would he help her like that – and at Fung's request?'

'Haven't you heard of the saying, there's no such thing as a free lunch?'

'But what purpose could he have in it? What possible gain was there for him – apart from the money?'

Tselentis looked straight into his eyes. 'Don't you see it? Don't you understand? Fung could only have had one purpose – to get to you.'

Dave's heart sank. But he still didn't understand, not fully. He wouldn't – *couldn't* – allow himself to do so.

'And so easy to do,' said Tselentis. 'It was perfect for

Khalil. He had the business contacts in New York, the access to finance. He must have known how vulnerable your wife was after the death of your son, how desperately she wanted to market her new collection. And if the collection was good – which it must have been – what simpler way to gain her trust and make a financial killing at the same time? A chance to score every way he knew. Has he had an affair with her?'

Dave nodded, feeling the pain deep inside.

'Yes, I thought as much. That's his style.'

'So he got to my wife,' said Dave, stumbling through the nightmare. 'But how could that help Fung?'

Tselentis gave a dejected shrug. Then he said, almost gruffly. 'Husbands talk to their wives – that's how.'

The impact of it was like a wave of ear-bursting concussion. Dave put his head back, closing his eyes. And spinning around in his brain in a jumbled, stunned kaleidoscope, were the memories of that afternoon when the decision was made to take him off the investigation. Husbands talk to their wives . . . oh God, yes – just as he had done.

All he wanted was to be alone with her that night. Hannah had appointments that evening which she agreed to postpone. But Ephram must have been scheduled to attend them with her, he had never considered that. When he had spoken to her, he had never thought – not for one moment – that she might say something to him. He had been too upset at the time, too disappointed. Oh God, he thought, so they were the leak, the two of them, he and Hannah!

And the words came back to him, words written now in tablets of fire – *I've done all the work with the witnesses. Their affidavits are finished. They sign them tomorrow morning at the Supreme Court.* In those few words he had given Fung's hired killer everything: the time, the destination, the perfect opportunity.

Dave shook his head, trying to clear it of all the guilt and anger; too late now for recriminations. He turned to Tselentis. 'Earlier, you said something about Ephram and Fung dealing in drugs.'

319

'That's how they both got started.'

'Fung I know about. But what about Ephram?'

'I don't know all the details – I was never close to him, not personally. Like I said, Khalil is Turkish. He was born in Istanbul. He made his first money peddling dope that came down from Pakistan but then moved on to the better quality China White that came from the Far East. That's how he and Fung met up. He was supplying Europe in those days, Holland, Germany, Denmark. His favourite method was to use female couriers. That's what Fung tells me. He would find women who were above suspicion, young girls on holiday, businesswomen with reputable companies. He would seduce them, be the perfect lover, show them a good time – the standard gigolo operation – then convince them to take a little package back home for him, a present for a cousin of his or a favourite aunt.'

'Did he ever come unstuck?'

'Yeah, badly. Just once. One of his girls got picked up with two pounds of the stuff concealed in cans of Black Sea caviar. Within five minutes of being caught, she had implicated Khalil. She stuck to her story too. Khalil was arrested in Istanbul, put on trial and sentenced to twenty years.'

'How did he get out?'

'Fung helped him there somehow, I'm not sure of the details. Some guards were bribed, some officials turned a blind eye. Khalil escaped from Turkey, changed his identity, became a respectable Jew by the name of Ephram and he has never looked back.'

'Did he continue dealing in drugs?'

'As far as I know, when the need arose – yes. Nothing helps you out of a financial squeeze quite like a couple of pounds of China White. You can clear a few million easy, tax free.'

'And what about his female couriers,' asked Dave, 'did he continue to use them?'

Tselentis frowned as if he didn't know how best to deal with the question. 'What are you suggesting?'

Dave's mind was racing now, probing every possibility.

320

These past couple of minutes had taught him that nothing was too far-fetched, nothing too remote to be feasible. 'I remember you telling me that Fung's arrest would have wrecked his money-laundering empire, hit him hard financially.'

'Put him on the rack, yeah.'

'Then he must have needed cash and needed it badly . . . and as you say, nothing helps you out of a squeeze like a couple of pounds of China White.'

'What are you asking me?'

'I'm asking you if it's possible that Ephram could be using my wife as a courier. She would *never* move drugs, not knowingly. But those women he used back in Turkey never knew they were carrying dope either.'

'Has your wife travelled to New York to meet him?'

'Yes. She's leaving today or tomorrow.'

'Has she shipped goods there?'

'Yes. Fashion samples.'

'Then maybe, yes, it is feasible.'

Dave fell silent. There seemed to be no limit to the dimensions of the nightmare. It grew every minute like some terrible fever devouring every cell of credibility, crushing every tissue of disbelief. He drained the whisky from his glass. A few minutes earlier the alcohol had made him thick-headed, ready to doze off. But now he was wide awake, cold sober. Sleep was impossible.

Dave looked across at Tselentis. 'I want you to tell me how Ephram first met Fung,' he said. 'Tell me how he managed to change his identity. Tell me everything you can about him.'

Somewhere around four in the morning, long after Tselentis and Nick Pangalos had fallen asleep, exhaustion must have got the better of him. Dave didn't remember falling asleep. All he remembered was the dream . . .

Two men were standing amid the carnage at Kai Tak Airport after the bomb explosion. Both were splattered with Danny's blood. One of the men was the assassin, a great sly cat of an individual, well over two hundred pounds with muscle-knotted prehensile arms, a face the colour of bruised peach and rust-red hair. The second man was Ephram. Nobody tried to stop them as they left the airport and Dave himself was trapped in a terrible vacuum of impotent invisibility, unable to speak, unable to intervene, capable only of shadowing Ephram like a ghost and witnessing what was done. Ephram took a car from the airport, a Mercedes, metallic gold, sleek and clean. He drove to the Regent Hotel and went up to a room. When he entered, Hannah was waiting for him. He began to undress her. Her clothes fell around her ankles on the carpet and her skin was a glorious satin, glowing pink and beige in the lamplight. When Ephram touched her breasts, however, he left an imprint of blood on her skin, Danny's blood, and Dave wanted so desperately to cry out to warn Hannah. But she could hear nothing. It was as if he was held, bound and gagged, behind a one-way mirror. They made love in front of him and Ephram was huge, the perfect lover, arrogant and oiled, and Hannah cried out when he entered her. And every time his hands touched her skin, there were smears of blood, burgundy red, as rich as altar wine. Afterwards, when it was done, Ephram handed her a box wrapped in black foil. It contained caviar, he said, Beluga caviar from the Black Sea. It was for a friend in New York. Hannah dressed while Ephram lay naked on the bed smiling at her, smiling all the time, filled with his own conceit. Dave tried desperately to call out: 'Don't take it, don't take it, can't you see what kind of man he is?' But his words remained trapped in his throat while Hannah, as meek as a handmaiden, went out to do his bidding.

Chapter Twenty-One

Dave awoke suddenly, sitting up with a jerk. He was still at the table. The pearl-grey light of morning came in through the kitchen window. A cockerel was crowing down by the mine compound. He rubbed his eyes. His head was pounding.

Nick Pangalos grinned at him from the stove. 'Coffee and aspirin time,' he said. He was frying bacon and eggs in a pan. The aroma of coffee filled the room. 'I've spoken to my night patrol men. They've done a sweep along the track, two miles out and more. Nothing, they say. Just your tracks from last night. So it's looking good – no reason I can see to stop us driving out.'

Tselentis came into the kitchen, slumping down at the table. He had slept fully clothed. His shirt and trousers were rumpled. He smelt of sweat. He said nothing, just took the mug of coffee that Nick Pangalos handed him and drank it in silent misery. He looked in a bad way. His unshaven cheeks were coal black, his eyes a puffed-up, rheumy red.

Nick Pangalos set out three plates of bacon, egg and local boerwors sausage. 'Ten minutes,' he said cheerily. 'Then we go. The sooner we get across the border, the better.'

Dave didn't realise just how hungry he was. The food was good and he wolfed it down. 'I'll go check on my vehicle,' he said.

'Get my foreman to fill up your tank,' Nick Pangalos told him. 'I've got my own storage facilities. Get him to check out my vehicle too, petrol and tyre pressure.'

Taking his mug of coffee with him, Dave walked out into

323

the soft morning air. The sky was a pale blue, as fine as Wedgwood porcelain. Autumnal-coloured leaves, russet and ochre, the colour of dried blood, lay scattered in the golden brown of the grass. He breathed in deeply, beginning to feel human. The coffee was strong and sweet, made with condensed milk.

Elias was waiting by the hired Mazda truck, smiling as always. 'Morning, Bossie,' he called. The mine foreman, Moses, a strapping individual, well over six foot, was waiting with him.

Dave passed on the instructions concerning the two vehicles. He finished his coffee then went back inside the house to collect his personal belongings. He checked that his rifle, the FN Nick Pangalos had given him, was firmly on safety. Then he went back outside to the Mazda, now fully fuelled and ready to go.

When they left Shamwari Mine, he and Elias drove ahead in the Mazda. Nick Pangalos and Tselentis followed fifty yards behind in a Land-Rover, an ancient gear-grinding relic of the Hemingway days, all dirt, grease and clouds of blue exhaust.

After a long night with precious little sleep, the track from Shamwari Mine seemed even tougher than Dave remembered it. In parts it was little more than two continuous ruts cutting a flinty groove up steep embankments or down precipitous slopes into dry riverbeds. It was hard going through the hills, slow and hazardous. He was surprised how broken the bush was; the ground scattered with ant-infested branches of long dead trees while others, still standing, jutted out of the thorn bush like grey gibbets.

'Elephant country,' said Elias happily. 'Elephants break everything.'

Forty minutes out, as if to prove his point, they came across a couple of old bull elephants standing just below the crest of a hill to the right of the track, huge animals, primordial and proud. They were browsing with unhurried deliberation. Dave watched them turn their heads lazily towards the clank and rattle of the approaching vehicles then move on up the hill, their great mud-brown flanks swaying

324

through the msasa saplings. In different circumstances Dave would have stopped the truck to watch them. He had never seen elephant in the wild before. But there was no time now for such luxuries and he continued on around a high rocky spur.

He followed the track down on to a flat open stretch that followed the low ground. At last he was able to increase speed and changed up into third gear. Red dust billowed up behind the Mazda, obscuring the Land-Rover that followed. Dave glanced at his watch. They were making reasonable time. With luck they would be in Kariba by early afternoon. There was a small rise in the road ahead and Dave came over it at full speed –

'Christ!' Coming over the rise, he saw it directly ahead, less than twenty yards from him. It was a dead tree, white as bone, that had fallen across the track.

He jammed on his brakes. But he was going too fast and the Mazda skidded crazily over the loose shale ramming into the leafless branches of the tree. Dave heard them break against the bonnet in a sharp shower of cannon cracks before the Mazda came to a jarring halt.

It's an ambush, thought Dave. Oh God, oh God! With every nerve in his body screwed to snapping point, he slammed the Mazda into reverse. The wheels spun, sending up a shower of gravel, and he shot backwards out of the web of petrified wood, back along the track in a wild, half-blind reverse that brought him hard up against a rock on the edge of the track. He heard the Mazda grind against it and slammed on the brakes again. Which way now? He was stuck here, stranded. Every second he expected to hear the first shot fired.

Jaw clenched tight, he looked for some way around the tree. But on the verge, to the right of the track, a hill rose up, a dense jigsaw of black basalt rock and thorn scrub. To the left the ground fell away sharply into a broken tumble of thorn scrub and termite mounds. The Mazda would never make it through either way. There was only one option – physically to manhandle the tree out of the way and clear the track.

325

Dave heard the Land-Rover come to a sharp halt just over the ridge thirty feet or so behind him. Then everything fell silent. He peered ahead into the bush but he could see nothing. 'Do you see anything?' he asked Elias, his voice constricted with tension.

Elias's big eyes were wide. 'No, bossie, nothing.'

Far off, a bird called; a sharp echoing trill that seemed to melt into the sun-drenched stillness of the morning. Dave sat, paralysed. Without realising it, he had taken his rifle and held it – safety off – across his chest, knuckles white from the fierceness of the grip. He waited, not daring to breathe. But nothing happened, not a thing. If it was an ambush, they would have opened fire by now, thought Dave. We wouldn't be left sitting here. Maybe – just maybe – it was nothing more than what it appeared to be . . . a dead tree fallen across the track.

Elias obviously felt the same because he climbed from the Mazda truck, smiling. 'It's elephant, bossie,' he said. 'Maybe those same elephants we saw on the hill. Sure thing, look around – dead trees everywhere.'

Dave climbed from the Mazda. The FN rifle was still in his hands, the safety still off.

'Dead trees everywhere,' Elias repeated. 'These elephants are like big bad children, sure thing.'

Dave could see more clearly now what he meant . . . the smooth, bleached grey of tree trunks flayed of their bark, broken branches in the grass and right there at the edge of the track the dried fibrous dung mound of an elephant. He smiled at Elias, mostly relief but part foolishness. 'Okay,' he said, 'let's pull this thing off the track.'

Elias walked over to the dead tree. Dave heard Nick Pangalos calling: 'What is it? What's the problem?'

'A tree across the track,' Dave called back. 'Elias reckons it's the elephants. There's elephant droppings here by the track.'

'Any way around it?'

'No. We'll have to pull it to one side. Can you give us a hand?'

Nick Pangalos jumped down from the Land-Rover, solid

326

and athletic, tanned as dark as the gravel. He carried his rifle too. He stared around him. 'Bloody strange,' he said. 'Tree fallen like that . . . too convenient by half.'

'Have you seen it happen before?' asked Dave.

'A few times, yeah. Just a few.' He turned back to where Tselentis sat in the front passenger's seat of the Land-Rover. 'Dimitri, stay there in the vehicle,' he said, 'this won't take a couple of—'

'*Tarisa, bossie, tarisa!*' Elias's high-pitched cry rang out across the morning air.

In his excitement Elias had lapsed into his tribal language. But Dave saw the agitated way he was pointing at the base of the fallen tree. His eyes followed Elias's finger and he saw what Elias had seen – the fresh cleavage marks of an axe. 'Ambush!' Dave screamed, swinging back towards the Mazda. 'Ambush!' But he hadn't made more than half a pace when the first rifle shot exploded.

Instinctively, he hurled himself sideways off to the left of the track down through shoulder-high elephant grass. His shoulder struck a rock as he hit the ground and he grunted with pain. He heard a second shot and then a third. Keeping his belly flat to the ground, he crawled furiously into the cover of a termite mound. He had no idea where the fire was coming from – that was the terrifying part of it – none at all.

But then he heard Nick Pangalos yell. 'The bastard's up there at the top of the koppie!'

What's a koppie, for fucksake? thought Dave, his face buried in the sand-beige clay of the termite mound.

'He's in the rocks up there at the summit! I saw his muzzle flash.'

So it had to be the hill, the one dominating the track. He heard Nick Pangalos fire two short bursts and heard the bullets whine off the rocks. Scrambling into a kneeling position, he stared up the hill for any sign of movement. But he could see nothing. A sudden, deafening silence settled on the scene. Nobody moved, nobody spoke. Dave could hear his heart thudding in his chest.

Nick Pangalos called out again in a strong, authoritative voice. 'Dave, are you okay?'

'I'm okay,' Dave replied.

'Dimitri, what about you?' Nick called.

There was no response.

'Dimitri!'

At first all Dave heard was a small whimpering moan. Then a weak voice answered. 'I'm hit, Nick, I'm hit.'

'How bad?'

'In the shoulder. It's gone clean through, I think. But I'm bleeding bad. Oh God, it's all over my shirt.'

'Okay, Dimitri, stay where you are, don't move.' Nick's voice didn't show a trace of fear. 'Don't worry,' he called, his voice very firm. 'We're going to get you out of this in one piece.'

Lying on the summit of the hill, Bruce Rexford heard the exchange of voices. So Tselentis was wounded – but still alive and only a shoulder wound; clean through too, no bones shattered, minimal shock. Would he never be able to kill the bastard!

But it had taken precious seconds to pinpoint him further back along the track in the second vehicle. The early morning sun had glinted off the windscreen obscuring his aim – worse than a damn mirror – and then that African screaming out a warning. If it hadn't been for the warning, if Tselentis hadn't dived sideways at the critical moment, he would have hit him four inches to the right, straight through the centre of the chest, and it would all be over now. As it was, Tselentis was cowering behind the Land-Rover out of sight: there was no way Rexford could get in a killing shot, not from his present position, and no way Tselentis was going to move.

There was an outcrop of rock further along the summit, just thirty feet away . . . thirty feet of open ground. If he could reach the outcrop, he would be looking down on the Land-rover like an eagle from its eyrie. Normally Rexford wouldn't have hesitated. But in a matter of seconds the odds had changed. Whitman was down there with another man, both of them armed, both of them holding their ground.

Very slowly, with the focused feline grace of a cat, Rexford came up on his haunches. He waited a moment, taking

328

one final deep breath, then – like a sprinter coming out of the blocks – he vaulted out of his shelter.

They both saw the movement at the same time, the same blurred silhouette high up in the golden haze of the sun. And both fired on reflex.

Dave's first shot was wildly high but the second, an instant later, he kept low, just a pace ahead of the running figure. Nick's fire came in simultaneously, two short stabbing bursts that tore up the ground around the running figure. The figure stumbled. In one half moment of elation, Dave thought he had been hit. But then the figure came up, crouching like a hunchback, and zigzagged back to cover.

'The bastard is trying to get to that outcrop to get a clear shot down,' Nick Pangalos called to Dave. 'If he tries it again, he's dead. He knows it too. He's only got one option, that's to cut down the back of the koppie and come around our flank.'

'What do we do?' asked Dave, his throat dry, sweat already beginning to sting his eyes.

'We can't sit here rooted to the spot. That way we're dead for sure. At the moment the bastard has got the initiative. He can move where he likes, come at us from any angle. He'll finish Dimitri and be gone without us even seeing him.'

Dave was prepared to take his word for it. Apart from the brief, disastrous gun battle outside Benevolence Villas, he had only ever been involved in a couple of shootouts as a much younger cop. But that had been in the back alleys of Hong Kong, sudden, erratic affairs with cornered robbers, the only weapons being pistols. The situation he faced now was different in every respect. This was rugged bush country, Nick's terrain. He had no choice but to trust him.

He looked around for any sign of Elias but there was none. Sensibly – it wasn't his fight – he had obviously fled into the bush.

'You've got to get Dimitri away from here,' Nick hissed. 'If he stays there behind the Land-Rover, he's a sitting target.'

'But where?'

'Anywhere – it doesn't matter – just get him away, out into the bush. You're safer there.'

'What about you?'

'One of us has got to take the bastard on. The longer I can keep him pinned down, the longer you'll have to get away. When I give you covering fire, get across to Dimitri. Do you understand?'

Dave looked desperately for the easiest route. The long way was best, further down the slope into the thicker bush, down towards a river line, then along and back up the slope to where the Land-Rover stood on the track.

He heard the first hard explosion of Nick's rifle fire, heard shots whine off rock, and set off fast, bulldozing his way through the bush. The thorn tore at his clothing, gouging his cheeks, each wound stinging with a fury. He was running low and hard, keeping his shoulders down, and all the time he could hear Nick's reassuring fire – short bursts, two at a time, double taps that echoed and re-echoed through the hills.

Closer to the river line, in sight of the tall green trees, he changed his course, still running until he calculated that he was directly below the Land-Rover.

Panting hard, he reached a small thicket of msasa and crouched down. Peering through the young leaves, he could see the Land-Rover thirty yards above him on the track and, huddled down behind the rear offside wheel, he could see Tselentis, face deathly grey, his shirt wet with blood.

The vegetation leading up to the track was sparse but there were broken outcrops of rocks all the way. If he just stayed low, he would be okay. He took a deep breath, summoned his courage and then came out from the lime green cover at a full sprint, bolting for the first parapet of rock. He reached it without incident and went down to ground. His eyes were stinging, his cheeks wet with sweat and blood from the thorn cuts. He sucked hard for breath, waited for a burst of Nick's covering fire, then sprinted for the next tumbled protection of black basalt.

The distance was ten yards, just three paces, but he had covered less than half when the first bullet whined by his

330

face. The second was so close it plucked a hole in his sleeve. Despairingly, Dave threw himself forward. He hit the ground flat on his belly as a third bullet hit the rock inches from his head and chips of stone flew into his face.

He was panting like a man who had run the marathon, sweat was sluicing down his unshaven face. But it was more shock than exertion, shock and anger, a boiling, surging rage that was suddenly drowning out all fear. Whatever the actual identity of that faceless, murdering bastard up on the hill, Dave would have a score to settle with him. He had no doubt he was the one who had murdered his son, the one who had killed Kit Lampton.

Up until that moment, Dave had aimed his wrath at Conrad Fung because Fung had been identifiable at least, a known quantity. But this man up on the hill, this assassin, this animal, would undoubtedly have been the one who had carried the bomb; he was the one who had cold-bloodedly set it down, he was the hired executioner who had taken Danny's life.

A deep silence settled again as Nick Pangalos reloaded. But Dave was barely aware of it. Chest heaving with anger, he twisted himself into a firing position. He looked up at the hill, and, as he did so, he saw the figure, clearer now, rising up again. He fired twice. Whether he hit him or not, he didn't know. He hoped to God he had. But he saw the figure fall, that was all that mattered. It had given him the chance he needed and, scrambling to his feet, he sprinted the last twenty yards up the slope. He reached the Land-Rover and dropped down beside Tselentis.

Tselentis gave him a beseeching look. 'I can't move my arm,' he said, his voice so low it was barely a whisper. 'Look at me, look how I'm bleeding.'

'Any pain?'

'No, no pain. It must be the shock. A kind of numb feeling, that's all. But I feel like I want to throw up."

'We've got to get away from here,' said Dave, 'out into the bush.'

Tselentis gawked at him.

'It's Nick's plan. Lying here on the track we don't stand a

331

chance. Nick is going to keep him pinned down. But we've got to move and we've got to do it now.'

Tselentis nodded.

'Good, just stay with me.' Dave put his hand on his shoulder. 'Are you sure you're up to it?'

With Dave there, Tselentis was now beginning to find some courage. He gave a brave grin. 'I'm shot through the shoulder, I've got high blood pressure, I'm fifty pounds overweight and I can't remember when I last walked more than twenty yards – of course I'm up to it.'

Dave grinned back at him. With that kind of spunk Tselentis might just make it. He looked towards Nick Pangalos and gave the thumbs-up sign. Then, rising to his feet, he let off a burst of fire into the summit of the hill.

As he did so, Nick Pangalos burst from cover, sprinting across the track and weaving his way up the rock-strewn slope of the koppie.

For a moment Dave was tempted to join him. There, that's where his revenge lay – up on that hill. But that was the rage inside him talking. Common sense – survival – dictated that he followed Nick's instructions. They were facing a professional, a man whose sole target was Tselentis. Keeping Tselentis alive, that's what mattered. Without his testimony, Conrad Fung walked free.

Dave fired an angry shot up into the hill. He estimated that he had about eight shots left. He would have to conserve ammunition. He ducked down next to Tselentis and searched for some way down to the riverline that provided better cover than the way he had come up.

Close to the track – just eight or ten yards from the Land-Rover – a long arm of elephant grass, a sea of silver-yellow bayonets, stretched down towards the riverline. Dave spoke rapidly to Tselentis. 'We're heading down the slope, down that way where the elephant grass is thickest. Keep low, stay in the grass and you'll make it. Don't worry, I'll be with you all the way. Are you ready?'

Clutching Dave's arm for support, Tselentis hauled himself to his feet. All the time he was breathing hard, wincing with pain.

'Now,' Dave urged him. 'Go, go!'

And Tselentis began to run. But it was all so terrifyingly lethargic, so cumbersome and slow. His short, dumpy legs were kicking up the dust, he was flailing his one good arm but out there on the track – frozen in time – he seemed to make the easiest target in the world. Dave heard the concussive explosion of a shot being fired and thought, oh God, that's it. But Tselentis was still running. It had been Nick Pangalos giving covering fire, doing everything in his power to keep Tselentis alive.

Tselentis was close to the grass now, stumbling and panting, and with a huge grunt, like a wounded elephant going down, he plunged headlong into the yellow screen.

Rexford caught a fleeting glimpse of the figure crashing into the elephant grass. He knew it had to be Tselentis and, throwing caution to the wind, rose up from cover to fire a long, raking burst. But f.re immediately came back at him, fire from two directions.

He had expected stiff resistance from Whitman, that was the way it had been from the beginning. But he hadn't counted on the aggressive bloody-mindedness of the other one, the one with the beard who was already halfway up the hill and threatening to outflank him. The man was good too, ducking and diving from cover to cover, obviously a man who knew what he was doing.

For the first time since Vietnam – a lifetime back – Rexford was facing an opponent on an equal footing, a man with training, a man willing to fight back, a man who knew his ground. In an unnerving way, after all the years of calculated murder, it was an exciting experience, one that made his heart beat faster. In this at least, as bizarre as it seemed, there was some kind of honour.

He came up again from behind cover just in time to glimpse Whitman diving headlong into the elephant grass too. He fired off a quick burst before his Dragunov suddenly stopped, the magazine expended. He dropped down, cursing, fumbling to reload. Keep calm, he kept repeating to himself, it's not over until it's over. Okay, so now you know their plan. Whitman is shepherding Tselentis off into the bush while this other one, the one with the beard, keeps you pinned down here on the hill. Okay, so you deal with the bearded one first. Don't let him get you from the rear, that's what he's trying to do. Then you set off after Tselentis. He's fat and unfit, he's wounded. How far can he get? You'll have him by the end of the day.

Dave found Dimitri Tselentis lying on his belly in the grass. His face and shirt were a mess of dust and blood and grass seeds. But he was alive at least. Dave tugged him to his feet. 'Follow me. Stay a couple of paces behind – and keep your head down.'

Pushing through the head-high grass was hard work for them both but the protective screen it provided more than compensated for that. Occasionally, shots fired from the hill cracked overhead but none came close to them and together they ploughed on down towards the thick, lusher greenery, the seventy-foot tamarinds and stiff-branched African mangosteens that crowded along the riverline.

Coming out of the elephant grass, Dave found a game trail that led to the river. He could see now that the river was dry. The river's edge was steeply enbanked but there was a great bulldozed section down into the bed, made by the elephants that came to drink at the few isolated ponds still left from the rainy season. He and Tselentis stumbled down the bulldozed section into the riverbed, then stood, their feet ankle deep in the white glaring sand, looking for the best way to go.

The opposite bank was too steep, Tselentis would never be able to climb it. Their best option was to head down river. That way at least the going was easy, just smooth rocks and sand. Further down, when they found the right spot, they would be able to climb out and head deeper into the bush.

Dave turned to Tselentis who had slumped down on a rock. 'We'll head this way,' he said.

Tselentis replied with an exhausted smile. 'You're the boss.' He climbed to his feet, grimacing with the effort.

334

'What about some water?' he asked. 'Just a couple of mouthfuls. Look at me, I'm sweating like a pig.' He made his way to the nearest pool, stumbling over dried-out elephant droppings, and it was then that Dave saw it . . . first, a dark glistening smudge on the rock where Tselentis had been sitting and then intermittent drops in the sand. It was blood from Tselentis's wound and it was leaving a trail that a child could follow.

In a matter of seconds the initiative had been wrenched from him. Bruce Rexford had lost sight of his attacker, the olive-skinned, bearded one, which meant the man could be anywhere by now . . . skirting around the back of the hill, coming up either side, even clawing his way up to the same rocky eyrie that he had tried unsuccessfully to reach two times himself. He knew only one thing – that the man was there to pin him down and the longer he was successful in that, the longer they hunted each other like cat and mouse, the greater the chance Tselentis would make it to safety.

Rexford studied the immediate terrain. He could remain there on the peak and wait, but that was just playing into his attacker's hands; giving him the advantage. If he remained static, he would allow himself to be pinned down, stuck there half the day.

No, if he wanted to get this thing finished, he had to be mobile, he had to find thicker cover. That meant making his way down the back of the hill, down into the rocks and the bristling, iron-grey clumps of jesse thorn.

Effortlessly for such a big man, Rexford emerged from his shelter, gliding over the broken ground. He crouched down a moment beneath a stunted tree, his mouth a little open to increase the acuteness of his hearing, and then – cautiously – stopping, waiting, listening every couple of feet, he began to descend the hill.

The grass was dry, it was winter grass that crackled and broke beneath his feet. There were dead leaves too and twigs. Every footfall – no matter what care he took – seemed to send out a deafening echo. He knew that he had to stay with the rocks where he could move silently. Silence and

335

surprise, in a fight like this they were everything: the difference between life and death.

A little way further down the hill, off to his right, stood a high pyramid of boulders striated with shadows. It was a natural ambush point, offering a dozen or more places to lie in wait. It was protected by thorn bush and had a dominating view of the lower reaches of the hill. Yes, he thought with satisfaction, and slowly, steadily, crouched low, he made his way towards it.

Rexford knew that any second a shot could ring out, a shot that he would never hear, the shot that would kill him. Cat and mouse, two men alone, two men intent on destroying each other. Nothing gave you quite the same exquisite sense of how fragile life was. It was like the old days again, the days of Vietnam, high up there in the hills on the Cambodian border with Johnny Dean and his SAS buddies. His pulse rate was high, the adrenalin pumping: that was good, it kept the senses sharp. But he was aware of a calmness too, a sense of detachment, no panic, no loss of control. If he was successful, good, his skill and training had earned it. If he had to die . . . then to hell with it, what better way?

He crawled on his belly the last few feet into the shaded cover of the rocks. He moved as slowly as a snake on the hunt, making barely a rustle in the grass. Then he came up, waiting and listening. But all he could hear were the crickets and far off the call of a bird. Everything else was silence. No smell either, no subtle perfume of rifle grease or human sweat. And yet he knew the man was near, he could sense it in the marrow of his bones. He took one pace, coming around the side of the rocks. He waited again. Still nothing, no sound, no smell. A single droplet of sweat hung on his lower lip. His concentration was wound to snapping point.

Ten feet ahead, under an overhang of rock, lay a dark, cool well of shadow. If he could just reach it, lie deep in its cover . . . yes, yes, then the initiative would be his again. He stood perfectly still, listening. He closed his eyes, letting the other senses – smell, hearing, primordial instinct – dominate.

The other man had to be out there, he had to be, and close too, so damn close he could almost feel him! Rexford took a deep, silent breath. His fingers wiped the sweat from his lips. Okay, he thought, here we go. He took one pace, just one – and they were facing each other.

For a moment – in less time than it takes to make a sound – their eyes were locked. Rexford saw the fierce look of anger on the man's face, the bulging veins in his neck, those dark Grecian eyes. They were six feet apart, almost close enough to touch. And they fired simultaneously.

The ragged volley echoing over the dry riverbed sounded like a distant firing squad. Dave stopped in his tracks. He waited, not daring to breathe, for the sound of further fire. But there was none. The deep, eternal, sun-drenched silence of the wilderness returned. He knew then that it must have been decided. So many shots so close like that . . . and then the shroud of silence. What else could it mean?

Tselentis understood the meaning of it too and, grimacing from the pain of his wound, he turned back towards the distant hill. 'What if Nick has killed him?' he asked in an exhausted voice. He dared not contemplate the alternative. 'If that's the case, we're running from nothing. I've got to tell you, I'm stuffed. I don't know how much further I can go. If we could just get back to the vehicles, get to a hospital . . .'

Dave saw the sense in it. But down there in the riverbed they could see nothing. On the opposite bank stood a giant tamarind tree rising sixty feet or more. Its trunk was gnarled and grey, encircled with parasite vines. It would be easy enough to climb. If he could just get up into the higher branches, he would be able to see back to the track where the two vehicles stood. The survivor – whoever he was – was bound to come down to them.

Many of the tamarind's roots had been exposed by the erosion of the river bank and Dave was able to use them to climb up on to the bank. Getting up into the tree itself posed no problem. Dave was fit and sinewy; at times like this the long years of running paid off, and he was able to climb quickly up through the branches.

Halfway up the tree, he flushed a couple of pigeon which flew off in a noisy flutter of wings. But that was nothing in comparison to what confronted him a second later . . .

A snake, a huge, fat, glistening thing, lay curled around a branch an arm's length from his face watching him with lifeless, onyx eyes. Dave recoiled. 'Oh Christ!' he muttered. He lost his grip and began to slip down the tree, tearing his arms on the bark. He found a footing in a lower branch and, blood racing from the shock, remained wedged there staring up at the reptile. He had always hated snakes. They turned his blood cold. But this one hadn't moved, it just watched him with those contemptuous eyes. Dave was amazed at the size of it. Its fat, yellow-brown length could have been part of the tree. It was an African rock python and pythons, he knew, weren't poisonous. He worked on the basis that if he left it alone, it would return the compliment, and, giving the python a wide berth, he continued his climb.

When he had climbed as high as his weight would take him in the thinning branches, Dave pulled aside the foliage and looked back towards the hill.

He could just make out the Land-Rover on the track, like a dusty toy. But there was no sign of movement. Dave looked at his watch. It was mid-morning. The sun was climbing higher, saturating the bush in a bright white light. He decided he would give it ten minutes. If he saw nothing in that time, he would head southeast with Tselentis to try and reach the main Kariba road. It would be an arduous trek. But it was too dangerous to go back to the vehicles. They could be walking straight into an ambush.

Tselentis had found a small pool of water down in the riverbed. His thirst was insatiable. 'Have you seen anything?' he called up to Dave.

'Nothing yet. Keep your voice down. Sound carries.'

'Can you see the vehicles?'

'Yes, I can see them.'

The minutes passed, each one seeming to take forever. Dave kept peering down through the branches of the tamar-

338

ind to where the python lay to ensure that it hadn't moved then looking back towards the hill. And all the time his mind was whirling. They had covered little more than a quarter of a mile as the crow flies, most of it relatively easy going along the riverbed. But Tselentis was already in a bad way, his wound beginning to bleed afresh. What in the hell did he do if Nick Pangalos was dead? How could they hope to stay ahead of a professional killer?

If he was alone – armed or not – Dave knew he could outstrip any pursuit. He had the stamina in him to run fifteen miles or more, even through the heat of the day, and keep up a cracking pace. But there was simply no way he could leave Tselentis.

'You must be able to see something by now,' Tselentis called up to him.

Shielding his eyes from the sun, Dave looked back towards the hill. 'There's nothing,' he replied. 'Not a thing.'

'But there's got to be something – look again.'

Dave stared at the track, moving his gaze slowly up the slope of the hill. But he could detect no movement. Everything was silent, everything still. But then suddenly – yes, there was something, a blurred kind of shape, a figure emerging from the bush. 'Yes, I see somebody now,' Dave called. 'He's coming down the hill.'

'Is it Nick?'

'He's too far away, I can't see from here.'

'Is he alone?'

'Yes, just the one figure.'

'Oh God save us, it must be Nick. Please, please.'

'He's coming down the hill towards the Land-Rover.'

'There must be some way you can see who it is!'

'He's too far away.'

'But does he *look* like Nick?'

'I can't see. I've told you, he's too far away!'

Dave watched the figure intently as it clambered down the hill. But at that great distance it was little more than a hazy, dreamlike figure. He could tell nothing about the man, not the height, the physique, nothing.

339

The figure reached the track, coming closer with every stride. If only he would stand still, if only he would lift his face! Then abruptly the figure stopped. The man, whoever he was, turned, gazing down towards the river line. For a moment he was looking in Dave's direction, face full on, and even in the shimmering heat of the sun there could be no mistake – no beard, no blackness at the hair line, just a lethal round blur.

Not since his SAS days in Vietnam had Rexford had to follow another man's spoor through the hot silence of the bush. In the years since then his killings had taken place in more prosaic locales: city streets, railway platforms, darkened rooms in cheap hotels. But as a boy back in South Australia he had gone hunting up in the Flinders Range – burnt out, hilly country not dissimilar to this – and the old skills remained.

Down through the elephant grass towards the green, riverine bush he was able to move at a steady jog following the bulldozed tunnel that Whitman and Tselentis had left behind them. When he came out of the grass, however, he had to slow down, searching for signs of their direction. He walked in a small circle patiently placing everything he saw under a mental microscope . . . each blade of grass, each sapling, each flinty trunk of a tree, the scrub bush, the Kalahari sand baked as hard as clay. He crouched next to a fallen tree trunk that now was almost eaten away by ants. A slow smile came to his lips.

Blood. A bright vermilion splash of it lay on the trunk like a red star. A pace or two nearer to the river were smears of it on the rose-russet surface of fallen leaves. Tselentis was bleeding badly. How far could he get? He had no bandages to stem the flow and no time to rest. He was bleeding his life away. Rexford rose to his feet, excited now. He wished Tselentis no pain, there was nothing personal in this. He was an objective, that's all, an objective which this time – come what may – would be achieved.

They had been moving now for over an hour, up and away

from the riverbed, up into the hills beyond, hills scattered with black rock and thorn scrub and fever trees. Dave was breathing hard. But it was not the physical exertion, it was the tension, that's what sucked the energy out of him, the knowledge that they were being hunted like animals.

Tselentis blundered along half a dozen paces behind, froth flecking his lips. They reached a steeper section. Dave scaled it easily, long legs stretching, but Tselentis had to haul himself up, half on his knees. 'Wait,' he called to Dave, sobbing with the effort. 'I've got to rest a second, I can't go on. I feel so dizzy. Look at the way I'm bleeding.'

Dave could see that he was close to collapse, clawing for the last agonised resources of his will. There was no way he could go on indefinitely, not like this. 'Don't give up on me now,' Dave said. 'Half an hour more, that's all.'

'But he's on our trail.'

'Yes, I'm sure he is. That's what I'm banking on.'

Tselentis shot him a look of perplexed delirium. 'Why? Every yard he must be gaining on us.'

'I'll tell you why,' said Dave, 'because we're moving ahead of him in a large circle, that's why – back towards our vehicles on the road. If we can just get there ahead of him, take the Mazda truck and immobilise the Land-Rover, if we can just manage that then we'll leave the bastard stranded.'

Tselentis lay back on the ground, his head against a rock. He closed his eyes, turned his face up towards the sun and there was a smile on his round, ravaged face, a smile that spoke through all the sweat and the blood and said more elegantly than any words: thank God, so there's still a chance to survive.

Rexford's only fear was an ambush. Pushed to the limit, with Tselentis ready to collapse, Whitman might just choose to drop down into cover and hold his ground. That's all that slowed his pace, fear of a sudden shot out of nowhere. But the trail Tselentis left was not difficult to follow and, even when it petered out, Rexford knew that Whitman must have taken the easiest route. Physically, Tselentis couldn't manage any other. Only once did

Rexford lose the spoor and have to cut back to find it again. That had delayed him a few minutes but since then every time he found a blood spoor it was fresher, brighter. He was gaining on them, gaining all the time.

As Dave came around the hill, he saw it five or six hundred yards away: the winding, olive-green strip of trees and scrub where the dry riverbed ran. They would have to cross it again but, once back on the other side, they would find the track and, somewhere along the track, the two vehicles. The going now would be easier too. Once they got to the foot of this hill, although the bush was thick with jesse scrub and termite mounds, it ran flat and even all the way to the river. Dave pointed out the river line to Tselentis. 'There, do you see it? The end is in sight.'

Tselentis was too exhausted to answer, barely comprehending. All he could do was nod his head. His face was deathly pale; his shirt was soaked crimson red and clustered with flies drawn by the sweet stench of the blood.

Dave gave him an encouraging grin. 'You're doing well,' he said. 'Hang in there. We're going to make it.'

And together they began the descent of that final arid hill.

Rexford reached the hill running at full sprint. He vaulted up the rocks, weaving through the thorn bush oblivious of the spurs that slashed at his arm and face, oblivious of everything except closing that final, tenuous gap. His body was slippery with sweat. It blurred his vision and stung the bleeding scratch marks across his cheeks. He could never remember feeling more tired in his life. But he was so close to Whitman and Tselentis now that he could almost smell them.

The years since Vietnam had added too much beef, too much bulk around his middle. The booze had sapped his youth. The young man's stamina wasn't there any more. But the grit in him hadn't changed, that cold inner core of determination that was unaffected by the aching muscles and the quivering legs and the rasping breath, and it was grit alone now that was keeping him going.

He climbed higher, following the red splash spots of Tselentis's blood, climbing up and around the hill, all thought of ambush forgotten. The heat was getting worse. Waves of nausea swept over him. His body cried out for him to stop but he kept pressing on. Not much further now and he would have them, he knew it. All he had to do was close the gap. He came across a small game path which swept around the hill and on its buff-brown surface, as powdery as talc, he could see the scuffed boot marks of his prey.

He slowed down, every instinct suddenly warning him to be cautious. His Dragunov was ready, held across his chest, his finger on the trigger. He strode out along the path, coming around the spine of the hill. He stopped again, chest heaving. They were close by now, every instinct screamed it out. He wiped the sweat from his eyes, took another cautious step, glanced down the hill – and there they were.

He could just make them out at the base of the hill, a hundred yards below him, heading into the flat bush that led back towards the river line. Through the rising heat haze and the first dust whirls of the day, they seemed to wave and shimmer before him like lost figures in a dream. But he had them, that's all that filled his mind. And this time there would be no mistake.

Tselentis could not run any more, not at the pace Dave was pushing. He was tottering on his feet like a drunk, arms slack, head rolling. The effort of getting this far had sucked him dry.

'Don't give up on yourself,' Dave urged him. 'Keep going until we get into the cover of the river line. A few hundred yards, that's all. You can do it.'

But Tselentis could only shake his head. He was leaning against the truck of a mopani tree, head down, lost in his own universe of exquisite pain. 'Just give me a couple of seconds, just to get my breath.' He tried to laugh but it was little more than an airless grunt. 'I've got to tell you Dave, I feel totally fucked.'

And out of nowhere the bullet hit him. It caught him in the lower back, hurling him against the trunk of the

343

mopani. He uttered no sound. But for one terrible moment he seemed to hang there, transfixed, arms thrown out like a man crucified. Then his legs gave under him and he fell.

Dave saw it all happen as if it was in slow motion. No, it was impossible, he couldn't be killed, not now; no justice on earth would let that happen. He threw himself down next to Tselentis, reaching out for his arm. 'Dimitri!' he called but there was no answer. Then he saw the great shot-torn hole of the exit wound in Tselentis's lower abdomen and thought he would throw up.

A second shot cracked overhead. In a wild panic now Dave looked for somewhere to drag Tselentis to safety. There was a large termite mound a few feet away. It was shaded by thorny sour plum bushes and, belly flat against the red Kalahari dirt, he crawled furiously towards it dragging Tselentis's inert body behind him.

He hauled him into the shaded protection of the mound. He lay him on his back and all the time he was saying. 'Don't die on me now, don't die, not when we're so close. Please God, you can't do this. No, for Chrissake, no. Come on, Dimitri, open your eyes!' But then he looked down at the face, at the swarthy, double-chinned, olive-eyed face, and it said everything. There was no movement, just a waxy stillness. The eyes stared up, glazed and unfocused, totally devoid of life. Dimitri Tselentis was beyond any miracle of modern medicine now, beyond all human hope.

A third shot ploughed into the termite mound. A fourth whined through the thorns of the soul plum bush directly above Dave's head and he crouched down, hugging the dirt, listening to the growling rumble of the echoes of the shots as they rolled out across the parched wasteland.

In a kind of trance, Dave reached out and closed Tselentis's eyes. Death was such a waste; flesh ruined, all spirit gone. What was left for him now? At that moment, huddled there behind the termite mound, exhausted, defeated, every hope smashed, it was the closest he had ever been to snapping.

He stared back towards the hill. That's where the shots must have come from. But he could see nobody, detect no movement. He knew, however, that this wasn't the end of it. The killer couldn't work on the presumption that Tselentis was dead, not seeing him dragged into cover that way. He had no choice, he would have to come down from the hill to confirm the kill. Only then could he be sure that the job was done.

Dave felt the panic begin to well up inside him, an almost uncontrollable desire to turn and run. He was no coward but no hero either, just an ordinary man possessed with a grand obsession, a desire to see justice done. But justice was dead. It lay next to him in a dusty, blood-soaked bundle behind the termite mound. Conrad Fung would never be brought to trial, not now. To believe otherwise was wishful thinking. Power had won the day again, power and corruption, influence, money, blackmail. How could he ever have dreamt of defeating all that? From the beginning it had been an exercise in self-delusion. What in the hell was he anyway? He had no money, no contacts, no influence, all he had possessed was a naive, old-fashioned belief that somehow honest principles would prevail. Honest principles – look where they had got him! At that moment, with the mopani flies flitting around his face, with his nostrils clogged with the smell of blood and dust, honest principles didn't seem to be worth the spit it took to pronounce the words.

Out there, down through the iron-grey scrub, down through the dust whorls, he knew the killer was coming. So what did he do? Stay here with the body and put up some futile, last-ditch stand against a professional? What purpose would be served in getting himself killed too? What kind of grand lesson would that teach the world? The panic was building inside him with the pressure of a million tonnes of water against a crumbling dam wall. Survival, that's all that mattered now – just as Tselentis had always said – staying alive to see another day.

Dave turned his face towards the river line. It was five hundred yards or more away and at least another two miles back to the vehicles. But the bush was thick, there was tall grass and termite mounds everywhere, more than enough

345

cover. On his own now, unimpeded, he knew he could make it. Why die for nothing? Why rot out here for a lost cause? Who was he going to impress apart from the hyenas? Maybe, if he could stay alive long enough, maybe he could still find some way to avenge himself on Fung.

He glanced one last time at the poor, dishevelled corpse of Dimitri Tselentis, filled with sadness, filled with pity. 'I'm sorry,' he whispered out loud. 'I truly am.' Then, in a swift, zig-zagging run, he burst out from the cover of the termite mound. He ran fast, clutching his rifle, running towards the river line. But he had made less than ten yards when the first bullet whined over his head and immediately a second puffed up the dust just twenty feet ahead. Dave threw himself down – Christ, the bastard wanted him dead too! – and rolled frantically into a tall clump of elephant grass. He came up on his knees just as a burst of automatic fire, echoing like a distant landslide, shredded the grass above his head. Bastard, he thought, damn you to hell!

He was crawling on his belly now, not daring to get up. He was still possessed by panic but another emotion – stronger, more powerful – was assuming its place. The anger was returning, the outrage, the wrath. He crawled faster, squirming through the bush like a snake, bruising his elbows and belly on the rocks, and the anger filled him, a sudden new determination to hit back. All right, you bastard, you murdered my son, you murdered my best friend and now my only witness. You want me to run, do you? Well fuck you!

And it was then that he saw it. It was set into the side of a termite mound directly ahead of him, little more than a shadow under an arch of thorn. It was the burrow of a warthog pirated off an anteater and enlarged . . . enlarged just enough for a man to wedge himself inside.

Rexford waited. Patience, patience . . . time was irrelevant now. Patience would keep him alive, patience would see this thing through to the end. A single bead of sweat rolled down the burnt bridge of his nose and fell salty-wet on to his lips. His pulse rate had settled, his head was clearing. He was certain he had taken Tselentis in the upper body, hopefully killing him outright. But he couldn't be sure. Maybe the hit had been the same as the first, into the shoulder or the arm. Maybe Tselentis was lying there now behind the termite mound a hundred and fifty yards away still breathing, still strong and capable of surviving. There was only one way to check it out, that was to get close to the body and put in the *coup de grâce*.

But what about Whitman? Where was he? He had seen him running – obviously fleeing – and had put in the shots hoping either to bring him down or send him even faster on his way. Maybe he had been successful, maybe not. Maybe Whitman was dead, maybe he was crawling away wounded . . . and maybe – it was a possibility he could never discount – just maybe he was lying out there waiting for him.

When you killed a man in a hotel room, it was simple. You put two bullets into his head and walked away. When you pushed him from a platform under a passing train, the results needed little verification. But bush skirmishes like this were never clean. You never knew the body count until you physically dragged the corpses out from cover. The ones you were sure you had brought down you never found, the ones you thought had got clean away you invariably found dead in the grass hit by a stray shot. Bush skirmishes were different: never clean, never easy.

Still no movement. A little way off he could hear the sharp insistent twitter of a Honey Guide. And looking down towards the flat land, he saw the bird, a dull, brown-coloured creature the size of a sparrow swooping from tree to tree. It seemed to be the only living thing out there.

Rexford looked up at the sun. It was nearing midday. It had been one of the longest mornings of his life. The bush down towards the river line was drenched in a harsh white light that seemed to suck it dry of colour. It was all bone whites now and bleached greys, parched sulphurs and brown.

It was time to move, he decided, time to come in from the flank and finish the job.

It was strangely cool in the confines of that narrow sandy

tunnel. Dave's shoulders were wedged against the sides but the rifle lay ready in his shoulder and from the dark pool of the burrow's entrance he had a good field of fire. He could see the termite mound where Tselentis lay, he could see the hill beyond and the sun-blanched scrub on either side.

There was no panic now, that had been a momentary fever in the wake of Tselentis's death. Now there was only a silent, grim resolve. If he died, he died. What did he have to live for anyway? No marriage, no child. The heart of his life had been ripped out long before today.

He thought of Danny; he saw his happy freckled face in his mind's eye and remembered those wonderful, timeless moments when they had been together. It seemed suddenly as if Danny was very close to him, all heart and pride and boundless, boyish affection. Before today ended, thought Dave, he would either have joined him or, in some small way, avenged his death. He was content with either result.

He turned his wrist so that he could see the face of his watch. He had been lying there in the warthog's burrow for two hours.

Rexford came in from the right in a broad outflanking sweep. He came slowly, step by patient step, content to crouch for ten minutes or more in one spot looking for any sign of danger, listening for any untoward sound. Sweat sluiced down his cheeks, down his neck and back. He was dehydrating badly. But it meant nothing. His concentration was focused totally on that termite mound now less than twenty yards away where Tselentis, he prayed, still lay.

This close, he was hoping he could see the man's form under the cover of the thorn bushes but he could see nothing he could identify as a body. What if Tselentis had managed to crawl away? What if he had only been winged and was across the river by now, halfway back to the vehicles? But no, that wasn't possible. He had seen the way Tselentis had been hit, he had seen the way he had gone down. That had been a full body shot.

Rexford looked around him. Hot shimmering silence shrouded the bush. Even the Honey Guide bird was long

348

gone. There was no sign of Whitman. No doubt he had reached the vehicles on the track and was going for help. But that would be many hours in coming.

Rexford stepped silently closer. He took three paces, four. Then he paused. He stared intently towards the termite mound and slowly, deep in the shade, a shape began to emerge; short and bulky, the shape of a discarded sack. He took another two paces nearer to be sure but there was no mistake. A look of satisfaction settled on his sunburnt cheeks. He could even see the mellow glint of Tselentis's gold Rolex watch on his wrist.

The shot caught Dave totally unawares. For a moment every muscle in his body stiffened, every nerve jangled. The shot had come from close by – God, just feet away! – but where was the bastard, where was he? There was only one answer, he had to be outside the narrow periphery of vision that the warthog's burrow allowed him. Oh God, thought Dave, what do I do now? I can't lie here squeezed into this damn tunnel while he walks away.

He had just one option. If he wanted wider peripheral vision, he would have to bring his head and shoulders out of the hole. Using his legs to force himself upwards, inch by inch, Dave emerged. All the time his eyes were desperately searching the bush but he could see nothing, nothing at all. Where in the hell was he? The man was a ghost.

Then suddenly, off to his left, his eyes caught the slightest movement. It was little more than the swaying of a sapling, the almost imperceptible movement when a bird settles on it. Perhaps it was nothing at all, just a trick played by the sweat in his eyes. But then – yes – he saw it again. It was twenty-five yards off to his left on the far side of a dense thicket of jesse bush. Dave froze. The rifle was pulled tightly into his shoulder, his finger curled around the trigger. The overwhelming temptation was to fire now but he knew he had to wait, wait and be sure . . .

He counted each second in the thud of his heartbeat. His mouth was dry, his fingers holding the rifle were beginning to tremble. Come on you bastard, show yourself! And in

349

paralysed amazement – as if the wish had been a telepathic command – Dave saw the man's face. All it had taken was a turn of the head as he looked around. He saw the skin, the profile of the mouth beneath the camouflaged bush hat, the soft blur of freckles, and the rest of the body took shape.

Dave aimed square at the man's chest, steadied his rifle, put the first pressure on the trigger and then, teeth gritted, gently squeezed. The rifle kicked hard into his shoulder but he barely heard the sound. All he saw was the man go down. He saw him thrown backwards, out into the open, he saw him hit the ground and, legs thrashing, try to crawl away.

Instinctively Dave fired again: a second shot and a third. The first was fired in wild, panicky reaction and went high but the second found its mark. The body rolled. Dave heard a high-pitched grunt and that was followed by the blood-curdling sounds of panting, hard, staccato breaths, ghoulishly like a man coming to climax. Oh Jesus, he thought.

Then abruptly all was silence. The body did not move. The rifle the man had been carrying, the one he'd used to kill Tselentis, lay four or five feet from him. Dave waited, watching the body and thinking all the time, part in horror, part in primal satisfaction: I've done it, I've killed the bastard!

There was still no sign of movement and, carefully, never taking his eyes off the body, Dave crawled out of the warthog's burrow. He rose up, legs stiff from lying so constricted for so long, and advanced on it. He could see blood now, a slow oily-thick ooze seeping from the man's shirt low down near the base of his spine. With his rifle ready to fire at the first indication of movement, Dave circled the body. He looked with surprise at the sweat-sheened dome of the skull shaved clean of hair. He looked at the face, at those cloudy green eyes – and to his horror, the eyes were open, unblinking . . . focused on him.

Bruce Rexford could not move. He knew that the first shot had hit him low down, smashing his spine. He was paralysed, unable to move his legs, unable to move his arms. The second shot had taken him through the buttocks and

350

his upper thigh. He would die, that was certain. But, unless he was lucky, it could take hours. He looked up at Dave and said in a surprisingly clear voice. 'So you waited for me. Yes, I should have known you wouldn't run. Stupid of me. That's all you need, isn't it, just one miscalculation.'

Dave looked down at him, eyes glazed with hatred. 'You murdered my son.'

'You want justice? Good. In your position I'd feel the same. So go ahead, do it. Finish it.'

Dave blinked.

'Kill me.'

But Dave did not react.

'For God's sake, man, I'm paralysed, can you see that? You've blown my spine away. You're not going to leave me like this, are you? I could take hours to die.'

Dave knew it would be easy to finish him, to exact his final pound of flesh. All he had to do was squeeze the trigger one more time. But something held him back, those damn principles of his. 'I can't kill you, not like this, not in cold blood.'

'So what are you going to do?'

'Get help.'

'How long do you think that will take, ten hours? There's no way you can drag me all the way back to the vehicles. You're going to have to leave me here. There's no way I'll last that long. Kill me man, go on, do it. Look at me, I can't move my legs, I can't move my arms, not even my head.'

Dave raised his rifle. Yes, kill him, have done with it. That was best. The man was an animal, ordinary rules didn't apply. The logic of it was screaming at him. But he still couldn't bring himself to pull the trigger. He couldn't shoot a man in cold blood, not a helpless victim lying there like that incapable of fighting back. It was murder, pure and simple. He shook his head. 'No,' he said, 'No, I can't . . .'

Rexford closed his eyes. 'The pain is going to come soon. Are you going to leave me no dignity? Do you have any water at least?'

'No.'

'All right, then drag me out of the sun at least, into the

shade over there next to Tselentis.'

Dave hesitated.

'It's no trick. I can't bloody move, you can see that. What do you think I'm doing, faking it?'

Dave drew closer, checking that he had no hidden weapon, no revolver or primed grenade. He could see nothing and from the way he lay, from the blood still spilling into the earth, it was obvious that he had broken his spine. 'Okay,' he said, 'I'll pull you into the shade.'

Placing his rifle on the ground, he grabbed Rexford's limp arms and dragged him slowly across the open dusty tract into the speckled shade of the termite mound where Tselentis lay. If Rexford had been able to reach out, he could have touched his victim's body. Dave walked back out into the sun to collect his rifle. It was all a dream, he thought, senseless, obscene . . .

He returned to the termite mound. So this was the assassin, the invincible killer whose shadow had haunted him all these weeks. He was florid in the face, bull-chested and strong but as mortal as any other man. He was vulnerable, he bled, he suffered pain. He was no different. A look of profound perplexity came to Dave's face. 'What motivates a man like you?' he asked. 'I saw you outside Benevolence Villas. You planted the limpet mine, you shot and killed my friend. That afternoon at Kai Tak, I saw you then too – I saw you walk away a few seconds before the bomb exploded. You must have seen my son, you were so close you could almost touch him. You must have known he was going to be killed. But you said nothing, you did nothing, you just walked on. How could you do it? That's what I don't understand. You must have known innocent people would be killed – women and children – you must have known it wouldn't just be Gomez.'

'Gomez?' Rexford gave a smile of exhausted irony. 'Gomez wasn't the principal target, not that day at the airport.'

Dave could hardly believe it. He had been so certain that it was Gomez. It all fitted, motive, everything. Incredulity was written all over his dust-caked face.

Rexford saw the look. 'Gomez had to go,' he said. 'But it could have been done any time. There were men back in Peru capable of dealing with him. Gomez was not the principal target at Kai Tak, he was a bonus, that's all. It was a coincidence he was on the same flight.'

'Then who was it?'

Rexford looked up at him, that ironic smile still there on his chapped lips. 'What do you want from me? A dying confession, is that it?'

'What difference does it make to you now?'

'It's the last bargaining chip that I have.'

'To bargain for what?'

'A quick, clean death. A bullet in the head.'

Hearing it said so prosaicly like that, as if it was a gift he could bestow, made Dave shudder. 'No,' he murmured. 'No.'

Rexford could not move, at that moment even the muscles in his face seemed paralysed. But the eyes, those green jade eyes, bored into him. 'I know what is in store for me. Once the shock has worn off, the pain will begin and it will continue growing. You have no morphine, no drugs of any kind. You don't even have any water. You wouldn't let a dog suffer this way. You want to learn what I know, you want to have some slim chance still of getting Fung? Okay. But in return you give me what I ask for. One quick bullet, that's all.'

Dave was silent, initially appalled then torn by indecision. He had never dreamt that matters could reach a bizarre impasse like this when to reward a man he had to kill him. What did he do? If he agreed then he was committing murder. He could dress it up a dozen ways of course, make a million excuses – putting a dog out of its misery, carrying out an execution – but it still amounted to the same thing, it was still murder. Nobody would ever know, he would never be brought to trial. But he would have to live with that knowledge the rest of his life. One murder balanced against one slim, fast-fading hope of bringing Conrad Fung to justice. What did he do? Did he go against the moral training of a lifetime or did he seek justice still . . . justice tarnished, justice in rags, but justice all the same.

'All right,' said Dave, after a long, troubled silence. 'All right, I agree. Now tell me what you know.'

Rexford smiled. Death he had never feared, only the gross humiliation of pain. 'The principal target was Gao Xin,' he said. 'The Chinese diplomat.'

'Why him?'

'I don't know. I was never told why I was assigned any target. It was not my place to ask. Fung instructed me to try and eliminate Gao Xin and Gomez together at the airport. But Gao Xin was always the priority target, the one I had to destroy.'

'Was the bomb your idea?'

'No, I was instructed to use a bomb, a powerful one. Whether you believe it doesn't matter now, but I was against it from the beginning.'

'But why a bomb? Why something so indiscriminate?'

'To blur reality, to make it look like an act of terrorism, work of the Japanese Red Army – to disguise the fact that it was a precise political assassination.'

'So the Japanese Red Army were never involved?'

'No. A decoy.'

'Who instructed you?'

'Conrad Fung.'

'Where?'

'Manila.'

'You say it was a political assassination?'

'That's right.'

'Then Fung must have been working for somebody or some organisation.'

Rexford blinked his eyes.

'Who?' demanded Dave.

And he answered, 'The Red Scroll.'

Dave had never heard of it. 'What kind of organisation is that? A terrorist group, what?'

'It operates out of Beijing. A terrorist group? Yes, maybe, that's how most people would see it. But sanctioned by the state.'

'Is it part of China's secret service?'

'It's a small, independent unit retained for special work, wet work,' said Rexford. 'Work that nobody acknowledges, nobody knows about. Who controls it, where its power comes from, I don't know. It's not an official part of the Chinese Ministry of State Security, not an official part of anything.'

'Red Scroll, what does that stand for? It must have some symbolic meaning.'

'God knows.'

'So Fung is Red Scroll?'

'From boyhood, yes, one of the elite brotherhood. Fung recruited me . . . if recruited is the right word – press-ganged is more accurate.'

'But Fung is a criminal, a drug dealer, a money launderer. Why would the Chinese Government – even some psychopathic sub-cell of its secret service – deal with a man like that?'

Rexford gave a weak, cynical grunt. 'Don't tell me you're surprised. The CIA worked with the Mafia when it suited them, they used gangsters when they wanted certain work done. The French Secret Service work all the time with organised crime. The killing of Gao Xin was a political act, an act of state. But you believed – everyone believed – that it was just another criminal killing. If you want to disguise a violent act of state, the surest way is to disguise it as a common crime. That's the reason the Red Scroll exists. That's why it was created.'

'They specifically employ criminals?'

'They *are* criminals, criminals working for the state. It was the Red Scroll Directorate that helped Fung to set up in Hong Kong, it was the Red Scroll people who gave him cash, cemented his early connections in the drug trade. The Red Scroll has done its best to protect him all these years.'

'Did you deal with anybody else in the Red Scroll?'

'Just Fung.'

'How do I find out more about it? What must I do to try and expose it?'

'It doesn't exist, not officially,' murmured Rexford, coughing up a small dribble of blood. 'How can you expose something that doesn't exist? Even if you got halfway there, what would you find? A loose amalgam of criminals . . . triads, Japanese yakuza, men like Fung, that's all.'

'What about you,' asked Dave, 'how were you press-ganged?'

'Me?' Rexford gave a small laugh that tailed away into a sigh. 'That was a lifetime ago.'

'In Vietnam?

'Yeah, Vietnam.'

'You're Australian. Were you with the forces there?'

'SAS.'

'Taken prisoner, is that it?'

'The beginning of it . . .'

'What happened?'

'You could say I was brainwashed. But that doesn't explain the half of it, doesn't even get close. You'd be amazed at the pressures that can be applied.' With a dispirited sigh, Rexford fell silent. He closed his eyes. What was the good of it? How could he ever explain those terrors that possessed him back then? How could one man explain to another why he had sold his soul? He had kept it locked inside himself all these years, let him carry it that way into death.

Dave waited for an answer but none came. 'Who are you?' he asked. 'What is your name?'

'I had a name that Fung gave me – Rexford, Bruce Rexford . . . it came with the bar in Manila and the cash in the bank. Part of my new life. My real name, the name I was born with, that you don't need to know.' He gave a sudden cough and bubbles of pink, frothy blood appeared on his lips.

Dave could see that he didn't have much time left. 'So Fung was your controller for the Red Scroll?'

Rexford smiled as if relishing some secret joke. 'Yeah, my controller . . . you could say that.'

'Everything came through Fung?'

'All the Red Scroll directives, yes.'

'How many people did you kill on Fung's orders?'

'Before the bombing at Kai Tak? Fourteen. But with the

356

bombing and afterwards, the numbers kind of blur.'

'Did Fung have other men he used, men like you?'

'I don't know. Maybe.'

'Fung must carry a good many secrets in his head?'

'Enough.'

'Enough to make the Red Scroll people nervous now that he's in American custody?'

'That's why I was brought in, to get rid of the witnesses against him, to make sure he got free. Killing Wong and Tselentis was a Red Scroll directive – it came direct from Beijing.' A spasm of pain hit Rexford. He winced, eyes screwed shut. He retched up pink, foaming bile. It was beginning to come now, waves of intensifying nausea. He looked up at Dave. 'It's time mate, time for you to do it.'

Dave's head was spinning. He was sure he had a thousand more questions that needed to be asked. But his mind had gone blank.

Rexford was moaning now, low, throaty moans of intensifying pain. He bit his lip until the blood came but it did no good. He looked up at Dave again. 'That's all I can tell you. I don't know what good it will do. Fung is one of the chosen. The Red Scroll people will protect him to the end, either that or slit his throat in jail.'

Brighter blood now, brilliant wet scarlet, dribbled from his mouth. His muscles were going into ugly spasms of twitching. 'Come on,' he murmured, 'Do it, do it! Don't be nervous, mate. Just pull the trigger. Get it done.'

Dave stepped a pace back. His fingers were trembling. This was crazy. Why should he care a damn about killing him? But he still couldn't bring himself to place his finger on the trigger.

Rexford could see the hesitation in his face. 'Remember,' he said, 'I killed your son. I knew the bomb was going off any second and I walked right past him. I was so close I could reach out and touch and I did nothing. Danny, that was his name wasn't it? Yeah, Danny. So go on, mate, do it for your son, do it for Danny and nobody will blame you, not me, not God . . . nobody.'

Dave stepped back one more pace. He raised his rifle. He

357

looked into Rexford's pain-filled eyes, he nodded his head, just once. Then he pulled the trigger.

When it was done, for a long time he just stood there, the sun beating down, the sweat blinding his vision, just stood there in the sun in a kind of trance. He looked down at the two bodies lying in the shade of the termite mound, shoulder to shoulder, blood mingling with blood, the hunter and the prey. Dimitri Tselentis was dead. His assassin was dead. But Rexford had been a functionary, in many ways a victim too. Dave could think of only one thing . . . out here in the dust of Africa, in this godforsaken wilderness, Conrad Fung had finally won the day.

He did not have the tools nor the strength to bury the two bodies. All he could do was remove his sweat-soaked shirt and tie it to the thorn scrub of the termite mound as a marker. Then, bare-chested, he made his way back to the river line, head bowed in the heat of the afternoon sun, one foot dragging in front of the other.

He found a way across the dry river and, on the far side, climbed back up to the track. It was late afternoon when he came across the two vehicles, the Land-Rover with its windscreen shattered and, a few yards further on, the Mazda truck.

He had steeled himself for one further task, a search in the surrounding bush for the gunshot corpse of Nick Pangalos. But, mercifully, as he approached the Land-Rover, he saw him lying with his back against one of the wheels – and there with him was Elias. It had been Elias who had found him unconscious near the top of the hill, it had been Elias who had staunched the bleeding, carried him down to the track and who had stayed with him.

Nick Pangalos watched Dave wearily drawing closer until he was able to look up at his face. There was no need for words; he knew. 'Dimitri is dead, isn't he?'

Dave nodded.

'The other man, what about him?'

'Dead too.'

Nick Pangalos gave the barest nod, his black eyes bright

with tears. 'We tried,' he said. 'We tried.'

'Yes,' said Dave. 'We tried.'

It was dark when they got back to Shamwari Mine. Nick Pangalos had been shot through the thigh and the wound was bleeding afresh. But there was first aid equipment there, bandages and morphine at least. One of the mine-workers' wives had been a nurse so they were able to clean the wound and bind it and give him something for the pain. In the morning they would set out for Kariba, to the hospital there.

It didn't take long for Nick to fall into a drugged sleep. But for Dave it was different. That day he had stepped beyond the limits of his endurance, physically and mentally. But sleep remained impossible. He sat in the small house, cocooned in the silence, alone as he had never been alone before.

What did he do now? He had no witnesses, no evidence. What was there left? There was only so much one man without influence or power, one ordinary man like himself, could do. Conrad Fung stood in the protective halo of the Red Scroll, he could twist the law to his advantage, he could turn important men to his cause. He could blackmail and intimidate, he could murder with impunity.

But the more Dave appreciated how futile it was to go up against him, the more he knew there was no way – no way on earth – that Conrad Fung could be allowed to go free. If Fung could not be punished *within* the system, according to the rules of law, then he must be punished *outside* it. Fung had murdered his only son, caused the death of his best friend and taken Hannah from him, the only woman he had ever loved. Dave didn't care what happened to himself, not any more. But to allow Fung to fly out of the United States, sipping Dom Perignon in the first-class cabin of some aircraft, smiling down with contempt on the world . . . no price was too high to ensure that did not happen.

Dave stepped out of the house, out into the night. He stood under the bright African stars. In all his career as a police officer he had never been forced to kill a man. But he

359

had killed his first man today and suddenly the killing of another did not seem difficult at all.

Chapter Twenty-Two

At eight-thirty that night, Scott Defoe dropped Hannah at Kai Tak. She was flying to London first to meet Joel Grossman for a forty-eight hour blitz of sales meetings before the two of them flew on to New York. Everything was happening with such alarming speed; pressure, pressure all the way, hardly a second to breathe.

Although she had departed with a smile, these last few days Hannah had not been herself at all, thought Scott as he drove back from the airport. She had been depressed, solitary, weepy. Nothing had been said, she had refused to confide in him, but he was certain there were problems with Dave. He just prayed to God their marriage wasn't breaking up, that would destroy her – and at a time when everything else was going so brilliantly well.

Her new summer collection was amazing, every cut and line created with stunning impetuosity. And her colours, oh God her colours, gorgeous corn yellow, crimsons, Prussian blues! Her colours were mesmerising! She was headed for the top, no doubt about it. Within two years she would be an international name and he was determined to be right there alongside her.

Scott knew he didn't have her genius for colour and line – if only he did! – but, with Hannah certain to be travelling extensively from now on, responsibility for the Hong Kong operations would fall increasingly on his shoulders, and that's where he would be able to prove himself.

He decided to call in at the factory on his way home to check that everything was in order. After all, he was in charge now. The factory was his responsibility.

361

Ephram's two people, Paco Lai and his wife Candy, had said they would be working late, packing a shipment of samples of the spring collection for New York. They had been given keys to the factory, they seemed responsible enough and he knew they liked to work alone. But there was something about them that made him wary. On occasions they seemed a little hostile, strangely cagey. It was difficult for Scott to put his finger on it but there was something about them that just wasn't right.

When he took the elevator up to the factory premises, he saw that the lights were still on. He used his own set of keys to let himself in. 'Hi, how are things going?' he called.

They both turned, a look of astonishment on their faces. Paco Lai had his back against the open carton, almost as if protecting it. 'Everything is going fine,' he said, his anorexic face, all bone and veins, suddenly flushed. 'What are you doing here? We thought you were at the airport.'

'I'm on my way home, just thought I'd call by and see how things are going.'

'We're on the last carton now. Don't worry, we'll lock up.'

Scott walked across to where they were packing the cartons. Everything looked okay, nothing out of place, everything neatly packed, yet the atmosphere was electric with tension. He looked a little closer. There was just one outfit, a boy's windcheater, which seemed a little . . . well, lumpy was the only way he could describe it. 'Is that windcheater lying okay? There's nothing wrong with it, is there?'

Candy, the wife, reached in to smooth it down. 'It's fine,' she said with a bluff laugh. 'I've checked every item. Don't worry, they're all fine.'

But Scott wasn't satisfied. 'We don't want to send stuff across that isn't one hundred percent,' he said. He reached into the carton to lift it out and examine it. But, before he could touch it, in a blur of movement, Paco Lai had seized his wrist. Scott looked at him in amazement. 'What are you doing?' he demanded.

Paco Lai smiled at him. He was a thin man, emaciated, but his grip was like a vice. 'My wife says it is fine. She is an experienced quality controller. She has checked every item. You shouldn't bother yourself with this kind of thing.'

Scott looked into his face. Paco Lai was smiling but there was a venom behind the smile, an unspoken message of violence. 'Let go of my wrist,' said Scott. 'Let go, I said.'

Paco Lai released his grip. 'This packing work is our responsibility,' he said. 'We've already done nineteen cartons. Sorry, I know I shouldn't have grabbed you like that.'

While he was speaking, his wife hurriedly smoothed down the windcheater and began to lay further garments on top of it in the carton.

Scott didn't know what to do for the best. He felt nervous, that was the truth of it. 'While Mrs Whitman is away, I am in charge here,' he said, trying without success to impose some authority. 'How dare you grab my wrist like that.'

Paco Lai smiled, the skin stretching tight across his cavernous cheeks. 'I don't know what made me do it. Please accept my apologies. It's been a long day. You get tired, a little irritable, you know how it is.'

'There,' said his wife, 'the last carton is packed.' She closed it and secured it. She said something to her husband in Cantonese and, while Scott looked on, she and Paco Lai stacked it with the other nineteen cartons.

Paco Lai lit himself a cigarette. 'Tomorrow we'll get this stuff out to the aircraft. Apologies again. I don't know what gets into me sometimes. Crazy Chinese, huh, hate to lose face on the job!' He laughed and his wife laughed with him.

Scott didn't know what to make of it. He felt humiliated, angry, impotent. But he had been in Hong Kong long enough to know that the Cantonese could get very upset – crazily so – over matters of face. Maybe that's all it was, a question of frayed nerves at the end of a long day. He gave a weak smile. 'Okay,' he said, 'let's lock up.'

But all the way home it bothered him. Should he report to Hannah perhaps? That would be the correct thing to do. But if so, report what? In the cold light of day it would sound so petty, as if he was unable to assert his own authority when she was absent. No, he thought, best to deal with it as an isolated, unhappy incident. They had parted on the best of terms: face regained. What would be the purpose of taking it further?

They left Shamwari Mine in the hired Mazda truck. Dave drove while Nick Pangalos lay in the back on a makeshift bed. Elias rode in the back with him with water, morphine and extra bandages. They set out at daybreak but it took until four that afternoon to reach the hospital high on the heights of Kariba overlooking the lake.

Nick's wound was bad but, luckily, no bones had been shattered and Elias had been able to prevent the loss of too much blood. If all went well, he would be left with a small limp and nothing more than that.

With Nick admitted into the hospital, Dave and Elias walked across to the nearby police station. Dave introduced himself to the officer in charge as a superintendent of police from Hong Kong and then made his report.

The news, of course, to a small country station used to cattle thefts and beer hall fights, was a bombshell. Dave, however, was able, in his own quiet way, to keep matters under control. He gave a detailed description of where the bodies had been left and then suggested that he type out his own statement and one for Elias too. He was given a desk and an ancient Imperial typewriter and while he pounded out the two statements, panic-stricken calls were made to Harare for instructions on how best to handle the whole affair.

Dave spelt everything out as it had happened. He started from the very beginning, the bombing at Kai Tak, and finished with his return to the Land-Rover to find Nick Pangalos wounded. There was only one thing he omitted . . . his conversation out there in the bush with Rexford, what the dying man had told him of the Red Scroll. For the moment, that was best kept to himself.

By eleven that night the two statements were finished. Elias went off to his uncle's house with a hundred US dollars from Dave and a promise of a job from Nick Pangalos. Dave drove himself down to the shoreline and booked into a small hotel called the Cutty Sark.

He was given a room in the gardens, a self-contained cottage that looked out over the water. The full extent of his exhaustion was now beginning to make itself felt but, before he fell asleep, there was one call he had to make. It was to Tom Mackay in Hong Kong.

As he had done with the local police, Dave intended to hold back only what Rexford had told him. It wasn't that he mistrusted Tom, far from it. But if that information was to be of any benefit, it had to be divulged sparingly – to the right person at the right time.

It was six-thirty in the morning in Hong Kong, seven hours ahead of Zimbabwe. Tom Mackay was already up. He listened in shocked silence as Dave reported, step by step, what had happened. 'You're lucky to be alive,' was all he could say at the end.

'It hasn't helped us get any closer to Fung, has it?'

'To hell with Fung, let the bastard rot!' said Tom. 'You've accounted for Kit's murderer, the one who planted the bomb at Kai Tak and killed your son. After what you've been through, isn't that enough?'

But Dave was unable to see it that way; in his mind that was a form of defeat. 'You know it and I know it Tom, Fung is the guiltiest of them all,' he said with exhausted doggedness. 'Why do we always take out a couple of the little men and say, okay, that's enough?'

'Be sensible, Dave. With Tselentis dead, what more can you do?'

'I've got a couple of options still. I need to speak to Mike Le Fleur. Can you get him to telephone me? And I want to speak to Stan Tarbuck too, that's important.'

'Stan left for London a couple of days ago,' said Tom. 'He's just been made legal attaché to the US Embassy there.'

'I'd still like to speak to him. There's got to be some way you can get hold of him.'

Tom Mackay didn't query it. 'I'll see what I can do,' was all he said.

'Hold the calls for a few hours. I'm dead on my feet.'

365

Tom Mackay chuckled. 'Okay,' he said, 'you've got an eight hour respite.'

Dave put down the phone. What he needed most was a long, hot shower. Every pore of his body seemed to be ingrained with dust. But he felt like he hadn't slept in a month. His head was thick, he could hardly keep his eyes open, his muscles ached. He kicked off his shoes and fumbled with his belt. But the effort was all too much. He flopped back on the bed and within seconds was lost in a dense, dreamless sleep.

He slept ten hours straight and would have slept longer if the harsh jangle of the telephone by his bed hadn't woken him.

It was Mike Le Fleur on the line, his broad Canadian accent ringing across the long-distance line. 'I've heard the news,' he said. 'Hell, what happened out there? Tselentis is dead, is that right?'

Dave sat up in bed, still groggy from sleep, 'I'm afraid it is. That's why I wanted to speak to you . . . it's about the Fung extradition.'

'Look, I know what you've been through, Dave, but we've spoken about this before. Without Tselentis, without his evidence—'

Dave cut across him. 'I appreciate that. But there have been a couple of new developments. They're long shots, I know. But I thought I should at least sound them out with you.'

'Okay,' said Mike, 'fire away. If there's any way we can get this bastard Dave, any way at all . . .'

Dave tried to get his scrambled thoughts in order. 'The night before Tselentis was killed,' he said, 'I got him to sign his extradition affidavit. It was signed before a local justice of the peace out here. I've got the affidavit with me now. It's a formal, official document made under oath. I know that Tselentis is dead but isn't there some way – somehow – that we can use it?'

'We could maybe use it for the extradition,' said Mike, his voice ebbing and flowing on the line. 'But I'm sorry, Dave, there's just no way it would be admissable at trial.

366

And where's the purpose in bringing Fung back if we can't try him?'

'Doesn't it fit the description of a dying declaration? Couldn't it be made admissable that way?'

'Not unless he knew he was dying when he swore it,' said Mike. 'Statements made by a man when he's at the point of death, when every hope is gone, when he knows he's facing eternity, yeah, those statements are admissable into evidence. But from what I understand, Tselentis was fit and well, hoping to make it out alive.'

'All right,' said Dave, switching tack, 'let me put this to you – I was with Tselentis's killer, Rexford, Fung's hired assassin, as he lay dying. The man knew he was dying too, he was under no delusions. While he lay there, he confirmed he was the one who had planted the bomb at Kai Tak. He told me he had carried the bomb on the express instructions of Fung – that Fung was the man responsible. Isn't there some way we can get that admitted into evidence as a dying declaration? I can testify to what he said, I can testify to the fact that he knew he was dying.'

'Hang on a second,' said Mike with a sudden spurt of interest, 'you might just have something there. Let me check.'

Dave heard him rustling through the pages of his law book, first finding the place in the index and then turning to the body of the text. But, as he waited, he knew there was going to be a hitch. The law never made things easy.

'No Dave, we're not going to be able to use any of it. Witnesses like yourself can testify to what they heard a dying person say. But it's only admissable when the death of that man himself is the issue at trial. It's not admissable as evidence of other deaths at other times. I'm sorry but it's here in black and white.'

'So that's it,' said Dave. 'With the dying declarations inadmissable and with Tselentis dead, legally, we've come to the end of the line. Is that what you're saying?'

'We both know the rules, Dave. Without evidence, even though we know the guy is as guilty as sin, what can we do? Our hands are tied.'

'So what happens now?'

'I'll have to contact Washington and tell them we're unable to supply sufficient evidence to support the extradition request, effectively withdraw it. Pull the plug.'

'Can you hold that back for a day or two, at least until the dust settles?'

'Okay, a day or two,' said Mike. 'But what difference is it really going to make, Dave? With Tselentis dead, Fung is going to walk free. We have to accept that fact. There's nothing you or I can do about it.'

At twelve that morning, Dave was collected from the Cutty Sark by a police Land-Rover and driven to the mortuary. An air force helicopter had been sent out early that morning to recover the two bodies and they lay now on aluminium tables, stiff and grey. Hyenas had found the bodies shortly before the arrival of the helicopter. Much of Rexford's face was gone, his belly had been opened. But Tselentis had not been touched.

'Are these the two men?' asked the officer in charge.

'Yes,' said Dave. He then formally identified the body of Rexford and the body of Dimitri Tselentis.

Afterwards, outside in the sun, the officer in charge spoke to him. 'You are required in Harare, Mr Whitman. The police there are better equipped to deal with important matters of this kind. Do you have any objection to flying down?'

'None at all,' said Dave. The quicker the investigation could be resolved, the better.

The officer smiled, patently delighted to be shifting the responsibility. 'Good,' he said. 'I have taken the liberty of securing you a seat on the plane. Your flight leaves in an hour.'

Harare was situated on Zimbabwe's central plateau. It had the air of an overgrown cattle town; good wide streets, space to waste, dusty and rough at the edges but with a sturdy, country elegance about it too. A room had been reserved for him at Meikles Hotel overlooking the jacaranda trees of African Unity Square.

There was a message waiting for him. A police officer would collect him at nine the following morning. Dave prayed he wouldn't be kept hanging around for days, unable to leave the country. Every day, every hour, was critical. Time was running out. It was just a matter of days now before Fung walked free.

For Edgar Aurelius it was a moment of triumph. As he waited in the small interview room at the Metropolitan Correctional Centre, the room he had come to loathe so much over these past few weeks, he could barely contain his excitement. At long last it was over, the battle was won. There was no way now – even if the State Department rejected the immunity claim – that the extradition could proceed.

When Conrad Fung entered the room with a guard at his side, Aurelius could not contain himself. 'Fantastic news,' he blurted. 'I heard first thing this morning. Tselentis is dead!'

Fung's first reaction, after the shock, was one of immense relief. But then, slowly, a smile settled on those pinched, parched features; a broad, open smile, the first smile of genuine, unadulterated pleasure he had shown since the day of his arrest. He waited until the guard had left the room then he asked. 'How did it happen? Where? When?'

Aurelius told him what he knew. 'It seems Tselentis fled to Africa, to some relative's mine way out in the back of nowhere. That cop, Whitman, found him there. They were on their way out, driving through the bush, when they were ambushed. Tselentis was shot and killed.'

Fung smiled thinly. 'So how much longer must I remain in this place? Without Tselentis, Hong Kong has nothing.'

'Zachary Hedgewood and I are speaking to the Justice Department in Washington this morning,' said Aurelius. 'Have a little patience, Conrad. It shouldn't be more than a few days.'

'I want you to check out the Philippines,' said Fung, already planning ahead. 'Speak to Paredes, I have to know in advance if I'm going to encounter any difficulties getting back in.'

Aurelius had pre-empted him. 'I phoned Eduardo in

369

Manila an hour ago, immediately before driving out here. He says there should be no problems. But there are a few reluctant officials. The recent publicity has got them a little skittish, apparently.'

'Which means he wants more money.'

'Of course.'

'How much?'

'He has to talk to a few people first.'

'I have to know as soon as possible. I don't care what it costs, just make sure I don't have any problems. The minute I'm released, Edgar, I want to be on a plane and out of this damn country. It's been nothing but bad luck to me. What about Khalil, have you told him the news?'

'Yes. He's delighted.'

'Did he say anything about our business venture?'

'The first shipment is due any day, he said.'

A look of supreme contentment settled on Fung's face. 'So everything is as it should be. At last some order is returning to the universe. I won't forget what you did for me, Edgar. You stood by me when many others would have run. The rewards will come, wait and see. Tell me one final thing . . . what happened to Whitman out there in there in the bush?'

'There were just two men killed,' said Aurelius. 'Tselentis and the man who killed him, some nightclub owner from Manila. Rexford, I think the name is.'

Fung nodded, not a flicker of emotion showing. 'And Whitman?'

'He survived, that's all I know.'

'A pity.'

'Forget him, Conrad. He might have been a threat to us before but he's burnt himself out. You're not concerned about a man like him, are you?'

'No, no, you miss the point,' said Fung. 'It's not a question of being concerned.'

'What is it then?'

'It's question of personal satisfaction, Edgar. Do you understand what I mean? The satisfaction a man gets from running over a snake in the road.'

*

370

Dave got up at seven that morning. No run today, his body was still too stiff, too sore. He shaved, showered and then dressed. He didn't have a tie in the holdall he carried with him. The best he could muster for his nine o'clock appointment with the police was an open-neck shirt, grey trousers and a sports jacket . . . like the rest of his clothes, all items Hannah had chosen for him. In so many things she was part of him still.

A complimentary copy of the local newspaper, the *Herald*, lay outside his door in the hotel passage. The Kariba story was its front-page headline –

BUSH BATTLE KILLS TWO
Paid killer and witness die

There was a photograph of the two bodies being carried from the helicopter at Kariba and a second photograph, smaller, taken from stock, that showed the aftermath of the bomb blast at Kai Tak. Dave skimmed through the article but suddenly it seemed to be such ancient history. Tselentis was dead. The past was the past. The only thing that mattered now were the critical days ahead.

Dave went down to the dining room for breakfast. At the entrance, he was met by the maître d'. 'Are you Mr Whitman?'

'Yes,' said Dave guardedly. 'Why do you ask?'

'There is a gentleman who would like to have breakfast with you, sir.'

Dave thought immediately it would be a journalist, somebody wanting to get the inside story. 'Where is this gentleman?' he asked.

The maître d' pointed across the room to a table on the far side next to the window. Dave looked across – and Stan Tarbuck was grinning back at him.

Dave went across to the table, delighted to see him. 'What are you doing here? Tom Mackay told me you were in London?'

Stan Tarbuck, the blonde FBI giant, the ex-gridiron player, held out his hand. 'So I was until fourteen hours ago. But your antics out here have had a few folks jumping

371

around. Tom phoned me, said you wanted to speak. Washington thought it was a good idea that I fly out. So here I am.'

'When did you get in?'

'About an hour ago.' He laughed. 'One breakfast on the aircraft and a second one now. No wonder my wife has me on a constant diet.'

Dave sat down, ordering scrambled eggs, tomato, minute steak and coffee.

'Sorry to hear about Tselentis. That was a rough break.' Stan Tarbuck showed a tired, jet-lagged sympathy. 'From what I hear, you were damn close to getting him home. So what is it we have to speak about?'

Dave sipped his coffee. 'There are certain things that I'm going to tell you, Stan, things that I've told nobody else, not even Tom Mackay.'

There was a grin from Stan. 'Why's that? You love the stars and stripes or you figure we can do something extra for you?'

'I love the stars and stripes.'

'Bullshit.'

Dave smiled. 'I don't know if you can do anything extra or not. Maybe it's just wishful thinking.'

'Give me the ball. Let me run with it. I'll see what I can do.'

Dave poured himself more coffee. 'It concerns Rexford, Fung's hit man.'

'What about him?'

'He didn't die outright Stan. He took a while. I was there with him. He had been shot through the spine. He was paralysed, dying, but he was lucid. His mind was clear right to the end. He told me things too, pretty startling things . . .'

Stan Tarbuck listened as Dave spoke; no interruptions, eating his eggs and bacon, just occasionally raising an eyebrow in surprise. He said nothing until Dave had finished, gave a small, impressed grunt and then asked. 'Is there any proof of what this guy said to you, any papers, documents, witnesses he told you about?'

372

'Nothing. Just his word.'

'Okay, so what do you want us to do with it?'

Dave gave a raw grin. 'I don't know. You tell me.'

'Throw a Hail Mary into the end zone, is that it, heave it up into the stratosphere and pray it comes down in the right hands?'

'Something like that, I suppose, yeah.' When it was spelt out, Dave knew how hopeless it sounded. But a refusal to give up on any opportunity, no matter how small, kept an edge of determination in his voice. 'There has to be something more than the straightjacket approach of the courts, Stan. I don't know what . . . maybe the FBI or CIA can exploit the information. Fung isn't some ordinary hood, the man is a state-backed terrorist. There's got to be some way of getting to him.'

'Clipping his wings maybe,' said Stan. 'But punishing him . . . that's a different ball game entirely Dave.'

Dave sat back on his chair. 'So long as you can get him somehow, screw him to the floor, I don't care.'

'Tonight,' said Stan. 'Seven-thirty at the US Embassy. We'll talk more then. I make no promises. I don't know what I can get done in a day. I don't even know if there is anything that can be done.' He wolfed down the last of his toast. 'Tell me something Dave, why are we always hanging on by the skin of our teeth in this case?'

Hannah was on the flight from London to New York with Joel Grossman that morning when she read the story. It was in the *Guardian*, one of the newspapers the cabin crew distributed. The headline caught her eye – 'Hong Kong Witness Slain' – and there, in the second paragraph, was his name.

Her first reaction was shock. Then came the relief, thank God at least he was alive and safe. Then last, but strongest of all, came a fierce sense of pride. She said nothing to Joel, who was next to her. How could she hope to explain the conflicting emotions that tore at her? Instead, she sat there gazing out of the cabin window at the endless azure sky and her thoughts were filled with Dave. What had she done to him? What had she done to herself? How, she wondered, would she ever learn to live without him?

Ibrahim al-Ghashmi heard the news that morning on the BBC World Service. He listened in a cold rage, unable to restrain his bitterness.

The granting of ambassadorial status to Conrad Fung had brought him immense trouble. The United States Government had openly challenged the good faith of the appointment, calling in the Yemeni Ambassador to express its concern. Of course, his Government had stood by the appointment. How could it do otherwise? But grave embarrassment had been caused. Members of the Presidential Council had openly castigated him, accusing him of selling diplomatic honours like melons in a market place. His political future was finished, he would almost certainly have to resign.

And Fung, what of him? The doors of his Miami prison were already half open. Soon he would walk out into the sunshine, smug and free. Ibrahim al-Ghashmi had trusted Fung and Fung had betrayed that trust. He had turned a bond of friendship, the most solemn of bonds, into an opportunity for blackmail. Fung was no better than a common thief, the kind of man whose hand you struck off. Ibrahim al-Ghashmi believed in an eye for an eye and a tooth for a tooth. He believed also that there were certain wrongs which could never go unpunished.

The United States Embassy in Harare was located just north of the city's central park on Herbert Chitepo Avenue. It was a three-storey block of a building painted a desert beige, the windows barred, the roof bristling with radio antennae; more like a Moroccan military barracks than a diplomatic mission.

That night, as agreed, Dave met Stan Tarbuck in the lobby behind the twelve-foot-high walls. As Stan signed him in, he told him. 'The man we're seeing is Winston Newman, Deputy Chief of Mission. He used to be an associate professor of international public relations at Yale

374

until he decided he wanted to play with live bullets and joined the Foreign Service. I can't promise anything but he's no slouch, perhaps even the ideal man. His last posting was Beijing. He speaks fluent Mandarin. Trust him, that's all I can say.'

They took the elevator up to the third floor. The lights were off, the place appeared deserted. 'He's at the back,' said Stan. They walked through an empty outer office and saw the light spilling out from under the door. Stan knocked and a sharp voice called. 'Enter.'

Winston Newman came around the desk from his high-backed leather chair to greet them. He was younger than Dave had expected, in his mid-thirties. He was tall, slightly stooped, with glasses and a frizz of prematurely greying hair, more the image of a benign, absent-minded chemistry professor than a diplomat. The office matched the man, an archivist's cavern, all books and manuscripts, old photographs, ink, papers and academic clutter.

'That was quite some story you recounted to Mr Tarbuck this morning,' said Newman. 'The stuff and substance of thrillers, Mr Whitman. We are doing what we can to check it out but you appreciate that these things take time. The Red Scroll . . . it is an interesting name, difficult to fathom its import. This nightclub owner, Rexford, you say, was an assassin for the Red Scroll?'

'That's what he told me.'

'A clandestine fraternity of criminals operating for Chinese Intelligence, is that it?'

'Essentially, yes, that's the way I understood it.'

Newman fumbled among the papers on his desk for a pipe and tobacco. 'I regret to tell you, Mr Whitman, that none of our intelligence experts in Washington appear to have heard of the Red Scroll. As far as we can see, it's not recorded anywhere, not even rumoured to exist. We have come up with a series of blanks.'

'New discoveries are made every day,' said Dave.

Newman responded with a bland smile, lighting his pipe. 'It does, however, give grounds for some initial scepticism. I regret to tell you also that we have no knowledge of Gao

375

Xin's intended defection, neither ourselves nor British Intelligence.'

'Why should he have given advance notice?' said Dave. 'I would have been surprised if he did. He was flying to England to meet his daughter at Cambridge University. Once he was there, it would have been a simple matter to contact yourselves or the British and request asylum.'

'Yes, I agree. But I must tell you, Mr Whitman, that Gao Xin was known to us as a staunch conservative, one of the old guard, a man of unflinching communist creed. There has never been the slightest suggestion that he espoused liberal beliefs.'

'Men change their beliefs, even old men.'

'Certainly. But again, you must admit, it does provide some grounds for scepticism.'

'Scepticism?' Dave's jaw tightened with anger. 'Do you think Rexford was making all this up, some last-gasp confidence trick? Or hallucinating perhaps?'

'Not at all,' said Newman airily. 'You're a policeman, Mr Whitman, you have experience in these things. I'm sure you know best whether a man is lying or not. I'm simply suggesting that Rexford himself may have been misinformed.'

'In what way?'

'I don't doubt that there is somewhere an organisation called the Red Scroll. I don't doubt that he has murdered on its behalf. But whether that organisation is controlled from Beijing . . . well, that is where my scepticism lies. The Chinese underworld loves symbols, Mr Whitman, you know that as well as I do. The Triads, the Tongs, they indulge themselves in ceremonies, myths and history, they love symbol and ritual, pretending it's all done in some higher cause. The Red Scroll has a ring about it, I admit. But so does the Wo Shing Wo, the Big Circle – and nobody suggests they are controlled from Beijing.'

'So the Red Scroll is nothing more than a parochial association of Asian gangsters, is that what you suggest?'

'It's a plausible theory.'

'Then why sell Rexford on the basis that it was something more?'

'To keep his loyalty, to make it seem that they were greater, more powerful, than they really were. Men will ally themselves to a grand myth far more readily than the reality of plain fact Mr Whitman.'

'Rexford was recruited from a North Vietnamese prison camp. How would that have happened?'

Newman sucked at his pipe, making no comment.

'If the Red Scroll was nothing more than an alliance of Triads, why would Rexford have been instructed to assassinate Gao Xin? There's no suggestion Gao Xin was involved in any criminal activity.'

'Ah, but Geraldo Gomez was.'

'But Rexford made it plain to me that Gao Xin was the principal target, not Gomez.'

Newman sunk deeper into his chair, the pipe held in the corner of his mouth. 'We can of course debate this for hours, Mr Whitman. But how far will it get us? We know next to nothing about Rexford, we know nothing at all about the Red Scroll. No doubt there will be some in the CIA and the Justice Department who will be happy to accept Rexford's claims. There will be others who will dismiss them out of hand. You would be amazed at the number of criminals who defend their actions on the basis that they are employed by one intelligence agency or another. Half the Israeli criminals in the United States, when apprehended, claim to be working for Mossad.'

Dave looked at him. 'What are you trying to tell me, that this will all go by default because a body of opinion has no faith in it?'

'We are all agreed on one thing Mr Whitman, all of us – Conrad Fung is a psychopath, a vicious criminal. But, as far as direct action against the man is concerned, we find ourselves in the same predicament as your own legal people in Hong Kong. All we have are the claims of a dying man, claims that are inadmissable in a court of law. There is no hard evidence, not a shred. What can we do, you tell me that? We can't bring him to trial, not without evidence. We can't simply detain him. If we deported him, he would be delighted, that's exactly what he wants. Even if we were able to put Fung on a plane straight back to Hong Kong, you could do nothing with him. You have no evidence either, no witnesses, nothing.'

'So my information is worthless?'

Newman puffed at his pipe, the room filled with the aroma of his tobacco. 'I regret that it is no elixir to cure all ills, Mr Whitman, but it does provide us with valuable intelligence. Now we can keep a close eye on Fung's activities, try and build some evidence against him. At the very least, keep him bottled up in harbour.'

'Pre-empt future Kai Tak outrages?'

'Exactly.'

'But Fung goes free, is that it? Back to the Philippines, back to his country estate, his servants and his bodyguards? Even though you appreciate what sort of man he is, politically, diplomatically, you are powerless to do anything. Is that what you are telling me?'

Newman took the pipe from his mouth. 'We are telling you that we have to operate within the confines of the law, Mr Whitman, no different from you.'

Stan Tarbuck escorted Dave down to the ground floor and out of the embassy. They stood on the pavement together while Dave waited for a taxi to arrive.

'Don't let yourself get riled up about Newman,' said Stan. 'I know he comes across as intellectually arrogant, too damn smug by half. But I've had it from my people in Washington that he's a top operator, a man who gets things done.'

Dave gave a disconsolate shrug. 'You heard him, he said there was nothing that could be done. It looked like he was washing his hands of it.'

'Maybe, yes. Maybe that's a hard fact of life in this case. But sometimes there are wheels within wheels Dave. Surprising things can happen. Don't give up hope, that's all I'm saying.'

The taxi drew up. It was a Renault R4, a dusty relic from the Sixties.

'One final thing before you go,' said Stan. 'I got news from Washington early this evening. Not too good, I'm afraid. With Tselentis dead and the Yemeni Government pressing like hell on the diplomatic issue, the State Department has had to bite the bullet. There's simply no legal basis for justifying Fung's continued detention, Dave. They're dragging their heels as long as possible to see if Hong Kong can come up with something. But arrangements have already been made to take Fung to court in Miami this coming Wednesday. The hearing is set for two in the afternoon. A formal application will be made for his discharge and after that he'll be set free.'

'Wednesday? That's less than four days away.'

'They just can't hold him any longer.'

Dave shook his head. 'Wheels within wheels, you say. Well Stan, if that's all I've got left to rely on, they'd better start spinning bloody fast.'

Dave slept badly that night in Zimbabwe, tossing and turning, haunted by failure, dreaming a lot of Danny.

In the morning, before it was light, unable to lie there any more, he got up, put on his running shoes and, barechested, set out into the empty streets. It was cold and brisk, dry as a bone. It took a little while for his breathing to adjust to the thin atmosphere of the plateau but, once it was done, the miles glided by.

The running for Dave was as much a mental thing as physical. In the easy, oiled relaxation of each stride, the despondency fell away. Slowly, stride for stride, his thoughts were set free, uncluttered again – and it was then he realised that one last, tenuous opportunity had been overlooked.

It was something Tselentis had said to him that night at Shamwari Mine when they had been drinking scotch, something about Ephram – Khalil Khayat, whatever his true name was – and the manner of his drug dealing. There was probably nothing in it, just another desperate attempt to slay Goliath with one small pebble of coincidence. But every last possibility, no matter how far-fetched, had to be explored.

He turned back towards the centre of town, increasing his

379

speed, sprinting the last quarter of a mile to the hotel, and went straight up to his room. He didn't bother to shower. He sat on the edge of his bed hoping like hell that, even though it was Sunday and nearly midday in Hong Kong, he would find Scott Defoe at home.

When he got through, however, an answering machine clicked into play. 'Hi, I'm out right now. Sunday, bloody Sunday, and it's mayhem at the factory. If you want me badly, that's where I'll be. If you're not that desperate, just leave your name and number—'

Dave put down the phone, got through to the hotel operator again and asked for a second number in Hong Kong, the number of Hannah's office in Tsim Sha Tsui. The number rang. Dave waited. But nobody picked up the phone at the other end. 'Come on, pick it up! Answer, damn you, Scott, answer, answer!' But there was no response, just that inane electronic beeping.

The hotel operator interrupted. 'There is no answer, sir. Do you wish me to try again later?'

'Yes please, if you would—'

But a voice cut through. 'Hullo, hullo. Can I help you?' It was Hong Kong, Scott's voice on the line.

'Scott, is that you?'

'Hi, Dave, yes it's me. I'm sorry I took so long to answer but I was across the other side of the factory in the fabric room. Where are you phoning from?'

'Zimbabwe.'

'Where!'

Dave laughed. 'I'll explain some other time. Scott, there's something I want to ask you. It's about the business. It's got nothing to do with the finances or anything confidential. I'm not asking you to go behind anybody's back. I'm not sure I even know where to begin. But okay, let me try and be as specific as I can. Recently, since Sam Ephram's involvement in the business, have you noticed anything . . . well, anything untoward happening?'

'Untoward?' Scott sounded puzzled. 'How do you mean exactly?'

'Any unexplained changes in routine, anything at all . . .

380

with the shipping of samples to New York for example? I know this must sound crazy to you but, believe me, there's a good reason—'

'No,' Scott interjected, 'no, not crazy at all. I'm glad you asked. You want the truth, it's been bothering the hell out of me.'

'What has?' asked Dave, his mouth suddenly dry with anticipation. 'Tell me.'

'It was a silly incident really but, at the same time, extraordinary, you know what I mean? When he was here, Ephram hired these two people, this husband and wife team. The husband is a shipping clerk. Paco is his name, Paco and Candy.'

'It was Ephram who hired them, definitely Ephram?'

'Oh yes. We had nothing to do with it.'

'What happened?'

'Well, the other night, after I had taken Hannah to the airport, I returned to the factory. It must have been about nine. They were working late, just the two of them, Ephram's people, packing this shipment of extra samples. They didn't expect me back, that was obvious. When I walked in, there was an atmosphere you could cut with a knife. They had just about finished their work. All the cartons except one were packed. But I noticed there was one garment, it looked badly sewn or something, and I wanted to check it. But they wouldn't let me—'

'What do you mean, wouldn't let you?'

'Exactly that,' said Scott. 'I couldn't believe it. Paco, the husband, grabbed my wrist and held me away. They wouldn't let me near it.'

That night, with the final police formalities cleared, Dave boarded an Air Zimbabwe jet, one of the old 707s, for the flight north to the British Isles. He would arrive at London's Gatwick Airport shortly after six the following morning, transfer to Heathrow and board a British Airways flight for New York. If all went according to schedule, he would be in the United States by late Monday afternoon, just forty-four hours before Conrad Fung's release in Miami.

New York was his destination for just two reasons. First, Hannah was there and, second, if what Scott told him added up, she was about to receive a shipment of heroin concealed in clothes dedicated to the memory of their son.

The Sheraton Hotel was a monolithic edifice of gold-anodised aluminium. It had been built by the Yugoslavs in the early Eighties when communist international cooperation resulted in half the Third World's buildings looking like the headquarters of the Bulgarian Secret Police. There was a reception that night at the hotel, a glittering affair hosted by ZANU, the political party that made up Zimbabwe's one-party state. As always on such occasions, the diplomatic community was there in strength.

During the course of the evening, somewhere after the display of traditional tribal dancing and before the President's speech, Winston Newman ensured that he had a few minutes alone with Lu Hai, a senior diplomat in Zimbabwe for the People's Republic of China, second only to the Ambassador.

They made an odd couple, the gangly professorial American with his sharp frizz of greying hair hovering over the diminutive, baby-faced Chinese. But they were known to be close friends. They both had academic backgrounds but, more important still, both men were dedicated to ensuring China's full place in the community of nations.

'A strange affair, that gunfight in the bush near Kariba,' said Newman, speaking impeccable Mandarin as he sipped a long glass of soda. 'What do you make of it?'

Lu Hai gave a disinterested shrug. 'They say it's to do with that gangster, Fung, the one who is supposed to be behind the bombing in Hong Kong. It's a bad affair. But criminals kill criminals. It happens every day.'

'Except this bad affair may be very different,' said Newman. 'There is something I should tell you in the strictest confidence. We have learnt that the assassin, the Manila nightclub owner, decided to unburden his soul before he died. And I must be frank with you, he made a number of startling allegations – allegations that might just cause us

382

both a great deal of unnecessary trouble.'

Lu Hai stared up at the American. Winston Newman was not an alarmist. If he said there was cause for concern, then he was to be believed. 'What sort of allegations?' he asked.

Newman replied in English. 'He admitted he had been employed by Fung to carry out the killing. But he went much further than that. He intimated that Fung was his controller, that they were both agents employed by some top secret cell, some dark inner sanctum in your national intelligence service. The Red Scroll, he called it, some secret fraternity of criminals controlled from Beijing.'

'The Red Scroll?' Lu Hai gave a thin, facetious smile. 'Surely, Winston, your people are not taking such nonsense seriously?'

'Regrettably, there are always people who will take such nonsense seriously. That's what troubles me. It seems that this killer, Rexford, even alleged that the real target of the Hong Kong bombing was not the Peruvian, that man who was mixed up in the immigration fraud, but one of your own diplomats – Gao Xin. It was a political assassination, he says, disguised as random terrorism. Gao Xin was intending to defect.'

Lu Hai looked genuinely shocked. 'Is this likely to come out, to be publicised in any way?'

'Yes, I very much regret that it may,' said Newman.

'But this is ludicrous! Unsupported allegations from some hired killer who is now dead. No reasonable person could take them seriously.'

'If only it was that simple. The power of logic. But you forget that Conrad Fung, Rexford's alleged controller and apparently a long-term member of this Red Scroll organisation, is in custody in the United States.'

'He's not saying anything, is he?'

'I'm afraid he may be, yes. Sources advise me that a couple of weeks ago, fearing the worst for himself, he negotiated a deal with elements of our Central Intelligence Agency – our own Red Scroll people.'

Lu Hai was looking more alarmed by the moment. 'What sort of deal?'

'Fung is going to be used for political advantage,' said Newman in a cryptic voice. 'In return for protection in the Philippines, he will be milked of information and used, at the opportune moment, as a propaganda tool.'

'Why are you telling me this?' asked Lu Hai.

'Why?' Newman smiled benignly. 'Because both of us know that the objective interests of the United States are not advanced by promoting some psychopath like Fung as a witness of the truth. The cause of the United States is enhanced by further cementing its legitimate ties with the People's Republic of China. As I said at the beginning, this man Fung can only cause trouble with his outlandish allegations, a great deal of trouble.'

Before either man could say more, there was a fanfare of trumpets. As Zimbabwe's President stepped up on to the podium, the two diplomats were separated. But Winston Newman was content. On instructions from Washington he had planted the seed. Whether he had done so in fertile ground, of course, was another matter entirely.

There was no Red Scroll. No such name was recorded in any government ministry, in any directory or ledger. The Red Scroll was a myth . . . officially at least.

But less than half a mile from Tiananmen Square in central Beijing, tucked behind the huge structure of the Museum of the Chinese Revolution, was a quiet tree-lined street named Zhengyi Lu. The buildings along Zhengyi Lu were hidden behind ivy-clad walls. Apart from the bicycles that were everywhere in Beijing, it could have been a street in one of the more elegant parts of Paris.

Some three hundred metres down the street, shaded by the feathery leaves of a birch tree, was a large red gate sewn with black metal bolts, the kind of gate seen in the Forbidden City. There was no nameplate by the gate, no indication what lay behind and only a few people were ever granted admittance.

That morning, however, a messenger arrived at the gate carrying an envelope. He gave his name and was granted admittance. Behind the gate was a stone-paved courtyard which led into an old double-storey building and at the back of that building, on the ground floor, was an office guarded by a stern woman in her sixties. It was to that woman that the messenger delivered the envelope.

The woman did not open the envelope. She waited until the messenger had departed, then she entered the office. The office had been occupied by the same man for over forty years, an old man now named Qu Zhe, and it was to him that she handed the envelope.

Qu Zhe opened it and read the decoded message inside. He poured himself a little jasmine tea and then, carrying the cup, walked from the office into a secluded garden that had its own small pond of green water. Carp swam in the pond. He stood for a time watching the fish then he sat in the shade of a lychee tree in an old weathered chair made of teak.

Qu Zhe had personally ordered the death of Gao Xin. He had done so for pressing reasons of state. Gao Xin, who for all those years had been a loyal party member, had been poisoned in his mind by a slip of a girl, turned to the ways of the West by his daughter. It had been Gao Xin's intention to seek political asylum in the United States and then to lobby the American Congress to cancel China's most-favoured-nation status in matters of trade, asking that it only be restored when Beijing bent its back to Western bourgeois ideas of democracy. Gao Xin had carried certain papers with him, judicial documents, letters smuggled from prisoners, photographs of labour camps and the like, all fodder for a gullible Western press.

If he had been successful in his aims, if China's special trade status with the United States and other capitalist countries had been lost, it would have cost the country untold millions. Qu Zhe felt no regret. There was now food in a hundred thousand bellies because Gao Xin had been stopped, there were now goods on the high seas, there were jobs for young men and women, there were smiles instead of tears. He felt no regret at all.

He had known, of course, of the risks. He had appreciated the probable repurcussions. That was why such painstaking steps had been taken to disguise Gao Xin's liquidation as a terrorist bombing: the work of those renegade Japanese.

It would all have gone smoothly too if only Conrad Fung had obeyed the one fundamental rule – that, without question, the work of the Red Scroll stood alone, above and beyond everything else.

It had been stupid of him, attempting to complete his own venal work that way in the same bomb blast. Gomez, the Peruvian, was too tainted, carrying his crimes with him like a bad smell. He should never have been killed at the same time. How could Fung have been so short-sighted? If Gomez had been disposed of elsewhere, back in South America, at another place, another time, there would have been no way of refuting the Japanese Red Army claims, no way whatsoever of discovering the truth. One mistake, that's all that was ever needed. That Hong Kong policeman, Whitman, obsessed with his vendetta, had seized upon it . . . and look where it had led.

Qu Zhe sipped his jasmine tea. It tasted bitter in his mouth. The old sages, the ancient Confuscist philosophers whom he read so much these days, had said it in a sentence: *Nobody is able to ride the horses of vengeance.*

So what was to be done with Fung? That he had brought these troubles down upon the Red Scroll was bad enough but now to hear that he had entered into some pact with the Americans, that he had betrayed the brotherhood – no, that was unthinkable. Such a thing had never happened before, never! Qu Zhe read the decoded message a second time as if to reassure himself that the words were truly there. He did not move, his eyes gave nothing away. But the disappointment coursed through his veins like poison.

Qu Zhe had grown infirm in these last few years. Arthritis caused him much pain; he had cancer too of the blood. The doctors gave him only a limited time. He was a little man, a toy Buddha with a round face and dimples in his cheeks. But, despite his infirmities, his hands were still thick and strong, a good peasant's hands. He was proud of those hands, proud of his humble birth. He liked to say that he had been born a farmer and raised a thief – a 'thief redeemed' was how he liked to put it. And he had memories, ah yes, memories that would be the envy of ten thousand men . . .

Back in 1934, as a young boy released from a country jail, Qu Zhe had accompanied Mao Tse-tung's Red Army on its epic Long March. Six thousand miles he had marched, six thousand blood-soaked miles from encirclement by the Kuomintang in Kiangsi Province to safe haven far north in the mountain redoubts of Yenan. That journey had gone down in history. It had forged the Red Army and it had forged him too.

As a convicted thief, a little urchin not worth a day's ration of rice, he had been unceremoniously dispatched to do what he did best, to scavenge ahead for food and supplies, to seek out Kuomintang ambushes. It had been dangerous work. Few in his position had lasted more than a few weeks. Most who were caught had been beheaded as common felons, many garrotted by the road. But so successful had he grown at his trade that, by the end of that six thousand miles, he had gathered around him his own small team. They had just been boys, vagabonds and cutthroats all of them, no different from him. By the end, however, not only had they been out there scavenging for supplies like crows but they had been stealing weapons too, sabotaging enemy positions . . . even isolating targets for assassination.

That is how it had begun, just a group of lice-infested kids, thieves, triads and pickpockets with angel eyes and big knives. And the name of each boy – each one who joined, each one who died – he had faithfully recorded. The written word was memory and Qu Zhe believed passionately in memory. It amused him to recall that the only paper he had been able to obtain had been rough local stuff pillaged from a tax collector's house, paper dyed a pinkish, ruby colour. That's what he had used, that's where the first names had been written.

Mao himself had seen the record one bleak winter's day in Yenan and had said. 'That red scroll of yours, some say it is just a list of thieves. But I say it's more than that now. I say it is proof that the revolution redeems us all. I wish you to inscribe my name in there with the others, no better, no worse.' And so it had been done; and so the Red Scroll had been born.

By October 1949, the month the People's Republic of China was proclaimed, Qu Zhe had extended his influence deep into the organised criminal circles in Beijing, Canton and Shanghai: if they had to exist, let them at least work in their own way to promote the new proletarian dictatorship.

Qu Zhe would have wished to grow bigger, to become a full arm of national intelligence. But Mao Tse-tung had other ideas. His small directorate, unacknowledged as thieves everywhere are unacknowledged, was to be answerable directly to him, available always to carry out those 'invisible tasks' for which it was most suited. Criminal elements were always used, of course. Criminal motives always disguised the true reason for such actions. Profiteers and slave dealers, drug lords and triads, scum of all kinds . . . Qu Zhe had been raised one and understood them.

He rose up from his weathered teak chair, looking, as if with regret, at the golden carp that moved with such tranquil grace in the dark jade waters of the pond. Conrad Fung had been recruited as a young boy, violent even then, but ambitious and bright, a person of great promise. He had trained him and helped him, protected him over all the years, forgiven his excesses, always gathered him back into the fold like a prodigal son. How could Fung even think of making a pact with the Americans? Surely he understood the inevitable result?

Qu Zhe walked slowly back into his office. What was he to do? He sat at his desk, shaking his head. Conrad Fung with the Americans . . . he found it hard to believe; it made no sense, no sense at all. But then, of course, good sense was not always a quality that marked the criminal mind, and betrayal was the worst of crimes, the only one beyond forgiveness.

Chapter Twenty-Three

All the way across the Atlantic in the long, dull, droning hours, one question dogged him: how, with the one card he had left, did he bring Conrad Fung to justice?

Dave sat slumped in his seat near the tail of the British Airways 747 nursing a glass of red wine. There was no way he could prove Fung's involvement in the Kai Tak bombing, not now, not with Tselentis dead and Wong Kamkiu dead before him. But what if he could prove Fung's involvement in another crime, a crime so serious that it would put him away for life? It may not announce him to the world as his son's murderer but at least it would prove him to be a criminal before a court of law and, at the end of the day, whatever the nature of the guilt, the punishment remained the same.

As lawyers liked to express it, there was good precedent. Al Capone had terrorised Chicago in the twenties – murder, corruption, intimidation, every offence known – but in the end they had only been able to convict him of one crime: tax evasion. What difference though? He still went to jail, he still died a lonely old man, shorn of power.

Yes, thought Dave, that had to be the way, second best perhaps but still good enough. And the crime that would destroy Fung, that would see him die lonely and embittered in some cell, was the felony of conspiracy to deal in narcotics. From what Tselentis had told him and what Scott Defoe had confirmed, it was almost certain that Ephram – or Khalil Khayat or whatever the bastard called himself – was smuggling heroin into the United States by secreting the stuff into Hannah's fashion samples. It was equally certain that somehow Fung was behind it.

Dave had no idea of the amount of narcotics involved but the extent of Fung's financial crisis indicated that the amount of drugs had to be substantial. If Ephram was caught with a large enough quantity, he faced life imprisonment without parole. United States federal law cracked down hard on drug dealers. There would only be one way Ephram could save himself, that was by cooperating with the police – and that meant pointing the finger directly at Conrad Fung.

Dave had worked with criminals long enough to be confident that a man like Ephram, too fond of the sweet things in life, knowing that he would die behind bars, would do whatever was necessary to save himself. He might bluff it out for the first few hours but, once the full reality of his predicament dawned on him, he would implicate Fung soon enough. In many ways it would be appropriate justice, thought Dave, the man who had taken his wife betraying the man who had killed his son. A nice, neat judicial package – or would it be?

What made it so certain that Ephram would only implicate Fung and Aurelius and perhaps a few henchmen? What happened if he spread his net of cooperation wider than that? Then the neat judicial package might just explode in his face. Dear God, he thought, what would happen if Ephram turned and pointed the finger at Hannah too?

If that happened, the DEA or FBI would have no choice but to pull her in for questioning. He knew she would never knowingly smuggle heroin. But why should the rest of the world be so certain? If a jury was going to be asked to believe what Ephram said in respect of Conrad Fung, how could they be asked to disbelieve what he said in respect of Hannah?

A prosecutor could put it so convincingly to any jury. And a jury might just be swayed.

Over these past weeks, in the dazzling stardust of a Cinderella story, Ephram had given her the world. Hannah owed everything to him. She was a changed woman. If the moral pressures were great enough, why shouldn't she agree to

390

help him? Just one or two shipments, that's all. It had happened hundreds of times before; girlfriends had been persuaded to act as couriers, lovers induced to hide the drugs in their homes. And after all, the heroin was found in her samples packed in her own factory. She was obsessed with the success of her collection. Would she not do anything to ensure that success?

Dave put his head back, closing his eyes, he felt cold inside. He had one final chance to destroy Conrad Fung, one final hope of justice. But, if he took it, he might just destroy Hannah too.

He landed at JFK in New York, cashed some of his last traveller's cheques and caught a yellow cab into Manhattan. He booked into a businessman's hotel on East Forty-Second, nothing fancy, just a place to put his head, and went up to the room.

He had two numbers with him, the Manhattan head-quarters of the DEA, the US Drug Enforcement Administration, and the number of Ephram's apartment, the place where Hannah was now staying.

If he telephoned the DEA and gave them the information, Ephram would go down but Hannah might just go down with him. Innocent or not, even if she was exonerated, the arrest and its aftermath might destroy her career, ruin her life.

But if he telephoned Hannah first, if he confided in her, how would she react? It was an incredible story, he knew it. Would she believe him or think it was some sick fantasy? She was living with Ephram now. She owed everything to him. If she warned Ephram, he would be gone and the last chance to bring Fung before a court of law would be gone with him.

Where would her first loyalty lie? So much had happened over these past weeks. He loved her, yes, nothing would change that. But could he still trust her?

He sat on the edge of the bed next to the telephone. It was an impossible choice. How did he make it? There was only one way. There was a simple question to be asked. At the

391

end of the day, what did he want more, justice for his son or the love of his wife?

Dave lifted the telephone and slowly, methodically, began to dial.

For those first few seconds when he heard her voice he was lost for words. It was the first time they had spoken since their separation. He could only manage to say in a dry voice. 'Hi, how are you?'

'Where are you?' she asked, surprised, her voice filled with hesitant affection. 'Are you in New York?'

'I arrived today,' he said, 'just a couple of hours ago. Is Ephram there with you?'

'No,' she said, 'no, I'm on my own.' Then she said. 'I read about you in the English newspapers, those terrible events in Zimbabwe. Are you all right? You weren't hurt in any way?'

'I'm okay,' he answered.

'Why are you here?' she asked.

'I'm here because I have to speak to you,' he said. 'It's important, Hannah. Is there somewhere we can meet?'

'Yes, of course,' she said without hesitation. She wanted so much to see him, to sit with him, so much to try and explain. And, oh God, she was terrified too.

'I'm in a hotel on the corner of East Forty-Second and Madison,' said Dave. 'There's a delicatessen opposite, a diner of some sort.'

'I'll meet you there in an hour,' she said.

He was already waiting, sitting in a cubicle with a coffee, when the cab drew up and she entered. She was dressed in a linen suit, tan in colour, with a single strand of pink-sheened pearls around her neck. Her yellow hair shone, her blue eyes – as blue as Arctic ice – seemed to swallow him. She looked vivacious and beautiful, more beautiful than he had ever remembered her.

At that moment all he wanted to do was reach out and take her and say, let's forget what we've done to each other, let's start again. Life is too short and we love each other.

392

But instead he sat there, rooted, as gauche as a kid on his first date. Hannah saw him and came across. He rose up from his seat, almost knocking over his coffee. All either of them could muster was a nervous smile, their eyes so full of regret.

'You look good,' he said. 'Success suits you.' Instantly he regretted the words. They sounded so bloody inane, smacking of envy.

But Hannah merely smiled. 'You look thin,' she said. 'You need somebody to feed you.'

They sat together in the cubicle, looking at each other across the narrow table. Dave had never felt so nervous. He thought to himself, how could it ever have got to this stage? We're sitting here like strangers. He thought of her and Ephram together and he burnt inside.

The waitress came across and Hannah ordered coffee. They spoke for a few minutes until the coffee came, a little about her business, how well she had done in London, a little about Africa and how Dave had got so close to bringing Tselentis home to Hong Kong. But it was all just words, empty and superficial, the smallest of small talk.

After the coffee had been served, Hannah said to him. 'You wanted to talk, you said it was important.'

Dave was silent for a moment. He knew how much this was going to hurt her. 'It concerns Conrad Fung,' he said. 'Fung and those who associate with him. I want to tell you in particular about one of those associates, a man called Khalil Khayat. Bear with me, please. The reason for it will become clear soon enough.'

Hannah waited, trusting him implicitly. She had no idea what was coming, Dave could see that. She had never heard the name.

'Khalil Khayat,' said Dave, 'was born in Turkey. His father was some minor civil servant in Istanbul, not poor but certainly not rich. Khalil, though, had a driving ambition, he still does. He got involved in the drugs trade when he was a teenager, moving heroin from the golden crescent in Pakistan through to Europe. But he learnt soon enough that nothing could match the quality of the Asian product, China White. That's what brought him first to Hong Kong and that's how he met Conrad Fung. They struck up a close relationship. Khalil, you see, had great business acumen and Fung saw that. The two of them went into business together. A lot of the drugs in those early days were shipped through the Middle East . . . the Yemen, the Lebanon, Turkey . . . and from there on to Europe and the States.'

Dave paused a moment, sipping his coffee. It was essential that the whole background be painted, brush stroke by brush stroke, full and complete.

'Khalil had a favourite method of moving the heroin. You see, he was very good with women, good-looking, charming. He would give them packages to take to relatives of his, small gifts, insignificant packages. But of course they contained heroin. Then, a few years back, I don't know exactly when, one of his unwitting couriers was caught and she agreed to testify against Khalil. He was brought to trial in Istanbul and sentenced to twenty years. That was when he appealed to Conrad Fung . . . and the machinery was put in motion. Nobody is too certain what happened but it seems that a prison official was bribed to move Khalil to a smaller prison upcountry. His escorts were then bribed, or cajoled some way, into letting him escape. Khalil had served less than six months. He was spirited out of Turkey and back to Asia. He was a wanted fugitive, of course, no good to anybody that way. So steps were taken to change his identity . . . to make him a new man.

'Fung arranged for Khalil to be admitted into a private clinic in Singapore, a clinic run by Chinese doctors. He underwent plastic surgery there . . . nothing spectacular, a slight adjustment to the nose, to the chin, a few other minor adjustments. He was given a new passport too, a new date of birth, new nationality, all the documentation a reborn man required. When that was done, Khalil – under his new name now – went to London where he set up a trading company. Drug monies were used to finance it but its day-to-day business was perfectly legitimate. And Khalil flourished, just as Fung knew he would. Khalil had a genius for the golden opportunity, you see. He made friends easily, he charmed people. He was a born trader. When the time was right, he moved here to New York and set up an office. But he never abandoned the drugs, not entirely. They were always there to provide a quick injection of cash if cash was needed.'

Hannah was listening intently to every word. She did not understand where it was all leading. How on earth could she? But when she did, Dave knew the shock would be devastating. That was why it had to be taken so slowly, with such care.

'Of course, Khalil's old identity could not be kept a total secret,' he continued, 'not from Fung and his inner circle of advisers, not from Dimitri Tselentis, for example. In private, they continued to call him by his old name. Maybe it was Fung's way of showing that he still had a hold over him, maybe it was just habit. But, outside of that small clique, that tiny coterie of Fung's advisers, the world today only knows Khalil Khayat by the name printed in his passport, that passport Fung gave him in Singapore.'

Hannah looked at him. She still had no idea, none at all. 'What passport is it?' she asked. 'What name does he go under now?'

Dave spoke very slowly. 'The passport,' he said, 'is an Israeli one.' He saw Hannah's eyes widen, the initial bewilderment. 'The name that Khalil assumed was that of a young Israeli soldier killed in a border clash. The name, Hannah, was Ephram . . . Samuel Ephram.'

For a time she could only stare at him; it was all too much to take in. She shook her head. 'Oh no,' she murmured. 'Oh no, no.'

Dave continued in a quiet voice. 'The man you know is a fiction Hannah. The man you're living with is not Israeli, his real name is not Ephram. He is a Turk by the name of Khalil Khayat. He's not a Jew, he's a Muslim.'

'But that can't be right,' she blurted. 'I've lived with him. I know he's Jewish. I've seen him. He's—'

'He's what? Circumcised?' Dave couldn't keep the hurt, the bitterness out of his voice. 'Muslims are circumcised too.'

Now Hannah was beginning to find her voice. 'Surely you

can't believe this, Dave? I know Sam has hurt you, I've hurt you even more. But he's a good man, he's kind, he's gentle. Who told you these things?'

'It was Tselentis,' he answered. 'I don't know how Ephram's name even arose but it did. And then he told me, he explained everything . . . the whole history, everything. Do you think I'd invent something like this? Dear God, Hannah, I'm hurt, yes, I feel betrayed, but I'm not sick in the head.'

She looked at him, her lower lip trembling. She had left her old world in rubble and now her new one was being torn down around her too. 'But it makes no sense,' she said, her voice barely a whisper. 'If Sam is the sort of man you say he is, why has he done so much for me? Why has he been so good? What possible reason could there be?'

Dave answered her, firmer now, more aggressive. 'He's a shrewd businessman, Hannah. As I said, he has a genius for the golden opportunity. He recognised your talent. I'm sure he hopes to make a great deal of money out of you. But the motive behind meeting you, the sole reason for that initial contact, had nothing to do with business – he was using you, Hannah, using you to get to me.'

'No, that can't be right,' she protested, fighting against the logic of it. 'I'm not that gullible. Don't you think I would have realised if he was pressing me for information? Don't you think I would have been suspicious? We hardly ever spoke about you. You want to know why, I was too wrapped up in my guilt, I was hurting too much, that's why. You never told me anything confidential anyway. If what you say is true, what could he hope to gain?'

'A couple of words spoken out of place Hannah, a hint of something . . . and, as it turned out, when the moment was crucial, when matters hung in the balance – everything.'

Hannah stared at him, her eyes glistening, now totally bewildered.

'I had just two witnesses,' said Dave. 'Without them I had no case. I had them both in a safe house. Okay, the safe house itself would not have been impossible to find. But the movements of those two witnesses – that was something else: Yet the very morning they set off for the High Court to sign their affidavits, as they came out, hidden in an ordinary commercial van, right at that moment they were hit. It was all set up Hannah, perfectly timed. The attackers had it down to the last second. They had to know in advance. It couldn't have been done any other way. They had to have prior information!'

'But half a dozen people could have known about that!' she said, close to tears.

'No,' he said, 'no, Hannah, that's where you're wrong. I knew, yes, Kit Lampton, Tom Mackay. But nobody else. I mentioned no names, I told nobody. Even the police in the vehicles didn't know where they were going or why until they physically set out and Kit gave them instructions on the radio.' He fell silent for a second, his eyes boring into her. 'Kit Lampton told nobody, Hannah, Tom Mackay said nothing. But I remember, I remember that evening . . . I remember telling you.'

Hannah said nothing. She had gone deathly pale. She was mute. A single tear had formed in the corner of her eye.

Dave continued remorselessly. 'We spoke on the telephone that evening, do you remember? I had just been taken off the case, I was upset. We spoke about it. You were upset too, you said I was essential to the case and I told you that most of the work had been done. I had finished the affidavits, the two witnesses were signing them at the High Court in the morning. Do you remember me saying that? We agreed to have dinner that night but you had to cancel appointments. Ephram was going to accompany you to those appointments, wasn't he? You had to explain to him why you were cancelling, you had to tell him about me. A few loose words Hannah, that's all it took. I'm not blaming you, I'm blaming myself. It's me, I'm the one responsible. I'll have to live with Kit's death the rest of my life. But you told him, didn't you? You spoke about me and somehow it slipped out.'

'I can't remember,' she said, 'I can't remember. But even if I did, it couldn't have been him, it couldn't. He's a good man, Dave. You don't know him. Sam is a good man.'

'A good man?' The words stung, they burrowed deep, deep down into the most vulnerable part of him. 'No, Hannah,' he said, angry now. 'Ephram is a confidence trickster, he's a fiction, he's a lie. Conrad Fung murdered our son, he murdered Danny, and Ephram is Fung's associate.'

'Oh God, what are you trying to tell me now, that I'm living with one of my son's murderers?'

'I'm not saying that, I'm not saying he was ever involved in the Kai Tak bombing. But I am trying to tell you he's an evil man, Hannah. He's used you, he's used me. Kit is dead because of him.'

She let out a small, terrified sigh. 'Oh dear God, how can you say that? How can you tell me these things?'

Dave leant across the table, his face a mask of unrelenting determination. 'I'm not asking you to accept everything I say on blind faith. Check for yourself. But do it, Hannah. Please, I beg you, don't let this go by default.'

Hannah was feeling suddenly light-headed; it was the shock of it all. She was spinning in darkness. She heard a distant voice and knew it must be hers. 'Check, you say. But how? How do I check?'

'There must be papers in his apartment, business papers, personal letters.'

She was feeling giddy. The air in the diner was hot. She couldn't breathe. 'But what good will papers be?' she muttered, feeling as if she was going to faint. 'You say he changed his name. Why would he have papers with his old name on them?'

Dave was pressing her hard. 'Not just the name. Check for papers addressed to Conrad Fung, papers with Fung's name on it, company letterheads, anything. Tselentis's name too and Aurelius – Edgar Aurelius, he's one of the inner circle, Fung's personal attorney. There's one company they have, they're all shareholders. It's registered in the Cayman Islands – Fate Incorporated.'

Hannah stood up, her face grey. In her heart she knew Dave had to be wrong. Sam Ephram was a good man, a kind man. Sam was honest, gentle. What Tselentis had said were lies, distortions, they had to be, everything – all vicious lies.

'No,' she muttered, 'I'm sorry, I can't do this. I can't betray him this way. I don't feel well,' she said. 'I must have some air.' She left the cubicle, swaying on her feet, making her way towards the door.

Dave followed her, throwing a ten-dollar bill down on the table for the coffees. 'Listen to me, Hannah, Fate Incorporated, that's what they call it. It's not just some melodramatic private joke. It's made up of their initials. Fung, Aurelius, Tselentis, Ephram – Ephram is the E.'

Hannah escaped on to the pavement. But the air was still so hot, full of pollution and noise. She felt Dave grab her arm. How could he be saying these things?

'You can't run away, Hannah. You can never run away from yourself. Don't you think I've tried. It's impossible. A time comes when you have to stand and face the world. Please Hannah, listen to me!'

'No,' she said, 'please let me go . . .'

'There's one final thing I have to tell you. I forgot to tell you inside. It's the most important thing of all. Please, Hannah, listen! Conrad Fung is in desperate financial straits. He has to acquire capital, millions of dollars, and he has to do it quick. He's smuggling heroin, Hannah, bringing it here to New York. And he's using Ephram to do it – just as they did in the past.'

Oh God no, drugs now! Hannah spun around, trying to shake off his grip. She didn't think she could take any more. Where were these lies coming from? 'Let me go,' she begged.

But Dave wouldn't loosen his grip. 'If you refuse to believe me, telephone Scott in Hong Kong. Ask him about the shipment of samples that's arriving here today. That's how Ephram is smuggling the drugs, Hannah – in your own clothes!'

That was it, that was the final allegation that broke her. Tears were streaming down her face. 'What are you trying to do?' she sobbed. 'Do you want to destroy everything I've built, every last thing?' She saw a taxi and, pulling free from his grip, staggered into the road.

Dave remained motionless. He did not attempt to follow

her. But his words carried clear on the air. 'The day áfter tomorrow, at two in the afternoon, Conrad Fung walks free. Together we can stop him. But you have to believe me. You have to believe what I say about Ephram. I'll wait twenty-four hours. You know my hotel. Don't turn your back on me Hannah, not a second time.'

Hannah stumbled into the cab, fumbling to close the door. She mumbled instructions to the cab driver and, as it pulled away, she buried her head, too frightened to look back to where she knew Dave would still be standing.

It seemed to take forever to get back to Sam Ephram's apartment. She had her own key now. She could come and go as she pleased. That was how much he trusted her. She entered the lobby, a fixed smile on her face for the attendants behind their marble desk. She took the elevator straight up to the apartment. A maid came in three times a week but she was gone. Hannah locked the door and stood for a moment in the hushed, austere luxury. Her whole body was trembling. It couldn't be true, it just couldn't.

She had to get control of herself, to think rationally. But it was impossible. A thousand emotions were spinning in her head. She could still barely comprehend the import of what Dave had told her. She sat for a time, her skin clammy, so nauseous with the shock of it all that she was afraid she would throw up. It couldn't be true, it just couldn't.

Then, in a sudden burst of determination, she rose to her feet and went through to the study. Dave had wanted her to check – all right, then that's what she would do! She would prove him wrong, prove it was all lies! She started with Sam's desk. She went through every page of his appointment book, she checked every name. Then she began with the drawers, scanning every document, scrutinising every photograph, opening every book. Nothing was locked. Everything was there for her to see. She went to every drawer, every shelf in the apartment. And there was nothing that supported the allegations against him. Nothing, not a single thing!

400

'Her head spinning, she went to the telephone. In Hong Kong it was the early hours of the morning but she was oblivious of time. She dialled the number of Scott's apartment, drumming her fingers on the desk top in agitation as she waited. But he was not there, just that damn answering machine of his – 'Sorry I'm not here right now. Buzzing around town again. The wicked East! I can't even give you a number where I'll be. So be patient please, just leave your name and number when you hear the beep—'

Damn him, she thought, unable to hold back her exasperation, damn him, he had found a new boyfriend. Sleeping around again. Oh Christ! She put down the receiver and dialled again. This time it was the home number of her Hong Kong production assistant, a woman called Lily Leung.

She heard a female voice, thick with sleep, answer in Cantonese. '*Wai?*'

'Hello, Lily, it's Hannah here, Hannah Whitman. I know it's the wrong time and I'm sorry but this is very important.'

'That's all right Mrs Whitman. What is it, what's the matter?'

'It's about the latest shipment of samples that were air freighted across to me here in New York.'

'Has there been any trouble?'

'No Lily, no trouble, not at this end. But I heard there might be problems across there in Hong Kong.'

'What sort of troubles, Mrs Whitman?'

'I don't know. That's why I'm telephoning you.'

'I'm sorry, Mrs Whitman, I don't know of any troubles. Everything was fine when the cartons left here.'

'Did Scott say anything to you?'

'No, nothing.'

'Are you sure, are you absolutely sure?'

'I promise you, Mrs Whitman, he hasn't said a thing. If there's any trouble, I don't know what it could be.'

'Thank you Lily, that's all I needed to know. I'm sorry for waking you.'

Hannah replaced the receiver and slumped down by the phone. She gave a small sob, her whole body flooded with

401

relief, every nerve alive with it. 'Thank God,' she repeated in a lilting litany. 'Thank God, thank God.'

Edgar Aurelius sat in the interview room, a strained look on his face. As Fung entered, he was polishing his glasses in agitation.

The look of concern transferred itself instantly to Fung. 'What is it? There's no problem with my release, is there? No new evidence?'

'No, it's not that.'

'What then?'

'I spoke to Eduardo Paredes this morning. He telephoned from Manila. He tells me that a growing number of politicians are worried about your return to the Philippines. It's all the publicity, he says, the killings in Hong Kong and now in Africa – the fact that Rexford, the killer, was from Manila. It's giving the Philippines a bad name. People are very reluctant, he says.'

'How much does he want? I know Paredes, I've known him too long. How much is it this time?'

'I warn you, it's stiff.'

'How much?'

'Half a million dollars.'

Fung blinked. He attempted to contain his anger but there was a visible stiffening of the face. White blotches appeared in his cheeks. 'Have you tried talking some sense to him?'

'None of it is for him, he says – none.'

'He's a liar. Thirty percent at least is always for him. When does he want it paid?'

'Before you land – within the next thirty-six hours. Otherwise there can be no guarantees, he says. It has to be there and it has to be in people's pockets.'

'Then we'll just have to pay it.'

'But where do we get half a million in cash in the next thirty-six hours? All our funds are committed.'

'There's still cash in the Fate account. Khalil has the signing powers.'

'But isn't that committed too?'

402

'Not all of it, not yet. Get Khalil to make the transfer. I want it done immediately. Paredes must have that cash.'

Hannah was in the shower, the water as hot as she could make it, attempting to scald away all the tension and uncertainty, when Sam Ephram came home. He came through to the bedroom. She heard him toss his briefcase on to the bed and he called to her, 'Hi, how was your day?'

'Okay,' she answered, her stomach twisted in knots again. 'And you?'

'I had a call from Joel Grossman this afternoon. He said he couldn't get hold of you. You must have been out. He has another of his business contacts in town, a Brazilian. He's seen your stuff, loves it and wants the South American franchise – Brazil, Bolivia, Argentina, Venezuela.'

'Great,' Hannah answered, forcing the enthusiasm into her voice.

'Subject to your confirmation, Joel and I have arranged a morning meeting – brunch at the Pierre at ten tomorrow morning. Any problems with that?'

'Fine. Just one thing, what about the new shipment of samples that's due to be delivered tomorrow morning. Does Joel know?'

'Don't worry, I'll deal with it myself. I've had the cartons addressed to our new Park Avenue showroom.'

Hannah was about to switch off the water but, when she heard what he said, she stopped, her hand frozen on the tap. The cartons contained salesmen's samples, salesmen employed by Pan-Perfect. They should have been sent direct to Joel Grossman. Sending them to the showroom made no sense. It created extra work, that's all. Why had he done that? What possible reason could there be? Did he want to have access to them first, was that the reason? Oh no, she thought, her emotions whirling again, oh no, what do I do now?

Sam called to her. 'How long are you going to be in there? Stay any longer and I'm going to have to come in after you.'

Hannah switched off the water. There was an abrupt silence. She summed up all her courage. Then she asked.

403

'Why did you have the samples addressed to the showroom? That's not the normal way. Why not direct to Pan-Perfect?'

'Because I like to keep my finger on the pulse,' Ephram answered. 'I know they're just samples, but we weren't there in Hong Kong to see the finished products. I think we should do so before a bunch of salesmen take them on the road. Maybe Joel could do it but he's busy all the time. And the people who work for him, well, no disrespect, but they're just staff. It means extra work for us, I know. I'm sorry. But control, that's the key to success. We're dealing in a brand name that denotes quality and quality demands one hundred percent care.'

Hannah knew what he meant; she wanted so desperately to agree. A few bad samples were all that was needed to destroy months of promotions and advertising. The tension began to ease out of her. This whole thing was crazy. She wrapped a towel around herself, her blonde hair wet and sleek, the steam rising from her skin.

When she emerged, Sam Ephram was sitting on the end of the bed, his tie loosened. He smiled at her, his eyes soft and liquid. Seeing that smile, reassured her.

'You look beautiful. I like you like this, no make-up, your hair still wet, your skin glowing peach-pink from the shower.' He reached out to take her hand. 'It feels so warm,' he said. He kissed her fingers, each one at a time, and then the inside of her wrist. Gently, he eased her down on to the bed next to him. The towel fell open so that he could see her breasts and, when he brought his lips down to them, they were warm too. He kissed each nipple, hearing the small throaty murmur of her desire. He kissed her throat, her chin and then her lips and nuzzled his face into her wet hair. But he could sense somehow that she was not relaxed, that in an indefinable way she was holding back. He sat up, puzzled. 'What's the matter?' he asked. 'What's wrong?'

Hannah looked up at him. 'Do you care for me, Sam?'

'Of course I do, you know that.'

'You wouldn't do anything to hurt me, would you?'

'What kind of question is that?' He reached down to kiss

her on the lips. 'Why these sudden doubts?'

'I don't know,' she said, concealing her true reasons. 'Maybe it's all come too soon . . . too big, too good. Sometimes I think it's just a dream, that I'm going to wake up and find it all gone.'

'It's not a dream,' he said with that soft, solemn smile. 'Nobody is going to take it away. You've worked for it, you deserve it. And I'm going to be here right next to you all the way. Do you think I could ever hurt you, do you really think I could do such a thing?'

Hannah looked into his eyes and there was such sincerity there that her heart melted. How could she ever doubt him? He kissed her, his hands on her breasts, and she came up tight against him. She wanted him so much, she wanted to make love to him, to do everything to please him, to prove – if only to herself – that she would never doubt him again.

The telephone rang. They grinned at each other, hoping it would stop. But the ringing persisted. With an exasperated moan, Sam Ephram rolled across the bed and picked up the receiver.

As she lay there Hannah heard him say. 'Yes, I appreciate the urgency of it. I'll arrange it first thing in the morning. Don't worry, it will get there on time. Hang on, let me get a pen so I can take down the details.' He reached across for his briefcase, opened it, taking out a pen and paper and began to scribble notes. 'How much did you say? Half a million? That's madness. No, it's okay, the account still has that much. Don't worry, Edgar, it's no problem. No, of course, Edgar, I'll see to it . . .'

Hannah heard the name, that single word – Edgar – and she froze.

Sam Ephram put down the receiver. He finished writing and tossed the paper back into his briefcase.

'Who was that?' she asked, trying desperately to make the question sound disinterested.

'A business associate, nobody special, an attorney.' Sam Ephram climbed to his feet, taking off his jacket and tie. He smiled down at her, none of his desire diminished by the call. 'I don't want you to get changed, I don't even want you

405

to move. Stay just like that. We've nothing to do all night, nowhere to go. Let me take a quick shower myself then bring through some wine. What do you say?'

Hannah smiled at him, not daring to speak. She watched him as he undressed and walked through to the shower. Then, as soon as she heard the rush of the water, she reached across to where his briefcase lay. He had not locked it. She opened it and removed the scribbled note –

Remit telegraphic transfer to Acc. 922–731–003-, Bank of Asia, Hong Kong. Funds ex Fate, Cayman Islands.

She read it again, her eyes swimming with tears, praying that she had made a mistake. But there was no mistake. The word was written all too clearly – Fate. And that proved it beyond all doubt.

In the coppery glow of the half-light, his naked body looked as dark as mahogany. He lay on his back, his hands above his head, his body stretched out, whispering through gritted teeth. 'You do such wonderful things to me. Oh yes, cover me, please.' Hannah touched the vaulting, veined tension of him and he groaned out loud with pleasure. Last night they had made love and Hannah would have done anything to please him. Every caress and kiss of his had set her on fire. But now when she looked at him, it was with revulsion.

What had ever been so special about him? He was built no different from other men, no better endowed, no more sculptured or beautiful. One special, intangible quality had captivated her, that's all . . . the magic he created in himself, that spellbound, brilliant anticipation of who he was and what he represented. His sexual potency lay in the promise of dreams fulfilled, nothing else. But now that promise was gone. Ephram had found her when she was at her most vulnerable, he had taken her trust and then he had desecrated it. He had used her as a man would use a prostitute. That's all she had been to him, that's all she was now, no better than a whore.

At first, lying there waiting for him as he showered, it had

406

been impossible to control the anger. There had been no fear, she was way past that. There had been only a frigid, lethal rage that built inside her like a great Arctic storm, all ice and white fury and clouds of cold despair. But she knew that if she let him see her feelings, everything would be ruined. All that was left to her now was her ability to hit back, to make him pay for the things he had done. And if to achieve that she had to play the whore just one more time then so be it . . .

Dave slept fitfully that night, exhausted beyond measure and yet incapable of rest. He dreamt of Hannah, he dreamt of his son. Finally, at around five-thirty, with sleep impossible, he climbed from his bed, put on his running kit and went down to the street. Dawn was rising, everything still framed in the colours of darkness. The garbage was being collected. A couple of winos huddled at the street corner. It was June weather, hot and humid, a thin drizzle of summer rain speckled his face. He didn't plan a route, just stayed on Madison and ran down towards Wall Street, wrapped up in his thoughts.

Yesterday evening a smouldering ember of hope had existed that Hannah would somehow see Ephram for what he really was. He had waited in his hotel room, sitting by the phone. But now that hope was gone. He had to face facts, he had lost Hannah long ago. And that, in turn, meant that he had lost the final opportunity of using the machinery of the law to bring Conrad Fung to justice. Without Hannah's cooperation, he dared not report the drug shipment to the DEA. The risks for her personally were just too great.

The law was of no use to him now – the law of legislators and courts, the technical law of evidence and the presumption of innocence – but the law was not everything. Even without the law there was still justice . . . and justice was all he had ever sought.

Tomorrow, at two in the afternoon, Conrad Fung would be released from custody. He would walk from the court, shake hands with his lawyers and drive direct to the airport.

A ticket out of the United States would have been booked for him, first class, of course. And once he was back in the Philippines with his private army of goons, entrenched behind the barricades of his corruption, he would be impregnable. So he had to be killed tomorrow, he had to be dispatched before he left Miami.

He had just two opportunities to do it, either as Fung left the court or at the airport itself. But having the opportunity was one thing, finding an effective method was another. The use of a firearm would be best. But how did he obtain one? No doubt Florida – like all the Southern States – had free and easy gun laws. But he wasn't a US citizen, he wasn't even a resident, he possessed no social security number, no identification card. There were other ways of course: black market purchases. But securing a firearm on the black market took time, it took cash and contacts, none of which he had.

That meant he had to look to another weapon, one more easily obtained. There was only one viable choice – a knife. Any sporting goods store would sell one to him, something solid with a bone handle, a heavy blade and serrated edge. A knife, of course, meant that he would have to get in close. That would make it more difficult. But he was fit, he was agile and he would have the element of surprise.

Effecting an escape after it was done would be difficult but that really didn't bother him. Once the killing was done, he didn't care too much about his own fate. Once Fung was dead – once justice was obtained – the rest was insignificant.

So that was it. The plan was formed. He would fly to Miami. He would buy himself a knife there, hire a car and be at the court when Fung was released. It was unlikely he would be able to get close enough to him outside the court. There would be guards, photographers, lawyers. It was almost certain that Fung would be ushered into a waiting car. But at the airport it would be different. At the airport Fung would be on foot, mingling with the crowds. At the airport he would have to check in, he would have to stand at the counter.

The airport offered Dave everything he wanted, the cover of the crowds, the element of surprise. There was also a poetic irony in the choice. Danny had been murdered at an airport. Now his murderer would be executed at one too.

Dave ran for over an hour. He got back to his room, stripped down and took a long cold shower. His purpose was set. Deep down he had known it would come to this: one upon one, no courts, no lofty conventions of civilisation to intervene. Somehow even the use of cold steel seemed appropriate, an Excalibur, symbol of long-forgotten ages when justice lay in the hand of each individual man.

Dave had no illusions about the consequence of his actions. He knew what the law would do to him. But then law was never intended to be the mirror of justice, it was a set of rules designed to keep some kind of order in society. No lawyer or cop pretended it was anything more. Enforcing the law was how he had spent his life. But then a set of circumstances had arisen which had forced him to look deep into his conscience, to make that fateful choice. Yes, he knew full well what the law would do to him. But, when he searched his conscience, he had no qualms, he had no regrets.

He scrubbed himself hard under the cold, stinging water. He stepped out of the shower, pacing the room, leaving wet footprints on the carpet as he dried himself. All doubts were gone. He went to the mirror, brushing his brown, tangled-wet hair. He had lost weight but he was looking fit, fit enough anyway to get the job done. He looked at his watch. It was eight-thirty. There was time for a quick breakfast before he took the bus out to the airport. He tossed his towel on to the bed, reaching for his shirt. And, as he did so, the telephone rang.

It was Hannah, he knew it. There was not a moment's doubt. He picked up the receiver, his chest tight with expectation.

'You were right,' she said in a hollow voice. 'He is with Fung.' There was a silence then, a deep pain-filled silence, before she asked. 'What do you want me to do?'

Dave tried to muster his thoughts. 'What about the

409

shipment, the sample shipment that's coming in from Hong Kong? Where is that being delivered.'

'We have a small showroom of our own now. It's below Ephram's offices on Park Avenue. The shipment is being delivered there.' She gave him the address, her voice slow and rational and yet filled with an infinite sadness. 'Ephram left the apartment a couple of minutes ago. He's on his way there now.'

'What about you, where will you be?'

'He's arranged it so that I will be at a business brunch elsewhere. He'll be taking delivery personally, that's what he said.'

'Okay,' said Dave, 'leave it with me now.'

'What must I do?'

'Nothing. Just go about your normal business. Try not to alert him in any way. I have to be able to get hold of you. Can you give me some contact numbers?'

She gave him Joel Grossman's business address and telephone number. 'My meeting will be at the Pierre Hotel,' she said. 'But you can always contact me through Joel. If there's anything else you want me to do, anything at all . . .'

Dave closed his eyes, took a deep breath to try and contain his emotions and said softly. 'I know how hard this must have been for you.'

But she seemed not to hear. 'I'm just so sorry,' she whispered as if lost in a world of her own. 'How can you ever begin to forgive me?'

The receiver was down. The call was finished. Dave sat there on the edge of the bed, naked, still unable to believe it had happened. But the address was there in front of him, the place where the heroin was going to be delivered. God bless you, Hannah, he thought, God bless you. Now at last there was hope again, hope for a million things.

He reached for the phone and began to dial the number of Group Forty-One, the South East Asian Heroin Task Force, on West Fifty-Seventh Street. He had a contact there, a man he had worked with five or six years back. He

410

was a veteran of the DEA, a damn good operator too, an old friend called Bud Immerman.

Hannah lingered for those last few moments in Ephram's apartment, looking out over the Manhattan skyline. It lay before her in the morning light suffused silver-pink, vast pyramids of mortar and mist, so dazzling it was impossible not to be enthralled. New York, the centre of her universe, the world's Camelot. All her hopes had been here. She had been ravished by its dream. But now for the first time she saw it in a different light. Those spires of opportunity, all those proud towers, were no more than concrete and glass. There was nothing mystical about them. They had been built on sweat, bankruptcies and deals gone sour. What made her think she was due some privileged place here? So she had been betrayed. So had a million others.

At what moment in time, she wondered, had her desire to remember her son become lost in her personal ambition? At what moment in time had that personal ambition blinded her to everything else that was good in her life? Sam Ephram had betrayed her, he had used her for his own ends. But, before he had been able to do that, first she had had to betray herself.

How could Dave ever take her back? How could he ever love her again? He was strong, he was good, he was forgiving. But look what she had done to him. Every man had his limits. No, she thought, there was no question of asking for his forgiveness, not now, not yet. If she sought redemption, she would have to redeem herself.

Sam Ephram's first priority that morning had been to arrange the telegraphic transfer of half a million US dollars out of Fate's account to the account of Eduardo Paredes in Hong Kong. The transfer had almost exhausted the account's funds but that was a temporary matter.

Now all that remained was to take delivery of the cartons, secure the heroin, pack it away and arrange for it to be collected the following morning by his wholesaler in Queens, a man he had dealt with since his days in Istanbul.

The man's name was Johnny Lim, Onion Head, they called him. He was Cantonese. And it was the Cantonese who controlled the heroin trade in the US these days. Johnny Lim was reliable, cautious and he paid top dollar.

Sam Ephram wasn't happy having to place his hands on the stuff physically. The later, much larger shipments, would be handled by middlemen ignorant of his role in the matter, hired hands who were expendable. But this first shipment of just twenty-five units had been required urgently, the first vital transfusion of cash. There had been no time to hire reliable men, the overheads were too high. This first small shipment he would handle himself.

All in all, he thought, in a strange way, Fung's arrest had turned out well for him. When Aurelius had passed on the request to cultivate Whitman's wife, he had had no idea – nobody had – of her true talents. It seemed extraordinary to him that nobody else had seen her potential. But he had seen it, that's what mattered. And he was going to take her to even greater triumphs. The children's clothing was just the beginning. Within ten years, Hannah would be one of the world's great designers and he would be financial controller, the power behind the throne.

He poured himself a coffee as he waited for delivery of the twenty cartons. The penniless young urchin from the souks of Istanbul hadn't done too badly, he thought, not too badly at all.

At ten the cartons arrived. He had them brought to an area at the very back of the showroom which could be curtained off. He had them stacked, all twenty, and then pulled the curtains around them. He checked each one. They did not appear to have been opened or interfered with in any way. He signed for them and, when the delivery team had left, locked the showroom doors. He telephoned his secretary upstairs in his office, instructing her that he was not to be disturbed. Then he set to work.

He didn't realise what a job it was just to open the packages. He hadn't done manual work like this in years. Using a knife and scissors, he hacked his way into the first carton and began to sort through the piles of clothing, examining each item for the tell-tale ink spot that indicated it contained

412

heroin. He found the first one, a boy's tracksuit, and cut open the seam. He reached inside, pulling out a transparent plastic packet. The packet was square, eight inches by eight inches, and had been flattened so that it was no more than a quarter of an inch thick. The contents looked like flour, snowy white, a little granular. So innocuous, he thought, the way uncut diamonds look before they are polished: wealth in the raw.

Hannah would not be happy when she learnt that fifteen percent of the samples had arrived in a damaged condition and would have to be returned. But she would be able to live with the delay. The samples could be air freighted to Hong Kong, repaired and air freighted back within two weeks. That was not a problem, the problem was the sheer physical labour involved in removing each packet of heroin from its seam.

It took him half an hour to complete the first six cartons. He was going to have to work faster. He removed his jacket and tie, a film of sweat forming on his brow. He took the seventh carton, unceremoniously ripped it open and began the same search. This one contained windcheater jackets, bright cotton garments in scarlet and blue with candy striped collars. He took the first one, found the tell-tale ink spot and, using his knife, tore open the inside seam. The packet of heroin slipped out of its own accord. Ephram picked it up and studied it a moment, smiling to himself. Nectar, he thought, pure nectar.

And the curtain was flung back.

He spun around, the packet still in his hand. He was staring at two men, both of them armed. 'Who are you?'

The older of the two men, ruddy-faced, built like an ox, gave a jocular grin. 'We are special agents of the DEA, Mr Ephram – the good guys, remember?'

The packet of heroin slipped from Ephram's fingers, falling into the torn rags of the samples piled around his feet. He gave a small, almost breathless sigh. 'There's been a terrible mistake, gentlemen.'

The DEA agent smiled. 'Oh hell yes, hasn't there just?'

Hannah's meeting at the Pierre was still in progress late that morning when she was called to the telephone. It was Dave on the line. 'What happened?' she asked. 'Is there any news?'

'It's done,' he said. 'They caught him red-handed.'

It was what Hannah had been expecting but even so the realisation that it had actually happened remained a shock. 'Was the heroin where you guessed? Was it in the samples?'

'Ephram was arrested in the showroom ripping packets of the stuff from the seams,' said Dave. 'He had a pile of packets on the floor next to him and one physically in his hand. He couldn't have made it much worse for himself.'

'How did they manage to surprise him like that?'

'The DEA broke in through the back, had to use arc welders, apparently.' Dave tried to keep his voice flat, neutral. But there was an edge of triumph that he couldn't disguise.

There was no way Hannah could blame him. He was entitled to crow. 'Tell me,' she said, her voice very quiet. 'Why did you come to me first? You didn't need to. You could have gone direct to the DEA. You must have known there was a chance I would warn Ephram. Why did you take that risk?'

'I didn't want you embroiled in something that wasn't of your own making,' he said.

'But I was living with Ephram.'

'You're still my wife, you're still the mother of my son.'

Hannah wondered how many men in his position would simply have said, to hell with her, if the bitch goes down in the crossfire, so be it. It was a mark of the kind of man he was, a mark of his feelings towards her.

'Those two people Ephram hired in Hong Kong are probably being arrested about now,' said Dave, 'I would suggest you get in touch with Scott, put some damage control procedures into motion. You must also expect some bad publicity here. Speak to Joel Grossman, see if he can't get some PR people on the job.'

Hannah laughed. 'You sound like my business manager.'

'Don't knock it. I may just be one day.'

'What about yourself?' she asked. 'Now that it's over, what do you intend to do?'

414

'I wish it *was* over,' said Dave. 'But it's not, not yet, not until Fung is stopped. I'm flying down to Miami this afternoon. Ephram may cooperate, he may not. Nothing is certain.'

'But even if he doesn't, what can you do?' she asked. 'What can you possibly hope to achieve in Miami now?'

Dave did not answer, not immediately. There was a brief, electric silence . . . and that silence said it all.

Bud Immerman liked to joke that he had been a Special Agent since the Jurassic Age, a little before the extinction of the dinosaurs. Since he had joined the DEA, he had put on thirty pounds, his golf handicap had dropped from three to eighteen and he had two torrid divorces to his name. He didn't regret a day of it. During his years in the DEA he had operated in most parts of the States, in Asia and Mexico. When it came to men like Ephram, Bud Immerman had seen it all before.

Their first interview took place in the lock-up processing area on the nineteenth floor of the building. There was one window looking out on to a back street but it hadn't been cleaned in fifteen years. It was a small room containing one wooden table and three chairs. Apart from a tin ashtray the room was unadorned. Ephram, however, rose above the tawdriness of his surroundings. He sat at the far side of the table, legs crossed, impeccably dressed, assuming an air of nonchalance.

Bud Immerman, built like a bull, passed a paper cup of coffee across the table to him. 'Black, no sugar, just as you asked for it. Sorry it's not bone china.'

Ephram accepted his coffee, blowing to cool it. 'I must confess,' he said, 'to being a neophyte in matters of this kind. It would seem to me, however, that there are occasions when silence is essential, there are occasions when legal barricades have to be built. But there are occasions also when a simple telling of the truth will resolve the matter.'

Bud Immerman drank his coffee; white, four sugars, enough caffeine and carbohydrate to poleaxe a horse. 'I'm more than happy to hear what you have to tell me, Mr Ephram.'

Ephram gave the smallest of shrugs, creating an air of reluctance as if what he had to tell was somehow distasteful. 'I must tell you, it grieves me to do this.'

'Do what?'

'Place a woman in difficulties.'

'Mrs Hannah Whitman, you mean?'

'As you know, they are her samples, addressed to her. I normally have nothing to do with such shipments. I'm a financier, not specifically a salesman of fashionwear. Mrs Whitman and I are, well . . .'

'Shacking up together?'

Ephram smiled thinly. 'This morning she had a meeting, a most important one, she said. For some reason she was anxious about the delivery of the samples. She wanted me to be there to ensure they arrived safely.'

'But obviously not to open the packages themselves, not if she knew they contained narcotics?'

'I presume not, no.'

'Then why did you?'

'I thought that perhaps she was worried about the quality of the samples or maybe the condition in which they had arrived. If the elements seep into the packages, the samples can be ruined . . . rain, moisture . . . it is not uncommon, I understand. I had some time on my hands, I have a great affection for the woman. And so, yes . . . I decided to open one of the packages to see if everything was in order. At face value, the samples appeared to be fine.'

'Then why didn't you leave it at that?'

'I noticed an ink spot on one of the garments. I lifted it to have a closer look and it seemed heavier somehow than it should be. Then I saw a small split in one of the seams. And that's when I discovered the first packet.'

'But you continued to go through the samples?'

'Of course. Wouldn't you?' Ephram's voice had taken on an emotional pitch, but not too strident, just enough to sound convincing. 'I was astonished. It had to be narcotics of some kind. I couldn't believe Hannah would be involved in anything like that. I checked further garments. You must understand, I was in a kind of daze at the time.'

416

'Shocked that your trust had been betrayed, is that it?'

'I was stunned, incapable of thinking straight.'

'Nice try, Mr Ephram, ten out of ten for sincerity.'

Ephram looked at him, his mouth tight shut.

'Why don't I tell you a couple of things, huh? Save ourselves a lot of time and bother and all this Oscar play-acting stuff. First, it was Hannah Whitman who reported the possible presence of narcotics in the shipment. That's why we were there. We were acting on *her* information. Second, leaving all bullshit aside, drugs are a tried and trusted commodity for you, aren't they, Mr Ephram?'

Ephram gave a look of stunned indignation. 'That's not true. How can you say that?'

'Then maybe if I use your old trading name . . . Khalil Khayat. Ring any bells?'

Ephram remained rigidly still, cut like stone.

Paralysed, thought Immerman happily.

'I have never heard of that name.'

'Come now, Mr Khayat, this is the computer age. I've been on to Interpol already. Tap into a computer and all sorts of information comes up. That's how you first broke into the big time, isn't it, peddling heroin in Istanbul? It was only after you had escaped from jail and decided it was better to undergo a few cosmetic changes that you became who you are now. I must admit, it's an interesting choice, from a Turkish Muslim to an Israeli Jew. At first it seemed a weird choice, couldn't figure it out.'

Ephram's eyes narrowed into an intense stare. He had balled his hands into fists so tight that the knuckles were white. But he said nothing.

'Then the computer told me why. You spent two years in Israel didn't you . . . way back when. There were plenty of poor schmucks there who needed a fix too. Two years in Jerusalem, learnt to speak Hebrew, got to know all the places. Peddled a lot of stuff on to the West Bank – until they deported you. Yeah, when I learnt that, it all made sense. Who in the hell would dream that an honest, hard-working Jewish businessman could ever be a Turkish dope peddler? Didn't even have to get your dick trimmed, Muslims and

Jews both follow the same practice. Yeah, ten out of ten. It's just a pity that a few people were in on the secret from the beginning . . . Dimitri Tselentis for example.'

'Tselentis is dead,' said Ephram with a cold smile.

'Ah yes, but what he told us before he died has all been checked. Like I said, it's the computer age.'

A look of deep concern had now appeared in Ephram's eyes. The mouth had opened slightly. But otherwise he clung to his composure.

'Let me put my cards on the table,' said Immerman. 'As far as we're concerned, this is a cut-and-dried case. We have the drugs, we have your fingerprints on the drugs. We caught you in the act. There's no question of entrapment, no messy fringe problems. Your only real defence is to blame it on the lady. But the lady was our informant in the first place, a neat little finesse that will stuff you with the jury. Add to that the fact that you're masquerading under a false name and frankly Mr Ephram a bookie would be nuts to give you better than a hundred to one on getting anything less than life. Think about that for a moment. Life. It has a kind of ring, doesn't it?'

Ephram was beginning to look sick.

'Under our Federal narcotics laws, that's without parole. You will sit behind bars literally until the day you keel over and they put you in a box. Where's the value in that, tell me? Why waste your life. Because, you see, there are other options.'

Ephram gave him a cold stare. 'Cooperate, is that what you mean?'

'You know the system. If you give us your full cooperation – hold nothing back – you'll still be able to live a life. Why sacrifice yourself for somebody like Fung? There's no way he would do it for you.'

Ephram thought for a moment, looking down at his hands. Now was the critical moment, Immerman knew it. Then Ephram asked in a low voice, almost hesitant, 'If I do agree to cooperate . . . if I agree to help you, what benefits will I receive?'

Immerman was silent for a moment, his battlefield of a

418

face outwardly impassive. Inside, however, he was grinning like a kid. 'You're going to be sentenced to a minimum of ten years. There's no way you can avoid that. But you won't have to spend all that in the pen. During the period of your cooperation, while we're investigating the case and you're testifying, you'll be kept downtown, close to the courthouse. Play your cards right and there's parole too. You could be a free man again in six or seven years.'

Ephram gave a small desolate shrug; it was still too high a price to pay. 'A great deal must depend on the value of the information I am able to supply, is that not so?'

'We already know the value.'

'Then surely a full immunity would not be asking too much.'

'Forget it. You have no chance of a full immunity.'

For the first time Ephram looked stung, some of the bland self-assurance fell away. 'I will have to think about it, discuss it with my lawyer.'

'The offer is not open-ended,' said Immerman. 'You know who we really want.'

'Conrad Fung?'

'And you know he'll be flying out tomorrow afternoon.'

'Yes, I am aware of that.'

'Before you talk to your lawyer, let me spell out one other thing,' said Immerman. 'If I get the idea that you're purposefully delaying your decision, not saying no but not saying yes, and you're doing it in order to give Fung time to get out of the jurisdiction, I'll take that as an act of bad faith on your part. Do you understand what I'm saying? Then the offer falls away.'

'All I wish to do is consult with my attorney. I assure you, I am not playing games.'

Immerman got up from his chair. 'Just make sure I have your answer by noon tomorrow. And if it's not yes, if you're not prepared to put your thumb right on Fung's forehead, then frankly, Mr Ephram, I don't give a damn . . . it'll be a pleasure to sit in court in a few months time and watch you get life instead.'

★

At eight-thirty that night Bud Immerman was in his office, feet up on his desk, drinking his fiftieth cup of coffee of the day, when Dave telephoned from Florida.

'What's the state of play?' Dave asked.

'He wants time to consult with his attorney.'

'How much time?'

'I've given him until noon tomorrow.'

'Shit!'

'I understand your anxiety Dave. But what choice did I have? That's the deadline, twelve noon. It will still give us time to have Fung arrested. Don't worry, everything is ready to run.'

'What do you think Ephram's answer will be?'

'He's no fool. He can read the writing on the wall.'

'So you think he'll come through?'

Bud Immerman had been in the game far too long to make predictions. 'Phone me tomorrow morning at twelve,' was all he would say. 'I'll let you know then.'

So that was it, still no finality. Conrad Fung's fate, his own fate, both now inextricably bound, remained tortuously in the balance.

Through the open window of his hotel room, out there on the Miami beach front, Dave could hear the laughter of tourists. A car cruised by, its stereo on full volume. A dog barked excitedly. People were finding restaurants, lovers were walking arm in arm. Alone there in the stillness of the room, suddenly, he needed desperately to talk to somebody, to reach out and feel the warmth of another voice – Hannah's voice.

He had the number; he had all her numbers. She was staying with Joel Grossman and his family in Scarsdale outside of New York.

When he got through, she answered the phone. 'How are you feeling?' he asked. 'Has the aftershock set in yet?'

'I'm coping,' she said, 'That's about it. Everybody is pretty shocked of course, Joel especially. But he says I mustn't worry, there's no problem. Anything Ephram could have done for my collections, he can do too.'

420

'He sounds like a nice guy.'

'The best,' she said.

'Just so long as the fashions continue to sell.'

'Don't you worry,' Hannah replied firmly, 'they'll sell.' Then she asked him, 'Have you heard anything further? Has Ephram agreed to cooperate?'

'I spoke to the DEA a little while back. He has until tomorrow, noon, to consult his lawyer and come up with a reply.'

'Cutting it fine, isn't it?'

'Too damn fine.'

'But he'll agree, surely?'

'You tell me. You know him best.' Dave immediately regretted saying it. 'I'm sorry, I didn't mean that the way it sounded.'

'No,' she said, 'you're right. Except, as from last night, I realise I've never known him at all.'

'So we sit and wait.'

'What else can we do?'

'I'll keep in touch,' said Dave.

'Please, yes . . .' And then quickly, her voice filled with caring, she said, 'Look after yourself. And please, please, don't do anything foolish.'

'Don't worry,' he said, an echo of bravado in his voice, 'I'm as cautious as an old cat, you know that.'

Don't do anything foolish . . . a knife lay on the bedside table. Dave removed it from its leather scabbard, turning it over in his hand. He had purchased it that afternoon in a hunting goods store. The salesman had described it as a bowie knife, a weapon, he said, used extensively by the American frontiersmen. It had a bone handle, solid to the grip, and a strong single-edged blade about ten inches long. The knife sat heavy in his hand. Used decisively – with force – it was as capable of killing a man as any gun. He would have to choose the point of entry carefully, the heart or the neck. He wouldn't have time for more than two blows at most. But he wasn't worried. He knew what to do. If it came to it, if Ephram did not agree to cooperate, he was ready.

Chapter Twenty-Four

The morning of Conrad Fung's release was perfect, warm, not too humid, with a soft breeze blowing in from the Bahamas. As always, Dave arose just before the dawn. He ran along the beach front, bare-chested, striding easily. At first, the sun was just a pale pink wash on the horizon but he was still running when it came into view, a great golden-red orb that set the sand on fire. He stopped and watched it, feeling the breeze on his face drying the sweat. He had barely slept, tossing and turning, besieged by dreams. But now in the morning light with that sun dwarfing everything, he knew, if necessary, he could go through with it.

Back at the hotel he shaved, showered and then dressed slowly with great care like a soldier preparing for combat. He had no breakfast, he was too tense to eat. Just coffee, black and sweet. At eight-thirty, he checked out of the hotel. He went out to his rented car, placing the bowie knife into the glove compartment and drove towards the downtown area, to the United States Federal Courthouse on 1st Avenue.

Fung's hearing wasn't scheduled until two that afternoon. But schedules could be changed, matters brought forward for the convenience of the magistrate or the attorneys. No hearing time was set in stone.

The Federal Courthouse was a large, square building built in white, sea-washed stone. It was about sixty years old, one of those grand municipal structures erected at a time when public dignity demanded Doric columns on the outside and marble halls internally. Dave parked his car in a side street and entered the building. He cleared the check-

423

point manned by Deputy US Marshalls and entered a long marble hall with a vaulted ceiling. His footsteps rang on the stone floor. A sign pointed to the duty magistrate's court at the back of the building. There were several courts, each numbered with Roman numerals. It was not yet nine, too early for them to be functioning but, looking into Court VII, Dave saw a woman preparing the day's papers. He entered the court room. It was large, carpeted in blue, with the chairs in black leather. The clerk looked up.

'Excuse me,' Dave asked her. 'Is this where the Conrad Fung extradition matter is going to be heard?'

The clerk checked her roster. 'Not until two this afternoon. A defence motion for discharge.'

'It's not likely to come on before that?'

'That's when it's set, two o'clock.'

'How long is it likely to take, do you know?'

'A couple of minutes. Doesn't look like it's going to be opposed.'

'Thank you.'

Dave walked back outside, out on to the street. It was nine o'clock. He had three hours to kill before he could phone New York to learn of Ephram's decision.

Bud Immerman spent his morning killing time too. He did so by drinking copious cups of coffee, eating sugared donuts and trying unsuccessfully to get some paperwork done. At eleven-thirty, half an hour before the deadline, he was advised that Ephram wished to see him. 'Thank God for that,' he said. 'Bring him up.'

Ephram had his counsel with him, a new guy on the block; young, aggressive, full of case law and principles. The man's name was Saul Epstein. He looked like he had been out of law school two minutes: the worst kind by far.

'I have discussed your proposition with my client,' said Epstein, the whine in his voice giving away his Brooklyn roots. 'Without making any admissions at this stage, I am sure we can accommodate you.'

'Accommodate me . . . the wording is a little fancy but I take it that means your client agrees.'

424

'In principle, yes.'

'In principle? What does that mean? Either he does or he doesn't.' Immerman didn't bother to disguise his anger. 'I need his answer now – and in plain honest English. Yes or no? I'm not here, Mr Epstein, to be hacked around.'

Epstein's face reddened. 'Nobody is trying to "hack you around", as you put it, Mr Immerman. But my client's interests demand clarification of a few matters before I commit him to an irreversible course of action.'

Immerman held up his hands. 'Clarification of what matters?'

'As I see it, there's just one major stumbling block.'

'And what is this stumbling block?'

Epstein sniffed. 'Turkey.'

'What?'

'The sovereign state of Turkey.'

'What are you talking about?'

'My client may further his own interests by reaching an agreement with you, Mr Immerman. But what happens afterwards if he is sent back to Turkey? According to you, he is wanted there to serve the balance of a jail sentence.'

'Turkey is not my problem, Mr Epstein, you tell your client that. I'm only concerned with the present crime, with US jurisdiction.'

Epstein cast him a look of blistering arrogance. 'Then what is the value in my client doing a deal? He puts his head on the chopping block and for what? So that Turkey can ask for his extradition when he has finished his sentence here.'

'I don't know that the US even has an extradition agreement with Turkey.'

'It does, Mr Immerman, take my word for it. Turkey has the right to extradite my client and make him serve the balance of his twenty years for his conviction there.'

Why did there always have to be an eleventh-hour complication? Lawyers, screw the lot of them, thought Immerman.

'Could you not approach the Turkish authorities to obtain some sort of undertaking?' asked Epstein. 'If they know he is cooperating with you and will receive a

425

minimum of ten years, they may be prepared to drop their own charges.'

'Okay,' said Immerman. 'No promises. I shouldn't even be bargaining with you this way. But I'll go this far at least, I'll make a call.'

When he got through to the Turkish Embassy in Washington DC, it took ten minutes to find somebody who was prepared to talk to him. Eventually he was put on to a third secretary or somebody with equal lack of authority. Bud Immerman explained his predicament. 'This man can be of great assistance to us, he's a vital witness. We'd like to offer him a deal but he's facing a long term of imprisonment in Turkey. We'd like to obtain some sort of undertaking from you not to seek his extradition to serve that sentence if he cooperates in our local investigations. Who would give such an undertaking?'

'Our Ministry of Justice back in Turkey.'

'How long would it take? Assuming we could fax all the necessary information back to your people?'

'A month at least. A report would have to be prepared—'

'I'm sorry, we don't have a month.'

'How long do you have?'

'About two hours.'

The man at the other end giggled. 'Two hours? You are joking, of course.'

Bud Immerman had his answer.

Saul Epstein, tie loosened around his neck like a noose, face flushed, came into Immerman's office alone. 'Have you been able to find out anything?'

'Yeah,' said Immerman. 'There's not a hope in hell you're going to get an answer out of the Turkish Government in the next hour. We're back to square one, my original position. Either your client cooperates now or the deal is off.'

'My client wishes to cooperate,' said Epstein, 'you know that. He will give statements, he'll testify – but only after this Turkish thing is clarified. Believe me, if he has to serve

426

twenty years, he would rather serve it here than back in Turkey.'

'Then there's no deal,' said Immerman flatly. 'I'm not interested. Tell your client we'll talk to him in court.'

'My client has indicated his willingness to cooperate, the court will be told of that.'

'The court will also be told that he waited until the big fat bird, the only one that really counted, had had a chance to fly the nest.'

'That's a collateral issue, totally irrelevant to my client's position. My client is entitled to know where he stands before he commits himself. That's all he's asking. He wants clarification of his position.'

Bud Immerman grabbed one last straw. 'If Ephram is that keen to cooperate, let him give me something to enable me to arrest Fung, just enough to hold him for a few days until this Istanbul matter can be sorted out.'

Epstein gave a facetious smile, shaking his head. 'We can't *provisionally* cooperate and you know it. I'm sorry, Mr Immerman, if you can't find some legitimate way of holding Fung yourselves, you can't blame us.'

'Sweet play, counsellor,' said Immerman, glowering at Epstein. 'I hope your client appreciates it when he goes down for life.'

'He won't go down for life, you know that,' replied Epstein. 'This screw-up lies in your camp, not ours. We're not asking for anything unreasonable. I think you'll find the judge will be firmly on our side. Clarify the Turkish issue and we'll do everything we can to help.'

'We could all be old men by the time that's clarified.'

'That's not our problem.'

Yeah, thought Immerman, screw you too.

At twelve-thirty, after trying for half an hour, Dave eventually got through to Immerman in New York. 'Has Ephram agreed to cooperate?' he asked.

'Sorry,' said Immerman. 'There's no deal.'

'What in the hell happened?'

'He wants a guarantee that, if he helps us, he won't be

extradited back to Turkey to serve that sentence he has waiting for him there.'

'Isn't there any way you can get some kind of undertaking?'

'Be lucky to get it in a month. Sorry, Dave, it just didn't come together. We ran out of time. Nothing we can do now, just sit back, grit our teeth and watch the bastard fly away.'

Edgar Aurelius was about to leave his hotel room for court when he received the news of Ephram's arrest. The call came from one of his associates in his New York office. 'But what was he arrested for?' he asked. 'Why?' He was stunned, it was too incredible to comprehend.

'Narcotics apparently,' said the associate. 'The information we have is sketchy. It seems he was caught unpacking a shipment of heroin that had come in from Hong Kong. The story is that his mistress, the fashion designer, went to the police. Sold him out.'

Then the pieces began to fit. So that was the business venture Fung and Khalil had together, that was how they were going to make so much in such a short time. Drugs! How could they be so stupid? And just when everything was going so well, when Fung was just hours away from walking free.

He sat for a moment, reeling from the shock of the news. He was bathed in sweat, it was sluicing down his temples. What if Ephram had been forced to cooperate with the cops, what if he had struck some kind of deal? There could be an arrest warrant out for him. The FBI could be waiting in the hotel lobby. He might not have known about the drugs but he knew about everything else. Did he make a run for it? Did he stay? How could Fung and Ephram have been so stupid to dirty their hands with drugs at a time like this? They had to be mad, totally mad!

It was one-fifty, just ten minutes to the court hearing. Dave stopped at the street crossing. He looked up. The United States Federal Courthouse, stern and white with its Doric columns, stood facing him. The building symbolised the system he had lived by for all his working life. But that system had failed him. So now it was left up to him. He was not surprised and only barely disappointed. He did not relish what he had to do but he did not flinch from it. If any man deserved to die it was Conrad Fung.

He made his way through the checkpoint manned by the Deputy US Marshalls. He was not carrying the bowie knife. That remained in the car. He walked through to the back of the building and sat on a bench outside Court VII reading a copy of the *Miami Herald*. A couple of minutes before two, he saw a small group, four men, obviously lawyers, enter Court VII. One of them was a small man with a hunched back. That had to be Aurelius.

He did not wish to enter the court himself. But the swing doors into the court possessed small square windows which enabled him to witness what occurred. Just after two, the magistrate, a woman in her fifties, entered. She sat flanked by the US flag on her right, the State flag of Florida to her left. An attorney wearing a blue pinstripe suit and silk floral tie – he guessed it had to be Hedgewood – approached the lectern and began to address the magistrate.

Dave looked to where he could see Aurelius and there, next to him, for the very first time, he saw Conrad Fung. It was an eerie sensation. He felt like a hangman peeping into the cell of a condemned man to assess his weight and height so that the gallows drop would work efficiently. Fung was smaller than he had imagined, more frail. The bowie knife would plough into him with the concussive force of a train.

Dave could not hear what was being said in the court but Hedgewood had completed his address and the magistrate was now speaking, no doubt ordering the formal discharge of the prisoner. Conrad Fung rose, bowing his head with deference towards the bench. The magistrate rose, took some papers and left the court. There was a brief celebration. Hedgewood, smiling broadly, went across to shake Conrad Fung's hand. Fung himself was smiling. Only Aurelius seemed to remain nervy, hanging at the edge of the group, face as pale as ash.

Dave moved away from the door, finding a spot where he

could sit pretending to read his newspaper. Hedgewood headed the group out of the court, talking to a reporter. Fung and Aurelius followed at the rear with a couple of Hedgewood's young assistants. Keeping his distance, Dave followed them out of the building, pausing on the steps as they paused. There was one last bout of handshakes, out there in the Florida sun, and then Aurelius ushered Fung down the steps to where a white stretch limousine with black-tinted windows was waiting.

Typical, thought Dave, the bastard couldn't just sneak away. He had to make his exit in style like a Mafia don or some Hollywood producer.

Edgar Aurelius waited until the limousine had drawn away from the courthouse and they were both alone, cut off from the chauffeur by a wall of glass, before he broke the news of Ephram's arrest. He was angry but most of all he was frightened. 'Honest to God, every second in that courtroom I thought the FBI were going to bust in and arrest us. How could you do it, Conrad, how could you take such risks?'

Fung was shocked, there was no doubt about it. But he wasn't panicking. 'Khalil will play for time, don't worry,' he said. 'He'll ensure I have enough time to leave.'

'I'm leaving with you,' said Aurelius. 'I've managed to get a seat on your flight, Lufthansa to Frankfurt and from there on to Manila. There's no way I'm staying here, not with Khalil in custody.'

Fung nodded. He was not happy but what could he do. 'What about the shipment itself, has it all been seized?'

'I don't know. Yes, yes, I think so.'

'How was it discovered?'

'Through the woman, I think.'

'Whitman's wife?'

'Yes, the dress designer.'

Fung gave a dry snort of anger. 'Then, in due course, I have another score to settle.'

Just as Dave had anticipated, the stretch limousine took the route to Miami International Airport. The road was not congested and he had no problem sitting fifty yards or so behind it, keeping it constantly in view. As they entered the airport precincts, the limousine took the ramp up to the departure concourses. Dave followed in his hired car. The limousine reduced speed to a walking pace as the chauffeur searched for the correct drop-off point, cruising past concourses A and B, past signs listing the airlines: Scanair, Air Jamaica, American, United . . .

Dave tucked himself in behind. The adrenalin was pumping now: sights, sounds, colours, his perception of them so much greater, his readiness complete. The limousine was approaching Concourse E. It slowed and pulled over to the side.

Dave pulled over behind it, parking behind a yellow and black Hertz pick-up bus. A sign said No Parking. But that was the least of his concerns right now. He reached across to the glove compartment, removing the bowie knife. He took it out of its leather scabbard, wedging it into the waist of his trousers. He climbed out of the car, checking that the knife was secure. He buttoned his jacket so that it could not be seen. He was ready.

The limousine had parked just ahead of the Hertz pick-up. He saw the chauffeur run to the boot, taking out a suitcase and two travel bags. Aurelius was the first to climb out, followed by Conrad Fung and – for one brief moment – Fung looked directly at Dave. Their eyes met. Dave felt his heart stop. He half turned away, cursing himself for the stupid jerkiness of the movement. Then he realised that neither Fung nor Aurelius had seen him before. To them he was just another faceless tourist.

Dave waited by his car while Aurelius tipped the chauffeur then, staying about ten paces back, followed the two men through the sliding glass door into Concourse E.

The concourse was crowded, the air-conditioning icy cold. There were people everywhere, passengers queueing at airline counters, slumped next to their luggage reading paperback books. Dave was conscious of the claustrophobic feel of the place, the low ceilings, the dark, green-grey carpeting, the square, black pillars. Despite the chill of the air-

431

conditioning, the palms of his hands were damp with sweat.

Fung and Aurelius walked ahead of him, shoulder to shoulder, threading their way through the crowds. They passed the Air France counter and made their way across to the far side of the concourse where Dave could make out the bold yellow lettering of Lufthansa. They stopped at the first-class check-in counter. There were no other passengers at the counter, no delays. Aurelius handed over two tickets and two passports.

Dave stopped a dozen paces back, leaning against one of the pillars. He could hear his heart thudding against his ribcage. He was about to kill a man, to kill him coldly and rationally with full knowledge of the consequences. The palm of his hand was so wet that he had to rub it against his trousers to dry it. He reached into his jacket, feeling the bone handle of the bowie knife, rough and solid.

He looked around, trying to work out where Fung and Aurelius would go once they had their tickets. The signs indicated that all passengers carrying boarding passes had to make their way to Gates E1 to E19. All of them had to pass through a checkpoint where their hand luggage was X-rayed. There were security guards on duty searching individual travellers. Dave made a rough calculation of the distance to the checkpoint. It was no more than sixty paces. Somewhere within those sixty paces he would have to do it. There was no way he could follow Fung past the checkpoint, not carrying the knife.

But the area was crowded . . . families gathering for tearful farewells, honeymoon couples, tourists lugging their holiday purchases. He would have the cover he needed.

At the Lufthansa counter, Aurelius, pallid, sweating at the temples, kept looking around like a frightened rabbit. He was clearly terrified of some last-minute disaster. But Conrad Fung seemed completely relaxed. He was talking to one of the Lufthansa ground crew, a pretty brunette. He obviously thought the day was his, that his escape was complete. Not yet, thought Dave grimly. There's still sixty paces more . . .

Fung and Aurelius had been issued their boarding passes

432

now. The pretty brunette pointed towards the checkpoint that led through to Gates E1 to E19 and, picking up their hand luggage, they started to make their way towards it. Dave dropped in behind them quickening his step until he was almost close enough to reach out and touch them.

Just ahead of Fung, a pace or two to his right, a group of Arab men were walking, a couple dressed in the traditional keffiyeh, they looked as if they came from the Gulf States, Saudi Arabia maybe. They were talking in their own language, laughing together, and with each step, as they centred in on the checkpoint, they pressed a little closer to Fung.

Dave, however, barely noticed. Everything outside of the target had become peripheral, the woman in the broad straw hat, the young girl carrying a huge Donald Duck, the Hispanic couple kissing and crying, the small group of Chinese. His focus was concentrated totally now on that point between Fung's shoulder blades, that point a little to the left where he would plunge the knife, heaving it through skin and nerve tissue, fat and bone and into the back of the heart.

He had another thirty paces within which to do it, another fifteen seconds at most. For a moment he felt paralysed, appalled by what he was going to do. But that emotion quickly fell away to be replaced by a cold, almost calm detachment. What the law dictated was irrelevant now. What he was going to do was above the law. This was for Danny and, yes, this was for himself too. A wild, bloody justice maybe but justice all the same.

He was just a pace behind Fung now. He glimpsed a woman to his right, the Arabs were pressing closer. He reached into his jacket, taking the knife. He eased it out, holding it tight against his chest. Now was the moment, within the next five to six paces.

The passengers ahead were bunching at the checkpoint. Fung and Aurelius, stopped, putting down their hand luggage. Fung was standing next to one of the Arabs. Dave turned the bowie knife in his hand, adjusting it for the swift thrust into Fung's back. He would never have a better chance. He saw nothing else, heard no sound. This was it, the supreme, terrible moment, the moment of no going back. Dave whispered a silent prayer – please God, forgive me – and pulled his arm back ready for the plunge.

A high-pitched gasp was suddenly heard. Dave froze. Then, amazingly, Fung started to turn. He staggered around clutching at his chest and the two men were staring at each other. Dave staggered back. His reaction was one of incredulity. What had made Fung turn like that? How in God's name could he have known?

But, as he stared at Fung's face, he saw that it was contorted with pain. Fung's eyes rolled back in his head, he was teetering on his feet. He tried to speak, but all that came out was a long, shuddering moan. Aurelius – shocked beyond belief himself – was calling to him. 'What is it, Conrad, please, what's wrong?'

The crowd fell back leaving Fung in a small lagoon of space. Dave saw the way he was still clutching at his chest. My God, he thought, he's having a heart attack! Fung reached out blindly for the person nearest him, a tourist in a T-shirt and red tartan Bermuda shorts. But the man backed away, eyes wide, as a person might shrink from a leper.

Fung let out a despairing groan, and turned again, back this time towards Dave, reaching out for him, while all the time Aurelius was calling to him. 'Please Conrad, what's the matter? Tell me, tell me.'

Then – in the form of a piercing scream – the answer came. A woman at the edge of the crowd shrieked. 'My God, he's been stabbed! Look, there on the floor – there's the knife!'

Dave looked down and saw it on the carpet, a long, thin stiletto blade, the steel made dark as pewter with the shadow of blood. What in the hell was happening? His mind couldn't grasp it.

Fung staggered the last foot or two towards Dave, grabbing him by the arms before he collapsed to his knees. 'Help me, please help me,' he gasped. Dave eased him down to the carpet. The man who, a couple of seconds earlier, he was going to kill was now cradled in his arms. Blood was spilling from Fung's mouth. He was struggling to remain conscious but rapidly losing the battle. His fingers tightened on Dave's arms. Dave heard him muttering words. It took a moment to realise they were in Cantonese, Fung's native tongue.

'A small person,' muttered Fung, choking on his own blood, 'A small person . . . yellow, yellow . . .' But no further words would come.

Dave looked around at each face in the crowd, at the circle of silent witnesses. 'Somebody call for help,' he said. 'Somebody call for an ambulance.' He looked for Aurelius but the man was gone. A couple of the Arabs stood looking impassively down at Fung's prostrate form. Then Dave saw the Chinese men. There were three of them, each wearing cheap grey business suits, three men standing in a tight knot; short, wiry individuals with sallow skins. And suddenly it all began to make sense . . .

A small person, Fung had said, yellow – Chinese. What else could it mean? So that was it, the Chinese had assassinated him. But why? There could only be one reason . . . the Red Scroll. The information he had given to the US Embassy in Zimbabwe must have been passed on somehow, turned against Fung himself. Wheels within wheels, that's what Stan Tarbuck had said. How those wheels had worked, what momentum they had generated to bring this about, he would probably never know. But it didn't matter, the consequence, that's all that counted.

Dave looked down at Fung. His eyes were closed, the fingers of his left hand were shivering slightly but otherwise he lay completely still. His shirt was now soaked in blood. Blood too, bright as scarlet dye, dribbled out of his mouth and across his cheek. Two security policemen in their brown uniforms broke through the silent crowd. 'Oh Lord,' said one. He knelt next to Dave, putting his fingers to Fung's neck, trying to feel for a pulse. 'I can't feel a thing,' he said. 'I'm sorry, mister, I think he's dead.'

'Yes,' Dave answered in a voice empty of emotion, 'I think he is.'

*

For an hour or more there was pandemonium at the airport. An ambulance arrived, sirens wailing and the paramedics came bustling through with a stretcher. Fung's body was hurried away. The blood-stained knife was taken as an exhibit. All that remained afterwards was a soaked patch on the carpet that could have been spilt coffee. People were questioned. Statements were taken. The press arrived en masse. But the airport could not stop functioning indefinitely, not for the death of one man. Scheduled flights still had to depart and one of the first was Lufthansa flight LQ320 bound for Frankfurt in Germany. Edgar Aurelius was on board, sick as a dog, wet with sweat, burnt up with a fever of unadulterated fear.

When he had boarded the aircraft, along with the other passengers, he had been asked if he knew Conrad Fung, that poor devil back there in the concourse who had been stabbed. Terrified that any admission would prevent him leaving, Aurelius had denied any knowledge of the man. A second time, when all the passengers were seated, a request had been made by the captain for anybody who knew Fung to come forward. Aurelius had remained in his seat. Fung, he knew, was certainly dead and in a strange, almost elated way, he felt suddenly liberated. He was free of him at last. What loyalty there was had died with the man.

In the concourse, Dave had to wait to give his name and particulars and to record a short statement before he was allowed to leave. Nobody had seen the stabbing, but several witnesses confirmed that Fung had staggered to Dave begging for help after he had been fatally stabbed. So there was no question of him being under suspicion. He had been an innocent bystander, that's all. Nor was he searched, thank God, or the tone of the questioning might have changed. But why search a Good Samaritan?

When the police were eventually finished with him, Dave made his way through the thick throng of passengers and curious onlookers, walking in a kind of daze, not certain now what to do or where to go. All that mattered was the fact that it was behind him at last. Fung was dead and somehow – miraculously – he was free. So there is a God in heaven, he thought, so there is some justice in the world.

He came out of the concourse, eyes blinking in the fierce glare of the afternoon sun. Great thunderheads of cloud were building to the south over the Everglades. Rain would come soon. Dave didn't know where he was going or why. He was just walking, one step following the other, all his thoughts focused on Danny who seemed suddenly to have been dead such a long, long time.

Would his son sleep more peacefully now? He would never know. But the living would. He would. And perhaps, when all was said and done, that's all that really mattered. Because the departed, if they lived on at all in the world, lived on in the memories of those who had survived them. Lived on in their love, lived on in their honour.

'I did what I could, son,' he whispered and, with a kind of half-hidden smile, said to him. 'None too elegant, I know. But at least I kept my head down, I slogged on, I never lost faith. And in the end, somehow, I muddled through.'

He stopped on the sidewalk, the crowds bustling around him, trying to get a grip of his thoughts. Best to head back into town, he thought, book into a hotel and then arrange a flight back to Hong Kong. There was no point in staying here at the airport. He turned back to where he had left his hired car – and that's when he saw her.

At first, still in a kind of trance, he thought he must be imagining it. But then she smiled at him, a smile so soft and uncertain, so intimate and knowing, that there could be no mistake. Hannah stood just a few feet from him, hands by her side, a look of deep fatigue on her face. But her blue eyes were alight. 'I flew down from New York this morning,' she said. 'I couldn't stay there, I had to be with you. I was here at the airport when I heard about the killing. I was so worried. I saw you with the police. Then I saw you walk away . . .'

Dave smiled uncertainly. 'Why didn't you come up to me?'

'I was trying to find the courage.'

'Courage for what?'

'To ask for your forgiveness.'

He shook his head. 'No, no . . .' He held out his arms and she came to him then, first one timid step, then as fast as she could. His arms enveloped her slim, lithe body. He nuzzled into her warm, golden hair. They hugged and he could sense the wetness of her tears on his cheeks.

'Oh God,' she said, her voice full of tears. 'What kind of nightmare have I put us through? How do I ever begin to make amends?'

But he placed a finger on her lips. 'Ssssh,' he whispered with a smile, loving her more than he had ever loved her in his life.

She looked up at him. 'I was blinded, Dave . . . ambition, greed, I don't know. It dazzled me. But under it all, no matter how crazy I was acting, I always cared. I always loved you.'

'In our own different ways both of us were blinded,' said Dave.

'So what now?' she asked, looking deep into his eyes.

'So now,' he answered solemnly, 'We close the book of the past and we start again.'

'You still want me?'

He gave a small sigh. 'How could you ever ask that?' He took her hand, squeezing it tight. 'Oh God, yes, of course I want you. Now and always, you know that, you're the only person in my life.'

Dave lifted her hand to his lips. Her skin was so warm, so softly scented, his own eyes so misted with tears, that he did not see the smudge. But he may not have seen it anyway . . . it was an insignificant stain, the barest smear of Fung's blood across her knuckles – the mark of Hannah's atonement.

More Thrilling Fiction from Headline:

QUILLER BAMBOO
ADAM HALL

'NOBODY WRITES BETTER ESPIONAGE THAN ADAM HALL' *New York Times*

QUILLER
'The best after Le Carré' *Guardian*

Summoned late at night to the Bureau, Quiller attends a secret conference with the Foreign Secretary and a surprise defector – the Chinese ambassador to Britain. Minutes later the ambassador is dead. So begins *Bamboo*, a mission that takes Quiller from London to Calcutta to Hong Kong and finally to the roof of the world, to Tibet, where he must take on the Chinese secret police and the People's Army in an effort to save the notorious dissident Dr Xingyu.

For the first time in his career, Quiller feels himself personally engaged in a mission, for the aim of *Bamboo* is to avenge the tragic bloodshed of Tiananmen Square and help the people of China to achieve the freedom and democracy they crave.

'Pure entertainment espionage at its best' *The Times*

'When it comes to espionage fiction, Adam Hall has no peer!' Eric Van Lustbader

'A writer with a secret formula for excitement' *Sunday Express*

'The most successful literary double-agent in the business' *Life*

'A brilliant practitioner' *Daily Telegraph*

Also available in Headline Feature
QUILLER BARRACUDA

FICTION/THRILLER   0 7472 3818 9

A selection of bestsellers from Headline

SEE JANE RUN	Joy Fielding	£4.99 □
STUD POKER	John Francome	£4.99 □
REASONABLE DOUBT	Philip Friedman	£5.99 □
QUILLER BAMBOO	Adam Hall	£4.99 □
SIRO	David Ignatius	£4.99 □
DAY OF ATONEMENT	Faye Kellerman	£4.99 □
THE EYE OF DARKNESS	Dean Koontz	£4.99 □
LIE TO ME	David Martin	£4.99 □
THE LEAGUE OF NIGHT AND FOG	David Morrell	£4.99 □
GAMES OF THE HANGMAN	Victor O'Reilly	£5.99 □
HEARTS OF STONE	Mark Timlin	£4.50 □
JUDGEMENT CALL	Suzy Wetlaufer	£5.99 □

All Headline books are available at your local bookshop or newsagent, or can be ordered direct from the publisher. Just tick the titles you want and fill in the form below. Prices and availability subject to change without notice.

Headline Book Publishing PLC, Cash Sales Department, Bookpoint, 39 Milton Park, Abingdon, OXON, OX14 4TD, UK. If you have a credit card you may order by telephone — 0235 831700.

Please enclose a cheque or postal order to the value of the cover price and allow the following for postage and packing:
UK & BFPO: £1.00 for the first book, 50p for the second book and 30p for each additional book ordered up to a maximum charge of £3.00.
OVERSEAS & EIRE: £2.00 for the first book, £1.00 for the second book and 50p for each additional book.

Name ....

Address ....

....

....

If you would prefer to pay by credit card, please complete:
Please debit my Visa/Access/Diner's Card/American Express (delete as applicable) card no:

Signature ....Expiry Date ....